All The Way

Canadä

The Publishers acknowledge the financial assistance of the Government of Canada through the Book Publishing Industry Development Program (BPIDP) for our publishing activities.

Library and Archives Canada Cataloguing in Publication

Keenleyside, T. A. (Terence A.), 1940-, author
    All the way / Terence Keenleyside.

Issued in print and electronic formats.
ISBN 978-0-88887-710-9 (softcover).–ISBN 978-0-88887-711-6 (HTML)

    I. Title.

PS8571.E4453A79 2018   C813'.54   C2018-904113-7

                                             C2018-904114-5

ALSO AVAILABLE AS AN E-BOOK (ISBN 978-0-88887-711-6)

Cover design: David Ross Tierney
Printed and bound in Canada on acid free paper.

All The Way

A Novel by
T.A. Keenleyside

Borealis Press
Ottawa, Canada
2019

To Dot
with love

Acknowledgements

I wish to thank Rick Archbold and Ramsay Derry for their comments on a much earlier version of this novel, produced when I had not yet reached the age where it made sense to write it. For her insightful observations on this book, as with all my previous publications, I owe a deep debt of gratitude to Sara Cummins, from whose advice I have profited almost as long as I have enjoyed her friendship. I also wish to thank another dear friend, Sandy Merry, for reading a draft of this book and offering valuable comments on it.

Once again, I am grateful to Frank and David Tierney of Borealis Press for their interest in publishing my work and to Janet Shorten for her expert editing of the manuscript, saving me from embarrassing errors. Several members of my family have read all or portions of this work, and I am most appreciative of their input. I wish, however, to thank in particular my wife, Dot, not only for her astute editorial assistance, but for her support throughout the long process of bringing this book to fruition. She has been my loving companion for sixty years, travelling with me all the way—not only through the journey of life, but to all of the places and experiences upon which this novel is based. I should add, however, that the events described in this book are fictitious as are all of the principal characters. Any resemblance they may have to persons living or dead is purely coincidental.

By the Same Author

Fiction

The Common Touch

In A Spin

Non-Fiction

Missing the Bus, Making the Connection

Roaming The Big Land

Around The Table

Chapter 1

"Do you think Lou's cancer may have spread?" Susie asked. "It was kind of out of the blue that Sally called us. They organized the reunion in quite a hurry."

"I don't think it has, but there's no question we have to be there. Everyone who can will be going."

"The gang of eight, you mean. No, I realize it's important that we're there."

Jack took his eyes off the road long enough to glance at Susie with an anxious expression, like a patient waiting for his doctor to finish studying his X-ray. "Sally didn't *sound* like anything was the matter."

"No, but she's nonchalant about everything."

"Like me, you mean?"

"Worse." Susie's response implied sublime indifference. "Lou could be dying, and we'd never know, not by the tone of her voice."

"He certainly wouldn't say he was. Lou doesn't talk about that sort of thing."

"Would Sally care even?" Susie wondered.

"Of course she would. You would if it were me, wouldn't you?"

"It would depend on your latest grade for behaviour. It would have to be at least a B."

"But you teachers are such tough markers!"

"What I mean is, it's not as if they're still really in love. They've gone through some rough patches."

"But Lou loves her, I'm sure of that, and they've stayed together through everything, after all. It would be awful for her to lose him. He's always been faithful and a good provider."

"Ouch! Chauvinist!" Susie slapped Jack lightly on the knee. "Is that all it takes to make a marriage work? More to the point is, how much do they have in common?"

Jack pondered the question for a moment and then laughed.

"Money. They've both always liked the smell of money. And the accoutrements that come with it."

"But Sally didn't need Lou for that, not with all the money her father had. She could have managed very well on her own."

"A feminist thanks to her father, you mean? My turn. Ouch!"

They'd left Higgins Beach, Maine, that morning to drive to the reunion. Early for them, around nine. No breakfast. They'd stopped instead at the first Dunkin' Donuts they passed so that Jack could declare once more, "Not as good as Tim Hortons," leading Susie to kick him under the table and reprimand him again: "Nationalist!" Then they'd continued over back roads through Maine and New Hampshire, stopping first for a bathroom break and then a picnic lunch in Old Bennington by the Battle Monument, which loomed over the wide, sparsely populated valley below that extended eastwards to the Green Mountains. Chance for Jack to remind them how lucky they were to have been born Canadian: fewer monuments to the dead, fewer wars. Fewer psychotic leaders. Another brief stop for coffee and a whiz and then on into New York state, crossing the Thruway near Albany and following back roads once again onto Route 20, paralleling the Thruway.

It wasn't the way they'd made the trip for all their working lives when, except for a quick bite at a Thruway gas station, they'd motored non-stop from Toronto to Higgins Beach. The route they were taking now was, however, much the same as the one Susie had travelled as a child every summer with her parents. Returning to it was part necessity: the speed and stress of motorway driving was too much for both of them, and their buttocks and bladders demanded frequent stops—"pee stretches," Jack called them. But it was a reversion for reasons of nostalgia as well, especially for Susie, but for Jack too, because they had been doing the trip by back roads again for a number of years now.

"Do you think Linda truly is a lesbian?" The upcoming reunion was still on Susie's mind.

"As opposed to falsely?"

"You know what I mean. Like has she always been?"

"Well, she's *always* been flat-chested, that's for sure."

"Jack!"

"No, I mean it. Maybe her hormonal count is low, and she's always been butch, I don't know."

"You're not being serious. She's never been a bit like that. If she really is a lesbian, she's the woman."

"What I think is that she's always been bent. She bends with the wind."

"But when she married Jay, it wouldn't have been easy to come out. She may have been suppressing her true feelings."

"No, you're right; being gay wasn't 'in' back then."

Sometimes Jack's flippant tone irritated her. "You think it's just a passing thing with her, a kind of fad? It's not. It's just that people are freer to be themselves now."

"No question, Susie, you're right." Jack backed off, but Susie knew he still felt that Linda's transformation was transient.

"You're slouching," she scolded. "Shoulders back. Chin in. Even when you're driving."

"Yes, sergeant-major. I can do the shoulders. Not sure about the chin."

Jack Sturridge was close to six feet, eight inches taller than Susie who always felt even smaller beside him. But she didn't really mind; she felt protected, shielded from adversity by his height and broad shoulders. She always had. Even now, though she knew he was no longer a match for a bad-tempered mongrel, let alone a determined mugger. When they walked together, the gap in height was not as great as it had been, for, unless Susie admonished him, Jack shuffled with a stoop. It was the same when he was painting, reading, or eating, and she was always after him to straighten his back. "Put your hands at the base of your spine and push out your chest."

"Show off my pecs, you mean?"

"Exactly. Show us who's boss."

The change in Jack's physique had, of course, been gradual, imperceptible from day to day, but persistent. At first, Susie had noticed that Jack was sometimes slow getting up and straightening out. Then later she had spotted an occasional bend that over time appeared with increasing frequency. Now, however, what had once been periodic was clearly permanent and it was a question of keeping it from getting worse. *We're old now,* she mused. *There's no doubt about it.*

In many respects, however, Jack still looked fit for seventy-eight. For the past ten years, he'd weighed the same as he had in his twenties, thanks to Susie's careful cooking—not much fat and only modest carbohydrate. Even Jack's face was relatively youthful once you got past the grooves chiselled into his forehead and cheeks. His hair was largely grey, but with traces of auburn still showing on his sideburns, and his dark brown eyes were clear, flashing refracted light the way they always did when he was trying to be funny. He had large hands with a patchwork of grey veins criss-crossing them and forming irregular shapes like little panes in a stained-glass window. His fingers were long, with square, stubby nails, good substitutions for brushes when he wanted to work his oils directly onto a canvas.

"So, when Linda married Jay, do you think she loved him or was he simply a useful cover for her real inclination?" Susie asked.

"I think she felt it was the thing to do. Everyone else was getting married. When she visited us in London, I guess she thought our life together in our little flat looked pretty good. And then Jay came down from Cambridge to visit; he seemed to have become a bit of an intellectual—not like I knew him as a kid or in his teenage years—so he struck her as the sort of person she could see herself marrying at that time."

"And keeping under her thumb?"

"Yeah, because she was going to be the *guy.*"

"Jack! You're impossible."

"Or realistic."

"At least let her be the woman!"

Susie sat quietly, admiring the scenery out her side window. And Jack stole glances at her, wondering what she was thinking. There was always something on her mind: the kids, grandchildren, friends, what to cook for dinner, her health, Jack's. Usually she told him what it was, but often he had to wait until the frown on her face vanished and she was ready. "Sally said Jay is coming, and Linda too apparently."

"With her new wife?"

"Jack, stop it!"

"That would be interesting, watching how the three of them interact. What new twists in the plot await us? Jesus, are we up to another round in the Linda-Jay title fight?"

"Oh, look! That's the road we drove down—that time we followed the car taking the bride to her wedding. Remember? We'd stayed overnight in Cazenovia and all the bride's family was at the same motel. After breakfast, we followed them."

"I remember. The kids thought we were nuts." Jack didn't add that on several trips now Susie had reminded him of that moment. "Wonder if they're still married. Or if they've split like Bev and Cass. Probably he knocked her up and her parents insisted they get married. While we were following the bride, maybe the groom was walking reluctantly into the church thinking, 'Fuck, I could be at the Big Red game.'"

"Big Red?"

"Yeah, Cornell."

"You're such a romantic!"

They were silent for several moments before Susie said, "I guess Bev will be at the reunion."

"For sure, she'd never miss it."

"Poor Bev. Things haven't exactly worked out for her, have they? I mean not the way she would have wanted, especially with Cass."

"No, but she's had a pretty interesting ride all the same. Everyone's Stampede Sweetheart."

"She's certainly resilient."

"'Look on the sunny side, always on the sunny side, look on the—'"

"Stop! We'll be hearing enough of that at Sally and Lou's."

"Cass won't be there, though," Jack said.

"You mean he's not fit enough to go?"

"No, not after that second stroke. Looks like he's on the slippery slide to the underworld."

"That's a fine way to talk about an old friend!" Susie changed the topic. "You know, I'm glad we're stopping in Cazenovia for the night. I've always loved it."

———

For Susie, the trip they were taking was full of images from the years before the Thruway was built: the sight of sailboats and water skiers on little rippling lakes in Maine, Vermont, and New Hampshire where simple wood frame cabins were for rent—cabins painted white with green or blue shutters and the sweet smell of pinewood and lemon oil inside. Fly fishermen in hipsters with wicker baskets at their waists, wading thigh-high in surging streams, whipping their thin lines over beds of boulders, expertly dropping their flies into limpid pools. A thick green forest rose behind them to mauve and blue mountains. When, years later, for the first time she pointed out these scenes to Jack, he commented dryly, "They look like glossy magazine adverts for the state tourism office."

"Not your kind of art, is it? It would sell."

Driving along Route 20, Susie loved the red barns on hillsides, their silos breathing easily before the autumn harvest. She loved the fragrance of freshly mown grass on summer evenings, the bleeping lamps of fireflies in the fields, the rich odour of burning leaves in late summer, and the aroma of fresh-picked corn at roadside stands—corn they could husk and eat the night they arrived home. And she loved the "I think I can, I think I can" hills, so steep before you started up them that her father would always say, "I don't think we'll make it. You may have to get out and walk to the top." And then there were the sudden dips in the old road that sent a little thrill through her body. "That's what an orgasm is like," her older sister Rebecca had said one time authoritatively, but Susie was pretty sure she didn't really know.

Susie loved it when all the family sang songs, and she and Becky leaned over the front seat to join in: "Roll Out the Barrel." "It's a Long Way to Tipperary." "This Land Is Your Land." Or when they listened to the Red Sox on the radio and Ted Williams hit another home run.

But what she enjoyed most of all each summer was watching for the advertising signs set out line-by-line along the edges of farmers' fields, especially the cautionary ones for drivers:

Altho insured
Remember, kiddo
They don't pay you
They pay
Your widow
Burma-Shave

Heaven's
Latest
Neophyte
Signaled left
Then turned right
Burma-Shave

The only thing Susie didn't like about those trips was being kicked in bed by Becky when they were little and sleeping in the narrow beds of those roadside cabins, or, when they had graduated to separate beds, being kept awake at night by Becky agonizing over whether she was going to go "all the way" that summer with the sandy-haired guy she'd met on the beach the year before.

———

Jack tapped the steering wheel lightly several times. "Shit, I hope Lou's okay. You know, when I first met him at the Ojibway Hotel in 1958, I never thought we'd become lifelong friends. As it turned out, I've known him as long as anyone else I still see, except for Jay. Well, there *are* two or three other guys from grade school I wish I never ran into. I don't need to be reminded how I barfed all over my desk in Grade Three. Filled the ink well even."

"Poor baby. How embarrassing! It's odd, though, that you and Lou have always got on so well. You're very different."

"I know. Why am I good friends with somebody whose main

objective his whole life has been to make big bucks and be noticed for it, who isn't too concerned about screwing people along the way?"

"I don't know. Why?"

"There's just something about him. Deep down he's way more than just a conniving, ruthless son-of-a-bitch in a dark suit with a leering grin. He's kind-hearted and generous. And he's really loyal."

"So was Stalin—to his first wife."

"But Lou likes everybody. He accepts people for who they are and isn't dismissive. No one gets dispatched to the Gulag."

"No, I guess not, not even Cass."

"No. Lou and Cass are still friends despite those attacks Cass launched on him in the media. But they wouldn't be if it weren't for Lou making the effort. Christ, I hope he's okay. It would be awful to lose him."

"He certainly likes you."

"Yeah. It's odd, but kind of flattering, too. Me, a failed artist who's lived off his wife's hard-won earnings for decades."

"Jack! You know that's not true."

"Of course it is. But it hasn't affected my relationship with Lou. He's always pulled for me, come to most of my shows, even though I'm sure a long time ago he figured, as Jay would put it, that I was a loser, that I'd never make it."

"It's not too late, you know."

"You kidding? At seventy-eight? I'm not Alex Colville or E.J. Hughes."

"You could still paint for years."

"Well, there's no chance I'll bat a century like Doris McCarthy. My hands already shake unless I settle them with a Scotch."

"You could try Pramipexole. It would be better for you."

"But what does it taste like?"

Susie laughed. "You might as well stick to Scotch."

Jack pulled into the parking lot of the Brewster Inn, an old but distinguished brown-stained hotel on Cazenovia's waterfront, built in 1890 by financier Benjamin B. Brewster, partner with John D.

Rockefeller Sr. in the founding of Standard Oil Company. No cabins or motels for Susie and Jack any longer. Recently they had started to pamper themselves with comfortable beds, freshly laundered duvets, and pillows that helped them deal with neck pain. It stretched their resources, but Jack claimed, "The actuarial tables say it's okay. We'll be dead before there's an issue, and it's cheaper than having to get rid of bed bugs."

Before dinner, the Sturridges had drinks at the gazebo bar on the inn's lawn, looking out onto the lake where several dinghies were flitting urgently across the ruffled water, going about and sailing back again, their courses little changed, as if looking for something they couldn't find. *For what?* Jack's thoughts turned momentarily dark. *The exit from the locked floor of a nursing home? The wing for Alzheimer's patients?* Then he caught himself and took a sip of his Scotch. "You know, we should visit Howe Caverns on one of these trips. It's time we did that if we're ever going to go before we're stalagmites ourselves."

"I'd love to."

"At least we went to Cooperstown that time with the kids."

"Yes. And it was much better than I expected. Not the museum. Too many bats, balls, and gloves for me. But the village was really pretty."

"And Cornell. I don't think the kids liked that much, though, especially Tom. No Big Red game."

In the dining-room, Susie chose a salad of mixed greens, topped with chicken, walnuts, pears, and a low-fat vinaigrette, Jack the tuna burger, a Monday night special. They shared a carafe of Sauvignon blanc, but Jack drank most of it.

"So, your relationship with Sally has never been like mine with Lou, has it?"

"No. I like her. She's always pleasant, but somehow I feel she just tolerates us, I mean everyone who'll be at the reunion. She does it for Lou, but really she'd rather not be there."

"'The Reluctant Hostess.' Not a bad title for a novel."

"I must say, though, I've always been impressed by her frankness, even about herself. She doesn't try to hide her flaws. But we're very different. It's too bad in a way because if we'd been closer, I might have been able to help her work out her differences with Lou."

"Maybe we both could have…should have tried harder to keep their relationship on course. Could we have prevented what happened?"

Susie sighed. "We'll never know."

"Well, whatever." Jack turned more cheerful. "She was the right choice for Lou, an asset he needed in his portfolio."

"You're such a cynic! But I think it's true she's always been a social climber, and she saw Lou as someone who could help her up the ladder."

"Well, it was never much of one for her to climb, thanks to her father… Funny, though, you're as different from Linda as you are from Sally, and yet you and Linda have always been good friends ever since you met on that trip to Europe in fifty-eight." Jack's elbows were on the table, his burger clutched before his mouth.

"It's like you and Lou, I guess. I didn't think it would be that way; it just happened, maybe because she liked me from the start and I found her fascinating. I must say, however, she does make me feel guilty sometimes—that I haven't been bold and independent enough, committed to causes the way she has. With Linda, you never know what is going to happen next. She keeps you guessing. You have to be on your toes to keep up with her."

"Well, you don't have to become a lesbian just because she says she is."

"Oh, thank goodness. That's a relief—for both of us."

Susie rested her fork on her plate as her mind floated back to that long-ago summer. "I liked the way in Europe she never stopped looking for new experiences. She was open for anything and wanted to absorb all she could of the local culture wherever we went. Most of the others weren't like that. They were more interested in just hanging out together, going to beaches in their bikinis, and drinking too much wine."

"Ah, bikinis! What a great invention that was!"

"For men, you mean." But Susie had bought one, too. She just didn't have the self-confidence to wear it on the beach at Nice like the others. She only admired herself in front of the mirror in her hotel room, her smooth, youthful breasts pushing against the flimsy fabric as she gathered her blonde hair above her head. *Brigitte Bardot, she would have looked like,* Jack thought as he painted that scene in his mind.

Susie's hair was grey now. Jack remembered when the first streaks had appeared he'd asked her why she didn't dye it the way her friends did. "I've always believed in just being myself," she'd answered. *Good old Susie. No slave to convention.* But that wasn't entirely true. Her hair was cut short, just below her ears, much shorter than she had worn it when she was young. "It suits me better that way now," she insisted. She had, however, never altered the gently curling bangs that tumbled down her forehead and that Jack liked to part in the middle when she stopped listening to him or was lost in reverie. "Hello, you still here?" he'd ask, brushing them off her eyebrows and exposing the worry lines he wished he could paint away. But then she would relax, her nose would wrinkle, and the creases would ease as she smiled. At those moments, her cobalt eyes always seemed to have a questioning look, or was it one of anticipation, as if there were something specific Susie was expecting Jack to say. But he was never sure what. When they had first met at the University of Toronto, he had thought—or hoped at least—that it was a signal that she liked him. He was glad that he had got that right and asked her out on a date. Then, when he saw that look again, he thought perhaps it meant that she was available sexually as well. But Jack had, nevertheless, moved cautiously because he wasn't sure. And he had been right to be patient. Susie was not what in those days would have been called "loose." Still, Jack was never entirely sure how to read that quizzical look in Susie's eyes. But he did know that it wasn't any longer a signal of availability.

"No, Linda was definitely different from the others. She'd read *H.V. Morton's London,* and Wordsworth's poem 'Upon Westminster Bridge.' So, we got up at five to watch the sun rise over the Thames. I'll never forget it. And in Rome, while the others shopped we went to Castel Gandolfo to see Pope Pius XII bless the faithful from his bedroom window. I remember we knelt with the others and prayed."

"But, you weren't carrying rosaries, were you?" Jack wiped his mouth with his white linen napkin.

"Just guidebooks. But I thought Linda was going to convert on the spot. And we went to the opera together at the Baths of Caracalla."

"While the others listened to 'Three Coins in a Fountain' on the radio." Jack had heard it all before.

"Yes. In Italian. You should leave the rest of that wine, you know. Remember what the cardiologist said?"

"No."

"Just one glass."

"I couldn't hear him. He mumbled."

"You're hopeless."

They finished their main courses and ordered one chocolate brownie with vanilla ice cream and chocolate sauce, Susie's favourite. "But two spoons please. He's bound to want a bite. And, oh, herbal tea. A pot for two, please… You know, when I think about it, I guess my closest friend was Becky actually. Not growing up so much, but later, as adults. Mmm. Delicious brownie. Want another bite?"

"Thanks. I thought you'd never ask."

"I always felt she understood me almost as well as you do. And she was really good to us, especially about the cottage."

"No question."

After her parents died, Susie shared ownership of the cottage at Higgins Beach with Rebecca. But Becky married a dentist from Bracebridge who had spent his youth at his parents' cottage on Lake Muskoka. In their thirties they had bought their own property on the same lake and, rather than Higgins Beach, they had spent most of their holidays in Muskoka, only going occasionally to Maine on short trips. So, while Becky paid half the taxes and maintenance, for years Susie and Jack had the cottage largely to themselves and their kids. And since Becky's own children stood to inherit two properties in Muskoka, when she was diagnosed with ALS, Becky left the cottage at Higgins Beach to Susie in her will. Now, on Susie's teacher's pension and Jack's modest income from painting, it was a struggle to maintain it, but their own kids, Catherine and Tom, helped a little. After Susie retired, they started spending most of every summer in Maine and much of September, too, when they had Higgins' half-mile of hard-packed, golden sand to themselves and the gulls pecking in pools for crabs and clams, undisturbed by dogs snatching Frisbees from the salty air with the deftness of NFL receivers. Now, because of the reunion, they had closed up a little earlier than they wanted in order to return to Canada.

———

"So, if you hadn't grown up as neighbours, but met later, do you think you and Jay would have become friends?"

"I'm not sure. We're very different, but it's hard to let go of friends who are a link to your childhood. And you know if it weren't for Jay I'd never have got that summer job at the Ojibway Hotel. In that case, I'd never have met Lou, Sally, Cass, and Bev, and we'd still be in Maine. Do you mind that we had to leave early?"

"No! Of course I don't. They've been my friends, too, for eons now. And there's Linda as well. I doubt she would be part of the group except for me."

It was the next day and Jack was turning up the ramp onto the New York Freeway. Buffalo presented a major traffic hurdle for them, so, as they approached the city and Route 20 became more congested, they needed to use the freeway briefly. Near Rochester, they would turn off again and drive cross-country to the Lewiston Bridge on the Niagara River not far from the Falls. Once he was comfortably on the freeway, Jack returned to the reunion. "You know, Jay is a lot like Sally. They would have made a good couple. He's a social climber, just like her. That's how he got us jobs at the Ojibway. In high school, he made friends with guys who had cottages in Muskoka and Georgian Bay. He even knew Sally vaguely when she was at Bishop Strachan School. Maybe she even mentioned the Ojibway to him. It was the kind of information that he would have filed away."

"I think Sally was always a reach for Jay. He's so obviously middle class."

"But Lou?" Jack interjected. "From a poor Italian immigrant family?"

"I know. But Sally was confident he'd make it. With Jay, she couldn't be sure."

"True. Jay always dreamed big, but he didn't have Lou's determination, nor his guile. I remember, when we were five or six, there was this airplane Jay was building in their family driveway. He'd wired two wheels off a broken wagon to the bottom of an old orange crate and nailed a long board across the top of it. Have I told you this story?"

"I think so, but go ahead. I don't remember the details."

"I asked him if the plane was almost finished, and he said it was getting there. But he needed a rest because it was hard work. He was stretched out on his back in the grass beside the driveway and there were tools scattered all around him: hammers, saws, screwdrivers, chisels. I asked him if he was sure the thing was going to fly. 'Of course it will,' he said defensively, 'you don't think I'd spend all this time building it if I wasn't sure it would fly, do you? We're going to fly it right over the city, and then we'll cruise over the harbour.' He got up from the grass and stretched out his arms. 'When the other guys are taking the ferry to Centre Island, we'll dive-bomb 'em.'"

"And that's when you said maybe the two of you could dump water on them," Susie intervened. "Right?"

"Yes, and Jay said 'no' very firmly. 'That would be illegal.'"

Susie broke into a big smile, and her nose wrinkled again. "I love it!"

You look so much younger now, Jack thought. *Almost like the girl I met at university and who went with me to London to do a Ph.T. while I was at art school. Jesus, that's really what everyone called it then. Putting Hubby Through! How far we've travelled!* "Yeah, that was Jay all right, always planning. Still is, I guess. I can't help but like him, though. He's open and gregarious, and he's always seemed vulnerable. In him, it's kind of an endearing quality, but it's what got him into such a mess, poor bugger, when Cass went after Lou in the media."

Bells chimed suddenly and near at hand. They startled Susie and Jack and, at first, they couldn't locate the source. "It's the phone! Where is it?" Jack cried.

Susie clutched her handbag, but the ring wasn't coming from there, nor from her coat pocket. "The glove compartment! It's in there." Susie pressed the latch, pulled out the phone and, as she put on her reading glasses, she ran her index finger along its base.

It was their daughter, Catherine. "Where are you? Why did you take so long to answer? I thought I'd have to leave a message."

"The phone was in the glove compartment, dear. It took a minute to find it."

"You ought to carry it on you, you know. And why didn't you answer the text message I sent you yesterday?"

"The ring tone was off. We only discovered that this morning. You know, that little lever on the side. It was showing yellow. So we didn't hear your message come in."

"So why didn't you text me when you finally saw it?"

"I don't know, dear. Maybe because I didn't know where my stylus was, and it takes so long to tap a reply without it. Sorry."

"Anyway, where are you?"

"At the moment, we're driving towards the bridge at Lewiston. We're going to Niagara-on-the-Lake for three nights for the Shaw Festival and then to Toronto. We'll be at home until Monday and then we'll drive to Georgian Bay for the reunion at the Pipers' cottage."

"Well, phone me when you get to Toronto."

"Okay, dear."

"Promise? Won't forget?"

"I'll phone for sure. Love you, sweetie. Bye."

Susie clicked the screen off and removed her glasses. "Catherine seemed upset about our not answering her message."

"Yeah, worried about two innocent old farts driving on their own through big, bad Trumpland."

Susie put the phone in her purse, but then, right away, she got it out again. "I better make sure I didn't inadvertently turn off the ring tone like yesterday."

Jack laughed. "Well, at least we have a smartphone, even if we're not very smart about using it. You know, I remember at the Ojibway Hotel all there was on the whole island was one radio phone in the office. If any of the staff wanted to call someone, the only way they could do it was from a pay phone at the Pointe au Baril Station."

Jack's remark brought them back to where they were heading. "So, if you hadn't bunked with Cass at the Ojibway along with Jay and Lou, do you think you would have become friends with him anyway?"

"Probably not. I mean, he's generous and he can be a lot of fun. But he always goes too far. You know what he was like at the hotel. I've told you about the Barbie Bigelow Affair."

"Yes. It haunts us to this day."

"Well, I don't think he's changed that much since then. And if he has another stroke, I don't expect a sudden deathbed appeal for forgiveness either."

"Jack! Ouch! That's awful."

Chapter 2

Jack was sitting on the rocks behind the hotel dock late that afternoon in 1958, sketching the wood frame buildings along its sun-bleached boards: the repair shop at the far end, then the gas pumps, warehouse, sports and gift shops, and finally the butcher and grocery stores directly below the hotel. On the bulletin board at that end, there was a sign advertising *Love is a Many Splendored Thing: Dance Hall, 8.00 p.m.* He drew it, too, that day. But not the hotel. He already had some pen and ink drawings of it towering behind the dock, looking elderly but distinguished in weathered cedar shakes, an octagonal tower at one end. The white pines in front reached beyond the third-storey windows, straight and tall, not like the bent and stunted ones in Group of Seven paintings. And their branches were long and healthy, heavy with India green needles. They weren't the scrawny, emaciated survivors of a glorious past that he lamented when he observed them in later years, ravaged by saw-fly caterpillars and other invasive species, stoically awaiting their demise. As the sun slipped from the dock that day, the pines turned golden and the hotel roof flamed a mix of scarlet and vermilion. In their presence, Jack felt a sense of youthful optimism. All the staff did in the summer of fifty-eight.

On the dock just below him, there was a row of deck chairs and two teenage girls were sitting in them, clad in Bermuda shorts. One was absently running a comb through her long blonde hair, the other, legs outstretched, was carefully studying her freshly painted toes. In front of them, their outboards were brushing gently against the dock; they were cottagers who'd come to the hotel to shop or just to gossip. Jack didn't know them, but their conversation was familiar.

"So, what do you think of Cass?"

A shrug.

"I think you're snowed."

"Ah, come on. Just because I think he's groovy, it doesn't mean I really dig him."

"Why don't you hang around after they unload the barge? Maybe he'll take you to the show."

"I'm going with Bruce."

"Bruce? He's a creep. All he wants to do is make out. He was all over Peggy Winslow at the wiener roast at Flat Rock."

The voice of someone singing reached them faintly from across the water:

Fucked last night, fucked the night before
Going to get fucked tonight
Like I never got fucked before.

By the buoys, marking the channel to the hotel dock, an old and battered workboat was chugging slowly towards the Ojibway Hotel, its engine throbbing under the strain of a heavy load. It was towing a cadmium orange barge riding low in the water, weighed down by a large container with an insignia painted on its side: the face of a First Nations Ojibway.

Glorious, glorious, one pack of safes for the four of us
Glory be to God that there are no more of us
Cuz one of us is fucking all alone.

Holding the wheel of the workboat lightly in one hand and jauntily swinging a bottle of beer in the other, Cass was paraphrasing one of his favourite drinking songs. As the boat approached the dock, he slowed the engine and in the same motion tossed his empty beer to Jay, sitting in the stern watching the barge. "Okay, Daddy-O," Cass shouted. "Up with the last of the brew."

Jay stirred and hauled in the long painter slapping against the side of the boat. Tied with clove hitches at the end were two bottles of beer—long-necked and green—their labels peeling after a couple of hours in the cold water during the slow trip out from Pointe au Baril Station. By now, Cass had slowed the boat almost to a stop as he brought it and the barge alongside the dock. The tow rope had slackened, and the barge was drifting closer to the boat, enabling

Jay to leap to it and walk along its deck to the stern to fend it off the dock. There were no fingers and slips in those days, just one long stretch of rough, sun-bleached planks from the grocery store to the repair shop. Later on, everything changed: all the services moved to different locations, more docks were added, and the cedar strips with 10s and 35s were replaced by fibreglass boats with 75s to 300s. More for Jack to lament.

The rocks leading up to the hotel were suddenly alive with activity as the kitchen staff hurried to the dock to help unload the barge. Jack put down his sketchpad and went over too, climbing aboard the workboat to help Cass and Jay.

When the unloading was finished, Cass untied the two bottles of beer that Jay had ostentatiously placed on the deck of the boat on the shore side. Pressing two of the bottles against his stomach, he hooked one cap inside the other and snapped a bottle open. "Here's to the Ojibway," Cass shouted. He tipped his soiled captain's cap to the staff on shore, chug-a-lugged the full bottle, and belched loudly. Jay used an opener for his and Jack noticed that he dumped half the contents between the floorboards. Then Cass reached under the bow deck for an empty twelve-pack and as he did so he muttered to Jay, "Look out Barbie Big Tits, here I come!"

"Barbie?" Jay sniggered, taking the twelve-pack from Cass. "Bullshit." He carried the empties ashore and placed them on their own away from the fresh supplies being lugged up to the kitchen. Cass had wanted to use a case of twenty-four, but Jay had insisted that they not exaggerate their prowess in case the hotel manager was alerted and they were fired. But only Cass, Jay, Jack, and Lou knew the true story—and Lou only because he looked twenty-one and was assigned to do the purchasing at Pointe au Baril: it was the same empty twelve-pack that was loaded in and out of the workboat every barge day.

As the last of the supplies were being hauled up the rocks, Cass and Jay swept out the container that was on the barge, but they saved a few chunks of dry ice for Cass to use later. Then they towed the barge to the boathouse at the back of Ojibway Island and Jack went back to artist mode. He'd never done a sketch of the kitchen staff crawling like a string of carpenter ants over the rocks to the back of the hotel.

When Cass and Jay returned in the workboat from the back of the island, they tied up at the gas pumps to refuel. Except on barge days, Jay was the hotel gas boy, so it was he who knelt on the stern deck of the workboat holding the hose into the tank. Six feet one and fair-haired, he was muscular back then. He'd been the quarterback at Upper Canada College the past two years and he was hoping to make the Baby Blues in the autumn at the same position. Unlike Cass, who was always sweaty after an unloading and splattered with grease on his face and hands, Jay looked as if he had just freshly dressed to take Sally to the show. He always managed to spend most of the unloading checking off items on the manifest as they were hauled out of the container, avoiding doing any heavy lifting himself. It wasn't that he couldn't have easily managed a sack of potatoes, but he preferred to stay fit with three daily swims and early morning work-outs in their cabin. There was less risk of a back injury that way, and Jay was ever cautious. Besides, having Sally or any of the other cottagers in the area see him perspiring over a crate of pineapples was not the image he wanted to project. That day he was wearing khaki shorts and a white T-shirt with *Yale* emblazoned on it. He'd bought it from an American cottager, and it was one of his favourites that summer, especially after Sally said she liked the way it fitted snugly across his chest, particularly when he flexed his muscles. Jay had already pre-registered at the U of T and, in fact, he hadn't applied to any American universities, but now he was having doubts about that decision. "I figure it would be really golden to go to an Ivy League school," he told Sally and Jack in his soft, confiding voice. "I'd be fat, man. Really fat."

By this time, outboards were arriving at the dock, bringing cottagers from the surrounding islands to the Ojibway for the Saturday night movie: an even mixture of prosperous young and old, brown and barefoot in Bermuda shorts or slacks, cashmere sweaters tied loosely around some necks. The gift shop was packed with eager customers and the grocery store was scooping out ice cream cones at a brisk pace. Two young boys carried theirs down to the gas pumps to see what Cass and Jay were doing. That was Cass's cue. Quickly, he tossed the dry ice he had saved from the barge over the side of the workboat and slipped a green garden hose lying on the floorboards over the transom. As he did so, Jack put down his sketch-pad and rejoined them in the workboat to see what Cass was up to.

"Hey, look at all those bubbles," one of the boys shouted. "What are they from?"

"We've got a diver down there," Cass answered. The boys must have missed the trace of a curl in his tightly set lips, the square, determined jaw angled slightly upwards, the arched eyebrows, and shifting ash-brown eyes that darted between them and the hose line. They were classic features of Cass at mischievous play.

The cone of the younger boy tilted at a precarious angle, dripping chocolate ice cream into the water as he leaned over the edge of the dock, peering at the hose and bubbles. "What's he doing?"

"Looking for a diamond ring an islander lost when they were getting gas this morning."

Ice cream trickled down the boy's chin from his wide, open mouth as his eyes moved uncertainly between Cass and the water.

"Yeah, sure," his older, freckle-faced companion said. "You're just jerking us around. I bet there isn't any diver down there."

"Guess again, Daddy-O." Cass suddenly jerked the hose. "Uh-oh. Three tugs. He needs me. Must be something wrong." He tore off his grey, oil-stained T-shirt and, in his khaki shorts, plunged off the stern of the workboat.

The older boy stopped licking his strawberry ice cream and stared at the spot where Cass had broken the surface. "What's he going to do?"

"Don't know yet," answered Jay, who had assumed Cass's position holding the garden hose.

Suddenly, Cass's head burst out of the water. "The diver's tangled in the crib. I gotta free him fast. He's getting low on oxygen." Cass quickly duck-dived to the bottom, located the dry ice, and swept it under the dock. Then he swam past the rock crib supporting the dock at the point where the stern of the workboat was tied and surfaced under the dock. For a few seconds, Jay and Jack could hear him gasping for air, but the boys couldn't.

"The bubbles stopped, the bubbles stopped!" the smaller one screamed.

"Hey, where's your buddy?" the other said, alarmed. "He hasn't come back up."

"Dunno, but I'm going to find out." Jay passed the hose to Jack and started stripping.

"I'm getting my dad."

"No! Hey, no, man. Wait a minute." Jay stopped undressing. His alarm bell was set way earlier than Cass's. "We're just horsing around."

"No way. Your buddy's drowned down there. And that diver, too. I'm getting my dad. Come on, Tommy."

"Naw, he's okay." Jay jumped off the workboat and put his arms around the older boy to restrain him. "There's no diver in the water and Cass has come up under the dock."

"No way. I'm getting my dad."

"Look!" Jack shouted at him, pulling the green hose out of the water. "See, it's just an ordinary garden hose. The bubbles were from dry ice Cass threw off the boat."

The boys returned to the edge of the dock, and the little one sucked the melting ice cream through the bottom of his neglected cone. "Whaddya mean?"

"Yeah, I knew you were joking." The older boy breathed easily again. "But you sure fooled Tommy."

"Listen," Jay spoke in his characteristically quiet, confiding voice again, but one that, this time, included a conspiratorial tone as well. "Jack and I gotta split. We're going to the show. You wait until our buddy swims back to the boat, and then tell him Barbie Bigelow was here looking for him, but since he wasn't here Jack is taking her to the movie. Then ask him for a buck each not to tell your dad we were goofing around."

"Yeah, man, no sweat."

"Whaddya mean?" the little one asked again, but by then Jay and Jack were already heading for Skid Row.

On reflection, Jack realized that it had been a stupid prank to pull. As he told Susie not long after they met, the three of them could have been in big trouble if the hotel manager had found out. But Jack hadn't really felt that way at the time. He had just thought Cass was a hell of a lot of fun. It was only later that he recognized that Cass had a chronic habit of pushing things too far. And it usually stemmed from his inherently competitive, even vindictive nature, especially in his relationship with Lou, and that all went back to the Barbie Bigelow Affair.

Skid Row was the name of the sleeping quarters behind the hotel: two rows of simple, one-room cabins, long gone now. The younger male staff lived there, while the older and married ones were on the top floor of the hotel with the girls. There were some guests on the second floor, but most were in the far more comfortable cabins strung along the shore of Ojibway Island. The Hungarian refugees who worked in the laundry slept in the small, stuffy quarters a floor above the washing machines. It bothered Jack that they were segregated from the rest of the staff, and sometimes he thought of raising the matter with the hotel manager, but, with characteristic reticence, he never did. In a way, however, the Hungarians were fortunate because their accommodation was clean and neat, especially compared to the mess at Skid Row. Smashed, empty beer bottles filled a gully behind the cabins and there were always soggy beer cartons outside the screen doors of several rooms. For weeks, a condom clung to the rocks beside one cabin, not far from a pink lump of vomit that had hardened on a swatch of green and black lichen.

When Jack and Jay got back to their cabin, Lou was there in his upper bunk, stretched out in his underpants reading *Playboy*. Like Cass, he had been at the hotel since pre-season, constructing docks, painting guest cabins, and doing other odd jobs in preparation for opening. How Lou and Cass ended up rooming together Jack didn't know, but the day he and Jay arrived, a week before the start of the season, Jay got talking to Lou in the staff dining-room at their first meal, discovered that Lou was Roman Catholic, and entered into the first of several discussions with him about religion. When Lou learned that Jay was an Anglican, he asked, "What about your friend here?"

"You mean Jack? Oh, he's nothing. An agnostic, I guess."

"Well, you guys better come and room with Cass and me. You'll be easier to convert than he is."

The rough plank walls of their cabin had been brightened with a summer's accumulation of artifacts, mostly supplied by Cass. There was a menu from the dining-room in which Cass had embedded his hatchet and scrawled in blood red "Chef's Delight." And there was a poster advertising the senior regatta of the Pointe au Baril Islanders Association that had been held at the hotel the weekend before the Barbie Bigelow Affair. Event number eight had been circled in black ink: *Bang and Go Back Race.* Beside it, Cass had scrawled, "I take the blue ribbon!" Nailed to the wall above his bed was, however, his prize possession: a metal highway sign with large black numbering: 69. He'd piked it from the road on one of his daily trips in the workboat to Pointe au Baril Station.

Jay's contribution to the décor was a spring chest expander that hung from a nail by the door, plus a red and black Princeton pennant, tacked to the wall by his bed. "Maybe I should have tried for a football scholarship to Princeton," he agonized more than once. "Spike's applied and he never played quarterback in high school. Besides, I did better in the Senior Matric than he did." The others never really learned who Spike was, or how much Jay really knew about his talent.

Jack's additions to the room slowly accumulated over the summer as he tacked up sketches, including ones of Jay pumping gas, Cass driving the workboat, and Lou carrying a bucket of ice to one of the guest cabins at the back of the island. Surprisingly, there was nothing of Lou's on the walls, except a small crucifix above the head of his bed. "It gives me the creeps," Cass said from time to time and invariably that would lead to a religious discussion:

Jay: "I know it's not that different from being high Anglican. But transubstantiation I just don't understand."

Cass: "Transubstantiation? What the fuck is that?"

Jay: "When you drink the wine at communion, you're actually drinking the blood of Christ."

Cass: "Holy vampires! So, what if you choke on a wafer while you're sipping the wine? Does blood come gushing out of your mouth?"

A chuckle from Lou.

Jay: "Of course, we don't have confession either. So that's another difference."

Cass: "Yeah, what the shit is that all about anyway? You don't really tell the priest everything, do you? I mean even that you use condoms?"

"No. I don't tell him that."

"Uh-oh! Naughty, naughty. You're a sinner like the rest of us. You're going straight to hell." Cass always warmed to the debate and by this point he'd be standing on his bed holding on to the railing of Lou's upper, so he could look him in the eye. "And what about this virgin, Mary? She gets more attention than Christ himself. I don't get it. An immaculate conception? What a downer. She went through a pregnancy, child labour, and all that shit and never even had the pleasure of getting laid."

"Yeah, just like you," Lou sniggered.

"Guess again, buddy boy. Hey, I bet at De La Salle you got math problems that went like this: 'If Jesus walks from Bethlehem to Nazareth twice as quickly as Joseph and Joseph is half again as fast as Mary, how many miles away will the others be when Jesus reaches his destination if the distance between the two cities is eighty miles.'"

Lou just laughed. "You dumb bugger. Jesus wouldn't have walked. He'd have ridden a donkey."

"Hey, did you guys hear that?" Cass guffawed with delight. "Jesus rode asses. Can you believe it? He rode asses."

One time, Lou attempted to shift the focus of the conversation by asking Jack why he was an agnostic, but Cass answered for him. "Because, he's a fucking fence-sitter; he always is."

Jack simply shrugged and told Lou, "I don't know. It was blank before I was born. I'm afraid that's what it will be like when I die."

"Yeah, so you're an atheist like me, but without balls," Cass interjected. "Come on, Daddy-O, when it's over, it's over. It's tits up and lights out."

Eventually, Jay would try to end the banter. "You know, Pinky [that's what everyone called Lou back then] I should go into the Station with you next Sunday. You could take me to the Catholic Church, and another week we could go to the Anglican, and compare." But Jay never got around to going with Lou. His interest in religion was only intermittent.

As soon as Jack and Jay got back to the cabin that infamous day, Jay told Lou about the prank with the dry ice. "You should have been there, man," he said, pulling briefly on his chest expander. "We really deked Cass. He's going to come flying in here flipping his lid."

Lou chuckled quietly but went on thumbing through his *Playboy* as Jay talked, and all he said when Jay was finished was "silly bugger."

Lou had constructed shelves at the far end of the cabin where he kept in neat rows his different brands of deodorant, after-shave lotion, and hair oil, as well as his sunglasses, portable record player, and transistor radio. He and Cass had originally occupied the two lowers, but when Jack and Jay arrived, he generously offered his to Jay, though he claimed it was because Cass kept using his bed as a couch and smelling it up. By default, Jack had the other upper. The major drawback was that Cass loved to lie on his bed passing wind and the putrid odour would rise and hang in the air around the uppers. But Lou was resourceful. He purchased a spray with a fresh pine fragrance and used it liberally to control the problem. It was also intended as a defence against the smell of fish guts emanating from Jack. He was the hotel's dock boy. Every morning he prepared the boats for the hotel guests who wanted to go fishing and arranged for guides from the Shawanaga Reserve. In the evening, he'd clean their catch, mostly smallmouth bass and perch, and take them up to the hotel chef in carefully marked bags to serve at dinner or breakfast the next day. Lou, however, never complained to Jack that he smelled. Jack was pretty sure that Lou liked him right from the start, but he didn't know why. Maybe, he thought, it was just because they shared the uppers.

Lou's real name was Luigi Piccolo. He was a year older than

After the movie, there were several minutes of talking and laughing all along the dock, and then the whine of outboards leaving, and the flicker of lights searching the black water for markers and shoals. Sally's 35 rocked in their wake as she, Jay, and Jack sat on the edge of the dock, holding the boat out with their feet.

"Gee, I don't know, Jay. But I think you're doing the right thing. If you went to Michigan, it might be tough to make the Wolverines."

"Yeah. I guess you're right."

"Besides, you'll find that Trinity College is pretty special. Everyone says so."

The swells from the departing outboards had subsided and Sally lowered her feet from the gunwales of her boat and tucked her long, slim legs up against her chin. She took a cigarette from the package she'd been clutching in one hand and held it between her index and forefinger.

"Yeah. I figure I'll take English and History. But you know, I may go into Theology after that. I'm more religious than I thought. I've been talking a lot with Pinky."

"No, Jay, I don't think so," Sally answered gently, but firmly. "You'd be wasting yourself. Don't you think so, Jack?"

"Yeah," Jack whispered, holding a finger over his lips and lifting his head to the stars. "Just hope there's no one up there listening to us."

"I don't know. I think I could write some pretty good sermons."

Sally laughed easily and deeply with a nonchalance Jack wasn't sure she really felt. He assumed she was horrified at the thought that, if their relationship lasted, she could end up married to a minister. That would never have been in her plans. Yet, there were doubtless moments, Jack was sure, when Jay could see himself in a mitre and gold vestments, kneeling on a hassock. It wasn't the most common image that rolled through his head that summer, but it was one that did get screen time, thanks to his discussions of religion with Lou. "No, Jay," Sally counselled in her deep, languid voice. She always seemed to grasp early the probabilities of life that others only slowly accepted. "It's just too much chapel. You'll get over it."

"Yeah. Going to church is like getting drunk," Jack joked. "It leaves you feeling awful, so you know you'll quit doing it some day; you just don't know when."

Sally had graduated that June from Bishop Strachan School where she'd been a boarder, since her parents lived much of the year in Bermuda. But, apart from her father who took only short vacations, the rest of the family spent the summer at their Georgian Bay cottage—in what was known locally as Cincinnati Bay. She had seen Jay a few times in high school, watching UCC football games from the sidelines, and her chums had rated him tops as a catch: handsome, athletic, intelligent, but not boringly bookish. So, on her first trip that summer from the cottage to the Ojibway, she'd been pleased to discover him working at the gas pumps. Pretty quickly, they had started hanging around together. No one exactly dated; they did things mainly as a group—at least until the end of the evening. But everyone figured that Sally was Jay's girl.

Sally was lanky, but not too tall for Jay. She had soft, light brown hair, worn shoulder-length back then, and it lifted gently behind her on breezy days. Her cheeks were lightly freckled and her nose narrow and unobtrusive, making her mouth seem larger and her lips fuller than they really were. Always her hazel-coloured eyes focused intently on whomever she was talking to, flattering them that she was intensely interested in what they were saying. Even in white shorts and one of Jay's UCC T-shirts, covered that night by a navy-blue sweater, she somehow looked more sophisticated than the others. They'd all concluded she wasn't loose, but the consensus was that for the right guy—and Jay seemed to be that person—she'd eventually go all the way.

Looking back, however, Jack figured they probably had it wrong. There was a lot of talk then about "doing it," but not many of them actually did, at least not before university. Sally may have looked the type: pretty, mature, confident, and relaxed with the opposite sex. But on reflection, Jack didn't think she really felt that way. In fact, he recalled her saying to him that summer in her self-deprecating manner, "I'm not the type guys groove on. Too tall, my nose is kind of short, and no one likes freckles. I'll probably end up an old maid. Headmistress at BSS or something. God! Can you imagine?"

"Why don't you take Soc. and Phil. the first year?" Sally suggested to Jay. "A lot of people do that while they're making up their minds on their major."

"Yeah, maybe I will. That's what Spike is going to take if he doesn't get the Princeton scholarship. And you are too, aren't you Jack?"

"Yeah," he answered. "It's there for the procrastinators."

Jay slipped Sally's cigarette from between her fingers, lighted it, and took a couple of drags before passing it back to her. "Hey, you coming over tomorrow morning?"

"Yes. Why?"

"It's Pinky's day off, and he needs a ride into the Station. He's going down to Gerry Dunn's in Bala. Duke Ellington is going to be there. Do you think you could take him in?"

"Sure." That was Sally. Always obliging, always ready to help out. She slid into the stern of her outboard. "Hey, listen, that was fun. I enjoyed the movie."

"No big deal. We'll do something better in the fall."

"Great. See you tomorrow. See you too, Jack. Don't you and Jay stay up all night now."

"Don't worry, I'll tuck him in early. After all, he's just a kid."

Jay and Jack watched her flashlight seeking out the two channel buoys and when they heard her shift to full throttle and head towards Cincinnati Bay, they got up from the dock. "Hey, whaddya say we cruise back to the boathouse and scope out Cass and Barbie," Jay suggested. "That's where Cass said he was taking her after the show."

"Cool."

Half way along the path to the back of the island, they could hear the voices of two people moving towards them. "Quick! Over here!" Jack whispered. They stepped gingerly over some blueberry bushes and ducked behind a clump of juniper a few feet from the path. "Lucky we didn't come down on a rattler."

By the light of a half moon, they could tell that the first person approaching them was a woman in a loose-fitting sweater with breasts that pressed firmly against it. Behind her was a short, stocky guy struggling to keep up with her fast gait. "So, what do you all think of the fellas up here in Canada anyway?" Cass was saying, overdoing Barbie Bigelow's Indiana accent.

"Oh, I think they're real fine, Bobby," She was mimicking Cass's attempt to imitate her and calculatingly employing the boyish form of his real name. "Almost as nice as my steady back home."

Their voices trailed away, and Jack and Jay followed them at a safe distance until they stopped at the fire escape at the rear of the hotel, used by the staff living on the third floor rather than the front entrance. Jack and Jay crept along the back of the staff dining-room until they were in hearing range again. "Sure you don't want to go over to the Rec Hall and play some ping pong?" Cass asked.

"Uh-uh. I gotta be at work at seven. Chef likes us to be bright-eyed and bushy-tailed." They could hear her start up the fire escape. "See ya tomorrow, Bobby boy."

For a couple of minutes, Jack and Jay could sense that Cass was still just standing there. He knew it was too early to go back to the cabin in case any of the others were already there and suspected he'd struck out badly. But eventually they saw his shadow as he moved slowly back along the path in the direction of the boat-house—back to the site of his intended conquest, the long cushioned seat in the stern of the hotel launch.

"Ping pong? Play some ping pong? See ya tomorrow, Bobby boy," Jay burst out at last. "No-o-o-o! What a loser. I wish Pinky had been here to see this. It's golden."

"Yeah," Jack agreed, but actually he felt sorry for Cass. He knew Jay was going to give him a hard time for years for going down swinging with Barbie.

Jay didn't feel like going to bed yet and he wanted to find some of the gang to tell them what had happened to Cass, so the two of them walked down to the dock to see if anyone was still around. No one was there, but a light was on in the repair shop, so they strolled down to that end of the dock, where the chief mechanic was working on the shaft of an outboard motor. His large room, heavy with the stench of oil and grease, was strewn with the half-dissected guts of long-cursed-at engines, chipped and bent propellers from careless picnics at Flat Rock, and batteries too weak to coax a fifty to life. The mechanic's assistant, known affectionately by all as "H-h-h-hap-p-py H-H-H-Harry," was sitting on a stool by the door, his work finished for the night. He had a beer beside him and his bristly, unshaven face, flushed from years of too much booze, was bent over his banjo.

Under the s-s-s-stones lies M-M-Mary Jones,
Under the s-s-s-stones lies M-M-Mary Jones,
B-b-but G-G-God only knows, those aren't the only s-s-stones
That Mary Jones lay under.

He always rushed the final phrases. It kept him from stuttering, but often made it impossible to catch the punch line.

"So, what's new?" Jack greeted him.

"Oh, n-n-nothin.' J-j-just a little quiet s-s-strummin.' T-t-tomorrow's my day. G-g-gonna go to P-P-Parry S-S-Sound to get d-d-drunk with the b-b-boys. G-g-gonna c-c-come home three sh-sh-sheets to the wind."

He pointed to the engine shaft his boss was working on. "B-b-bottom end c-c-country, I c-c-call it. Those sh-sh-shoals are m-m-mines of silver."

Harry and the mechanic were too old to mix with the summer staff and there was always the risk of anything they heard being relayed to the hotel manager. Jack could sense Jay's disappointment that they were the only people around he could tell about Cass's misadventure, but he was prudent enough to avoid the subject, and simply asked Harry for another dirty ditty.

Oh, the r-r-roosters they grow t-t-tall in ole M-M-Mobile,
Oh, the r-r-roosters they grow t-t-tall in ole M-M-Mobile,
Oh, the r-r-roosters they grow t-t-tall,
They eat' em b-b-balls 'en all
Down in ole Mobile.
By the light of the s-s-silvery m-m-moon,
By the light —

Suddenly Cass was at the door. He'd changed his mind and reversed directions on the path. Harry stopped strumming. "So, what the f-f-fuck's a g-g-guy like you d-d-doin' here at this t-t-time of n-n-night? How come you ain't g-g-givin' it to some b-b-broad in your b-b-bunk?"

Cass's thick eyebrows had arched in surprise when he saw Jay and Jack in the repair shop, but he recovered quickly. "Aw, I've already had my ass," he boasted. "I had to poke it in early. She's gotta be up early." Obviously, he didn't share Jay's and Jack's reservations about being frank in front of the repairmen.

* * *

Later, when the three of them got back to their cabin, Lou wasn't there. The next day, Jay and Jack calculated that it must have been while they were in the workshop that Lou had slid out of his bunk, washed and deodorized himself, and then glided over to the fire escape at the back of the hotel. Half an hour later, lying on the cushioned seat in the stern of the hotel launch, he was running his slender fingers gently over the ample breasts of Barbie Bigelow, stroking them with the same skill he hit a cue ball.

A loud fart exploding out of Cass awakened them all the next morning. "Come on, you lazy tits," he shouted. "If you got more ass you'd sleep better and be up earlier."

"So how did it go last night?" Jay asked yawning, as he rolled over to look at Cass. "Seriously now. Not the bullshit you were stringing us in the repair shop."

"Daddy-O, you shouldda been there. She was so hot there would have been seconds for you."

"Come off it. You didn't even get to first base."

"You kidding? I'm serious. She's loose, man. Well, at least for me."

Lou stirred in his upper. "Yeah? Well, how about proving it? Let's have a look at your safes."

Suddenly, Cass remembered he'd forgotten to open the package and take one out before picking up Barbie Bigelow. It was a pretty careless mistake when he was always so careful about reloading the empty carton of beer into the workboat every barge day. Involuntarily, Cass reached under his pillow for his condoms. "Hey! What the shit! They've been opened," he shouted without thinking. "Who's been into my safes?"

There was a short silence and then, at the same moment, they all heard Lou, still stretched out in his bed, chuckling softly. It was impossible to tell who was the most surprised to discover what had happened, Cass, Jay, or Jack.

"Piccolo, you fucking bird dog," Cass glared at him, his face flushed and contorted. His dark eyes narrowed, and he pointed a shaking index finger at Lou. "I'm gonna fucking get you."

Chapter 3

Eyes fixed on the highway ahead, Susie reflected on all that she had heard over the years about that summer at the Ojibway. "Do you think Lou was actually interested in Barbie Bigelow, or did he just want to put Cass in his place?"

"I don't know. It can be hard to tell with him. Maybe a bit of both. He certainly chased a lot of women that summer, but I'm sure he was also tired of Cass's boasts and digs at Catholics. And, he's instinctively competitive, not just with Cass—almost anyone. I don't think it's ever a vengeance thing with him, though. He can take a lot, but sometimes he likes to dish it out, too."

"No wonder Cass always wanted to get him back. But why did he go as far as he did? And why did he hold onto his grudge for such a long time?"

"I think it's because he's always had an inferiority complex and getting even helps alleviate it."

"But why does he feel that way?"

Jack shrugged. "Lou's made a ton more money. Jay got into the foreign service. I'm happily married; he's on his own. Who knows? Maybe his father verbally abused him as a kid, made him feel like a shit."

"Poor Cass. He could have been quite likeable if he'd just let things go. I mean he *was* fun back then. That prank with the dry ice was pretty hilarious. But, were all the guys like that—always talking about 'getting it' and treating girls as sex objects?"

"Yeah, pretty much. It was a different era. Male predators were rarely exposed. To be fair, though, Cass did back off when Barbie made it clear she wasn't interested in sex."

"And proposed ping pong instead. I love that. But what about you?" Susie was confident she knew the answer. "Did you behave like a typical male?"

"What? Me, too?" Jack laughed, but then he hesitated. *Jesus!*

I wasn't like the horrible guys we're hearing about now. But was I sensitive to women's vulnerable situation—to their unequal treatment? I don't think so. Not until much later. And I certainly didn't make any effort to restrain Cass. I'm guilty too, I guess.

"Yes, you. Was there anyone you went after?"

"Hey, I was the dock boy. I had to clean the guests' catch every evening. That was hardly the way to score with the girls."

"But I bet you were so cute some of them found you irresistible anyway."

"Well, there was one girl. I've told you about her. Mary-Anne Thompson, I think her name was."

"You think?"

"She had a classy chassis, as they said, and breasts even Barbie Bigelow couldn't beat. But I never touched them. We made out one night at a campfire party; that was all."

Susie pouted and frowned. She knew he was telling the truth, but still she wanted the reassurance she always sought. "That was all? You didn't love her or anything?"

"No. You know that. I was waiting for you to come along."

She leaned over and kissed him on the cheek. "I was waiting for you, too."

Jack chortled. "I guess, though, I was still a little naïve about girls and sex that summer. Remember the Everly Brothers song 'Wake Up Little Susie'? It was really big that year."

"How could I ever forget it? In Europe, Linda kept kidding me, 'Wake up Little Susie. You're *so* clued.'"

"Well, I remember we were lying in our bunks one night talking about girls and Cass sniggered, 'You know Jack believes that Susie and her date actually fell asleep at the movies.' Then he lowered his voice and whispered, but loud enough for me to hear, 'He doesn't realize that at four in the morning they were humping big time in the back row of the theatre.'"

"And no doubt right after that Jay called you a loser," Susie added, "my innocent little angel…well, with a devil's fork in one hand."

Jack patted her on the shoulder. "I may have been naïve and

shy that summer, but when at last I saw you, I sure woke up."

The Sturridges reached Canadian customs at the Lewiston Bridge. The satisfied smile vanished from Susie's face and her forehead wrinkled into an anxious look again. "Okay, please behave yourself this time."

Jack lowered his window and the officer asked, "Anything to declare?"

"Yes, as a matter of fact." Susie tightened involuntarily. "I'd like to declare that I love my wife."

The officer hesitated, momentarily disconcerted, but then he smiled. "I think you're telling the truth," and he waved them through.

"Jack, I declare you an idiot!"

"Yes, but a lovable one, right?"

"Most of the time."

It was still early in the afternoon, so they took a short detour to Niagara Falls. Susie's idea—they hadn't been there in over ten years. Jack parked as near as he could to the Horseshoe Falls and they walked over to the railing at the point where the water was plunging into the rocky chasm below. A curtain of mist was hanging above the American Falls to their left as if suspended from an invisible ceiling, but the sky was clear above them and the teal blue water at the lip looked like smooth, iridescent ribbon candy racing into a rapacious mouth that was devouring the treat at a mesmerizing speed.

"I wish we had something we could throw in," Susie said. "It would be like playing Poohsticks with Catherine and Tom."

"Not much of a game here. They'd vanish instantaneously. Snuffed out like the lives of so many who went over the Falls in barrels and other contraptions, seeking a moment's fame."

"Well, the Falls are certainly putting you in a morbid mood," Susie scolded.

"No. Actually, I was thinking of that boy who survived in 1960. The boat he was in had engine trouble and then capsized. He was hurled into the rapids along with his sister. She was plucked from the river by onlookers twenty feet from the edge, but he went over with no protection other than a life jacket, yet all he got was a mild concussion. What were the odds of that?"

"Not good. I never heard that story."

"He was only seven, and he was rescued by the *Maid of the Mist*. What a fairy tale ending!"

Susie cast her eyes around the Falls and the foaming water in the menacing river above them, and then turned to Jack. "You know, for all its sad history and its tacky tourism, this is still a stunning place. I'm surprised you've never painted here."

"I thought of it once." The impish grin resurfaced. "A large oil canvas of newlyweds, wrapped in rubber tubes, plunging to their deaths over the Horseshoe Falls." He stopped himself from adding that they could choose that themselves as a dramatic way to go rather than ending up in a nursing home.

"How lovely. Yes, your kind of art. Never anything pretty."

"Maybe I'll have a crack at that scene one day."

"Who would ever buy it? Not that you care."

"Maybe a Niagara Falls marriage counsellor."

"An undertaker more likely. Let's go. You're making me feel depressed."

On their way to Niagara-on-the-Lake, Susie returned again to the reunion. "Jay has certainly changed from the way he was at the Ojibway, hasn't he? He's much less caustic now, not so hung up on other people's faults. More forgiving, I think."

"No question. Life does that to you, especially if you hang out with chameleons."

"Like Linda you mean?"

"Yeah. You know her name came up once at the Ojibway—before I met her at Trinity?"

"I didn't know that."

"Really?" *That's odd. I'm sure I told her.* So Jack reminded Susie how, at the Ojibway, Sally told him and Jay about Linda pretending to take an overdose of sleeping pills during the Senior Matric exams just to get attention.

"Gosh, that's news to me, but it sounds like Linda, always pretending, always searching for her true identity."

"Ah, so you agree with me that she's not really become a lesbian!"

Susie frowned. "I didn't say that."

Jack let it go, adding only, "Know what Jay said to Sally when he heard about the pills? 'How come all the losers went to Europe this summer. But maybe I should have gone. It's the sort of thing to do before starting college.'"

"Sounds like Jay." Susie fell quiet for a few minutes, admiring the flowerbeds she could see out her window as they drove along the Niagara River Parkway. Eventually, she sighed, "We were always planning to rent bicycles at Niagara-on-the-Lake and ride them through here to the Falls. Remember?"

"Yes."

"Now, it looks like we'll never do that—at least not without a couple of cans of oil to lubricate our joints."

"So, who's the morbid one now?"

More quiet reflection until Susie spoke again. "Georgian Bay has had a hold on you ever since the Ojibway, hasn't it?"

"Yes, I guess so. It's a fun time when you're eighteen. You're bound to feel nostalgic about wherever you were at that age—me on Georgian Bay, you in Europe. But it wouldn't still be a big draw if it weren't for Lou and Sally and our trips to their cottage. They remind me of the Bay's appeal, its elemental beauty."

"I think I like Muskoka better. Especially Lake Joseph, ever since we were there for Linda and Jay's wedding. It's gentler. The water is warmer and it's often calm. The woods are better for walking, too. The Bay often seems menacing to me—the high winds and waves, the dangerous shoals, the freezing water."

"They're all things I love about it. They make it wild and unpredictable, a moody bitch."

"You like bitches? I don't feel flattered. So, if you really love it there, how come you've never painted on the Bay?"

"It's all about landscape."

"And that's not your thing."

"Besides, how could I compete against Tom Thomson's trees and Ed Bartram's rocks? No way."

"No-o-o... Loser!" Susie poked Jack in the ribs.

"Hey, I've never painted on the Maine coast either, and I love it just as much as you."

———

Susie was never sure about that. Maybe the coast in general, but she wasn't convinced Jack loved Higgins Beach as much as she did. For him, it had not been a part of every summer since early childhood as it had been for her. He knew it only as an adult when, for Susie, it had already lost some of its quaint New England charm.

Higgins had a gentle sloping beach, safe for body-surfing, and the shore front was lined with brown-stained cedar-shake cottages, most proudly flying the stars and stripes. They had porches that were half enclosed behind large windows and half open to the elements. Old men and women sat there in wicker rocking chairs, looking, in Jack's view, "smugly satisfied in the knowledge that the Lord had rewarded them for their faithful adherence to the Protestant ethic." Several narrow streets ran up a gentle slope behind what Jack called the "front pews" and on these there were more modest homes, often with kitschy names painted over their doorways: *Linger Longer; Last Resort; Heaven-on-Earth*. Jack awarded them gold, silver, and bronze stars for their inventiveness—and for their owners' promise as "members of the aspiring middle class." It was a habit that sometimes irritated Susie because it was on one of these streets that her parents had eventually bought their family cottage.

Susie was missing Higgins already, especially pining for the days when you could walk up the main road from the beach and buy lobster rolls and Len Libby candies. There had also been a general store with a bowling alley on one side that had dim lighting and uneven lanes. It had employed pin boys at a wage of ten cents a game. Until much later, there had also been a gas station where you could rent rubber mats for surfing and buy drinks and snacks, but now that, too, had gone.

Still, there was much that remained unaltered and appealed to Susie's longing for simpler times. Across from the tidal Spurwink River at one end of the beach, there was the weathered hut of a lobsterman, salt- and barnacle-encrusted pots and red buoys stacked up against its walls. Part way along the beach, at low tide, you could still see the skeletal hull of a cargo ship that, in 1897, had run aground in a dense fog. And at the other end black rocks, covered in slippery green and brown seaweed, surfaced as the tide ebbed. Then, scattered around them were shallow pools where kids would wade with plastic pails, searching for shells, crabs, and starfish.

Whenever they had lobsters for dinner, there was always the custom of wading into the ocean with a large metal bucket to collect sea water for boiling them, since Susie insisted they were much better cooked that way. And every day, there was the pattern of carrying chairs, umbrellas, books, balls, and towels down to the beach. Like other families, they would toss a football, play beach tennis or softball, and sometimes, unlike the rest, they would make stumps and bails out of driftwood and use a tennis ball to play cricket, for Jack had studied art in London, England, while Susie taught primary school and they had at least a rudimentary knowledge of the game.

But most of all, the Sturridges just liked to lie on their towels and listen to the conversations of the locals "beaching it" just as they did. Every day, every summer, youths who never aged, lightly clad in swimsuits or cut-off jeans, would arrive in large numbers from Portland, parking their cars in lots on the road to the waterfront and carrying the same gear down to the beach as Susie and Jack— often radios and surfboards as well. The two of them would catch snippets of their conversations and music, trying to plug into the changing concerns of youth decade to decade: Vietnam war—"San Francisco"; Watergate hearings—"Song Sung Blue"; Monica Lewinsky—"The Boy Is Mine"; Twin Towers—"A Thousand Miles"; Isis—"Dark Horse."

———

Jack sensed that Susie had drifted away, but they were approaching Niagara-on-the-Lake, so he let her enjoy her reverie and didn't bring her back to their central conversation until they sat down for dinner that night. They were staying at the Oban Inn, built in 1824 as the residence of Duncan Milloy from Oban, Scotland, captain of the first steamship launched at Niagara. They ate in an intimate nook of the dining-room, its walls painted in cherry red and covered with photographs of stars from various performances at the Shaw Festival. "Did you know that Jackie Burroughs' brother, Gary, owned this place for thirty years?" Jack asked.

"Jackie…?"

"Yeah, Burroughs. She was at Trinity. Maybe she was never around when you came over."

"The name sounds familiar."

"She became an actress. Had a pretty successful career. Stage, movies, television. Hetty King in the CBC series *Road to Avonlea?*"

"Oh, the school teacher. Now I remember."

"She was a friend of Linda's at Trinity."

"Part of the literary and dramatic society crowd?"

"Yeah. Long, stringy hair, grey sweaters and black skirts. Flakey."

"Jack! Stop it."

"Anyway, did you know the inn burned to the ground in 1992 just as the guests were sitting down to dinner on Christmas night? Fortunately, no one was injured, and Gary Burroughs had it rebuilt the next year exactly as it had been. For the opening, he invited back any guests who had been at the inn the night of the fire to finish their dinners."

"What a lovely gesture. I must say they did a beautiful job with the reconstruction. It's just as nice as the Brewster Inn, and the lake view is better."

"Better food, too. More international. So, let's talk about Linda and how she was when you met her on that trip; it always amuses me. That way I'll shut up and finish my meal—before another fire breaks out. I'm not sure we can afford to come back for a second dinner."

"Okay. But first I want to hear about Beverley Scott at the Ojibway. When you talk about that summer, her name hardly ever comes up. Poor, forgotten Bev."

"Well, she was never part of the Barbie Bigelow Affair. Maybe that's why. But I remember she was down on the dock the next afternoon in the area beyond the grocery store where the staff were allowed to sun and swim in off-hours." Jack's mind flashed back to that spot.

———

It was where the chambermaids gathered after work, and some of the waitresses as well with time off before dinner. They played bridge or gossipped about the size of the tips they'd received. Wafting lazily along the dock, there was always the scent of summer — of suntan lotion, turning girls bronze and beautiful, *Mary-Anne Thompson, too!*

Some of the male staff were there that afternoon as well, including Cass, behaving as if nothing at all had happened the night before, no hint of mortification. He was jumping at the end of the diving board, arms outstretched as his body sprang higher and higher off the board. Then, as he reached his limit and a half gainer into the water seemed imminent, he abruptly stopped, and the board shuddered to a halt. Jack never saw Cass actually dive. He didn't know if he even knew how. It was at that point that Bev rushed down to the dock, wearing a one-piece pale pink bathing suit with buttons on the shoulder straps. At five feet even with a freckled face, thick thighs and the start of a stomach, she looked ridiculous in it, Jack recalled thinking. *Jesus! I guess I was as bad as the other guys. Everyone was always joking about her.*

Bev spread out her towel and skipped over to Cass at the diving board, crying. "Cassie-pooh." She pecked him on the cheek as he walked, hands on hips, off the diving board to meet her. "Scottie, baby," Cass answered. "Where have you been all of my life?" Bev wiggled her hips imitating Elvis before dropping to her towel for Cass to rub his bare foot in her short, curly brown hair.

———

"So, were they really in love back then?" Susie asked.

"No, it was just a game they played. Mind you, I think Bev would have liked the undivided attention of Cass or some other guy and at least an attempt to round second and head for third. I could tell from the postcard she inadvertently left on the dock one day.

'Having a blast. Wish you were here,' she had written in perfect penmanship. 'The guys are fab. I mean really fab.'"

"Oh, that's so sad. Poor Bev."

"Jay was always making fun of her, talking about how she went to Etobicoke Collegiate and was a cheerleader, as if that explained everything. 'I bet the guys shouted, "cartwheels, cartwheels,"' he sniggered, 'and she innocently obliged.' Once he joked that she was the one who did the write-up of the winter prom in the school annual that said 'a good time was had by all.' Cass was no better. When Bev suddenly jumped up from her towel to sing the song she'd composed for the farewell party she was planning for the end of summer, it was he who egged her on. The tune was from the musical *Salad Days*. It was big that year."

Jack ran through the words in his head.

The summer quickly is ending,
The Ojibway is ready to close,
We look back with fondest memories
To those first days in June
When we froze.

We'll always remember the corn roast
And the hot dogs out at Flat Rock.
These and other happy memories we'll
Take from the Ojibway dock.

"When Bev finished all Cass said was, 'Oh, that's groovy, honeychuckers. Really groovy. It'll move Pinky to tears.'"

"People can be so cruel. It's amazing Bev's survived it all… well, outwardly at least."

"No question. She's resilient." *But what did I ever do to help her feel better about herself? Nothing. I just saw her as good old lovable Scottie. I never made an effort to understand her, to boost her sense of self-esteem. Susie would be right to shout "Chauvinist!" Is it too late to make amends?*

"You know, to be fair to Cass, he wasn't crude and tasteless with everyone. It's just that he was a showman and he hid his insecurities in bluster. He was great with the hotel guides, for instance. He knew how to kid around with them without going too far. I was too tight-assed even to try, so, while I worked with them more than Cass did, he was the guy they really liked... Hey, how's your salmon?"

"Very nice. How's your soba noodle and miso?"

"Very flavourful. A lot of different spices. But I'm talking too much. I'll never finish it."

Susie eyed the almost-finished carafe resting between them. "You seem to be enjoying the wine as well."

"Oh, sorry. Do you want another glass?"

"No thank you. But it was nice of you to ask."

For some reason, Susie's gentle rebuke made him think of Bernard Shaw whose work they would watch and especially listen to the next two days. "Do you know what Shaw once said of marriage? It's an alliance entered into by a man who can't sleep with the window shut, and a woman who can't sleep with the window open."

Susie laughed. "I'd be more inclined to say it's an alliance that depends on the presence of a snoring room."

"Agreed. But for either partner."

Susie kicked him gently under the table. "I think I *will* have a little more of that wine."

"Anyway, back to the Ojb," Jack said. "I think it was just after Bev finished singing her composition for the farewell party that Sally showed up in her outboard. She'd just taken Lou into the Station on his way to Bala. So far as I know it was the only time they were alone together all summer."

"Wonder what they talked about."

"Whatever it was, I'm sure Sally found it hard going. Anyway, she landed near our end of the dock and I saw Jay walk over from the gas pumps to help her tie up. It was pretty quiet by that hour and Jay had unclipped his green bow tie and stuffed it in his pocket, at the ready if a boat happened to come in for gas. With his khaki shirt also unbuttoned at the collar, he looked less like Murray

Westgate in those old Esso ads and more like a handsome quarterback relaxing in the off-season."

Susie laughed. "How do you remember all that?"

"Painter's eye. Anyway, Jay and Sally sat down together near us on the rocks. Then it was their usual conversation and went something like this: 'I'm not so sure about Soc. and Phil. after all. Kind of an option for losers. Guys who don't know where they're going.'

"'Why not go into Commerce and Finance? I think you'd make a good businessman.'

"'Like your dad, you mean? Build a string of resorts in Bermuda and the Caribbean.'

"'Well, he certainly enjoys a nice lifestyle.'

"They were quiet for a moment while Jay pondered Sally's suggestion, and then he answered he'd have to consider the idea, because he thought he could be as good a businessman as Lou. I guess maybe the others overheard some of their conversation, too, because Bev and Cass started amusing everyone by imagining what their graduation yearbooks had said about them and their futures."

Jack drifted off, trying to dredge from his memory their quotations.

––––––

Cass describing Lou at De La Salle: "Pinky is the quiet, loner type, but he is also a schemer and his eyes are always open for the big chance. Outside of school, he keeps busy souping up his '46 Chevy and listening to music. Future: Commerce and Finance, and then owner of a sleazy nightclub that makes book at the back."

Bev about Sally: "Sally was our beloved head girl this year, captain of the field hockey team, and a stalwart in the choir. Everyone turned to her for advice, so Psychology is a natural for her at Trinity. She's popular with the guys, and maybe Mr. Right will come along this summer."

Bev again with Jay: "Jay led the football team to another winning season, but he had to fight off the girls as much as the opposition. Left wing on the hockey team and highest point total at the annual track meet, Jay was voted athlete of the year and most likely to succeed. Future: Undecided."

Cass for Bev: "Voted most enthusiastic student in the graduating class and every jilted guy's choice for a blind date for the spring prom. Future: head of a girl guide camp in Algonquin Park."

Bev laughed as if she weren't hurt. She flicked her towel against the seat of Cass's bathing suit, wiggled her hips at him, and started up to her room to change. "Well, we all know your future, Cassie-pooh. Driving a delivery truck for Labatts."

"Yeah?' Cass retorted. "Know what my yearbook said? That I was into everything and probably always would be.'"

"No-o-o!" Jay snorted. "We all know *that*'s bullshit."

––––––––

"So, what did they say about your future?" Susie finally terminated Jack's reverie.

"I can't remember."

"You can't remember? You with the photographic memory?"

"Honestly, I can't. Probably something like 'future: cynical, crotchety old geezer.'"

"You can come up with something better than that."

"Maybe impoverished painter? With loving and supportive wife?"

"Well, at least that's an improvement."

"You know, that conversation at the Ojibway that afternoon was the kind you tend to have at that time of year, often just with yourself. For me, the end of August is the real New Year's. There is time in the lazy dog days of summer to reflect on the past and contemplate the future. I always think of the CNE as the tinsel and horn that ring in the New Year. Then, on the Tuesday after Labour Day as they dismantle the merry-go-round, January begins." Jack paused, quietly reflecting on the youthful aspirations of their friends and how life had actually turned out for them. When he spoke again his voice was lower and husky. "I guess the dreams and promises of summer tend to meet cold winds—winds that are too chill for the pink-painted horses of summer."

"My, you're turning poetic!" Susie cried. "And sombre again, too."

"Yeah. So, let's talk about that trip to Europe and Linda. Thinking about her in that gondola always cheers me up."

Chapter 4

They're long gone now, those floating hotels of romance and anticipation, the lesser ships that crossed the North Atlantic from Montreal to England: the *Saxonia*, the *Ivernia*, the *Carinthia*, the *Empress of Canada*, and the *Empress of England*. Gone, too, are the interlopers in what was largely an Anglo-Saxon fleet, ships like the *Homeric* on which Susie sailed in 1958. Ah, the little *Homeric*— 40,000 tons of fun, carrying bunk loads of students to wine and lust in Europe. Employing an all-Italian crew was genius—sailors adept at liberating their charges from overweening parental control and instilling in them a desire for previously unimagined adventures.

The mammoth cruise ships of today usually shun the North Atlantic route of their forebears, but then, once you reached the Gulf of St. Lawrence, part of the adventure was fighting seasickness and keeping track of the missing faces at the large, circular tables of former strangers, now, briefly at least, intimate friends, drawn together by travel and the battle against the swell. "Hmm. I think I'll go on deck," Susie contemplated. "I'm not feeling hungry anyway."

"The best thing to do is to eat regularly," Godfrey Wincanton answered authoritatively. Susie noticed that one of the girls at the table rolled her eyes at his comment, and she was pretty sure the look was intended for her to see.

There were ten people on the Ulysses tour at their table. The girls were simply dressed in drip-dry A-lines or sheaths and pumps with bows on the toes, but their faces, flushed by a hint of make-up and the excitement of the voyage, offset their plain attire. The boys wore lightweight, checkered sports jackets, slacks and loafers, except that is for Godfrey Wincanton. He was in a tan-coloured three-piece suit with a white handkerchief in his vest pocket. His perfectly knotted brown and gold tie had an exaggerated loop before it disappeared inside his vest. His hands were delicately clasped at the edge of the table and he sat erect like an English gentleman of leisure favouring the dinner table with his informed company. But from the neck up, Godfrey was a complete contrast. He had a bad case of acne which had defied the best dermatologists in Toronto and, between frequent red blotches, his skin was pale and flakey. His watery, brown eyes, enlarged and blurred by the thick lenses of his horn-rimmed glasses, stared slightly cross-eyed at Susie with all the power of an aging, myopic dachshund. It was a face that wasn't helping her cope with her nausea.

Godfrey looked dismissively at the two flasks of red and white wine on their table, provided gratis by the ship. "What we need is something better for you than this rotgut. Antonio!" Godfrey summoned their waiter from another table as he raised the two flasks above his head. "Would you ask the wine steward to bring us two bottles of Châteauneuf-du-Pape, please?"

"Certainly, sir."

Godfrey patted Susie on the arm. "That will settle your stomach better than a walk on deck."

"You could have waited until Antonio came to our table," the girl with the rolling eyes hissed at him. It was not only his supercilious and rude behaviour that irritated her, but also his open flaunting of the guidelines set out in the brochure for their tour. Parents had been urged not to supply their children with more than $300 spending money so as not to create an unfair hardship for those of modest means. "Would you like some Gravol?" she asked Susie. "I have some in my cabin."

"No thanks. I think I'll try other means first," and Susie rose from the table.

"Well, don't just lie down in your cabin," Godfrey Wincanton lectured. "That's the worst thing you can do. Walk around on deck."

"That's what she said she was going to do. Are you deaf?" The Gravol girl correctly read the shocked expression on Susie's face. "Sorry. Not true. Here, I'm going with you. I can feel the ship slowing. I think we've reached Father Point."

"I'm Susie, Susie Goldsmith," Susie said as they reached the boat deck. "I'm sorry, I didn't catch your name when we sat down for dinner."

"I'm Linda. Linda...umm...yes, Linda Loony. That's what others would say. Linda Osterman actually. It's nice to meet you."

"You don't seem loony," Susie smiled. "You seem nice."

"Well, I'm not loony like that creep at our table. Sorry about the way I snapped at him, but I know him better than I'd like to. Our parents are friends. His are filthy rich. I guess that's obvious. Well, mine are too, I suppose. Anyway, when Godfrey's mother learned I was going to Europe, voilà, she decided he should go, too. I suppose so that there would be one person at least obliged to talk to him and try and be nice. Gad, what a challenge it's going to be. You'll help me, won't you?"

"I'll try," Susie laughed, brushing her blonde bangs to the side. Her blue eyes widened, shining at Linda the way they would at Jack just three months later.

"I could tell right away I was going to like you." The *Homeric*'s engines were barely audible now, and only the ship's momentum seemed to be still pushing it slowly through the gently rolling sea. "Look! There's a boat coming alongside. It's come out from Father Point Lighthouse to pick up the pilot; he's been with us since Montreal. I love this moment."

"You've crossed the Atlantic before?"

"Yes. Twice. But with my parents. All my grandparents lived in England then."

Leaning forward at the boat deck railing, the girls could see that a rope ladder had been lowered over the side of the ship at the point where the pilot boat was slowly moving at the same speed as the *Homeric*. A man climbed down the ladder, was helped aboard, and the little boat sped away. "Now, we're totally on our own," Linda announced dramatically as the *Homeric*'s engines throbbed again and the deck under their feet vibrated once more. "We'll be plying the ocean alone until we reach the pilot station at Brixham. Did you know that this is a tragic place in Canadian history? It's where the *Empress of Ireland* collided with another ship in a fog, in May 1914. It sank in fourteen minutes and over a thousand lives were lost, more passengers than on the *Titanic*. It was the worst maritime disaster in Canadian history. Can you imagine the terror on that ship?"

"Gosh, I'm not sure I needed to hear that story right now," Susie answered. "I thought icebergs were what the ship had to look out for."

"Well, they will be until we're well past the Newfoundland coast."

"How do you know all this, especially about the *Empress of Ireland*?"

"I can't remember. I guess my parents told me. But I love history—history and art. That's what I want to study at university. What about you?"

"I'm not sure yet. I think I'll do Soc. and Phil. the first year."

"What college?"

"Victoria."

"Oh, too bad. I'm going to Trinity. Maybe we could have roomed together at St. Hilda's. Hey, were you on deck when we passed Quebec City?"

"No. I missed it. I must have been in my cabin unpacking."

"Too bad. If I'd known you then, I would have come and got you. We could have gazed together in awe at the cliffs leading to the Plains of Abraham and thought of General Wolfe and all his men scaling those heights before the battle. As we sailed past, I imagined myself there in 1759, a nurse maybe, succouring the wounded soldiers, holding Wolfe in my arms as he died."

"You certainly have a vivid imagination!"

"I have. And I would have assigned you a role if you'd been with me. Binding up the wounds of General Montcalm."

Susie laughed. "I don't think my French is good enough to have done that."

Linda *did* have a strong imagination. Later that autumn, when Susie first visited her at her Rosedale home in Toronto, Linda's mother told her how, as a young girl, her daughter had often pretended to be Queen Elizabeth I. She would wrap an old blue curtain around her shoulders and place on her head a cardboard crown decorated with translucent marbles. A boy, assigned the role of Sir Francis Drake, would kneel on a dog's blanket in front of her to be knighted before being dispatched abroad. Once, a boy with a yardstick rapier as long as he was tall had had the temerity to ask if he could accompany Sir Francis on his voyage. But Linda had declined, saying that she required him at court. When the boy complained that Queen Elizabeth never let him do anything, Linda apparently rose regally from her orange crate throne and, swiftly removing a tattered white garden glove, flicked it across the chest of her recalcitrant subject. "How dare you argue with your queen?" she apparently shouted at him. "Do you want to be banished from the kingdom?" It required Mrs. Osterman's intervention to break up the argument that ensued and to remind her daughter that they were just playing a game.

When her mother had finished recounting the incident, Linda had said to Susie, "I would have let you be queen if you had been there."

"Sure. Mary Queen of Scots. So you could have had my head chopped off."

"Ah, so you *do* know some history!"

It was growing colder as the *Homeric* ploughed on into the Gulf of St. Lawrence." How's your nausea?" Linda asked. "Feeling any better?"

"Yes, thanks. I'm fine now. The fresh air really helped."

"Or maybe it was just getting away from Godfrey. Hey! Now that you're okay, let's see if we can sneak into the first-class lounge and have a drink. I'm dying to see how different it is from the Taverna." For the first time Susie noticed a strange glint come into Linda's dark brown eyes, almost as if they were being lit by an invisible candle held to the side of her oval-shaped head. It was the look of a person who, though certainly not mad, was wild and unpredictable.

"Gosh, do you think we can? They'll know we're students and obviously tourist class."

"You'll see. It's too early in the crossing for them to know who all their first-class passengers are. Besides, the waiter will be Italian. He'll be dying to have someone other than old maids to serve."

They climbed to the Lido Deck, and as they were working their way towards the bow, they passed Freddie Finchley from Table

Number Eight. He was stone drunk as he would be every night of the tour, released from the restrictive grasp of his over-protective parents. "Hey, you going to the Taverna? Which way's the goddam stern?"

Freddie leaned into Linda who held him off like a manikin being readjusted in a store window. "No, Freddie. Just taking a walk around the deck. It's about time you went to bed, isn't it?"

Freddie pulled away from her and staggered off. "Hey, see ya' later, you fuckin' alligators."

"Alligators?" That unseen, lurking candle lit Linda's eyes again. "We're tigresses on the prowl."

A ship's officer was standing near the entrance to the first-class lounge. Linda nodded at him and confidently held her gaze until a waiter swiftly approached them. Linda stood close to him, the front of her dress brushing against his chest so that she could be sure he would feel the soft, supple tissue of her breasts, disappointing as they might be to him, as they were to her. "My mother should be joining us a little later," she said to the waiter and pointed to a table in a far corner of the room. "Could you show her where we'll be sitting? Oh, and two Singapore Slings, please."

"Sorry, I didn't ask what you'd like to have," Linda said to Susie as they sat down. "I just felt we should get our order in right away, you know, and take control."

"I don't mind," Susie answered. "I wouldn't have known what to order. I've never had an alcoholic drink before. I mean, it *is* alcoholic, I assume."

"Oh, it *is* alcoholic."

Susie felt excited and anxious at the same time. *Well, if I'm ever going to have a first drink, this seems like the time, and Linda the person to have it with. Somehow, I feel safe with her. I'm not sure I should, but she seems older, more experienced.*

So they sat in the lounge for half an hour, chatting together as they sipped their Singapore Slings, the highball of the uninitiated, growing high for the first time as sweetly as possible. "Gosh," Susie exclaimed as the lounge gradually filled with ladies in floor-length evening dresses and men in white dinner jackets with black bow ties. "They certainly look different from us. It's clear we don't belong."

"Yes, dreadful, aren't they? It doesn't look as if any of them has ever got a hand dirty working. They look so smug and self-satisfied. Do you think any of them cares at all about the poor, about people starving to death in Africa, about all those displaced in Europe by the war?" Susie was pleased by Linda's reaction, but also surprised, and Linda sensed that. "Of course, who am I to talk. I grew up in Rosedale and went to school at BSS. Was sent there, please note. It was not my choice. How about you?"

"St. Clement's. My family lives in Lawrence Park."

"Oh, so you're privileged too. But we're both rebels, aren't we? Let's get out of here and go to the Taverna before this place makes us both sick."

When they reached it, the band was playing "Volaré" for the fifth time that night and the small dance floor was jammed with young people, mostly students, staggering to left and right in rhythm with the rock of the ship rather than the music. They found a table near the back and Linda ordered another Singapore Sling, Susie a ginger ale. "See that tall guy three tables over?" Linda asked her. "His name is Bill Hunter. Handsome, don't you think?"

"Sort of, I guess."

"Let's dance. Maybe we can get his attention." Linda finished her Singapore Sling and led Susie onto the waxed and polished floor. There, they jived together with feminine ease, no awkward young men treading on the toes of their pumps, no tiresome Godfrey Wincanton droning arrogantly in their ears. Linda took the lead as they spun happily across the floor, passing close to Hunter's table. "If I were wearing a formal, I'd do what I did at a dance in Grade Twelve," Linda whispered. "I'd snap a shoulder strap to get his attention."

That had contributed to her growing reputation among her school mates of being a bit of an oddball, unconventional if nothing else. It had started a few months before when she had attended a Billy Graham crusade at Maple Leaf Gardens. Much to the embarrassment of her school chums, at the preacher's bidding she had been one of the first to march onto the platform and commit herself to Jesus. Her friends acknowledged, however, that with her pale, slender body, long straight black hair, and sometimes unnerving eyes—a diminutive, dark figure on that expansive stage—she had not looked at all out of place.

Then, that spring, there had been the sleeping pill episode, though the account Sally had given Jay at the Ojibway Hotel had been blown out of all proportion. Linda hadn't been able to sleep the night before the first of her Senior Matriculation exams and at about two in the morning she had popped one of the pills she had lifted from her mother's medicine cabinet weeks before and stashed in an old aspirin bottle in preparation for just such a crisis. It had taken her roommate at BSS a long time to shake her awake at seven-thirty, and she'd grown alarmed when she spied the empty bottle of pills on Linda's dresser. The suicide rumours had followed, and Linda, rather enjoying the notoriety, had done nothing to dispel them.

Hunter never asked either of the girls to dance, and eventually they sat down again while Linda consumed two more Singapore Slings. At last, her stomach rising, she got up. "The swaying dance floor is getting to me. I'm feeling seasick." The girls hurried on deck, Linda barely making it to the railing before vomiting. Susie helped her find her way to her cabin where she was sick again in the sink while Susie held her hair back. She undressed her and got her into a nightgown. "Thank you, Susie, you're a saint. I should have your picture in a locket around my neck."

There were four berths in the cabin and Linda had one of the two lowers. Sitting on the side of her bed, she looked across to the other one where a girl she had met only that morning was fast asleep, her blonde hair swimming seductively over her pillow and cotton batten stuffed in her exposed ear. "I'm sick," she called to her. "Would you mind moving to an upper so my friend can sleep here?" The girl didn't move, prompting Linda to stumble out of bed and pull the cotton from her ear. "I'm sick, damn it," she shouted. "Show some sympathy."

The body stirred. "Antonio?" The girl breathed deeply again.

Linda and Susie both laughed. "Antonio! My, my, lucky her. That certainly beats getting Bill Hunter. No wonder she needs her beauty sleep! Well, Susie, I better get some, too. Thanks again. See you tomorrow. Well, maybe not at breakfast."

* * *

The girls were together on deck when the *Homeric* reached the Needles and sailed up the Solent to dock at Southampton. In London, they managed to arrange to share a room at the hotel and everywhere they visited they went together. Looking back, what they both liked best was Westminster Bridge with its sweeping view of the city along both banks of the Thames, the elegant gilded Parliament Buildings soaring beside it and Big Ben looming above. Linda woke Susie before dawn the morning they went there, so that they could admire the view as the first, weak light of the sun touched its solid girders and while the city was still asleep. When they arrived, however, there were already people on the bridge and red double-decker buses too, adding colour to a bleak, grey morning. Still, these were not tourists, but Londoners, mostly coming from Waterloo Station on their way to work. The girls walked to the middle of the bridge and stood at the railing for some time, admiring the quiet majesty of the city at daybreak. It was then that Linda impressed Susie once again, this time by reciting lines from Wordsworth.

> This City now doth, like a garment wear
> The beauty of the morning; silent, bare,
> Ships, towers, domes, theatres and temples lie
> Open unto the fields, and to the sky;
> All bright and glittering in the smokeless air.

"Well, not so smokeless any longer, I guess," Linda added.

"No," Susie agreed. "But still impressive. Just like your memory."

Two German buses were waiting for the tour when they crossed by ferry to Dieppe, and they headed south through France, the women in one bus and the men in the other, staying at night in the same hotels. Godfrey Wincanton regaled his unimpressed companions with facts memorized every evening from his Michelin Guide. "It's certainly not one of the better châteaux," he noted, gazing at a faded tapestry at Château Loches. "It's a pity we didn't go to Chenonceaux." Freddie Finchley amused himself tossing empty wine bottles out a window, asserting that it didn't matter because, with their German vehicles and licence plates, the French would blame the litter on their erstwhile enemies. Bill Hunter tried to doze, stretched out across the rear seat, wondering at the same time if Linda were after him and if he should try to score.

In the women's bus, Linda's high school flirtation with religion was revived by the dark blue windows of Chartres Cathedral, and the bus had to make several unplanned stops while she photographed the facades of previously unsung churches. Every time, Susie got off the bus and accompanied her, enjoying the enthusiasm with which her new friend greeted every discovery.

When they reached Spain, they went to the bullfights at Plaza Monumental in Barcelona. Freddie was slugged by an angry Spaniard he'd squirted with sherry from his newly purchased wineskin. In the middle of the commotion that followed, perhaps to divert attention from Freddie, Bill Hunter suddenly shouted, "Down with Franco! Freedom for the Basques!" His intervention caused Godfrey to choke on the anchovy he was swallowing—either from embarrassment or surprise that Hunter knew anything at all about Spanish politics. Linda had to slap Godfrey hard on the back to dislodge the anchovy—unduly hard, Godfrey thought.

Throughout Spain, Linda took to photographing paintings of crucifixions. At dinner one night in Madrid, she described to the table the practice in some outposts of Christendom of nailing a person to a cross during Easter pageants. "What a brave way to show your devotion to your faith," she exclaimed.

Susie shuddered at the thought, while Godfrey retorted, "Don't worry, my dear. I'd never expect you to show that kind of devotion to me."

"Don't worry, I never would," Linda shot back, rolling her eyes at Susie. In fact, however, while she barely tolerated Godfrey's presence, she was finding him somewhat useful as a male companion when they went out for dinner. So long as she wasn't left like some of the girls with nothing to do at night but wash out her underwear, there was no telling what adventures might arise.

And in Italy, such a moment at last arose. Linda and Susie were together in the Uffizi Gallery in Florence where Linda had moved on to sketching ascension scenes in medieval paintings. Hands suddenly rested on both their shoulders, gently placed by someone standing behind them. They turned to face a smiling young man with swarthy skin, dark curly hair, and large oval eyes that looked like black, ripe olives. "Che bella! Non?"

"Si, bella, bella," Linda responded.

"Ah, you're not Italian. American?"

"Non, Canadese."

"Ah, bene, bene."

Discussing the encounter afterwards, Linda always insisted it was simply because she was the one who answered him that thereafter Dominic focused his attention almost exclusively on her. Susie wasn't so sure. She didn't have the courage to answer him in Italian the way Linda did and that was undoubtedly a factor that influenced his subsequent behaviour. But it was also clear to Susie that Linda was more interested than she was in having an encounter—in having some sort of relationship while abroad, an adventure with an uncertain end. Consciously or unconsciously, Susie believed, Linda had signalled that to Dominic.

The next day, Dominic followed the women's bus to Venice on his motorcycle and that evening appeared at their hotel to ask Linda to dinner. She wasn't yet prepared to go out with him alone, so she begged Susie to accompany her along with Godfrey as, in effect, Susie's date—both for security and to satisfy her mother that she wasn't neglecting him. They ate at a restaurant just off St. Mark's Square, and it pleased the girls to have an Italian to do the ordering, to talk to them knowledgeably about the country, and especially to treat them in a solicitous but unpretentious manner. Godfrey, however, was put out by having to defer to the Italian's choice of wine, and by being gently corrected for confusing a Titian with a Tintoretto when he recounted for the girls his impressions of the paintings in the Doges Palace. "Whatever, I think the Venetian painters' blues surpass those of all the others," Godfrey recovered quickly. "Look at Veronese, for instance. Wouldn't you agree that the pigments for his skies are masterful?"

"Si, si," Dominic grinned, winking at Linda. "Ah! Attenzione. Ascolta!" he cried, leading the conversation away from Godfrey. An old Italian with a grey beard, a club foot, and darting eyes was crouched by the table next to them, speaking to a fat man in a red sports shirt gaily painted with a large blue shark. "You wanta to buy the guide book. Best book for Venezia. Only one thousand lire. Very good price-a."

"It sounds high to me," the tourist answered.

"Americano, non?" Dominic nudged Linda.

"Si."

While he spoke to them mostly in English, Dominic threw in a little Italian. Susie suspected that it was to flatter Linda that she was making progress learning the language. But she also assumed that he had calculated that Linda was seeking an authentic Italian adventure that involved a man with a romantic tongue.

"Look at the colour. Alla the pictures have-a the good colour. In the square, they wanta fifteen hundred. I no cheata."

The American doled out the money. "Non!" Dominic cried incredulously to the girls. "Mille lire? Troppo costoso!"

The old Italian's eyes were gleaming now. "You wanta postcards? Look." He unfolded a pack of connected cards with too-blueish scenes of Venice. "For you special price-a because you buy-a the guidebook. Only eight hundred lira, okay?"

It was not okay. The American couple *did* know the price of postcards, and they got up to go. But the Italian grabbed the man by the arm. "Pssst," he whispered to him. "How abouta the dirty pictures. I have all kindsa. You like-a them?"

The American pulled away to catch up to his wife who had already hailed a taxi. "Hey-a," the Italian shouted, limping towards him. "You come back-a later. I take you for good time-a. I know lotsa girls. Very pretty. You'll like them. Very hot-a."

"Magnifico!" Dominic clapped his hands and started enthusiastically to devour his veal parmesan. Linda laughed with him, but not Susie. She was beginning to doubt the real intentions of Italian men—all of them, including Dominic.

After dinner, they threaded their way along the narrow back streets of Venice to the Rialto where Dominic hired a gondola for them. The boatman's name was Alfredo, a powerful man with bulging biceps and a broad chest that stretched his blue-and-white striped jersey taut. His athletic build made him look faintly ridiculous wearing a straw hat with a scarlet tail on top of his thick black hair. Linda and Dominic sat close together under a blanket on the cushioned seat in the bow, Susie and Godfrey decorously in the stern with the boatman just behind them, standing on a sloping deck, sculling. At first, Alfredo took them along winding, narrow rios near the Grand Canal. As they passed into the black, echoing water under a small stone bridge, Dominic drew Linda closer to him and kissed her on the cheek. She turned her face squarely towards him and this time he kissed her softly on the lips. Linda opened her mouth, enticing him into a deeper embrace. It continued as the gondola slipped from under the bridge, and Linda's frail fingers were now working their way through the black strands of hair at the back of Dominic's head.

Godfrey cleared his throat and started to explain to Susie why all the gondolas in Venice were painted black. Suddenly, however, Linda was aware of Susie watching her, disapprovingly, she assumed. Momentarily, she turned away from Dominic and shrugged her shoulders at Susie. "Well, when in Rome, do like the Romans."

They reached the Grand Canal again by the Rialto and the boatman turned in the direction of the open sea. Linda and Dominic were close together again, their tongues playing at the edges of each other's mouths. Dominic started gently stroking the insides of Linda's thighs and Alfredo from his perch on the deck was giving as much attention to the action in the bow as he was to the heavy traffic in the canal. Godfrey tried to divert Susie's attention from Linda by reciting Shakespeare. "Many a time and oft upon the Rialto, you have spurned me…"

Susie ignored him as best she could, and, stifling a yawn, gazed in the other direction at the solid phalanx of shuttered and sinking palaces of a bygone nobility. Wounded and ill at ease, Wincanton tried another tack. "Would you please ask the boatman to sing for us," he called to Dominic. "They usually do that, don't they?"

Linda and Dominic's mouths parted long enough for him to speak to Alfredo, and right away the boatman broke into a mournful love song.

"Ah, that's better." Godfrey tried to sound relaxed as he diffidently placed an arm around Susie's shoulders. But she shivered involuntarily and pulled away from him. "Sorry, Godfrey. I don't want to be mean or to disappoint you, but I'm not interested. Let's just enjoy the ride. It is so beautiful on the water."

She sensed that Godfrey was actually relieved. "Yes, the view is superb, isn't it? This whole trip has been an unforgettable experience. It makes you long to travel still more." His sense of self-importance restored, he spouted poetry for Susie's benefit, but without the effect Linda had achieved in London.

I am a part of all that I have met;
Yet all experience is an arch wherethro'
Gleams that untravell'd world whose margin fades
Forever and forever when I move.

"Phony," Susie wanted to say. The lines were from Tennyson's *Ulysses* and they were in the brochure for their tour. But she simply smiled and let him have his moment.

They were by now opposite St. Mark's Square and ahead of them lay the wide expanse of the inner harbour. Gondolas, launches, and ferries were criss-crossing the bay through a sea of psychedelic lights manufactured by the rising moon. But suddenly, the boatman stopped singing. "What's happened?" Godfrey called right away to Dominic. "Why has he stopped?"

There was a short exchange in Italian between Dominic and Alfredo and then Dominic answered. "He says the song was making him sad because he has no one to love." Alfredo spoke briefly again, and Dominic translated for Linda alone as he nibbled at her ear. "He says what's the matter with the other two, aren't they in love?"

Linda rubbed her cheek against Dominic's as she whispered her answer. "What? With that weirdo?"

Dominic translated what Linda had said for the boatman, who laughed uproariously. Then there was a longer exchange between the two Italians at the end of which Alfredo climbed off the deck of the gondola and said to Susie and Godfrey in faltering English, "Excuse me, I get mandolin. Under seat."

"Ah, that will be nice," Wincanton answered, and they both stood up. The boatman bent over the seat, his hands brushing against the back of Godfrey's legs. Suddenly, he jerked up and outwards, pressing his full weight against Wincanton, who tottered backwards. His hands flailed the air as he desperately sought to regain his balance. But it was hopeless, and he toppled into the murky water sprawled out like a sky diver. Momentarily, he disappeared beneath the choppy waves, but then he resurfaced, coughing and sputtering.

"My God! Godfrey? Are you all right?" Linda shouted as she pulled away from Dominic and peered at Godfrey over the side of the gondola. She put her hands over her face half in horror and half to conceal the smile that uncontrollably appeared at the ridiculous sight of Godfrey, floating awkwardly on his back, his vest and carefully knotted tie just breaking the surface.

Alfredo leapt back to his position on the deck and vigorously worked the gondola away from Godfrey. As he did so, he began to sing again—this time a loud, triumphant aria that boomed across the gleaming bay.

"Help! Somebody stop him!" Godfrey screamed, but Linda and Susie just stared at him dumbly, too surprised at what had happened to take any action. And then Linda felt Dominic's arms wrap around her as he pressed her gently but firmly downwards on the seat. It was then, she told Susie afterwards, that she had her first doubts about his intentions and she didn't know how to react.

The gondola had been only about twenty feet from shore when Godfrey was knocked overboard, and swimming on his back, he soon reached the wall of the canal where a crowd of spectators had quickly gathered and he was helped ashore. He pushed his way through them and ran along the wide esplanade abutting the Grand Canal. "Help! Stop that gondola. Those girls will be raped! Help! Help!" He scrambled over one bridge and then another, his soggy pant legs flapping noisily, leaving behind him a trail of muddy water. "Help! Police! Stop that gondola!"

Out in the middle of the bay, Alfredo dropped from the deck and sat close to Susie, breathing heavily, his brow dripping with sweat. "Now I happy, too. I have-a someone to love."

"No," Susie said firmly, attempting to pull away from him. "No. Let go of me. I don't want to. Please let go." He loosened his grip and Susie said, "Please take us back to shore now. It's not funny what you did."

In the bow, Dominic was on top of Linda, trying to work a hand inside her white rayon panties. "No," Linda said, doing her best to sound as convincing as Susie. "I like you very much, but I don't want to…not now. We're both worried about Godfrey."

"Shhh. Don't worry. He'll be fine." Dominic searched for her mouth again. "I know you want to. I love you, and I know you love me, too."

Just at that moment, a broad beam of light swept over the gondola. "There they are!" the women could hear Godfrey shout jubilantly from the deck of the police boat—Godfrey the valiant rescuer. He was wrapped in a blanket, his hair wet and uncharacteristically mussed, but he looked more masculine than usual, like a prize fighter just out of the ring in the care of his seconds. The police boat slowed and drew alongside the gondola.

Susie sighed with relief, and Linda with what Susie surmised was a vague feeling of frustration.

Chapter 5

"I've always kind of wished that I had been on that trip—that that was how we met."

"Well, it's not as if we've never been to Europe together."

"No, but we've never taken a gondola ride." Jack cast a quick, sly glance at Susie.

"It wouldn't have turned out differently... Well, maybe you wouldn't have ended up in the water like Godfrey, but..."

"Weren't you scared that something awful was going to happen?"

"Not really. I would have been a few years later. But we were so young and innocent."

"Linda? Do you think she really was ready to have sex with that guy?"

"I'm not sure. I didn't ask her until much later. When I did, she admitted she did find him attractive and enjoyed his attention, but she also said he had terrible garlic breath!"

"Oh, no!" Jack roared. "Saved by a bud of garlic."

"But then she added, 'I don't really know. I mean, we were in a gondola in Venice. What could have been more romantic? It would have been hard to resist him.'"

"Sounds like Linda. And certainly not like a lesbian talking."

"Jack!"

"So, whatever happened to the others on that trip?"

"Well, I heard that Freddie Finchley had a drinking problem the rest of his life. He died of cirrhosis of the liver years ago."

"Bill Hunter?"

"No idea. Probably half of them are dead by now."

"And what about Godfrey Wincanton? We never saw him again after university, did we?"

"Yes, we did. Once in England. He moved to London about the same time we did and worked in an antique store until he started his own. It was a good choice for him. He was an antique himself really. Linda told me he died of AIDS in the late eighties. We never suspected he was gay, or at least I didn't. I think we would have been nicer to him if we'd known. Poor man. It must have been very hard for him back then. Not like now. Linda is very lucky."

"Linda...well..." Jack stopped himself. "Who knows?...except Linda...maybe."

It was a long, tortuously slow drive on county roads from Niagara-on-the-Lake to Toronto. The network that had been constructed took no account of the needs of the aging, Jack complained—those who shunned at all cost highways like the crowded and dangerous Queen Elizabeth Way. And apart from the orchards they passed, their trees laden with ripening fruit that hung like gleaming Christmas decorations, there wasn't much to see. There were, of course, some wineries they could visit as they zig-zagged their way eastward towards Burlington to pick up Lakeshore Road for the final, tedious leg into the city. They stopped at one for a "pee stretch" and to select a case of wine to bring to the reunion.

"Lou and Sally drink mostly red," Jack said, testing another varietal. *Of course, it could be the doctors aren't letting Lou drink at all, poor bugger.* "With Jay and Linda, it used to depend on what was for dinner, but Christ knows what their preference is now. Could be Linda's only drinking bottled water from her favourite mountain stream in Nepal. And, as for the new temptress, I have no idea."

"New temptress?"

"Yeah, Linda's latest paramour. Goddam, it will be unfair to Jay if they both come. In that case, he might just get right back in Lou's boat and leave. On the other hand, if he stays, he's going to need plenty of wine to get through it. What colour?"

"I say we get eight bottles of red and four whites."

"Sounds good. Of course, if Cass shows up—"

"He won't."

"Well, if he does, he might go through more than a case of beer whatever *his* doctor's orders. But Lou can easily get that in Pointe au Baril."

"Wouldn't empties do? Of course, as usual, you've left out Bev."

"Shit, I did, didn't I? Well, good old Bev, she'll drink whatever's in the greatest supply."

"No, not that red." Susie pulled out two of Jack's selections. "Look at their screw caps. They're covered in that awful metal foil. You'll cut a finger opening them and curse the way you do at the flaps on milk cartons."

"Well, if we can make robots that put millions out of work…" With Susie, he didn't need to finish the thought.

"Singapore Slings, eh?" Jack commented as they started driving again. "That's what you drank all the time on the *Homeric*? I'm glad I saved you from type two diabetes."

"Well, I drank rye and ginger ale when we first went out. So did you, I recall."

"Touché" Now Jack drank only rye and water or Scotch and soda, sometimes a Manhattan if they were in a bar. "I like a simple palette, just varied shades of amber." Susie drank only wine, and very little of that any longer. "You're right about the rye, but that was on dates; the rest of the time we drank beer. Same in London. That was all we could afford."

"Yes, I remember we bought quart bottles at the off-licence and put a stopper in so that they'd last for two or three nights."

"Yeah, flagons they were called."

"So, now I get it. You seduced me with rye, but then you switched me to beer."

Jack just laughed. "You know that first year at university was really great, especially after we met. I'll never forget that day you came over to Trinity to see Linda. I was infatuated with you the moment I saw you."

"What do you mean? You barely spoke to me, you were so busy talking to your Ojibway friends."

"Hey, that's not fair. Afterwards I asked Linda all about you — what college you were at and what courses you were taking. I dropped Introduction to Geology and enrolled in that horrible sociology course just to see you."

"So why did you sit in the back row then, and not join me in the front if you wanted to get to know me?"

"Because Jay switched courses at the same time to lighten his workload and he always liked to sit there."

"Yes, so that he could talk all through class with his buck shoes resting on the top of the seat in front. 'What a farmer!' I bet that's how he described the professor."

"Well, his lectures did seem trite. All I remember is there was a lot of obvious stuff about the roles in a family—all dressed up in a bunch of academic jargon."

"I guess you didn't get it, though, did you? As I recall you both got Ds. Not the bird course you were hoping for."

"That's not true." Jack tried to sound offended. "I got a D+! Hey, remember the old Buttery in the basement at Trinity where we first met?"

"You think I've forgotten?"

———

The Buttery was packed every morning, especially early in the term. The air was thick with cigarette smoke and the tables covered with half-finished cups of coffee and clipboards with timetables scotch-taped to their centres and important phone numbers inked along the edges. Piled on top were books like Plato's *The Republic*, *King Lear*, and the *Wealth of Nations*. The boards were hopelessly over-loaded, but everyone used them, at least at Trinity and Victoria. At University College, it seemed to Jack that there were mostly brief-cases, cheap brown plastic ones with straps and buckles, and they sagged to one side stuffed with books and papers. What they used at St. Mike's, he had no idea.

On the tables in the Buttery there were always copies of *Salter-rae*, coffee-stained and covered in doodles, or maybe a map of how to get to a classroom at McMaster Hall for a language course. The college paper was full of juvenile, undergraduate humour with statements everyone thought were hilarious like "Hang down your dooly, Tom Boy," and "A bird in the bush is worth two in the hand." *It's hard to believe it was the same college that published that literary journal Linda helped edit,* Jack mused.

But then there was more than one Trinity, and more than one conversation in the Buttery. Some talked about "acing" last year's final, or failing because the professor "threw a curve"—about toga parties at the fraternities, who was "pinned" to whom, and who had puked in the quad the night before; others about Marcel Proust, Shakespeare's sonnets, and the auditions for the next production of the Trinity Dramatic Society. And then there were the worldly-wise, discussing the prospects for nuclear disarmament, France's Fifth Republic, and the conclave that was choosing a successor to Pius XII. Jack himself shifted around, but at the outset he conversed mostly with the superficial group because he sat with the Ojibway gang.

The first time he went to the Buttery he was alone with Sally and Jay. Sally was wearing a reversible skirt with a matching sweater, and she was on her third cup of coffee and sixth cigarette. She'd missed both her morning classes and felt bad about it, but she had a lot of friends to talk to and didn't want to offend any of them by rushing away. Over his black College gown, Jay wore a beige crew neck sweater that conveniently concealed all but the knot of his black and red-striped "worm" tie. He hated that freshman label and was anxious for the end of the Trinity initiations when, in keeping with College tradition, he could burn it. Custom also dictated that students don their black gowns while on the Trinity campus. Jay's was already chewed and threadbare. He'd bought it second-hand because he knew the worn look was what was "in."

Sally and Jay dominated the conversation that day and the topics were predictable. Holding her head in one hand with her elbow resting on the table, Sally used the other to flatten her soft, wavy hair, while, in her mellow voice, she reassured Jay that the Dekes were the right choice of fraternities for him to join. That was good news to Jay because he was impressed by the fact that six guys playing for the Blues were Dekes, but, nevertheless, he was concerned that it was too early to be pinned as he hadn't yet checked out the Zetes. Sally told him that she thought they were too wild for him, and Jay's amber caution light flashed on, the same one that had finally led him that week to choose Soc. and Phil. rather than Commerce and Finance. Still, he told Sally he thought he'd go to the Zetes' stag along with Jack because they'd already accepted an invitation. "You went to the Zetes with Jay?" Susie had been surprised the first time Jack had told her about that conversation in the Buttery. But, in fact, he hadn't gone. Before the stag he had met Susie, and it was clear she didn't approve of fraternities. "Hmm. I'm impressed," she had responded when he had initially explained his decision to her. "I didn't know I had that much influence on you. I'm not sure I still do," to which Jack had retorted, "You're kidding, of course."

From rushing, Jay and Sally turned to football, Jay explaining to Sally that he'd decided to play for the Trinity football team instead of the Varsity Intermediates. He was afraid if he spent too much time practising he might mess up his grades. Besides, he figured that someday an employer would be more impressed if he'd quarterbacked a college team for four years than simply warmed a bench at the Varsity level. Jack could tell that Sally was disappointed. She liked the idea of dating a guy good enough for the Intermediates. Who knew? By second or third year, he might be ready for the Blues.

"I remember that first day in the Buttery I had been talking to Sally and Jay for some time when, suddenly, we heard a shriek from across the room: 'Jay-Jay! Jackie! Sally! Hi.'"

"There's no doubt who that came from," Susie commented.

"Bev rushed to our table and jumped into my lap. Hanging from her neck over her front and back were large squares of cardboard, edged in red and black paint. Bev's name and major, English Lang. and Lit., were printed on them, and suspended above her head by a wire was a halo, made out of bent coat hangers, covered in yellow crepe paper."

"I'd forgotten about that garb. You could spot Trinity freshies wherever they were on campus."

"No question. Bev wore that stuff proudly, not like Sally. She

had taken her halo and placards off when she sat down in the Buttery and draped them over a chair. But Bev liked the way the cos-
tume identified her as someone new to be checked over, and I'm
sure she hoped it would get her a date for the Saturday football
game and the parties that would follow. The problem was it made
her look like a jack-in-the-box that had sprung open unexpectedly."

"Jack! Please."

"Sorry. That's awful, I know. But that's what I thought at the
time. Anyway, she jumped off me and pecked Jay on the cheek.
'Isn't it fab? Isn't it just fab?' she jabbered, or something like that.
'Aren't you having a ball?' Jay patted her on the back and told her
to slow down or she'd fly through the ceiling even without wings.
He sounded affectionate but condescending, as if he were talking
to his kid sister. As Bev sat down with us, she asked Sally what was
new and said that she assumed Sally was being rushed all over the
place. Sally wasn't, of course. She was more interested in going to
parties at the fraternities, the Dekes and Kapps in particular. To her,
sororities were for women who needed their dates shipped in in
bulk for the Saturday night dances like steer corralled and ear-
marked for Chicago, New York, or—"

"Jack! Really!"

"Well that's how she saw it, I'm sure. But not Bev. She was
going to join, but she wasn't sure where. 'It's really exciting,' she said
to Sally. 'I think the Pi Beta Phis are really neat, but the Delta Gam-
mas are pretty cool, too. I can't decide. But what's the hurry. I'm on
cloud nine, aren't you?'"

"Do you think she really was?" Susie asked.

"I doubt it. I suspect she was confused. Her enthusiasm netted
her a lot of friends, but the relationships were superficial."

"Except with Cass."

"Yeah, but what a disaster that turned out to be. And we did
nothing to try and stop it. Anyway, at some point while we were talking, Linda walked up to our table with Godfrey Wincanton in tow.
That's the first time Jay, Bev, and I met either of them. As they
approached us, I distinctly remember Sally whispered to Jay that
Linda was her classmate from BSS who had gone on the Ulysses

tour to Europe, but that she didn't know the creepy-looking guy with her. Jay appraised them quickly and said he hoped they'd keep on walking, but they didn't. They sat down at our table, and Sally introduced everyone."

"I'd forgotten you met Linda before that day I came over to Trinity to call on her," Susie intervened.

"Yeah, I saw her a few times, but I think she managed to shake free of Wincanton pretty early in the term. Whenever I saw her in the Buttery later, she was always with her long-haired female friends, and I noticed that, like them, she sometimes spoke with an affected English accent. In fact, even that day I first met her, she was in the Trinity College Dramatic Society uniform. You know, long charcoal-coloured dress and wrinkled grey sweater, black hair trailing half way down her back, matted and unwashed."

"Jack!"

"Well, that's how she looked. In fact, later at lunch in Strachan Hall, Jay remarked that without the halo and name cards she could be mistaken for a witch."

"Gosh!" Susie cried. "I wonder if Linda knows he said that."

"So who's the real Linda? Back then, of course, it was clearly the artsy Linda of the *Trinity University Review*. In fact, she told us at one point that she was working on her first literary contribution, 'An Ode to Trinity Chapel.' Apparently, she spent a number of hours there during that first week in quiet contemplation. I guess all those crucifixions and sculptured pietàs in Europe really did get to her."

"Well, briefly at least."

––––––

It wasn't just Linda's phony English accent that bugged Jack back then; it was also her manner of speaking. He remembered Linda asking Sally what she planned to "read" at university. Sally looked at her quizzically, but she was only momentarily caught off guard before she answered that she was taking Soc. and Phil. in first year and then Psychology. "Oh, perfect!" Bev clapped her hands and explained to Linda that Sally had been the resident counsellor for the lovelorn over the summer at the Ojibway. That led Sally to quip that she thought she might as well be in a position to start charging for her advice, which in turn brought Godfrey Wincanton into the conversation, pompously suggesting that Sally was confusing the fields of psychology and psychiatry. Sally proceeded to anger Godfrey by nonchalantly tossing the matter lightly aside with the admission she probably was confused, because she wasn't much of a student, and then turning to Linda to ask her about her major. Jack remembered clearly the turn the conversation took then; Linda answered that she was taking English Lang. and Lit., although, during the summer in Europe, she had contemplated Art and Archaeology. "Coming in contact with the students at the *Trinity University Review* and the Trinity College Dramatic Society has altered my intention," Linda explained. "Everybody there is so interesting and eclectic. They read Goethe and Sartre. They go to Chekhov plays."

"Ah! But do they understand them?" Jack intervened, eliciting a withering, dismissive look from Linda. He hadn't got off to a good start with her. In fact, he was sure she regarded them all as vacuous and uninteresting, even Sally. So far as Jack could recall, she didn't speak to him again until the day Susie visited Trinity to see her. And she avoided Jay as well, let alone Bev. Of course, Bev didn't help herself by bringing to Linda's attention that she, too, was taking English Lang. and Lit. Linda looked sceptically at her plaid skirt, yellow sweater, white socks, and tennis shoes—obviously not the appropriate attire. Still, she gave Bev the benefit of the doubt, and asked if she were writing anything. Bev's freckled face wrinkled into a big smile as she answered that she was working on a new Varsity cheer. Before anyone could answer, she was crouching on the floor, shooting her left and then her right leg out while she did half-turns, hands on her hips. "The Blues, the Blues, the Blues are best" she cried, slowly standing erect, arms rising above her head. "They're worth, they're worth, they're worth all the rest." She dropped quickly into a crouch again, and then leapt high in the air, arms outstretched. "Yeah, Blues." Wincanton's bleary brown eyes bulged like a bullfrog's as he stared incredulously at Bev. Linda was motionless—far away as if in a trance and willing the encounter with all of them to be over. Bev sensed their reaction and sat down abruptly, explaining almost apologetically that she was trying out to be a Varsity cheerleader. That led Jay to snigger, "Why not for Trinity instead? I hear they're having a hard time getting a group together."

It was obvious to Jack even then that Bev was wounded, but now, looking back on that day from afar, he realized it was a kind of hurt she was already used to. Doubtless she had heard her mother say things like "Beverley, dear, you have such a sweet voice. Why don't you do something about your appearance," or her ballet instructor plead with her to hold her stomach in and feel like a swan. Unfortunately, Bev made things even worse for herself that day. In an effort to change the subject, she asked Linda if she were joining a sorority, but Linda said she wasn't—that the *Trinity University Review* and the TCDS were what interested her. "The TCDS? Oh? Who are they?" and without waiting for an answer, Bev added, "I think the Pi Beta Phis are fab. Just fab." *Poor Bev. It pains me remembering that moment."*

For several seconds now, Jack and Susie had been stopped at a busy intersection on the outskirts of Burlington, waiting to turn right as pedestrians sauntered slowly across the road. "Look at them! They're almost all on their cellphones!" Jack impatiently tapped the wheel. "They're blissfully unaware that they're holding up traffic and creating a dangerous situation. We could be rear-ended."

"If you were the one walking, you'd be complaining about drivers almost running you over."

"Pedestrians, drivers. It doesn't matter. They're all self-absorbed and oblivious of others."

"Get over it, dear. It's a different era."

Jack nevertheless persisted. "So what the hell are those people talking about that's so important it can't wait until they reach the curb, assuming they actually get there alive?"

"You can go now," Susie interrupted. "Don't miss your moment."

Jack made his turn but didn't let go. "You know, whenever

I eavesdrop on people on their cellphones, it's always some silly conversation about a relationship that's in trouble, or where the caller is and when they'll be wherever it is that they're supposed to be going. Sooner, if only they'd just shut up. And does everyone really need to have all these different ways of staying in touch? Emails, iPhones, iPads, Facebook, LinkedIn, YouTube, Twitter, Snapchat, Instagram. Maybe if they cut a few devices out of their lives, they'd have time to look around as they cross the road. Maybe they'd even notice that the sun is out and that there are flowers blooming in people's gardens."

"You won't start talking that way at the reunion, will you?" Susie admonished him. "You'll sound as bad as you would giving an organ recital."

"I'll try not to, but remind me to find out from our grandsons what the specific attraction is of each of those apps on their cellphones that they're so focused on every time I try to engage them in conversation. Doodle Jump, Cookie Clicker, Pokémon GO, Flappy Bird, Angry Bird—"

"Stuffed bird! Just stop it! Angry old bird!"

They fell silent momentarily while Jack fumed to himself about the present, and Susie rummaged for memories from the past. Finally, guessing where Susie's head was, Jack said, "You know, it wasn't just Linda, Godfrey, and Bev who joined our table in the Buttery that day. Just after Bev put her foot in her mouth once again, we noticed Lou standing in the doorway in the same sunglasses he wore at the Ojibway and with the same knowing grin. 'Pinky-pooh!' Bev rushed to the door to greet him, throwing her arms around his neck. I think we were all kind of flattered that he'd come to see us. It was only then that we realized he saw us as more than one-time, summer friends.

"'So, this is where you heathens hang out,' Lou chuckled, as he sat down at our table.

"'Yeah, you better cross yourself a few times for protection,' I joked. In fact, Lou already had all the protection he needed. His latest pungent deodorant encircled him in a six-foot ring.

"'So how are things at St. Mike's?' I think Jay asked. 'I've been meaning to get over there, you know, see more of the campus, but it's been busy here.'

"Lou said nothing much was happening, but that he'd come over because he had something for us, and then, from under his arm, he pulled out two brown bottles filled with a pink and white powder and handed them to Jay and me. He'd bought the stuff at the CNE, he said. It would help us develop our muscles and was good for our sexual prowess as well—that we'd have the pick of the freshies. Lou told us he had bought a bottle for Cass too, in case he ran into Barbie Bigelow again. Jay guffawed with approval at that, but I remember Lou apologized to the women for sounding crude. Lou was an avid fan of the Exhibition. Did I ever tell you that?"

"I don't think so."

Funny, I could have sworn I did. "Anyway, the day he got home from the Ojibway, he'd rushed out to the CNE before the closing. What he liked to do was listen to the barkers hawking their new-fangled appliances; you know—magic peelers for three dollars, or two for five, peelers that never worked at home as easily as they did on show. Most of all, Lou liked the barker with the python in a cage. For thirty minutes, he talked about the snakes of Africa and how to handle them as the crowd grew larger, anticipating the release of eighteen feet of twisting hose. Then out popped the bottles of magic potion. Lou was so impressed by the performance that he bought three.

"'God, Pinky,' I remember Sally exclaiming as she examined the powder. 'What are you doing wasting your money on stuff like this.' Lou just smiled. He knew he'd probably wasted his money, but not his time. He rarely did. The wheels were always turning. Already he could have written Terry O'Reilly's script for the *Age of Persuasion* or *Under the Influence.* Lou just stood there silently grinning, and appraising Sally. I guess it was the first time he'd seen her in a skirt and he seemed to like what he saw. It was Bev who finally ended that revealing moment. 'Hey, Pinky. Give me your address and telephone number,' she asked, 'so we can stay in touch.'"

Jack stopped talking as they turned left onto the Lakeshore, momentarily lost in reflection. "Everything started changing after that. Life slowly got more serious."

"You mean because you met me the following week?" Susie asked. "Was I that much of a downer?"

"No, no. It was just that we started to grow up. After that, lots of things trod over our ties. Ambition. Anxiety. Insecurity. Frustration. Failure. Gradually, we became more circumspect. We hid our feelings."

"Linda?"

"Well, maybe not Linda. I think the remarkable thing is that we're all still friends. There have been conflicts and ruptures, but we've always managed to weld the links together again. Maybe that says something about old friendships. They're a bit like those buoys marking the safe route in to the Ojibway dock. They get roughed up by the wind and waves and have to be repaired and repainted. But they're always there, a comforting reminder of the past. Maybe they are markers that can never be safely removed."

"Well, you're not removing this one," Susie interjected.

"I could never have made the trip without you. You've buoyed me up the whole way."

"Ouch! What a terrible pun!"

"Sorry. But when I met you in the Buttery the next week, it was the most important moment in my life."

Susie leaned into Jack. "For me, too."

Chapter 6

Susie was right. Jack had hardly spoken to her the day she visited Linda at Trinity College. Before she arrived, he was deep in conversation with Jay and Sally—well, listening actually to one of Jay's monologues. "You know I'm thinking that, after a B.A., I'll go into law. I'd like to get into politics one day, and law would be a good launching pad. I was talking to Henry Phillips about it over lunch at the Dekes. He's being rushed there, too. He figures it this way. There's little real difference between the Liberals and Conservatives, so you don't want to commit yourself too early. You've got to base your decision on where you're living when the moment comes that you want to run and on which party is on top at that time."

"Isn't that what's wrong with politics?" Jack interjected. "All pragmatic calculation, no passionate commitment?"

"Jack has a point," Sally agreed. "And I don't think you should choose law because it might be advantageous later for a political career. All the professions are a tough slog. You need to be really interested in whatever you choose."

"Oh, I know. That's what Henry says, too. He's a fantastic guy. He's got a great future. You know, the other day I was putting together a list of the winners and losers. I know that sounds a bit obnoxious, but it's kind of interesting to do. It helps you think about where you're going. Now, Godfrey Wincanton, there's your classic loser. Totally out to lunch. He'll never get out of the starting gate. Then there's Bev. I like her, and I count her among my friends, but if she doesn't tone down, it's game over for her before the end of the first quarter. Cass? A great guy, no question. Always the life of the party, but he goes too far—the kind of guy who might suddenly pull a 'drop trou' right in the middle of class. Then, there's Pinky. Clever as a fox, no doubt about that, but what kind of a future is there for a guy with greasy hair who rarely talks and has a name like Luigi Piccolo? Now you," Jay said to Sally, "you're a real winner for sure. You've got your head screwed on right. And you, Jack, you—"

It was at that moment that Linda walked by the table where they were sitting, and Sally motioned to her to join them. Jack noticed how she hesitated and stole a glance at her watch. He was sure Linda didn't want to be caught again in his company, nor that of Jay. She might even have felt the same way about Sally, but Sally was perceived as a class leader at Trinity just as she had been at BSS, so she wasn't someone Linda could dismiss lightly. She reluctantly sat down and Jay abruptly terminated his insensitive personal assessments. "So, Linda," Sally quickly filled the void, "have rehearsals started for *Murder in the Cathedral?*"

"No, we're still auditioning. There's so much talent in the society that it's very difficult to assign roles."

"I can imagine. I'm really looking forward to seeing the play."

"Murder in the cathedral? I thought it was just a chapel," Jack quipped.

Linda gave him another reproachful glare but didn't respond. Her attention was diverted by Susie walking into the Buttery. She was standing by the door searching the room when Linda spotted her and waved her to their table.

For Jack, it was as close as one could possibly come to love at first sight. Although Susie told him later that he was mistaken, Jack had the impression that, when Linda introduced them, Susie's deep blue eyes fixed on him with unusual intensity and sparkle, almost as if she recognized him—as if they had encountered each other before and she was delighted to see him again. And when Susie ran her fingers through her bangs, as if brushing them to their most enticing angle, it only served to confirm Jack's initial mistaken impression. He was pretty sure she liked him and wanted to get to know him better. And there was no doubt in his own mind that he felt that way about her.

Now, however, conversation at the table split. Susie and Linda fell into a long exchange about what they had been doing since returning from Europe, and Jay and Sally reverted to a discussion of the first-year students at Trinity, albeit in a more subdued manner. For his part, Jack was bored by the latter conversation and eager to join the former to get to know Susie. As he remembered that first meeting, he made several attempts to intervene, asking for their impressions of different places they had gone in Europe. The result, he always contended, was simply an extension of their own dialogue without attempting to include him. That was not, however, Susie's recollection of their first meeting. She claimed that Jack asked only one feeble question—"Which country did you like best?"—and then returned to talking with Jay and Sally.

What was indisputable, however, was that Jack did seek out Linda at St. Hilda's later that afternoon to confirm Susie's name and learn what classes she was taking. Linda did provide him with the information he desperately wanted, but it came with what he regarded as a scathing indictment. "I don't think she's your type. She's a very nice person, you know. And she's bright and eclectic."

Jack and Jay quickly dropped the introductory course in geology which neither of them liked and enrolled in Sociology. At their first class, they sat in the back row in Jay's preferred location. "See that girl at the front?" Jack whispered. "She's Linda's friend, the one we met in the Buttery the other day."

"Just what you would have expected of a friend of Linda," Jay snorted. "A front row brown-noser. What's her name, I forget?"

"Susie Goldsmith."

"Susie, eh? Not Susan or Sue, but Susie. Cutsie! But I'll say this much: she is kind of pretty…well, cute at least."

"Kind of? I think she's gorgeous."

Jay looked at him quizzically. "No-o-o," he breathed. "You learned about this course from Linda, didn't you? But it's because of Susie that we're here."

"Partly," Jack grinned. "Don't worry, though. Sociology *is* supposed to be easy."

"And is Susie supposed to be easy, too?"

"I doubt it."

"Me too. Not someone who sits in the front row when they don't even need to wear glasses."

When the lecture ended, Jack walked down to speak to Susie, while Jay headed back to Trinity to see what Sally was doing. "Hi,

I'm Jack Sturridge. You're Linda Osterman's friend, aren't you? We met briefly in the Buttery at Trinity."

"Oh yes, I remember. Hi. I didn't know you were taking this course."

"Well, I wasn't actually. Jay Walters from Trinity and I just enrolled." Jack couldn't tell if the little curl in her mouth suggested she'd guessed the motivation for the switch. He hoped it did, but in case he was wrong, he decided to add, "We both hated Introduction to Geology. I love the rock formations on Georgian Bay, but the science of it all wasn't for me."

"So you know Georgian Bay. Do you have a cottage there?"

"No, Jay and I just worked at a hotel on the Bay this summer— along with Sally Macdonald. She was at our table, too, when you came in. Do you know that area?"

"Me? No. I've never been there. My parents have a place in Maine. I would have been there this summer if I hadn't gone to Europe."

"That sounds pretty neat, too."

"Yes, I love it. Lots of great rocks along the coast there too."

"But you don't need to be a geologist to enjoy them, right?"

"No," Susie laughed. She was finding that conversation with Jack seemed easy and natural. And he wasn't bad-looking either. Maybe a little tall for her, but not excessively. "So, you've already missed several classes. Would you like to borrow my notes to catch up?"

"You mean you wouldn't mind lending them to me?"

"Not if you return them at the next class."

"Gee, thanks. That would be great. It looks like they're extensive."

"They're almost verbatim. But I get a break whenever he digresses to tell a story."

"Wow! That's amazing. I know a guy who would pay you good money to get his hands on a full set for a term. I'm afraid my own notes are pretty incomplete."

"Oh? So how many pages did you take today?"

"Only three."

"Three? That's all?"

"I try to get down just the essence of the lecture. Want to see them?"

Jack handed over his three sheaves of paper. Right away, Susy's cheeks flushed, and she started to giggle. "You call these lecture notes?"

"Well, like I said. I record only what seems essential. Which page do you like best?"

"Gosh, I don't know. I like them all." Susie pressed a hand over her mouth. "I have to say that I've never experienced a come-on like this before. Hmm. The middle one, I think."

"Then it's yours."

Jack handed over the sheet, pleased that his flirtatious gambit had worked so well, for he had spent the entire class doing three charcoal sketches of Susie. Indeed, he and Jay had seated themselves at precisely the right angle for him to capture Susie's face in profile—her slightly pudgy, wrinkled nose, her feathery bangs, puckered temple, and eyes concentrated on the professor at the lectern. "Would you like me to sign it?"

"Yes, of course. I didn't know that you're an artist."

"Well, I don't know if I am really." For a moment, Jack couldn't decide how to sign the sketch. He thought of writing "To Susie, Love, Jack," but decided that was dangerously forward. So he wrote simply, "To Susie. Thanks for exchanging notes! Jack."

The room was empty now and a custodian had come in to clean the boards and the floor. It was the moment when they would go their separate ways unless Jack took another bold step. He was anxious about the outcome, but he felt he had to risk it. "Hey, you wouldn't like to go for a coffee or something, would you?"

"I don't drink coffee…" Susie left her answer hanging and Jack held his breath. "But sure. A tea maybe."

"You drink tea?"

"Yes."

"Well then, it's clear we're meant to get together."

The lecture had been at Falconer Hall, so the obvious place to go was the Wymilwood Café at Susie's college. "Hey, this doesn't look much different from the Buttery," Jack said as they sat down with their cups.

Susie laughed. "What did you expect? Coffee and tea dispensed from a canteen on the street?"

"No. A couple of thermoses on a bench in Queen's Park."

"It's funny, Linda seemed as surprised as you the first time she came over. You know, Trinity doesn't have a monopoly on everything good. Linda didn't realize, for instance, how strong Vic is in the literary field. This is Northrop Frye's college after all, and there is a lot of budding talent at *Acta Victoriana*, our literary journal: Peggy Atwood and Dennis Lee, just to name two."

"Oh, I know," Jack answered defensively. "Lots of famous people from other fields went to Vic, too, like E.J. Pratt, J.S. Woodsworth, and Lester Pearson."

Now it was Susie's turn to sound surprised. "So, you know a bit about Vic? You're not the narrow-minded social snob from the Trinity jock set Linda warned me you might be."

And then it was Jack's. "So you know I went to see her about you?"

"Yes," Susie confessed at last. "She said you might show up in one of my classes, but just to ignore you."

"But you didn't exactly... Well, I guess I don't know, since I approached you. But at least you didn't tell me to get lost."

"No." Susie smiled impishly. "I have a mind of my own."

Those glowing, azure eyes were focused on him so intensely Jack felt there must be a message in them, but how to read it. "Would you like another cup of tea?"

"Sure. Thanks."

"How about a cookie with it?"

"No, just tea, please. But get one for yourself if you like."

Jack bought two more teas and a cookie. As he sat down, he split it and handed Susie half. She didn't refuse. She simply looked at him with those intriguing eyes that seemed to search deep into his own, as if trying to peel away a veil that hid his inner self. "Mmm. Chocolate chip." Susie nibbled on the cookie. "My favourite."

"So that's really how Linda described me, eh, as a snotty-nosed Trinity jock. It's a wonder you didn't throw my sketches back at me."

"Linda would probably have viewed you differently if she'd known you're an artist."

"I may just be someone who gets bored in class and doodles."

"I think you have talent."

"Hey, don't get carried away. And I have to confess. Actually, I don't know that much about Victoria College either. It's just that I have relatives who studied here."

"Really?"

"Yes. One of them was in residence at Gate House when Vincent Massey was dean of men. He was regarded as a stuffed shirt, so, once, when he was passing under the arch at Gate House, a bunch of students standing at a residence window dumped water and ashes on Massey's head."

"Oh, so you come from a family of pranksters. Linda didn't tell me that. I better watch out." Jack wasn't sure what Susie meant by that. Was she brushing him off, or, more hopefully, hinting that she might be open to seeing him again? "So, why didn't you choose to go to Vic if you have relatives who studied here? Is your own family Anglican?"

"Only my mother. My father is a lapsed Methodist—lapsed since the church union. In 1925."

"And you?"

"I'm an agnostic. What about you?"

"Lapsed United Church, I guess. So, if religion wasn't a factor in your choosing colleges, why Trinity?"

"I'm not sure. I knew some people who were going there, and it sounded pretty cool. But coming from Leaside High and not a private school maybe Victoria would have suited me better."

"We have good cookies. And there are a lot of nice people here."

"Well, I only know one of them, but she seems pretty special." Jack felt a soft kick on his ankle. A good sign! "I guess I don't always make the right decisions."

"So, for instance, how do you feel about fraternities? Are you going to join one?"

"I'm not sure. I know a lot of guys who are—Jay Walters, for instance. Why do you ask?"

Susie frowned. "Because I think they're discriminatory, and the way they select members is distasteful. The university environment should be open and socially inclusive."

"True, but they have a lot of good parties."

Jack felt another kick under the table, a little harder this time.

After the next sociology class, Jack returned Susie's lecture notes to her with another sketch tucked inside. It was a portrait of her drinking tea and eating a cookie in the Wymilwood Café to which he had added a caption: *Party Time!*

"Oh, I like that kind of party," Susie said, thanking him. "But I think your drawing flatters me."

"Well," Jack joked. "I told you I don't think I'm much of an artist." Susie poked him in the ribs. "Hey, *Gigi* is on at the Odeon Varsity. Would you like to go tomorrow evening?"

"I'd love to."

The following week, Jack asked her out to dinner at Diana Sweets. Again, she accepted without hesitation. At the next class, they started sitting together—at a location delicately negotiated. If they sat at the back, Susie said she couldn't concentrate properly on the lecture and take good notes, especially if Jay were there, which was only intermittent. Jack, on the other hand, contended he would feel uncomfortably conspicuous in the front row. Besides, the classroom lacked any perspective from that location. Susie was responsive to this argument because she felt it reflected Jack's artistic sensibilities. So they reached a compromise, agreeing that they would sit in the fifth row. And there they remained together until the end of the course. In fact, they were largely inseparable from that point on until they graduated.

When they finished their first degrees, Susie went to the Ontario College of Education to get her teacher's certificate. Jack was uncertain what to do, but Susie pushed him to enrol at the Ontario College of Art. "I doubt I could make a living as an artist," he said. "I should probably go to law school or something like that."

"You'd hate it. And I don't think you'll be happy with yourself if you don't at least try to become a professional artist. After all, if you have only modest success, you can always teach to supplement your income." She didn't say that, with her salary as a teacher and whatever he made as an artist, they could get by. But that's what she was thinking and that's how things turned out. After graduating from OCE, Susie taught high school in Toronto to complete her teaching qualifications, while Jack finished a Bachelor of Fine Arts degree at OCA. They married the spring they finished, with Susie's sister Becky serving as her maid of honour. Linda and two friends from Victoria College were bridesmaids. In deference to the fact he had known him since childhood, Jack chose Jay as his best man, while Lou and Cass were ushers. "We all wondered just how long it would be before Jack popped the question," Jay said in his toast. "I thought I'd have to do it for him," to which Jack retorted, "It would have happened much earlier, but you know me, I don't know much about etiquette. I was waiting for Susie to propose."

They were both still virgins when they married because Jack had never learned how to read Susie's enigmatic eyes. And it wasn't until they had been married for several months that she told him approximately when she would have consented to sex. "Probably in the spring of second year. Maybe sooner."

"No-o-o-o!" Jack breathed, aping Jay. "So many good times missed."

Right after the wedding, they left for London, England, where Jack had been accepted into the Slade School of Fine Art and Susie had landed a position at a comprehensive school in Battersea. A number of friends bade them farewell at Union Station where they boarded the boat train for Montreal. "I hope she'll find him interesting enough," Linda commented as Susie and Jack disappeared up the stairs to the platform. "Perhaps if he flourishes as an artist…"

"I'm not worried about them at all," Sally answered. "They look like a 'happily ever after' couple to me."

Chapter 7

In the end, influenced by his conversation with Susie over tea in the Wymilwood Café, Jack decided not to go to the stag party at the Zete House with Jay. So Jay went with Cass instead. As Jay reported to Jack afterwards, Cass was in top Ojibway form, showing off to the brothers scrutinizing the rushees. Standing on a second-storey patio roof, beer in hand, he bellowed out a song for passers-by on St. George Street.

> Screw them all, screw them all
> The long and the short and the tall
> Screw all the loose ones and all of the prigs
> Screw all the virgins and even the pigs.

The Zetes guffawed with approval, but Jay's antenna started bleeping a cautionary yellow again.

Two of the drunker brothers trotted onto the deck, carrying balloons filled with water, and waited crouching by the patio wall for the right person to pass. "Hey, no-o-o! That's Godfrey Wincanton," Jay wheezed in surprise. "He's at Trinity." Three young men were passing the fraternity, Godfrey in his usual three-piece suit and the others in crew neck sweaters and slacks.

"That's Rusty Jones from the Kapp House in the middle," one of the Zetes said. "Perfect." The heavy balloons wobbled through the air and burst on the sidewalk, one of them close enough to spray all of the target. Four angry eyes immediately lifted to the rooftop patio, while two others, large and filmy, searched aimlessly to left and right and then slowly followed the others upward.

"That you, Finletter?" Rusty shouted. But there was no answer from the rooftop; everyone was now crouching behind the wall. "Okay, you've fucking asked for it." The three walked on towards the Kapp House.

The Zetes were out of balloons. But Cass dove into his pants pocket and handed out a package of condoms. More pizzazz than balloons. Cass had just "chalked up ten points" with the Zetes, Jay was certain. But why was a loser like Wincanton being rushed by the Kapps? It was Sally who, the next day, provided Jay with the answer, aware, it seemed, of everything going on at Trinity. "Apparently, Wincanton's uncle was a Kapp, and he wanted Godfrey to follow the family tradition. His mother thought it would be good for him to join and broaden his university experience. They're very rich, you know, and Godfrey's uncle has given a lot of financial support to the Kapps. So they have no option but to accept him."

"Hey, no-o-o," Jay exhaled hoarsely in his "best-bit-of-gossip-I've-heard-today" voice. "He'll be a backdoor Kapp for sure, and not the first, from what I've heard. They'll keep him hidden away during rushing." Jay was leaning more than ever towards the Dekes.

It grew cool on the rooftop after the sun set, so everyone moved downstairs to the living-room where another group had already gathered by the piano.

There once was a professor named Hall
Who had a rectangular ball
Now the cube of its weight
Was his penis times eight
Plus four times the square root of fuck all.

Aye, aye, aye, aye
In China they do it for chili
So here comes another verse
That's worse than the other verse
And waltz me around again, Willie.

Cass chug-a-lugged the rest of his beer and plunged in.

There once was a man on a heath
Who got himself stuck in a sheath
Wasn't the hair on his prick

That made him stick
But the virgin who clamped underneath.

All the Zetes roared and Jay heard one whisper to another, "We gotta get this guy pinned right away."

The raucous singing drowned the voices of the eager Kapp rushees, minus Godfrey Wincanton, marching down St. George Street under the watchful eye of a vengeful Rusty Jones. The Zetes didn't hear them, but the song was a familiar one along fraternity row.

Let's all go and piss on the Zete House
Piss on the Zete House
Piss on the Zete House
Let's all go and...

The Zetes were too slow responding to avoid a liberal, yellow washing of their front steps, and, when they finally did respond, in the commotion they missed altogether the two Kapps who snuck up a fire escape and entered the house through a second-floor bathroom window. They locked the door and disconnected the floating bulb in the back of the toilet, flushed the toilet, and retreated out the window.

It was after midnight when the stream of water tumbling down the staircase was spotted. Five minutes later the Zetes had rammed the bathroom door open and stopped the flood—in time, it appeared, to preserve the first-floor ceiling, but the hall carpets were oozing water like giant, soggy dish cloths. There were no clues as to who had entered the house. One of the Zetes, fully dressed, was sleeping soundly in the empty bathtub, but he had passed out before the assault and, when he was shaken awake, he could tell the brothers nothing.

In the end, Cass didn't join a fraternity. He made it onto the staff of the *Varsity* as a reporter, and its editorial position was strongly anti-fraternity. This time prudence trumped partying, and Cass did one of his infamous about-faces. His first byline story, under the banner headline "I INFILTRATED THE ZETES," was a scathing exposé of fraternity life, complete with an account of the water bombing, the urinating, and the blocking of the toilet. "No-o-o!" Jay exclaimed to Jack as he read it. "I'm glad I've chosen the Dekes."

It was the article in the *Varsity* that brought Cass in contact with a fellow student at University College, Marcia Feldman, who was already active on the Students' Administrative Council. She stopped by the newspaper's office to congratulate him. Marcia, Cass soon discovered, was the daughter of a senior editor at the *Toronto Evening Telegram*. How much that was a factor in the attention Cass showered on Marcia thereafter was always a matter of conjecture among his Ojibway friends. Jay also contended that it was only to please Marcia and align himself with the thinking of the *Varsity* that Cass joined the Campaign for Nuclear Disarmament and proudly wore the organization's black and white peace button. Jack and Lou, however, disagreed. From their conversations with Cass, they were convinced his commitment to the movement was genuine even if it seemed to come out of left field.

Whatever the true explanation for his behaviour, Cass and Marcia got engaged the year Cass graduated, marrying soon after. And right away, Cass went to work at the *Telegram* as a reporter.

***

"No, I mean it, you *really* are pretty," Jack was trying to reassure Sally as they sat in the Buttery the fourth week of classes, waiting for Jay's football practice to finish and Susie's class at Vic to end. "And I've always liked your hair—the way it bounces when you walk. I noticed it the first time I saw you walking along the Ojibway dock." Sally enjoyed the few times she was alone with Jack. It was an opportunity to talk about themselves rather than be a couch for others. "And when you're speaking to someone, you look at them intently. It makes people feel they have your undivided attention."

Sally roared with laughter. "What does that have to do with looks?"

"I think it does. Beauty is a product of many qualities." Sally still looked sceptical, so he added, "You've got great legs, too."

"Yeah, like a giraffe's." She frowned as she scratched away a flake of skin from the fading tan of one calf. "God, look how my kneecaps stick out. It's awful."

"I'm looking, but I don't see any problem."

Startled that somebody had overheard their conversation, Sally and Jack turned, and there was Lou standing by their table in his habitual sunglasses and with another of his infamous bags under his arm. Jack was not particularly surprised to see him. There had been something about the way he had looked at Sally the first time he had come into the Buttery. And the week before, when he and Lou had gone for a drive together in Lou's old '46 Chevy, he had wanted to go by Sally's parents' home on Old Forest Hill Road, just to have a look. When he discovered how close their house—well mansion really—was to Lady Eaton's, he just nodded his head slowly and said, "Yeah-h-h."

"So, where's Jay?" Lou asked, sitting down.

"At practice," Sally answered. "He's quarterbacking the Trinity team."

"But worrying he should have played for the Intermediates," Jack added.

Lou chuckled. "So how is he anyway?"

"Oh, he's fine, Pinky, just fine." It was Sally's good old, just-the-same Jay voice.

"He's taking Soc. and Phil., right? So what about next year? Has he decided on a major yet?"

"No-o-o, Pinky, no-o-o-o." Sally dragged out the words even more than usual. "We haven't crossed that bridge yet... So, how are you?"

"Great. Oh, here. I've brought you something."

"Oh, no!"

Lou pulled a bottle of a white, creamy liquid from the bag under his arm.

"What's this? Another of your famous potions?" Jack kidded him.

"No. I got it at a drugstore. It's a new lotion for moistening the skin. Just out. It'll keep your complexion soft and youthful for years."

"Geez, Pinky, are you trying to tell me something?" Sally laughed.

"No, no! I just noticed at the Ojibway how concerned you were about your skin—you know, about getting it tanned just right."

There was an awkward silence. Lou took off his sunglasses, polished the frames carefully with a cloth, and then laid them on the table as he laid out a proposal to Sally. "Say, what are you doing Friday night? There's this dance at St. Mike's. Would you be interested in going?"

"Gee, Pinky, that's really nice of you to ask." It was clear to Jack that Sally had been taken completely by surprise. After all, once the Deke initiations were over, it was pretty well assumed at Trinity that she'd be pinned to Jay. Sally closed her eyes and raised her head towards the ceiling, her soft brown hair teasing the back of her neck as she feigned careful deliberation. "Let's see, that's the third of October, right?"

"Yeah, the third."

"Awe, gee, no! Isn't that too bad." She sounded as though she really meant it. "I can't. I'm busy that night. The social life around here is pretty hectic, you know."

"Yeah. I didn't think you'd be free. Anyway, it was just a thought."

"Well, thanks. I'm really sorry."

It looked as if Lou were about to go, but Sally didn't want the conversation to end on a sour note. That was not in her nature. "So how is your new business going?" she asked.

"Oh, fine." There was another awkward pause until Lou added, "I'm getting a little heat from the university administration, but I think I can weather it."

Lou had started up a textbook exchange on College Street, making much of the fact that his shop was the first to cater to poorer students by organizing the resale of used books. The shop had a small front, but was at ground level, and the windows were completely plastered with advertisements.

WHY PAY MORE? PUT YOUR FOOT IN OUR DOOR
YES, WE BUY AS WELL AS SELL

WHO ARE YOU GOING TO IMPRESS WITH A DEN OF DATED TEXTS? BUY FROM AND RESELL TO US!

A homely, unemployed music graduate managed the store for Lou and lived in a room above it. The pay was pittance, but Jack was pretty sure Lou also compensated her with sexual attention. "Lou's going to put Coles Notes out of business one of these years," he said to Sally.

"I'm sure he will," Sally answered.

In one corner of the store window in much smaller print than the other advertisements was a sign that read:

EXPERT ESSAY COUNSELLING. INQUIRE WITHIN

That was the side of the business that Lou was banking on to turn a good profit, and for which the book exchange was principally a convenient cover. Lou was in the process of amassing a collection of undergraduate essays, carefully cross-referenced and filed according to grade. On each was noted the date of its original bona fide submission and the name of the recipient professor. They were always carefully described by Lou as "research aids," and their price ranged anywhere from five to twenty-five dollars depending on the paper's quality. At that time, his collection encompassed only courses in Commerce and Finance, Political Science and Economics, History, and English, but, as his network of suppliers expanded, he expected within a year or two to be servicing all disciplines of the university. "I'm collecting lecture notes, too," Lou said, "but there's not as much money in them unless they're really good. Hey, guess who came in? Cass."

"Really?" Sally and Jack said at the same time.

"Yeah. I sold him two 'A's." Lou chuckled again. "At a discount, of course. Cass said he just wanted to get an idea of the standards in first year."

"Sure, sure," Jack responded. "I've got to hand it to you. Someday you're going to know a hell of a lot about everyone in this town."

"God, Pinky, you certainly will!" Sally agreed.

Lou just grinned and then got up to go. "So, when am I going to get to meet this new love of yours?" he asked Jack.

"Gee…I don't know. I'm thinking I'll keep her away from guys like you." Lou grinned at that and patted Jack on the shoulder.

"She's sweet, Pinky," Sally said. "You'll really like her."

"I'm sure I will. Well, say hi to Jay for me, eh? Too bad I missed him."

"Will do. Sorry about the third."

"No problem."

"And thanks for the lotion. It was very thoughtful of you." When Lou had reached the door, Sally said, "Well that was certainly a surprise visit. Imagine people buying essays to submit, even Cass. You never would, would you?"

"Never."

"Nor Jay?"

"No. I don't think so."

"God, Jack, what do you suppose Jay *is* going to do with his future?"

"I think he'll probably become a lawyer."

"Really?"

"That guy Henry Phillips at the Deke House is planning on law, and Jay is pretty impressed by him."

"God only knows, Jack. God only knows." She laughed, but not in her usual, hearty manner. "Maybe he's going to be the perpetual undergraduate, collecting a string of degrees."

"Maybe. Or a football coach."

"Oh, not that, surely… Funny thing Pinky asking me to a dance, wasn't it?"

"Yeah, I guess." But Jack wasn't really surprised by either the invitation or the rejection. He was sure the last thing Sally could imagine herself doing at college was going to a dance at St. Mike's with a stick of deodorant for a date.

"Do you think I should have accepted? I hate to hurt his feelings."

Jack shrugged his shoulders. "Pinky's not easily hurt. Besides, you were very nice about it."

"Can you imagine if someone else from Trinity were there?" Sally dug out her cigarettes from her purse and lit one. "You know, he really wouldn't look too bad if he didn't use so much hair oil, and if he'd just get rid of those ridiculous sunglasses."

"No question. They make him look sinister, but he's not really."

"He's going to be pretty successful someday, don't you think?"

"Not much doubt about that. He's very determined."

"God! What would you ever talk to him about? At a dance, I mean."

"Business, I guess. It wouldn't be easy. But you know, I've learned to feel comfortable with him even when there's silence."

"Really? I don't think I would. Of course, I listen more than I talk. But that requires someone blabbering at me."

"Well, it's not as if he doesn't talk. It's just that he doesn't unless he thinks he has something worth saying."

"It would be interesting to see what St. Mike's is like, wouldn't it?"

Jack didn't answer. Sally took a long, pensive drag on her cigarette and, with her head tilted backwards, blew the smoke out towards the ceiling. Then she firmly butted her cigarette in her saucer. "Maybe it's stupid. But I'm going to go. I hate to let him down."

She got up. Jack straightened his books on his clipboard and followed her out of the Buttery. At the telephone in the hallway, she stopped abruptly. "I'm going to phone him right away before I lose my nerve. He ought to be back by now. God! This is crazy. Do you have his number?"

Jack wrote it down for her on a slip of paper.

"Hello, Pinky?" Jack heard her say, standing in the hall at a discreet distance from the phone. "It's Sally. Hey, listen. I got out of that date on the third, if you're still interested."

Jack could almost feel Lou grinning through the wire.

Sally and Lou only went out a couple of times over the ensuing weeks, but by the Saints in late November—the big dance of the year at St. Hilda's—Sally was in a real dilemma over whether to ask Jay or Lou. In the Buttery, she discussed the matter more than once with Jack, but he stayed rigorously neutral out of deference to his two friends. In the end, however, it was Lou who got the important call. In January, she and Jay broke up completely, and by March, Sally and Lou were really going steady, although they never called it that. Lou never joined a fraternity, so he didn't have a pin to give Sally. Jack figured he never would have in any event; that was too conventional for him. But on Sally's birthday, in October 1959, a year after they first went out, he gave her a silver bracelet, engraved "I love you…Lou." She wore it without fail the rest of her days at university.

When Lou graduated, he went to work initially for Sally's father, managing the Toronto office of his chain of holiday resorts. At the same time, he changed his legal name from Luigi Piccolo to Louis Piper, though everyone used only the short form of his first name. And, just after Sally graduated, in June 1962, they were wed in the Trinity College Chapel. Lou's mother was upset that it was not a Roman Catholic wedding, but Lou didn't have a problem with the location himself. He was happy to please Sally and her family. "Besides," as he put it, "I've already sinned enough that if I confessed everything to a priest, I'd be excommunicated anyway."

Jack was best man at the wedding and Lou, in a gesture that reflected his conciliatory nature, invited both Jay and Cass to be ushers. "Fuck," Cass whispered to Jay as the men were standing near each other by the altar, "It's a wonder Barbie Bigelow wasn't asked to be a bridesmaid. Then Lou would have had three people here all of whom he screwed in the same year."

Chapter 8

"Poor Jay. It must have been awfully hard on him, losing Sally in first year and then, later, seeing so many of his close friends get married."

"No question. Being the one standing on the sidelines was a real blow to his ego." Jack shifted uncomfortably in the driver's seat, his buttocks aching from so much time in the car. "But he tried to hide it. I remember by January of first year he was saying that Sally was fun to date, but not right for him for the long haul; she was too superficial. Sally? What about himself? Well, to be fair, Jay did get more serious after they broke up. Not that he stopped judging people, not for a while at least. When Sally and Lou were clearly a couple, he announced that that was great; Lou was a diamond in the rough, but Sally would polish his edges. Anyway, after the breakup, remember how Jay dated a lot of different women? But no one seemed to suit him, maybe because his selection criteria kept changing."

"So did Linda's."

———

At first, she went out with an actor in the Trinity Dramatic Society. Then, she joined the peace movement and dated a pacifist at University College. When she went to Thailand with CUSO, she was attracted to Buddhism, and keen on an American she met who had become a novice in a Bangkok wat. As the Vietnam War heated up, however, he went home to join the protests and about the same time Linda landed on the Sturridges' doorstep in London. "The detritus of war," Jack called her.

———

It was already six o'clock, so Jack asked Susie to try to get the CBC news on the radio. "I think it's FM 99.1."

"Didn't Catherine fix the buttons so that we could press 'one' and go straight to the CBC?"

"She did, but somehow I fucked it up."

Susie found the station, but they were doing yet another item on the Trump administration. "Jesus, I can't listen to any more of that crap." Jack pounded the wheel with one hand. "The Bush years were bad enough, but this is a nightmare. Makes me glad to be home, even though Maine seems a world away from Washington."

"It wasn't when the Bushes were at Kennebunk." Susie turned the radio off. "Remind me to ask Catherine if she can program it again."

"Maybe at the same time she can show us how to plug in the iPod so that we can listen to some music if I forget again to bring some CDs. No wonder the kids figure we're in our dotage."

"You know that's not fair."

They were on the outskirts of Toronto now on Lake Shore Boulevard as it passed the old bathing pavilion at Sunnyside, a landmark that Jack had painted several years earlier. He had depicted it with a long line of cars and trucks stuck in traffic in the foreground, and in front of them several railway tracks. Jack had hoped that the painting might be purchased by a city gallery and have some impact in generating support for moving the road and tracks farther north to enhance the waterfront environment in the area of the pavilion. But it never sold, and lay buried deep in his attic studio in his collection of unappreciated paintings.

"You know, those were incredibly quiescent years in the fifties when we were at university." With the radio off, Jack's mind wandered backwards. "The only time a building was closed was when a band of drunken engineers iced over a doorway as a practical joke. There were no sit-ins, no evacuations because of bomb scares."

"No. And the pinned co-ed in a strapless formal, looking for a husband, was a long way from the women who burned their marriage certificates a decade later."

"While guys were burning their draft cards. They were confident years, too, when even a degree in Greek and Latin could land you a decent job on Bay Street. I remember talking with assurance about things that, just a few years later, seemed far less clear: the global spread of democracy, the efficacy of the free enterprise system, the resilience of the planet."

"The elimination of racial and economic inequality," Susie added. "The sanctity of marriage, even the nature of male and female sexuality."

"Back to Linda again!" Jack laughed. "No wonder by the time we saw Jay again in London, he was a changed man. It was a new era. We were all different by then. Jesus, I've got to stop for a break. My sciatica is killing me."

They parked in a lot on Queen's Quay and took a stroll through the Music Garden, resplendent in late-summer ochres, pinks, and scarlets, dripping petals on paths that curved like notes in a score. It was one of the few features of the waterfront of which Jack wholeheartedly approved—apart, of course, from the fact that, just past the garden's far end, there still loomed the stolid, gloomy silos of the long-abandoned and decaying grain elevators of the Canada Malting Company. Jack had once painted them, too, in all their gigantic, concrete ugliness, adding to the right of the silos an enormous red, festering eye. That work never sold either, but Susie so detested it that Jack eventually threw it in the trash. "Still no decision has been made on what to do with those silos." Jack shook his head with disgust. "You know, one idea was to convert them into a giant mausoleum with space for thousands of coffins and urns. Wow! What creative waterfront thinking! If that ever happens please make sure no one gets into our backyard and digs my ashes out of the garden."

"Stop it! Let's go get tea at the Music Garden Café."

Susie sat at a small outside table on Queen's Quay while Jack got them a pot of Earl Grey. Early evening sunlight was still falling on their table and they found it comfortable and relaxing sitting there after so much time in the car. "This is nice. No laptops on the tables. I don't feel like I'm in a classroom."

"Maybe going back to school would be good for you. You'd learn a bit about contemporary culture."

"I don't want to know more than I already do."

"Neanderthal!"

Susie noticed Jack frowning as he gazed across the wide expanse of Queen's Quay where cars and streetcars were steadily streaming by. "Please don't tell me what you're thinking."

"Because you know, right?"

"Of course."

"But I don't want the Music Garden disrupted by having cafés directly on the other side of the road. I just think there's space for a couple of nice ones just to the east and west of the garden, if only—"

"So, are you going to paint a proposal?"

"Maybe... Sorry?" Jack was suddenly distracted by a man, shirt open to the sun, sitting alone at the table next to them and apparently speaking to him. "Pardon?" The man wasn't, however, looking at Jack and seemed oblivious of the fact Jack had spoken to him.

"Silly! He's on his cellphone. He's talking into a microphone."

"Jesus. You're right. They aren't as many nut cases on the streets of Toronto as I keep thinking."

"That reminds me. I think I'll text Catherine now rather than phoning her when we get home. That will impress her." Susie unzipped her purse and got out the phone and stylus. As she tapped her message, she recited it to Jack. "Hi, love. We're at the waterfr... Oh, look, the sweeties! They've finished the word for me! ...waterfront having tea. Will be home shortly. Will phone in the morning... Oh, and now they've corrected my spelling!"

"Yes, those little people inside *are* nice, aren't they?"

"Maybe I should have invited Catherine and Alan for lunch tomorrow," Susie said after putting the phone away. "And the girls. After all, it's a Saturday. They may all be home."

"I imagine Alan will be playing golf, and Alison will be with her boyfriend."

"Well, at least Catherine and Mary-Anne might want to come over." Susie studied her tea cup, frowning. "I wish I liked Alison's boyfriend better. I don't think he's right for her."

"He doesn't seem that bad to me. He's quiet, but at least he's not like that last guy. All he ever did was talk about himself. That seems to pass for conversation today."

"But this one's parents are divorced. That's never a good sign. We've been so lucky with our own kids. I hope it lasts for our grandchildren as well, but I don't know..."

"Well, Tom and Narinda have had their rough patches."

"Yes, but they've stayed together, and they've been careful never to fight in front of the boys."

"Good thing for Tom. If he went toe-to-toe with Narinda, she'd deck him with blistering verbal punches."

"Jack!"

"No, no. I mean that as a compliment. You know I love her. In fact, even if they did have a spat in front of the boys, I'm sure they wouldn't notice. They're always too busy fighting invading aliens on their apps."

"Well, that's better than each other. You know, when I think about it, our friends have been pretty lucky with their kids, too, except for Cass that is, with Stephen an alcoholic—"

"Worse. He's a coke addict, too."

"With divorced parents. So, there you are. It's a factor."

Jack finished his tea and stood up. "Shall I get us a couple of cookies to take home?"

"If you like." When he returned, Susie continued. "Look at the others. Lou and Sally's boys are fine. They're like clones of their dad."

"Is that good?"

"Well, at least they're doing okay and seem happily married." They were walking to the car now. "And considering the turbulent nature of Linda and Jay's relationship, Sigmund and Elizabeth have turned out pretty normal."

"I don't know. Sigmund gets regular counselling and Elizabeth is a professional agitator."

"Jack, Elizabeth is an environmental activist like her mother. What's wrong with that?"

"Nothing, if she stays at it." Jack patted Susie on the shoulder and started the car. "Gee, I'll never forget that weekend that we had both Linda and Jay staying in our little flat. Unwittingly, we were the ones who brought them together, weren't we?"

"Yes." Susie closed her eyes and sighed, wading back to their years in London.

————

She loved their Battersea flat despite the floral wallpaper that was always damp and bubbly from the rain and fog, and the coal fires that were almost impossible to light. Of course, they could be replaced with paraffin heaters, but that risked other problems. Sometimes Jack started one in his greenhouse studio to warm the space while he had breakfast, but if he lingered too long in the kitchen, the heater filled the greenhouse with smoke. As a result, some of his paintings ended up so covered in soot that he had to throw them out. Still, the greenhouse was the perfect place for him to work—plenty of sunlight and lots of room for his supplies. Susie believed they might have stayed in London their whole lives except that, as Jack put it, they always felt as if they were camping out.

London proved good for Jack's career. Early on, he sold a painting of then Prime Minister Sir Alec Douglas-Hume, dressed in a tweed jacket and breeches, out on a moor shooting grouse. Jack pictured him with a bowler hat twirling on the barrel of his gun. It paid their rent for weeks as there was a good market in England in the sixties for canvases that satirized the establishment. That success encouraged Jack to do similar paintings with good results, but sales weren't as brisk after Labour came to power.

For her part, Susie loved teaching in London—mud-splattered little urchins in striped football jerseys and short pants, their mouths stuffed with candies from the local sweet shop: gobstoppers. jelly babies. drumstick lollies. "Please miss," they would ask her politely, "'Ave you got a plaster? I've scraped my knee, I 'ave." Or "Please miss, I need a new biro. Mine's as buggered as me dad's sore arse." They were always coming into the classroom with jars of little fish they'd caught in Battersea Park and thrusting them in the faces of the girls, freckle-faced little mischief-makers with pigtails and big red bows in their hair. They would shriek with feigned alarm until Susie shooed them out to the playground to skip rope.

I had a little puppy, his name was Tiny Tim.
I put him in the bathtub to see if he could swim.
He drank all the water, he ate a bar of soap.
The next thing you know he had a bubble in his throat.
In came the doctor, in came the nurse,
In came the lady with the alligator purse…

A couple of the boys would stop playing conkers and have a try, but they were hopeless at timing their jumps and would end up holding the rope ends while the girls whispered snide remarks about them. Later, when she taught in Toronto, Susie found the kids weren't that different, but they never spoke as colourfully as her biro boy: "When I get home from school, me mum's always busy in the kitchen, but me dad's just kippin' on the settee."

"I remember so well that time Jay came down from Cambridge to visit us in Battersea," Jack said. "We hadn't seen him in a year and a half."

"He'd changed a lot, hadn't he?"

"No question, but in some ways he was still the same. After all, he'd gone to Cambridge because he figured it would be prestigious to have an Oxbridge degree."

"Well, it was also because he didn't like law school. And at least he didn't say that it would be 'golden' to have an M.Phil."

"True. What I noticed most was that his interests were really different. I thought we'd take him to see a football match at Stamford Bridge or White Hart Lane, but that didn't interest him. He wanted to go to the British Museum to see the Elgin Marbles and to the Tait to admire Turner's paintings. I took him to both and to the Courtauld Institute as well. He asked a lot of questions, even about my own work, good ones too."

"We talked a lot about art over dinner too, didn't we?"

"Yeah, post-Impressionism, surrealism, that sort of thing. At one point, Jay said that, when he looked back at the way he was at Trinity, he couldn't believe how shallow he was, and how tolerant we had all been to put up with him."

"And you agreed we had been."

"I did? How did he take it?"

"I can't remember."

"Well, I know he did talk about what he'd do after Cambridge, but he didn't go on endlessly about himself and his future the way he used to, and he even asked you about teaching in London and how it compared with Toronto. He looked different, too. I mean he still had a boyish face and it was exaggerated by that lock of blonde hair that hung, slightly curled, to one side of his forehead. But when he put on the black-rimmed reading glasses he'd just started wearing, he suddenly looked older and far more serious. Wiser even. A scholar."

"Maybe that's what did it for Linda. She was there too, wasn't she?"

"No. It was the second time that Jay came to visit that Linda showed up unexpectedly. She was on her way home from her CUSO assignment."

"Oh, yes, I remember now. She called us from a phone box at Waterloo Station, didn't she?"

"Yes, and less than an hour later she was at our front gate, looking like an unwashed peasant who'd just crossed the bank of a rice paddy. She was wearing brown leather sandals and a homespun batik sarong, and she lit joss sticks in the living-room while she meditated an hour each morning. The whole flat smelled like the Temple of the Emerald Buddha."

"Well, that was nicer than the odour of coal and paraffin smoke."

"I'll grant you that, but she didn't seem very changed!"

"How can you say that? She was very nice to you. She took a real interest in your painting. She even bought one—a black family looking in a shop window plastered with advertisements of flats for rent: 'Europeans Only.' 'Please no coloureds.' She still has it hanging."

"Yeah, but in her attic hideaway. I don't think she ever really liked it."

"Well, she did its message. She said it showed you had a conscience even if you were reticent about displaying it. The truth is she's always been supportive of your work. If there were more people like her with a taste for your art, you would have done very well."

"Better, anyway."

"Linda took an interest in my teaching, too. She came to the school to talk to the kids about Thailand. Some of them had seen *The King and I*, so they were very excited about having a visitor who had been there."

"Even though she hardly looked like the Queen of Siam."

"They were in awe of her all the same. I remember she had them sit on the floor in the lotus position like novice monks while they watched her joss sticks burn. Then she taught them how to chant a prayer. She had the room humming like a wat on the Chao Phraya."

"And did any of the kids attain enlightenment?"

"Well, they finished the day with more open minds than yours."

"Ouch! But weren't you afraid some of the parents would complain about what you were doing in the classroom? This wasn't exactly Church of England stuff."

"Not back then. Not in London."

"Shit! This traffic is terrible." They had been stuck on Avenue Road north of Bloor for several minutes. "Worse every year. Guess we shouldn't have stopped on the waterfront. Remember how we worried about dealing with Jay and Linda in the flat at the same time? We had only that one roll-out bed in the living-room and even it was pretty awful."

"Yes. Linda got it, and we had to put Jay on the floor in a sleeping bag with just a mat under it. But, as it turned out, they were fine with that and not at all concerned about sleeping in the same room."

"In fact, the real worry was that they got on so well together. It wasn't at all like Trinity, was it? Jay asked Linda lots of questions about Thailand and showed a real interest in her passion for Buddhism. He admitted that it took a while for him to reject the Anglican faith, but now Buddhism really attracted him because it appealed to the intellect with its focus on selflessness and attaining enlightenment. Linda was not only surprised but delighted."

"And at the attention he gave her. When Linda and I decided to get up at dawn and go to Westminster Bridge for old times' sake, Jay said he wanted to go with us. Not like you, you old lazy bones."

"I was tired. They kept us up late every night."

"Anyway, at the bridge, I asked Linda to recite Wordsworth's poem just as she had done in fifty-eight. Jay was really impressed when she did it flawlessly, and said he'd have to get a copy of Wordsworth's collected works. Linda promised to mail him one, and that's when I first sensed trouble ahead."

"For me, it was hearing them in the living-room talking late into the night. And especially the third night they were there together. We heard them whispering and laughing, but only for a few minutes, and then it went silent for well over an hour before we could hear them talking again. We were sure that was the night Linda invited Jay to share the bed with her."

"And that's why the next day I had a frank talk with Linda. I warned her that, while it was true that Jay had changed a lot since college, she needed to be careful about getting too attached to him. I was sure he was still too conventional and career-driven for her, and that a long-term relationship wouldn't work."

"Remind me how she reacted?"

"Oh, she took it pretty well. She thanked me and said not to worry; she wasn't planning on marrying anyone. She just found Jay surprisingly good company now."

"Funny, isn't it? At the same time that you were talking to Linda, I was with Jay at the Beacon Arms, advising him to be careful about Linda. He was still very impressionable, and I was afraid he wasn't forming a rounded picture of her. I don't think he understood that her attachment to Buddhism was probably transitory. I told him I thought he'd find her quixotic nature too much to handle. But he wouldn't buy it and told me he looked forward to seeing her again in Canada."

"Well, we both tried," Susie sighed, as Jack parked the car in their driveway.

"Yeah, but did we try hard enough?"

"Oh, look! The shrubs have been trimmed and the Japanese maple pruned. Must have been Alan. How nice of him."

"Not much to do, though, and now he's free to play golf tomorrow."

"Jack, that's not fair!"

"I know. Sorry. It just came out." He carried their larger bags to the front door, Susie following him with lighter cases. "So, after that visit in London, we didn't see Linda again until the wedding, right? Of course, Jay stayed with us a couple more times—when he came down from Cambridge to write the foreign service exams and then when he was in London for his interview." Jack dropped the bags at the front door and fumbled in his pocket for the key. "He talked a lot on those visits about how good it had been to see Linda again and he wondered what she would think if he joined the foreign service. I told him I thought that was way too conventional an existence for her—that she'd feel restricted by the protocol and niceties of diplomatic life." As Jack unlocked the door, he added, "But Jay thought she'd enjoy living abroad, especially if he were assigned to a post in a developing country."

"So, again he didn't listen." They deposited their loads in the hallway and returned to the car. "Nor did Linda when we talked on the phone after Jay went home. She told me they were driving back and forth between Toronto and Ottawa to see each other."

"Seeing? They were already sleeping together at our flat. Christ knows what they were doing by then!"

"Wow! It's lovely and cool inside, isn't it?" They'd returned to the house with their second loads. "Theirs was some wedding, though, wasn't it?"

"No question, it was the best."

"If you like the bizarre."

"Of course, it wasn't just the wedding that I enjoyed," Jack answered. "It was great, too, to see all the old gang again."

"Well, that wedding ceremony certainly made clear that Linda and Jay should have taken our advice and, after London, gone their separate ways."

"Yeah, that's why I always follow yours."

Susie rolled her eyes at Jack and picked up their accumulated mail from the hallway floor. "Please."

Chapter 9

When Susie and Jack went home for Linda and Jay's wedding in the summer of 1970, they flew first to Boston and then Portland, Maine, to spend ten days at Higgins Beach with Susie's parents. Jack had been there the year they were married and one other time on holidays from England, but that was all. Still, it already appealed to him. He loved to walk the beach from end to end with Susie in the early morning when mist often swirled along the shore, washing everything grey, and in the evening when sunlight, glancing off the slick black rocks at the southern end, dazzled their uncovered eyes. Those were the hours when the daytime crowds from Portland left Higgins' packed white sand to the locals and a small knot of determined surfers, lying patiently on their boards for a breaking wave large enough to give them a decent ride.

Like Susie, Jack enjoyed the beach in the middle of the day as well when they would plant an umbrella in the sand, spread out their towels, and sit and listen to the conversations of those around them. Now thirty, they felt, however, that they were observers only, not an integral part of the youthful scene. Yet, that summer, there were among the sunbathers some men who looked much older than their years—men on crutches with half or whole legs missing, others with bandaged foreheads and eyes, amputated hands or arms. Most were with family—parents, siblings, friends, lovers—helping them move to and from the beach, buoying their spirits with jokes and laughter.

While there had always been lots of flags flying from mast-heads on cottage lawns, Jack was sure there were more now than he had seen before—especially hanging vertically from cottage windows flat against the weathered cedar shakes, their red stripes like streaks of blood dripping to the sandy soil. On his previous visits, Jack had enjoyed poking fun at the kitschy names of cottages painted above their front doors, but now some seemed to him darkly ironic: "Rocky Rest," "Heavenly Haven," "Welcome Respite." They made both of them feel uncomfortable—so far from the battlefield of Vietnam, yet so near its tragic consequences.

The feelings those names engendered did not, however, keep them from the beach games they always played, including, for the first time that summer, cricket. It seemed well suited to Higgins' smooth, firm sand, and Jack and his father-in-law had no sooner pounded the makeshift stumps into the sand and perched driftwood bails on top than a crowd of mystified onlookers gathered. Two of them obligingly agreed to play at slips and silly mid-off, and one of them, a middle-aged man from Boston, became an enthusiastic convert to the sport. He even promised to bring a visiting English friend with county-level experience to play the next day—"a ringa," he called him in his infectious Harvard accent. The Englishman came, but his off-spin bowling was no more effective than anyone else's in the abnormal conditions. "Not your fault," Jack tried to comfort him and sound knowledgeable at the same time. "Doesn't matter who's bowling. On this pitch, the only thing that works is a full toss, though that makes the game like playing baseball."

"*Rather*," the Englishman responded. "And then they would be batting sixes off me into the ocean." It wasn't clear to Jack if he declined to change his delivery for this tactical reason, or because of the importance to him of preserving tradition by continuing to bowl in an orthodox manner. "Odd duck, wasn't he?" Jack commented to Susie after the match.

"I say, rather!" It was then, as they gathered up their belongings and started back to the cottage, that Susie told Jack that she had missed her period.

"Really?" He stopped suddenly and dropped the umbrella and bag he was carrying in the sand. "You're sure? How late are you?"

"Two weeks now."

"Two weeks? Jesus!"

"You're not upset, are you?"

"No, no! Not at all. Just surprised. Here... Here, give me that bag with the stumps."

"Jack! It's only two weeks. I'm not about to deliver."

"Holy shit! You're sure about this?"

"Yes, I'm as sure as I can be until I see a doctor."

"Where? Here?"

"No. I'll wait to we're back in England. It won't be that long."

"Holy shit! We're going to be parents!"

In bed that night they spent a long time talking about the future and how the time was right if they were ever going to have a family. It would be tough financially, they knew, but Jack's paintings were still selling reasonably well, and they calculated that income plus their savings would get them through while Susie took a leave of absence from her school. With all its social services, England was as good a place as any to have a baby, better than most, especially in the working class neighbourhood where they lived with its strong sense of community. The next day they told Susie's parents, who urged them to move home. "We're still not ready to," Susie responded. "We do miss you very much, but we love London. You'll just have to visit us more often."

* * *

From Higgins Susie and Jack flew to Toronto where Bev had urged them to stay with her for two or three days. From there, they planned to go by rented car to Pointe au Baril to visit Lou and Sally, and then to Linda and Jay's wedding in Muskoka.

"Hey! Jackie! Susie Q!" Bev screeched as she flung open the door of her old duplex near Eglinton and Avenue Road. "What a surprise. I didn't think you'd be here until much later."

She planted her short legs wide apart and spread out her arms to welcome them. *It's like walking into the Buttery again*, Jack thought. "We managed to get an earlier flight out of Boston. I'm sorry, but we didn't get a chance to call."

"Hey, no problem! Wow! It's great to see you. You both look terrific. It's been, what, six years since you moved to London? You don't look a day older, either of you."

"Nor do you," Susie responded quickly.

In fact, however, it was hard to tell because Bev's face was plastered with make-up and her lips lustrous from a fresh application of cherry red lipstick. She was in a floor-length pink satin dressing gown, slit up one leg, and slightly unzippered at the front. "You've probably guessed, I'm not alone," she said apologetically, and then giggled, "I was…we were…well…you know…"

"Oh, we're so sorry," Susie cried. "We really should have called. Why don't Jack and I just go out and get a bite to—"

"No, no! Don't be silly." Bev took Susie by the hand and led her towards the living-room. "Oh, it's so great to see you!" From the living-room to the right of the hallway, Jack and Susie could hear Bev's hi-fi bellowing one of her favourite, carefully selected tunes, Buddy Holly's "Oh Boy."

At the living-room door, she stopped and said, "You're in for a bit of a surprise, I'm afraid. I hope you won't mind."

As they entered, Susie and Jack saw a man with his back to the door, standing next to an eiderdown that had been spread out by the unlit, tile-lined fireplace. He was tucking his dark green shirt into his unzippered trousers, and, as he heard them, he turned to face them.

"Cass!" they shouted together, and Susie covered her face with her hands.

"Hi you guys. Long time no see." Cass hugged them both, while Jack explained how they'd arrived earlier than expected. "Well, who gives a shit? Great to see you."

Jack and Susie both thought he looked older. His sideburns were already greying, and permanent dark circles were developing under his eyes. But more than that, it was obvious that he had put on weight; his stomach was pressing against his shirt above his belt buckle, creating a distinct bulge. Yet, standing there grinning at them, it was clear it was still the same old Cass. In fact, Jack could almost hear him saying defiantly, "Yeah, and you, you dumb bugger, you never thought I did it with Barbie Bigelow either, did you?"

Jack and Susie were at a loss as to what to make of the situation. Had Cass left Marcia? Were he and Bev together now and that was common knowledge? Or were they having an affair? And, if so, did Marcia know anything about it? But no answers were offered. "Come on in," Bev cried. "Have a seat. Hey, how about a martini? We've got a jug of them in the refrigerator."

"Just a beer would be great," Jack said, and Susie agreed. Bev bustled off to the kitchen to get them while they sat staring at Cass, speechless at first.

"So, what do you think, eh? Great house, no?"

"Gosh, it looks lovely."

"Yeah, Scottie has done a lot of work on it."

Indeed she had. Bev had bought the narrow duplex several months earlier. It was on a street that had not yet caught the eyes of developers, so she had purchased it relatively inexpensively. Nonetheless, it had stretched her teacher's salary to the limit. But Bev had decided that even if she never married, she wasn't going to live in an apartment all her life. The third floor of the house had a separate entrance and that part she had rented out, but the rest was for her own use and she had already redecorated it in a spotlessly cheerful *Home and Gardens* fashion. Bright chintz drapes on the high bay windows reached all the way to the fawn pile carpeting that in turn blended into the green velvet of the armchairs and sofa. Earthenware pots hung from thick, knotted ropes in the windows, spilling over with white, red, and orange impatiens. It was, Jack thought to himself, perfect downtown Toronto chic, except for the bookcases. Where he figured normally you would expect to find the complete works of Shakespeare, Churchill's six-volume history of World War II, and a random selection of book club choices, there was instead a solid phalanx of vinyl records: five rows of 33s within Bev's limited reach and five more of 45s and 78s. The collection included virtually every popular song of the fifties and sixties, and space had been set aside for the seventies as the new decade gradually acquired nostalgia for Bev.

"Thanks, Scottie," Jack said as Bev returned from the kitchen with two beers, turning off the stereo as she came in. It seemed clear to both Susie and Jack that no explanation about Bev and Cass's relationship would be forthcoming and they had by now been living too long in England to pry, so Jack simply inquired obliquely, "So, how are things with you both? How has life been treating you?"

The result, however, was only a summation from each of them about their careers. According to Cass, everything was "great" at the

Telegram, though that was a perspective at odds with the actual financial state of the paper. It had, in fact, been bleeding financially for some time and was shortly to close its doors, leaving Cass to find new employment. It was true, however, that he had done well himself, bringing to the *Telegram* the aggressive approach to reporting he had taken at the *Varsity*. It wasn't so much that Cass had stylistic flare; rather, what he possessed was an ability to ferret information out of reluctant sources and uncover stories that others missed. So far, he viewed his greatest triumph as his coverage of the Paranopulos murder in Toronto just two years earlier, and he gleefully recounted the details for Jack and Susie.

————

Cass was on the *Telegram*'s rewrite desk around four-thirty in the afternoon when, over the police radio in front of him, he heard cars summoned to the scene of a shooting on Broadview Avenue. Cass left for the destination with a photographer right away, but the police were there ahead of them and the victim had already been bundled into an ambulance that was just speeding away. "Ahh, fucking shit," Cass apparently cried in frustration at their failure to get the photographs he wanted. Instead, he approached the police officers at the scene to find out what had happened, but they were tight-lipped and told him simply to phone the station later.

Cass was not, however, the type to sit back and wait for the police to issue a release. Beating them at their own game was one of the challenges of his trade that he relished, so he set about learning what he could from available witnesses. Before long, Cass established that the victim was George Paranopulos, long-time proprietor of a Broadview Avenue grocery store and a beloved fixture in the neighbourhood. Apparently, a man in a black woollen jacket had come into the store shortly after four—too late for the *Telegram*'s final edition, Cass had noted with frustration; now the *Globe* would be the first with the story and he figured they would screw it. The assailant, whose name was apparently Nick, asked for a pound of feta cheese and, as Paranopulos had his back to him slicing it, he pulled a meat cleaver from under his coat and demanded the contents of the cash register. At first Paranopulos had resisted, but when the man brought his cleaver down hard on the long, wooden counter just inches from the shopkeeper's hand, he relented and emptied the contents of the till into a plain brown grocery bag as instructed. Nick grabbed the bag and rushed from the store with Paranopulos pursuing him until the robber turned and shot him in the chest. It looked pretty bad, the witnesses all agreed.

"Why was he carrying a meat cleaver as well as a gun?" Cass pondered as they sped in their car to the Wellesley Hospital. "It doesn't make sense." His photographer thought it was probably to scare Paranopulos into handing over the contents of his till without having to use a gun. "Maybe," Cass agreed, "and that may prove to have been a fatal error."

Dead on arrival, the hospital desk reported to Cass, and he and his photographer immediately rushed to the Paranopulos residence after Cass coaxed the address out of the hospital staff. There, they camped out for several hours, periodically ringing the doorbell in a vain attempt to persuade the family to give them photographs of Mr. Paranopulos. On the last attempt, Cass simply pressed the bell in and held it in place until a second-storey window flew open and a pail of water splattered onto the front porch, mostly missing him. Shielding his face with his forearm, Cass looked up at the man at the window. "Hey. Come on! I'm going to be bugging you every twenty minutes right through the night," he shouted. "You might as well give us a photograph now and we'll leave you alone."

"You dirty, rotten scum. You got no feelings?" the man at the window yelled back. "You get out of here or I'll call the police."

"Motherfucker," Cass exhaled in exasperation as he climbed into their car again to try a different tack, a long shot that miraculously worked. At the fourth drug store they visited, Cass once again told the clerk behind the counter that George Paranopulos had left a roll of film to be developed, and he'd been asked to pick it up.

The clerk opened a drawer stuffed with white envelopes and thumbed through them. "Paranopulos? Here you are. That will be five eighty-five."

Cass grasped the envelope almost too eagerly, handed over six dollars and, without waiting for the change, hurried back to the car. Together he and his photographer sifted through the photographs until at last Cass shouted, "There! That's gotta be him. Probably his old lady with him. Looks like a holiday picture, in Florida maybe."

"Not very good quality," the photographer commented.

"No. Sorry about that, but it will do, buddy boy, it will do! I think we've got a scoop." And they hurried back to Paranopulos's street to show the photograph to neighbours to verify that it was a picture of the slain man.

The next day the *Telegram* ran the photo on the front page, while to Cass's and the city editor's delight the *Star* and the *Globe* had nothing. Cass still wasn't finished with the story, however, for the police had not yet found the killer, and to reach him before they did, Cass recognized, would be an even bigger scoop. That was the kind of moment reporters like him lived for, and he had another scheme to implement that he thought just might work. It was after more than two hundred phone calls by Cass, an assistant, and his photographer to grocery stores, restaurants, and butcher shops all over Toronto, and after checking out half a dozen false leads that Cass got the break he was looking for. It was on a call to a restaurant some distance from Paranopulos's grocery store and that is why it took so long to find the right place. "Hello, I'm Bob Cassidy, and I'm trying to get ahold of an old friend by the name of Nick. I believe he works for you as a cook or something."

Cass learned that Nick did indeed work there, but he hadn't shown up for his shift for three days. Another employee at the restaurant knew, however, where he lived and gave Cass the address. Not surprisingly, the murderer had fled his apartment and it was not until the next evening that Cass, with the help of the killer's neighbours, was able to trace his movements to a friend's bungalow in Oshawa. Cass and his photographer drove there immediately and parked a few doors away from the home. There they waited through the night before alerting the police—waited until it was well past the *Globe*'s deadline and it was light enough for his photographer to take good pictures.

When the police arrived, to Cass's delight they sealed off the suspect's street at both ends, making it impossible for other media, if they'd heard the police call, to get their reporters to the scene. After surrounding the bungalow, the police used a loudspeaker to urge Nick to come out. When at last he did, the police escorted him, handcuffed, to their car, obligingly stopping beside Cass and his photographer so that they could get good close-up shots. "I NABBED MURDER SUSPECT" was the three-inch headline for Cass's front-page byline story that appeared later that day.

—————

The headline was a bit of an exaggeration of the truth, Jack and Susie realized when Cass had finished, but for him it was only a modest one. "Isn't he something, you guys?" Bev kissed Cass on the cheek. "There's no one else in the business that clever."

Yeah, Jack thought. *Still aggressive, still a ruthless schemer determined to win at all costs*, but all he said was "That's certainly quite a story." Susie agreed, but added, "That poor old shopkeeper. I feel so sorry for him and all his family."

"Hey," Bev interjected, coming to her lover's defence, "Cassie didn't tell you, but he attended Mr. Paranopulos's funeral and he sent a big cheque in his memory to his Greek Orthodox Church."

"It would have been bigger still if that fucking guy who splashed me with water had given me a good pic."

"Oh, Cassie. You know that's not true. You were very generous. Oh, hey, you guys! I'm sorry. I bet you haven't had any dinner. You must be starving."

"Just a snack would be great."

"I've got spareribs for tomorrow, but little I can get you quickly now. There's leftover pizza in the fridge, but that's not much of a treat."

"It is for us. Not what you'd call a standby in England, like bangers and mash or bubble and squeak."

"Jesus! Those are foods?" Cass snorted. "They sound more like toys kids play with in the bath."

They walked down the hall to the back of the house, Cass

padding along in his stocking feet. Buried in the freezer, Bev found several slices of pizza, and put them in the oven. Like the living-room, her kitchen had been completely refurbished. A sharp glare bounced off her pastel-coloured appliances, but it was relieved by the spindly green plants in red clay pots that lined a window sill. A delicate pink and yellow orchid sat demurely in earth and moss in a wire basket suspended from the ceiling. And there was a large, pressed cork noticeboard beside the refrigerator to remind Bev of the activities and movements of her fantasy family. That night, it contained the best of the water colour paintings her Grade Three pupils had done following a year-end picnic on Centre Island. There was a notice from her principal's office that listed the dates for special school events and professional development days in the coming term, though Bev already knew them all by heart. There were several postcards from friends travelling on holidays and one from Susie of Tower Bridge announcing their impending visit home. Finally, there was a sheet of pale blue paper, decorated with yellow ducks, that she had tacked to the board. On it in ramrod straight characters, she'd printed with a magic marker: "Cass, 6.00 p.m. Thurs. Susie and Jack, 9:00-10.00 p.m."

"I just love my kids," Bev said to Susie who was studying her pupils' paintings closely. "They're all so adorable. I couldn't be hap-pier than I am being a teacher. I bet you feel that way, too."

She and Susie talked about their respective jobs until Bev took the pizza out of the oven. As she slid slices onto plates, Cass grabbed her around the waist and held her tightly to him. "Sorry, babe, but I've got to go."

"Oh, Cassie-pooh. So soon?" Bev pouted. "Are you sure?"

He looked at his watch and shrugged his shoulders. "Yeah. I've got to. There's a big report I have to read before a Red Cross meet-ing tomorrow." Bev knew that Cass had to leave, but that the meet-ing was not the real reason. He had a brash exterior that concealed a vacillating conscience, but his sense of guilt about Marcia meant that he rarely stayed at Bev's for more than an hour or two at a time. Cass put on his shoes, grabbed his sports jacket from the living-room, and they said their goodbyes at the front door. "Gimme one more kiss. One more kiss," Bev begged, and she threw her arms around Cass's neck, drawing him into a long embrace.

"See you at the wedding, eh?" Cass said to Jack and Susie as he went out the door. "And tell Lou to bring his racquet. We might get a chance to play over at Cleveland's House."

After they finished the pizza in the kitchen, Bev led the Sturridges back to the living-room where she seated them on the green velvet couch. "Hey, how about a nightcap?"

"No thanks. Really. It's getting late. We should let you get to bed."

But Bev ignored the comment and sat down in an easy chair near her guests. "Well, now you know. We're having an affair."

"For how long?" Jack asked.

"One year, three months, and six days," Bev giggled. "Not that I'm counting... Oh, I love him so. Ever since the Ojibway. I don't know why he had to marry Marcia. They're not at all suited. She's not like me. She never wants to go out and have a fun time. She's just a boring homebody and she's dragging him down. But I don't think he'll ever leave her." Bev's lower lip curled, and she started to cry. "He's too nice to do that. He wouldn't want to hurt her."

"So, she doesn't know about you two?"

"No. Cass is very careful to keep it from her. But I wish she *would* find out. Maybe then they'd break up and I could have him all to myself. I do love him more than anyone and I'd be good for him, I really would." Bev covered her face with her hands, and Susie got up from the couch to comfort her, placing an arm around her shoulder. She let Bev sob quietly for several minutes until she finally recovered her composure and looked up. The flush that had lighted her cheeks while Cass was there had vanished and her make-up no longer concealed her fatigue. Susie imagined that handling thirty eight-year-olds took a lot out of her and that most nights, during the school year at least, after a couple of drinks and a makeshift dinner, she probably collapsed with exhaustion in her bedroom by nine or ten. The nights that Cass came, Susie guessed, Bev managed to psyche herself up and draw on some inner reserve. She had to because she dreaded his not coming more than putting on a charade of boundless energy.

"We ought to all go to bed," Susie said. "I'm sure you're tired. You've probably had a very long day." She let go of Bev and at the same time Jack stood up.

"Hey, guys! Sorry. I'm okay now." Bev dabbed at her eyes with a facial tissue, but then she too rose. At the foot of the stairs to the second floor, she stopped, however, a big smile planted on her face again. "You know that summer at the Ojibway and the years we spent at college, those were the greatest, weren't they? I mean, I'm really happy now. I could hardly ask for a better life. I love my job. I've got a great house, lots of friends, and most of all guys like you two and Cass…well at least some of the time. But those years were outta sight, don't you think? I mean really fab."

"No question," Jack agreed, deliberately overlooking the period since. "They were fab."

* * *

Lou met Susie and Jack in his Boston Whaler at Pointe au Baril Station. He seemed to them a mix of new and old: sunglasses as always hiding his eyes and thoughts, same enigmatic grin, same warm welcome. But his clothes were different, casual yet stylish. He was wearing long, freshly pressed white pants and tennis shoes and a white, collared T-shirt with the top two buttons unfastened. Over it was a knitted, off-white woollen sweater with a V neck. On one side, it sported the crest of the Toronto Lawn Tennis Club.

"Good to see you," Lou said as he kissed Susie and gave Jack a hug. "Welcome home. In fact, welcome to the real Canada."

"It's good to be back," Jack said. "I haven't been on the Bay since fifty-eight."

"So, Susie, you've never been here, eh?" Lou asked as he stowed their luggage in the Whaler and started the engine.

"No, but I feel as if I have. I've heard so much about it."

"Well, we'll go out by the main channel and past the Ojibway so you get a look at the whole area."

The Whaler sped along a snaking channel that was much narrower than Susie had expected from Jack's descriptions of the Bay. All along the way, they churned past red and green markers, some only a foot or two from the outboard and one so close that it brushed their bow. Navigation on the Bay, Susie realized, was rather complicated—something that required the undivided attention of the skipper. While Susie noted that there were long, wide stretches of water, especially to port of the Whaler, there was never, as she had anticipated, an open view to the horizon until Lou cut the engine in a bay dotted with pine-covered islands and old, wood frame cottages, mostly painted brown with green-shingled roofs. About a hundred yards off the shore of a large island to their port, Lou turned the Whaler's bow to face it squarely. And there was the Ojibway Hotel in all its majesty with its octagonal tower at one end and its long dock, lined with service buildings, gas pumps, deck chairs, and happy vacationers loading groceries into their outboards. *The grand duchess of the Bay*, Jack thought to himself. *One of the last survivors of a gracious and elegant era…but also of enormous privilege. Working class London has opened my eyes.* "It looks larger even than I remember," he commented to Lou. "Do you come here much?"

"Not really. I play tennis occasionally, and Sally does a little shopping. I guess we'll use it more when the boys are bigger. They'll want to come for ice cream cones—with staff portions like we got. It's no longer a hotel, eh? They closed it in the late sixties. It's just a club now."

"So where is the infamous boathouse?" Susie asked. "You know, where Cass intended to make his conquest."

"That's on the other side."

"Oh, right. I'd forgotten that detail."

"The Barbie Bigelow Affair." Lou grinned again. "It's always with us," and he started the engine.

The Pipers were staying at a second cottage on Sally's parents' island in Cincinnati Bay, but that would be their last summer using it. They had just bought an island of their own at the outer end of Hemlock Channel with an uninterrupted view of the open. "I sold gold at forty bucks an ounce and bought granite at fifty thousand an acre," Lou told Jack and Susie. "Crazy, eh?"

"Knowing you, I bet it will prove a smart investment."

Sally greeted them at the dock and led them to the cottage porch where they settled in wicker chairs to talk, but right away she left them to Lou. Now that they were in the shade, Jack noticed that Lou had removed his sunglasses and set them on a table beside him. When Jack kidded him about no longer wearing them all the time, Lou fetched a copy of the *New Yorker* magazine from under the coffee table in the living-room. "Actually, I have several pairs now— Ultra Ray's. I have their account," and Lou opened the magazine to the page with his advertisement. "WHAT ELSE COMES IN A SIX PACK BESIDES BEER?" the headline read. "THERE'S MORE THAN ONE KIND OF SUNLIGHT, SO YOU NEED MORE THAN ONE PAIR OF SUNGLASSES." Below it was a bikini-clad blonde stretched out on a white sand beach: "For brilliant mid-day glare try Ultra Ray's Riviera XL-88 with protective G-15 lenses for super-deflection of harmful ultraviolet rays." There was another image of a man in a grey suit on the floor of the stock exchange with the caption: "For indoors and those irritating twilight hours, you need the Ultra Ray Senior Executive with photochromic, swift-adjusting lenses. Comfortable vision under changing conditions."

"Cool ad," Jack said, "But how much are they?"

Lou just laughed. "If you need to ask, you can't afford them. The more the jargon, the higher the price."

Sally brought them beers and then the boys to meet. Scott was a toddler of two and a half and Jeff only ten months old. Susie took the baby from Sally's arms and rocked him gently to keep him asleep. She exchanged a glance with Jack that he correctly read as wondering if she should tell the Pipers she was pregnant, but he shook his head gently in response. She knew he was right; it was too early to be sure. Jack brushed a hand through Scott's light auburn hair. "Hello, young man. So, what are your plans in life? Business like your dad? Politics? Or a loafer like me!"

An au pair whom the Pipers had hired for the summer appeared on the porch and took the boys away. "She's terrific," Sally said. "We're hoping she'll stay with us in the fall, maybe even for a year or two. God, I can do with the help!"

"We're feeding her well to keep her happy," Lou said. "Lots of croissants, steaks, frites, and red wine."

"Add some tartes au fraises," Jack said. "That ought to do it."

"Of course, my mom has been a great help. She always comes over when I have a meeting of the Garden Club." Sally got up from her chair to lift one of the collars of Lou's shirt out of his sweater and align it with the other. "But there's a limit to what I can expect of her."

"So, what's up with you guys anyway?" Lou changed the conversation to something less personal. "When are you coming home to stay? Soon, I hope, or you'll lose your citizenship."

"Nothing very exciting to report," Jack said. "We're pretty busy with work and tight on money. But we love London. You can get by without very much. Sprats are less than a shilling a pound and the parks and the banks of the Thames are beautiful for walking."

"No shopping?" Sally asked.

"Not much for us," Susie answered. She looked at Sally, casual but smart in tight-fitting blue corduroys and a cashmere sweater of a heather hue with a long pearl necklace hanging low in front. "But you'd probably like it: Harrod's, Liberty's, Fortnum and Mason's." *Sally looks the same*, Susie thought. *Maybe a little tired under the eyes. Probably the kids. She seems a bit distant, though.*

They had dinner at an antique pine table in a dining-room where pewter pots and plates were strung out on one shelf of a matching sideboard and old duck decoys on another. The main was fresh Georgian Bay pickerel that Lou had barbecued, accompanied by a bottle of white wine. "Hey, this stuff is terrific," Jack exclaimed. "You couldn't get anything like this in Pointe au Baril in our day."

"It's from Toronto actually," Lou answered. "A Burgundy Chablis, premier cru, I think. One of Sally's parents' recommendations."

"Well, it's certainly better than the plonk we have in London from Algeria."

"God!" Sally exclaimed without elaboration.

"So, I didn't realize before Cass mentioned it in Toronto that you play tennis," Jack commented to Lou.

"Yeah. I used to bang a ball against a wall when I was kid, but that was all until we married. Sally's father got us into the Toronto Lawn Tennis Club, so I took some lessons there. I'm not bad now and I find it's good for business. Doesn't take as much time to play as golf. Of course, it helps if you let the other guy win sometimes."

Then Lou told them about playing with Cass shortly after his Paranopulos media triumph. "There was something I was after from him, so I let him win that day. It's not hard to do. He calls a lot of good balls out and sometimes messes up the score. We were at five-all and after two deuce points I'd just netted a backhand. He was standing at the baseline, puffing hard and sweating."

"I'm not surprised," Jack intervened. "It looked to us as if he's put on some weight."

"Yeah, I'm a little worried about that. He's drinking too much as well and pigging out on junk food. Anyway, Cass shouted to me, 'So what's that? Game and set, isn't it?' It was only his ad and in games we were even, but I told him I thought he was right, and he staggered slowly to the net, mopping his forehead. 'Fuck, that was a tough set. I was afraid you might come back and take it.' I told him he'd played well and that I couldn't handle his volleys. 'Yeah, they were really working for me today,' he boasted. 'So was my serve.'

"We showered quickly and sat down on the patio by the pool to have a beer and a sandwich." Susie could picture them sitting there, Cass in a frayed shirt, sweater, and creased slacks, and Lou perhaps in a pale blue and white-striped seersucker suit that Sally had just bought him at Harry Rosen. "So that's when I congratulated him on his byline stories about the Paranopulos murder. 'Don't forget about our pic of the guy,' he responded. 'That was a real bugger to get.' I figured a little more flattery wouldn't hurt, so I pulled out of my briefcase a bottle I'd brought him."

"Oh, no! Not another concoction from some barker!" Jack interjected.

"No. It's called Super Vision. Terrific stuff. Another product of Ultra Ray. Keeps glass surfaces from fogging up. Great for tennis. Anyway, Cass seemed appreciative, so that's when I hit him with a request. I asked him if he could arrange a meeting for me with the

Telly's new head of advertising—lunch maybe, just the three of us, and if he'd put in a good word for me beforehand."

This is amazing, Jack thought. *I've never heard Lou talk for so long.* But he still wasn't finished.

———

Lou went on to explain to the Sturridges how he had just been given the account for Ripples chocolate bars—not a bad product, he said, "if you want to kill yourself on that kind of crap." In fact, he had wangled the account away from Max Gardner, his arch-rival at the advertising firm Warnick and Redfern, the company he had joined after a year working for Sally's father. Lou had been in George Warnick's office receiving congratulations for the recent success of his advertising campaign for Suncrest, a manufacturer of home, in-ground swimming pools. It seemed an opportune moment to make a pitch. So he drew to his boss's attention some problems with Gardner's Ripples account, including cost overruns, and even hinted to him that word was out that the client wasn't too satisfied with the work the firm was doing, relying on Warnick's faith in his pervasive, enigmatic knowledge not to question him too closely about his sources. Then Lou had sketched out for his boss some of the ideas he and his hot-shot young colleague in Creative, David Jones, had quietly worked out for turning the account around. Right there on the spot, Warnick had asked him to take it over and "pick this one up off the floor for the firm." From his meeting with the boss, Lou had walked down the hall to Gardner's section, lifted a box of Ripples Chocolates from his secretary's desk, and pranced unannounced into his rival's office. "Ah, a chocolate, Max?' Gardner's face apparently went as white as poor Paranopulos's must have been lying on the sidewalk outside his store.

———

"Anyway," Lou continued, "I told Cass that if we were going to hold onto the Ripples account, we had to really prove ourselves, show the firm that we could go that extra mile for them. What I was after was a commitment from the *Telegram*'s advertising head to run our

Ripples ads in a conspicuous location, preferably as close to the comics section as possible, if not actually in it. 'What?' Cass whinnied at me. 'You mean even if the Canadian Dental Association doesn't approve of Ripples, Rex Morgan M.D. does? No problem, old buddy. I'll talk to the boys. We'll have chocolate plastered all over the good doctor's face.' And that they did."

Amazing, Jack thought, *that Cass would do that for Lou despite what happened with Barbie Bigelow. Guess he can't resist any kind of competitive scheming if it has a place for him.*

Shortly after dinner, Sally excused herself; she felt very tired and was going to bed. So, the others settled in easy chairs in the living-room to talk some more. "I'm thinking of leaving Warnick and Redfern," Lou told Jack and Susie. "I've got as much as I can out of the experience there. It's time to go on my own. I'm a bit tired of advertising, too. I want to branch out and do public relations and management consulting as well. I'll take David Jones with me; he's Warnick and Redfern's future. And probably Jerry Langford as well if he'll come; he's good with numbers." Lou paused, looking thoughtful. "Trouble is Sally doesn't want me to do this. She thinks all I need is to threaten to leave and I'll be made a partner. She's not a risk-taker."

"No. I don't think she is either," Susie agreed. Like Jack, she was astounded that Lou had gone on for so long and so openly, especially about himself. For Jack's sake in particular she was flattered and wondered if it was because there were, in fact, few people in whom he could confide. His father had died recently, his mother had moved in with her sister in Burlington, and his siblings were scattered across the country. There were, it was true, other friends he could talk to, but Susie calculated that Jay for one was too preoccupied with his own concerns to be very helpful and that Lou would be cautious about revealing much of himself to Cass.

"With Sal, it goes back a long way," Lou continued. "It was hard having her family live in both Bermuda and Toronto. She never knew which was her real home. And she hated being sent away at so young an age to board. She still has nightmares about it. I know outwardly she seemed to thrive at BSS. That's the side of her that her friends saw, but inwardly she felt insecure. Still does."

"Poor lamb." Susie was amazed at Lou's perceptiveness.

"Anyway, I'm thinking when I go on my own, I'll open an office in New York. We'll get an apartment there. Sally would like that. She's a big city girl."

"Gosh, what about the kids? That would be hard on them if you live in two different places, same as it was for Sally."

"Yeah. Maybe." Lou sat silently for several seconds staring at a wide plank on the polished cedarwood floor. "We'll figure it out somehow. I want them all to be happy. That's the main thing."

"Sure," Susie and Jack agreed. But that wasn't exactly how it worked out for Lou and Sally.

Chapter 10

The wedding guests gathered in a grassy clearing near the water some hundred yards from the Ostermans' cottage. White birch logs had been laid out in several rows lengthwise facing the lake and in front of them was a tall, antique side table with a copper bowl sitting in the centre. It was filled with bird feathers—from local gulls, loons, ospreys, turkey vultures, and, in deference to the groom, blue jays. Gazing at the arrangement from his log seat, Jack couldn't help but wonder if Linda had deliberately and symbolically set the feathers so that those of the jay were next to the vulture's. That the marriage was happening at all had been a near thing. By 1970, influenced by Gloria Steinem's article *After Black Power, Women's Liberation*, Linda was having serious doubts about the institution itself. Had Jay waited any longer to propose, there was a strong possibility that she would have declined. Jay was still not one to make decisions quickly, but professional circumstances had led him to act when he did. He had finished his probationary period in the Department of External Affairs the year before and had now been offered an assignment in Vientiane, Laos, with the Canadian mission to the International Commission for Supervision and Control, charged with the hopeless task of reporting on violations of the non-existent 1954 ceasefire in Indochina. He was to leave in September and would be away for up to two years, so he had been prodded into making a decision by this looming deadline. His inherent caution had also been offset by the realization that Linda's incipient reservations about marriage might be dispelled by the opportunity marriage to Jay offered of returning to Asia. That it was caught up in a bloody and protracted war was admittedly a negative, but from distant North America, Vientiane seemed very much at the edge of the conflict, especially to someone who was preoccupied with other issues. So, Linda accepted Jay's proposal and the wedding had been arranged somewhat hastily, but with careful attention to detail.

In front of the pine table there was a mound of soft green moss on which Linda and Jay were kneeling, holding hands as they gazed up at Bev standing beyond the table with her back to Lake Joseph. Ripples were forming on the water as a light afternoon breeze stirred the surface, and the occasional brown maple leaf, left over from the previous autumn, was being set adrift. The leaves had been swept to the shore during preparations for the wedding and the thought passed through Susie's mind that Linda had anticipated what was happening now—that the leaves would appear as makeshift boats carrying imaginary friends to her wedding. Linda knelt on the moss, erect and motionless, covered in a long deerskin cloak. Jay was beside her, fidgeting. There was no doubt in Jack's mind that Jay felt self-conscious and was probably having a hard time resisting the temptation to turn around and appraise the reaction to the ceremony of the guests sitting behind him. For the wedding, Linda had wanted him to wear buckskin trousers and a fringed and beaded jacket, but Jay had resisted her request, strenuously arguing it would be a condescending gesture, not a meaningful affirmation of support for Indigenous rights. His preference was for informal cottage attire: long white pants and an open-neck pale blue shirt, perhaps with an ascot to mark the occasion as special. Linda would have none of that sort of conformity, so they had compromised on blue jeans— slightly faded but no tears—and a blue and white-striped T-shirt. *I wonder if the T-shirt was Linda's idea*, Susie pondered. She and Jack were sitting on front row logs at Linda's request, for Susie was the unofficial maid of honour. *Is the T-shirt a wistful reminder of her unconsummated affair with Dominic?*

Love one another, but make not a bond of love:
Let it rather be a moving sea between the shores of your souls.
Fill each other's cup, but drink not from one cup.
Give one another of your bread but eat not from the same loaf.
Sing and dance together and be joyous, but let each one of
you be alone,
Even as the strings of a lute are alone though they quiver
with the same music.

Bev brushed a mosquito from her puffy, sunburned cheeks, but without hesitating in her recitation. Her rich, expressive voice conveyed the verse to the guests with her usual enthusiasm, and they, squatting uncomfortably on the logs in varied, casual summer wear, listened with the same rapt attention as her Grade Three class. She was squeezed, not altogether successfully, Jack thought, into an all-white, one-piece bathing suit, purchased especially for the occasion, the only guest to have taken seriously Linda's suggestion that they dress as informally as they liked. Not many years before, Bev wouldn't have anticipated even being invited to Linda's wedding, let alone asked to deliver the first reading. Lately, however, as Cass explained it to Jack and Susie before the ceremony started, Linda had displayed a sisterly affection towards her. It was a result, he said, of her moving from "the woods to women"—from nature to feminism. "She sees Scottie as a victim of sexist exploitation. Men take advantage of her craving for companionship to the point where she doesn't know her real self. According to Spooky, her identity is obscured by a male-induced veneer of garrulous superficiality. All bullshit, if you ask me."

Linda and Bev's new relationship had already become apparent to the Sturridges that morning. Sitting on the porch of the Ostermans' cottage talking to Lou and Sally, they had seen Linda and Bev stroll past in bare feet at the end of a walk in the woods along paths covered in blankets of soft pine needles. Linda had been pointing out to Bev her wilderness friends—the chipmunk and red squirrel, the sumac and cardinal flowers. "I see us guarding this property as a sacred trust for future generations," Linda had said as they stopped near the porch. "Of course, if the cottage were mine and not my parents', I'd tear it down and we'd live in tents."

"Far out!" Bev had responded excitedly. "It would be like Girl Guides." Bev had realized immediately that what she said had not been to Linda's liking, for, right away, she had added, "I mean, that would be the right thing to do, wouldn't it? Return the property to its natural state."

"Or to the First Nations."

Give your hearts, but not into each other's keeping.
For only the hand of Life can contain your hearts.
And stand together yet not too near together:
For the pillars of the temple stand apart,
And the oak tree and the cypress grow not in each other's
shadow.

"Who the fuck wrote this shit?" Cass whispered loudly to Marcia. They were sitting in the row behind the Sturridges along with the Pipers.

"Shhh," Marcia hissed at him. "Look at your program."

Cass glanced at the curling skin of birch bark that had been deposited at his log before the ceremony started. "Kahlil Gibran? Who the fuck is he? Doesn't sound like he's hot shit on marriage."

"Very nicely done," Jack heard Lou whisper to Bev as she returned to her seat. Jack couldn't see his face, but he was sure Lou was grinning broadly, amused by the whole ceremony—maybe even impressed by its creativity.

"Not your kind of wedding, is it?" Cass whispered to Lou. "No crosses. No holy water. No priest. Shit, there isn't even a minister."

Lou, of course, didn't care about any of that any longer. And Jack was sure that his compliment to Bev was genuine. He liked her earnest enthusiasm as much as her sense of nostalgia. In fact, he'd taken a fraternal interest in her welfare ever since university. He'd even got her her first job—in the Creative Department at Warnick and Redfern. However, a year of bottom-pinching and advances at office parties by young, drunk executives who didn't recognize her the next day had driven her back to college and a second degree in education. Lou had been sorry to see her go. She had been quick to learn, and he thought she had a bright future in advertising.

Hold on to what is good,
Even if it's a handful of earth,
Hold on to what you believe,
Even if it's a tree that stands by itself.

Hold on to what you must do,
Even if it's a long way from here.

It was Sally's turn now, her deep, lackadaisical voice effectively concealing her embarrassment at being a participant in an unorthodox wedding. If one of her boys married some day at the cottage the Pipers were building, Susie was sure the ceremony would not be at all like this one. They'd inveigle an Anglican minister into presiding on unconsecrated ground.

Hold on to your life,
Even if it is easier to let go.
Hold on to my hand,
Even if someday I'll be gone away from you.

Cass unfurled his birch bark program. "Pueblo Prayer? Jesus! When did Spooky get into all this pagan stuff anyway? If she's not careful the Muskoka Mafia will drum her family off the lake." Linda was a total enigma to Cass, the Sturridges realized, but carrying on about her seemed to help him deal with her vaguely threatening personage. "I wish I had a cameraman with me. I'm sure Spooky would be happy to do some dances for us while we sit around a campfire and smoke a pipe. Yeah, something to anesthetize me, that's what I need. When the shit do we get a drink?"

This time Marcia poked Cass hard in the ribs and at last he shut up.

Let me not to the marriage of true minds
Admit impediments. Love is not love
Which alters when it alteration finds,
Or bends with the remover to remove

It was Susie's turn now. As *ex officio* maid of honour, she was the only one who had been allowed to choose the piece that she would read. But after the other recitations, she was feeling embarrassed that she had made such a conventional choice, let alone a sonnet with an orthodox perspective on love and marriage. Yet, she had no option now but to carry on, taking some heart from the fact that at least Linda's mother was beaming at her with approval. Indeed, she noticed that even Linda herself was smiling, so tolerant was she of her old friend's frailties.

> Love alters not with his brief hours and weeks,
> But bears it out even to the edge of doom:
> If this be error and upon me proved
> I never writ, nor no man ever loved.

Jack squeezed Susie's hand when she sat down next to him again. "Beautifully done. And the reassuring message we needed!"

Linda had intended that Susie's would be the last reading. But Linda's mother had insisted that someone from her generation must be a participant. Linda had reluctantly concurred on the condition, however, that it was a woman who spoke, and the passage was from Indigenous literature. So, Linda's mother decided to assume the function herself in order to have influence over what was said. She spent considerable time searching for a passage that struck the note she wanted, but at last she found it, a Cherokee blessing with a cheerful and innocuous message.

> May the Warm Winds of Heaven
> Blow softly upon your house.
> May the Great Spirit
> Bless all who enter there.
> May your Moccasins
> Make happy tracks in many snows,
> And may the Rainbow
> Always touch your shoulder.

Then, at Linda's insistent urging and with Bev's eager support, the guests began to sing "We Shall Overcome"—at first reluctantly, but gradually with increasing zest, especially as Cass and then Lou joined in, provoking Linda to go as far as she dared in shocking her guests.

Now, with the formal part of the ceremony over, it was Jay's turn to speak. "Ahh... Gee, I want to thank you all for your recitations... They were... I mean, Linda and I very much appreciated them." His face was flushed, and Jack and Susie could tell he was both distracted and embarrassed. "It was terrific of you all to come. I know it was a long way for many of you to travel—for Susie and Jack Sturridge in particular who flew from London, England, to be with us on this special day. And we know that for many of you, it disrupted one of those precious summer weekends, so we are grateful for the sacrifice you made on our behalf. All I can say in consolation is that it was a smaller sacrifice than if we had waited longer and then expected you to fly to Vientiane for our wedding." Jay waited for a rumble of laughter to abate and then finished. "Anyway, our thanks to you all for coming, and for your wonderful presents as well... Ah... Champagne is about to be served down on the dock, so if you'd like to make your way there—"

"Wait a minute! Wait!" Linda was suddenly on her feet, using a hand on Jay's shoulder to press him back onto the mound of moss. She tore off the beaded headband she had been wearing and threw back her head, shaking her long, dark hair free. "Hey, listen you guys. This has been neat. I mean really neat. This hasn't been a wedding wedding. It's been a real wedding. And you've all been a part of it."

Jack turned around in his seat to look at Lou, who winked back at him. It was clear the guests were about to be treated not to the literary Linda of university days, nor the religious one of Europe and Thailand, but someone else, and Jack knew that Lou was eager to see the Linda of the moment fully revealed.

"We've made an important statement here in this little clearing. We've said 'screw you' to organized religion, and to all the social hypocrites."

Mrs. Osterman gasped and cried, "Linda, no! Linda, dear. No! Please."

But Linda ignored her. "I mean it. The churches with their cushioned pews and smug sermons are finished. This is where it is at: Right Here in the Bush!" Her voice was loud and shrill now.

"The trees, the rocks, and the water, these are our real saviours and what we've been celebrating is our union with them, Jay's and mine, and all of yours." Linda glanced at Mrs. Osterman as her face transitioned from shock to anxiety. "Our eternal bond with our true mother, mother nature."

"Your bond with the loony bin," Cass sniggered loudly, and once again Marcia poked him in the ribs. Jack had turned his head and caught her admonition. *It's clear their relationship is in trouble, but I wonder if she suspects Bev is part of the problem.*

"We've said 'fuck you' to tradition, 'fuck you' to pretence."

"Oh, Linda!" Mrs. Osterman cried, covering her mouth with her hands.

"And we've opened our arms to each other and to our true saviour, Our Mother Earth. I wish... I wish we could all do it right here together. I wish we could just take off our clothes and—"

Quickly, Jay reached for Linda's arms, fearful of what she intended. She shook herself free of his grasp, however, and glared at him disapprovingly. Momentarily, several of the guests thought they were about to witness the couple's first post-nuptial spat. But then Linda continued in a softer voice. "But we can't. Not yet. What we have started here today must grow, even if only slowly. We must nurture it patiently. Just as a tree grows stronger and outward with age, so, too, will this thing that we have done today."

"Just what the fuck is this thing that we've done?" Cass asked of no one in particular. This time Marcia just ignored him because Linda had almost finished.

"Gee, you are all so great. I love you. Thank you for doing this with us."

Silence fell over the clearing for several seconds, a hushed mix of shock and relief. Then Bev began to clap; Lou quickly joined in, and soon all of the guests were politely applauding.

Linda took Jay's hand and together they walked to a small beach near the Ostermans' dock where a freshly varnished, red canvas canoe was resting upright in the sand, paddles leaning against its bow and stern seats. The newlyweds launched the canoe, gliding onto the placid lake to symbolize their oneness with nature, Linda taking the stern and Jay the bow. Meanwhile, the guests had walked onto the dock where they were handed not only glasses of champagne, but scented bags of pine needles with which to shower the bride and groom as their canoe slid by the end of the dock.

At that point, with one wide sweep of her paddle, Linda turned their craft in the direction of the open lake. But when they were only some fifty yards from shore, she suddenly grasped the gunwales on both sides and, leaning hard to the right, capsized the canoe, spilling herself and a startled Jay into the water. She grabbed him by the arms and pulled him under the canoe with her. There, as Jay explained it later to Jack, treading water on opposite sides of the centre thwart, they awkwardly embraced.

When they emerged a few moments later, it was Bev and Lou who once again led the guests in a round of applause, while, over the water, they heard Jay complain to Linda, "Hey. That wasn't an agreed-upon part of the ceremony."

"No, it wasn't," Linda laughed, sweeping her wet black hair from her face. "It was impromptu. And that's how I like my sex to be, too."

"Hey," Cass exclaimed, taking a swig from his glass of champagne. "That's the broad for me after all!"

Chapter 11

"Do you think Jay had doubts about his decision to marry Linda right from their wedding day?" Susie asked.

"No, not really. He was fascinated by her, kind of under her spell. Besides, he wanted to get married—everyone else was—and I think he felt he needed her—someone strong and creative, someone who would stimulate him. He knew it would be good from a career standpoint as well—to have a spouse to help with the social side of the job, and especially someone who was bright and engaging."

"In that case, he got way more than he bargained for... I've forgotten now exactly what happened in Vientiane that led to his career ending so early. Was he fired?"

"Not exactly. The Department didn't like messy departures. It was suggested to him that both he and Linda might be happier if he pursued a different career."

The Sturridges were sitting on the rear, second-storey deck of their Summerhill Avenue home, having a pre-dinner drink, a Scotch and soda for Jack, and half a glass of white wine for Susie. It was the night before they were to leave for the reunion at the Pipers' cottage. They had bought the attached Victorian brick home, painted desert sand with white trim, when they had first returned from England, in 1980. It had been an astute move as prices in the neighbourhood were relatively modest at that time but had skyrocketed since. So, they were perched on a small pot of gold that gave them some financial security despite their modest income. Sometimes, especially when he was working on their annual tax return, Jack felt it was time to sell, especially now while the market was particularly hot. They could move into an apartment or condo and, with the revenue from the sale, increase their disposable income. But Susie didn't even want to contemplate selling. She loved the house—always had—and she hated apartments and condos. She found them claustrophobic and impersonal and she despised the lingering odours of other people's cooking. On top of all of that, she distrusted elevators and was not assuaged by Jack's argument that they could move into an old, low-rise apartment building and reach the ground and freedom by a stairway. "You'd hate it, too, you know you would," Susie would retort. "Imagine yourself in a building with a concierge you had to greet every time you went in or out. You'd exhaust yourself always trying to think of new, clever things to say."

Jack knew that Susie was right. He didn't like apartments and condos either, and he loved their house almost as much as she did. It was in a quiet location with a rectangular-shaped parkette, shaded by old trees right across the road. Just beyond it was James A. Balfour Park and the underground Rosehill Reservoir where he and Susie liked to walk in the afternoons and evenings. There was always something to look at—kids playing in the sand of a wrought iron enclosure filled with flowers and shrubs, teenagers absorbed in games of Frisbee, kite flyers, dogs in joyful pursuit of balls and other breeds, and aging men and women like themselves, wandering slowly along the park's paths, looking, Jack contended, as if they had just climbed out of the ravine and were waiting for a drug drop. What bound Jack most to their home, however, was its third-storey loft which, for the past fifteen years, had served as his studio. When they first returned home from England, Jack had rented space with two other artists in an old warehouse on Spadina Avenue. But when Susie eventually retired from teaching, he gave it up as an economy measure and ever since he had worked in the loft at home. While he certainly wasn't painting as much as he had in his prime, and selling even less, Jack wanted to continue as long as he could. Moving into an apartment or condominium, he knew, would not help. But most of all, he knew it wouldn't suit Susie. She liked to read on their open deck, putter in the garden, and take on minor repairs and improvements. So, whenever the subject of moving arose, eventually they dropped it, putting it off, at least in Jack's mind, for as long as they could.

"You know, I wish you'd thanked Alan for cleaning up the garden for us rather than leaving it to me to say something." Susie was standing now, looking down from the deck on their small backyard, filled with neatly trimmed shrubs and flowers, carefully chosen to be in bloom when they were home in the spring and fall.

"I knew you'd do a better job praising him than I would."

"It would have meant more coming from you."

"Well, I did praise him for his golf game. Apparently he shot an eighty-nine last time out."

"But did you thank him for coming for lunch on Saturday? He passed up a game to be with us, you know. Catherine told me."

"No. What I should have thanked them both for was not bringing Alison and her mute boyfriend."

"I thought you said before he wasn't that bad." Susie turned and walked off the deck. In the dining-room they had a light supper, a salade niçoise that Susie had made from supplies bought at the Harvest Wagon. Being frugal, she normally shopped at a supermarket on St. Clair Ave., but since they were home only briefly, it was more convenient to pick up the few things she needed locally—at "The Five Robbers," as they were known in the neighbourhood.

"So, what did happen in Vientiane for the Department to suggest that Jay leave the foreign service?" Susie asked.

"Well, the problem was Linda had no idea what they were getting into. I mean, she knew about the war and, of course, she was opposed to it. But she wasn't following developments there closely. To her, war was a guy thing. Juiced up on testosterone, men were always fighting."

Susie nodded in agreement. "I don't know much about the details either. So Laos was involved in the fighting, too?"

"You bet it was. In 1954, a ceasefire was negotiated in Geneva that ended France's colonial rule in Indochina, but it quickly broke down and fighting resumed in all of the successor states created by the 1954 agreement: Vietnam—divided into North and South—and Cambodia and Laos. You know, from 1965 to 1973, U.S. B-52 bombers unloaded eight million tons of bombs on the Communists in Vietnam alone, more than three times the number dropped in Europe in the Second World War. But for its size Laos was hit even harder. It still has the dubious distinction of being the most bombed country in the world. Linda told me that."

"Gosh, and she knew nothing about this beforehand."

"No... Mmm. Great salad. Love those anchovies. This meal always reminds me of the trips we took to Paris from London, our outdoor lunches in cafés, watching the world stroll by."

"And eavesdropping."

"Yeah, we learned the sordid details of more than one affair and of several quarrels. It's time we went back to learn how they turned out."

"If we could handle the flights."

"Right... No, Linda thought we were the good guys out there, trying to end the war—that we were investigating violations of the 1954 ceasefire. But the International Control Commission had been a total failure for years."

"So then why were we there?"

"Ah, that's a good question. Not easy to answer. And you know Linda even better than I do; she may not have known much about the war before she got to Laos, but once there, she threw herself into learning as much as she could. And she didn't like at all the things she was learning—like that the Canadians were using their position on the International Control Commission to convey messages to the Communists on behalf of the United States, maybe using their presence on the ground to pass intelligence information to the Americans about the accuracy of their bombing. She learned about the military supplies and raw materials we were exporting to the U.S. like napalm and Agent Orange for jungle defoliation. Christ, even the berets U.S. marines were wearing were manufactured in Montreal!"

"No! Really?"

"Really. So, the more Linda learned about the war, the angrier she got, and the more she pressed Jay to raise objections about Canada's involvement with his superiors in Vientiane and in telegrams home to Ottawa. He was persuaded by her arguments, but still, he was wary about saying anything that might affect his career. That frustrated her, so Linda began speaking out herself, especially at social functions where Canadian and other Western diplomats were present. Apparently, she got increasingly strident, shouting at a room full of people that they were lily-livered toadies. 'This isn't 1950,' she argued. 'What are you afraid of? The witch hunts are over.' Actually, she wasn't quite right about that. Gays were still being drummed out of the foreign service in 1970. Anyway, eventually Jay was asked to put a lid on her. But of course he couldn't."

"Or wouldn't!"

"No, and I guess that's why his superiors came to believe that Linda was acting as a kind of surrogate for him. Eventually they told him that they had concluded he wasn't really suitable material for the foreign service. He was devastated at first when he heard this, but he didn't immediately give in and resign. Instead, at first, he followed the course Linda advised. 'Make the fuckers squirm as long as you can,' she told him. 'Force them to fire you and then go public with all you know about this pointless, dirty war.'"

"Would you like something else?" Susie interrupted. "Some cheese maybe? It wasn't a very big meal."

"No thanks. It was perfect."

"So how do you know all about what happened anyway?"

"Jay told me. Remember how they stopped off in London on their way back to Ottawa? Most of it came out over a pint at the Ancient Oak while you and Linda were at home, working on a school project, I think."

"I really can't remember. But poor Jay, he must have been humiliated by it all."

"Yes, I'm sure he was. But, as he saw it, at least he'd worked it so that he wasn't fired. His assignment was simply terminated, and he was recalled to Ottawa. There he negotiated an arrangement whereby he would stay on in the Department for another year, doing research in the Historical Division on commercial relations with Southeast Asia. But a condition of the agreement was that he would resign quietly at the end of the year, with no public outburst."

"I'm sure Linda didn't like that."

"No, she didn't. But at least Jay saved some face. He appeared to be leaving of his own volition, and that was important to him."

"Well, he certainly wouldn't have wanted people snidely suggesting that the Department had fired him because he was gay."

"Not that Linda would have cared."

"Aha!" Susie cried jubilantly. "You're admitting that she may well have been a lesbian all along."

Jack just laughed and finished his wine. "Anyway, when Jay and I discussed what happened, he said he thought the foreign service hadn't really been the right choice for him after all and certainly not for Linda. He was already talking about going back to law school—about how well Henry Phillips was doing and how law had probably been the right profession for him all along."

"Oh, no! Not Henry Phillips again?"

After their supper, Susie cleaned up in the kitchen while Jack climbed to the loft to go over their monthly accounts and pay some bills. Nowadays, he used the space as much as an office as an art studio, but in appearance it still looked more like the latter. It was filled with unsold paintings, leaning against the walls in simple frames, and there were at least three on easels that he was still working on intermittently. Not long after they had returned from London, Jack had held an exhibit at a Yorkville gallery: "The Satiric Paintings of Jack Sturridge." It was not unlike several he had staged in London with reasonable success, though now the themes depicted were largely Canadian. The Toronto event had been well attended and had garnered positive media coverage, but his sales had been light. One of his own favourites from that exhibit was still in his studio. It was a large caricature of René Levesque smoking a cigarette as always but bearing the features of a bullfrog. He was poised to leap from a large lily pad, roughly the shape of Canada, to a much smaller one.

There were as well oils from later shows that also had not sold—one of the UN General Assembly building in New York totally immersed in a martini glass. And one he had done recently for his last show: a parade of stick figures with bodies shaped like cellphones, goose-stepping and waving large red banners with the Apple logo in white and black. Of their friends, Linda was still his greatest supporter, but she had already purchased as many of his paintings as she thought she could without appearing to be treating him as a charity.

When sales were particularly light, Jack sometimes did commissions — usually portraits or scenes of families at work or play. But he hated doing them. "It's like prostitution. The money may be good, but there's no creativity to it, no excitement, no thrill at completion."

"Oh, my poor gigolo," Susie had kidded him. "I had no idea you were so frustrated."

Later that night, lying in bed, Jack asked, "I wonder what Linda's parents thought when she and Jay ended up back in Toronto with Jay in law school again, the perpetual student."

"I don't think they were worried. Money wasn't an issue, and I know Mrs. Osterman saw Jay as a stabilizing influence on Linda. That's what really mattered to her."

"It was harder on Jay's parents, though. They were pretty middle class. Success was important to them. They were financially comfortable, but they didn't need Jay complicating things by screwing up." Jack rolled over and adjusted his pillow, trying to avoid the neck pain that had been nagging him in recent months. "Anyway, it all worked out…well, sort of at least. Jay finished his law degree, worked with a firm for a year, and then realized it wasn't the thing for him. He complained that he could never catch up to Henry because he had too big a head start, so he decided he should go into business where there were big bucks to be made. It was Lou who got him the job at Universal Consulting Services, did you know?"

"If I did, I'd forgotten."

"Jay was to be their legal counsel, but he was to have broader responsibilities as well, and that's why the position appealed to him."

"It certainly wasn't what Linda wanted for him. But she was stoic about it."

"Well, he got her on side by arguing the job would entail spending time in Asia where Universal was exploring new contract possibilities."

"That never really happened, though, did it?"

"No, before long, Lou's Mapledome project came along and buggered up everything. Still, things have never been that bad for them, have they? When Linda's dad suddenly died of a heart attack in 1978, her mother moved into an apartment and she and Jay inherited the house on Chestnut Park."

"Yes. I remember they were happily ensconced there when we came home in 1980."

"Yeah, living their contradictory lives. Jay was doing okay at Universal, but not exactly making a bundle, and Linda was working part time as an editorial assistant and spending the rest campaigning for the NDP. Not your typical Rosedale couple."

They lay silently for some time thinking of that year and of Jay and Linda, contemplating whether in the end one or both of them would show up at the reunion. "Ever wonder what our parents thought of us back then?" Jack asked at last. "Like when we came home to Toronto to stay?"

"Mine were really pleased. And, yes, I think of them often and how they would feel about the lives we've lived, and, you know, how we've handled the things that have happened along the way."

"Like, how I've treated Alan, you mean?"

"Yes, and what we've both said about Alison's boyfriends."

"Well, I can tell you one thing, I know my parents were delighted when we hooked up. Mom adored you from the start, so did Dad, and he was doubly pleased to discover that you had a sensible head on your shoulders. I think he was afraid that I would always be a financial burden for him, but you relieved him of that anxiety."

Jack thought Susie had at last fallen asleep, but then she said softly, "I wonder what our kids will say about us after we're gone."

"That you were a police helicopter pilot and I was a criminal court judge who usually misconstrued the evidence."

"How bleak!"

"And I'm sure Tom's boys will always think of us as incomprehensible aliens from the Planet Zero."

Susie laughed. "Whatever it is, I suppose it's bound to be different from anything we might imagine."

"Anyway, it's irrelevant. I'm not planning on going and that means you can't either. You know, if we end up in a retirement home someday, this is how I'm going to pass my time: lifting weights and riding a stationary bicycle. I want to hear the caregivers complain, 'What the hell is that guy doing here?'"

"Entertaining me," Susie answered. Several minutes of silence passed and then she asked, "Are you afraid of dying?"

"Petrified. Aren't you?"

"Yes. I want to be with you always."

"Well that's a pretty long time, wonderful though I may be." Jack wrapped an arm around Susie's shoulder. "Infinity is a scary concept, alive or dead. I can't grasp it either way."

"Let's not talk about it. I'm sorry I brought the subject up." She rolled over to end their conversation, but then added, "It must be wonderfully comforting to be religious."

"Yes," Jack agreed. "But that requires being irrational, like believing in an overweight Santa Claus who can stuff himself down every chimney in the world in a single night. And you have to be ready to spend a lot of boring time kneeling in old, gloomy buildings with poor heating. My knees can't take that."

"Thank you," Susie yawned. "I feel much better about dying now. I think I may even be able to fall sleep."

But Jack knew he couldn't. His mind was still on 1980, the year he and Susie had at last moved home. He slipped quietly out of bed and tiptoed up the stairs to his loft, returning a little later with a large blue binder under his arm. Susie was still awake and heard him come in. "What's that you're carrying?"

"Lou's promotional material for the Mapledome project."

"Oh. That! You're not going to sit up reading it now, are you?"

"No. I browsed through it upstairs. I'll show it to you tomorrow." Jack put the binder on his dresser and climbed back into bed. "That's what really changed everything and everybody, though: Lou's big fuck-up. He launched it just months after we moved back to Toronto. If we'd stayed in London a little longer, we could have avoided the whole bloody mess."

Chapter 12

It was in part the altered political climate that led Jack and Susie to move home in 1980. The Thatcher government had come to power in the United Kingdom in May 1979 and they anticipated a long period of right wing government that would challenge the existing economic and social order to which they had grown accustomed. They were, however, influenced by personal considerations as well: the realization that if they didn't return to Canada soon they probably never would, the desire to be nearer to their aging parents, and to experience again central heating and moderately reliable sunshine. So, over the winter of 1979-1980, the Sturridges took the difficult decision to return to Canada at the end of the school year, and Susie applied for a position with the Toronto public school board. When she was offered a job late that spring—and at a school in the centre of the city—they felt a little less conflicted about leaving London and the friends they had made there over so many years. At least Susie would have a reliable income and they were moving back to a city that was becoming increasingly dynamic and multicultural, and to old friends whom they had managed to see only intermittently since university. As it turned out, it was, indeed, good to spend time with them all again, but Jack and Susie were not prepared for the entanglements and stressful situations that also entailed.

In November of 1980, several months after they arrived back in Toronto, Lou invited Jack to his office to introduce him to his proposal for a major sports complex on the Toronto waterfront. When the Blue Jays were first stretching their wings at Exhibition Stadium, Lou calculated that it was not an adequate long-term home for the team, and he wanted in on the action to build a replacement. His Mapledome proposal was not the first scheme advanced—there had been several since the early 1960s—but his was the most technically sophisticated. He got everyone thinking retractable roof in 1980 and, after that, the idea never went away.

The offices of Piper, Langford and Jones were on the twenty-fourth floor of the Toronto Dominion Tower, and Lou met Jack in their reception area. Lou was dressed in a dark blue suit with thin red stripes, a red and white-striped, button-down shirt, and a scarlet tie dotted with little blue images of a domed stadium. Lou had had dozens of them made for a group called "Citizens for the Complex," but that was the only time Jack ever saw Lou wear the tie himself and only while he was in his own office. Lou's once black hair was still thick and fashionably long, but it was greying on top and along the curling edges of his sideburns. It was blown dry and carefully combed with a small wave at the front; clearly he was in the hands of a professional stylist.

There was only a vague scent of cologne in the air as he steered Jack through the lobby to his own office, a hand affectionately placed on his old friend's shoulder. Jack noticed that Lou still walked with a spring to his step as if his feet were coming down on foam rubber, his eyes shone as always with warmth and clarity, and there was the same enigmatic grin on his face that Jack had first observed at the Ojibway.

Lou's office was tastefully furnished in Swedish modern with a plush teal carpet and walls of a complementary shade, lined with black and white prints of street scenes in early Toronto. The curtains on the glass exterior walls were open so the room was full of light and cheery, but it was also crowded that morning with mockups for an advertising campaign. On one board, there was a glossy photograph of a handsome, young executive and his beautiful wife in bathing suits on a stretch of exotic, tropical, white sand, and on another a black and white shot of a dowdy, middle-aged couple in street clothes at what Jack thought might be Wasaga Beach. "YOUR VACATION REFLECTS YOUR PERSONALITY," the opening text asserted.

Where you go to relax, what you do with those invaluable vacation days is a statement about you. You're no ordinary person, so why take an ordinary vacation? Visit NEW ADVENTURES and let us plan a holiday that will say something different and exciting about you.

"What do you think?" Lou asked.

"I like it."

"Good. So do I." Jack knew, however, that Lou himself was impervious to that kind of advertisement. Whatever holidays he and Sally took, they almost always spent them on Georgian Bay. Lou walked behind his desk and pressed a button on his console. "George, it's great. Tell everyone in Creative I like it. I'm setting up a meeting with Richard Harris at New Adventures for Friday to go over the magazine coverage Russ has worked out. I'd like you to be there... Good. Good."

Things had been going well for Lou over the preceding decade. Piper, Langford and Jones was now one of the larger agencies in Toronto, and five years earlier Lou had finally decided the time was right to open an office in New York City. While he had considered working from there himself, in the end, because of the kids, he had decided to stay in Toronto. Ironically, he'd enticed Max Gardner, his arch-rival at Warnick and Redfern, away from that firm to head up Piper, Langford and Jones's New York office. It was a move that surprised everyone in the industry, but it was typical of Lou; he liked to win, but he was good at mending fences. Lou did maintain an apartment in New York in the company's name, but almost exclusively it was used by him and Sally for short visits that were as much social as they were related to business.

An Oscar Peterson tape was now playing softly in Lou's stereo at the precise volume he liked, controlled by his secretary in her office. Lou motioned to Jack to take a seat on the far side of his desk, and, as he sat down himself, he handed Jack a large, blue suede binder. Lou had had several hundred copies made for select distribution. "Here. This is for you to read at your leisure." At that moment, the music faded out; Lou's secretary had an important call for him. "Sorry, Jack. It's Matt Dunlop at the *Toronto Daily News*. This is going to take a few minutes." He motioned to him to go ahead and read through the binder. Jack obliged, but it was hard to give his full attention to the contents, knowing that Lou was talking to Cass's sports editor. After the *Toronto Telegram* folded, Cass had been hired by the *News*, and recently appointed Managing Editor.

"Listen, Matt, I just want to make sure you're going to be at the reception at the Harbour Castle this afternoon for the unveiling... Good... Good. I'm glad you like the binder." Lou nodded at Jack, smiling. "Wait till you see the presentation. So, what time is your editorial meeting? Okay, good. Listen, I'd like you to work on Bob Cassidy to make sure the project gets front page coverage as well as in the sports section. The presentation has been timed so that you can make your late editions with the story. I'd rather you had it first than the G and M... Good. I know you'll do your best."

Jack was sure that Dunlop would, indeed, do all he could to ensure the *News* gave the unveiling of Lou's complex proposal extensive and favourable coverage. Lou tended to know about the skeletons in everyone's closet. What Matt's was, Jack didn't learn until later, but it was, in fact, a gambling problem. Lou knew about it because he sometimes played tennis with Dunlop at the Toronto Lawn Tennis Club just as he did with Cass. It was there that he had learned that Dunlop gambled heavily on the horses and placed wagers almost daily through the *News's* track reporter, who wrote under the pseudonym King Quinella. King, however, didn't have the means to float Dunlop the loans he needed when he hit a bad streak. Lou did, but he expected favours in return for not revealing Dunlop's betting habit to his boss.

"Bob doesn't know I'm in any way involved with this thing, does he?"

"No. I don't think he does."

"Good. That's good." While he talked, Lou was fondling an eighteen-inch model of the Mapledome's proposed retractable roof which was lying on top of his desk. *He's like a kid playing with the lever on his favourite dump truck,* Jack thought.

"Let's just keep him out of the loop for now, okay?"

As soon as Lou hung up, his secretary had another call for him — from the head of the construction firm Taylor-Steeles, about the reception at the Harbour Castle. So, Jack turned his attention more intently on the binder Lou had given him. On the cover, embossed in gold, were the words "THE MAPLEDOME: TORONTO'S TOMORROW." Inside, each page of sketches and text was protectively sealed in a transparent, plastic pocket. The opening one was a summary of "palaces of sport" through history:

> From the earliest times, we have built temples to the gods of athletic prowess, reflecting our insatiable love for physical combat. They stand on the pages of history as testimonials to the skill and courage of those who did battle there and to the ingenuity and daring of those who built them. Among these monuments that reflect our devotion to sport, the ancient Colosseum in Rome still stands to this day, visited by countless tourists who walk the streets of the eternal city, a tribute to the foresight of its imaginative citizens. Begun by Vespasian in A.D. 72, it took eight years to complete the four-storey oval with all-marble seats. Measuring 250 by 151 feet and with a seating capacity of 50,000, the arena is dwarfed by the stadiums of the twentieth century, but remains to this day a proud example of the playing fields of ages past.

> The ancient stadium in Athens, Greece, erected in 330 B.C. and completely restored to serve as the site for the first modern Olympic Games in 1896, is another fine example…

Lou's historical survey concluded with some subtly disparaging remarks about the Olympic Stadium in Montreal and its flawed retractable roof which was not in place in time for the 1976 Games. And then came the climax: a sketch of the Mapledome under the heading "A PEEK AT TOMORROW."

> The Mapledome will represent an entirely new departure in the construction of sports facilities…

A list of the "radical innovations" envisaged for the Mapledome followed, with particular focus on its proposed transparent, retractable roof, which, it was contended, could be slid on and off along runners in eight minutes, "more swiftly than a grounds crew can move a tarpaulin." Of course, this was simply Lou's estimate. The design was based on the premise that glass fibre roofs were too frail for the ice and snow experienced in northern cities. A stainless steel roof, on the other hand, would be strong enough to withstand the elements, but would not let in the natural light necessary to grow real grass. According to the information in the folder, the Mapledome roof would combine the advantages of the two systems, since it would be made entirely of "duraplex, an amazing new fabric ultrasonically fused by a process patented by the engineering firm Globaltech." Purportedly, it had the texture of fibreglass, but was considerably stronger, yet transparent enough for light to pass through it.

Lou had spent many hours with the senior brass of Globaltech and the construction firm Taylor-Steeles, discussing this "revolutionary new fabric and roof design," but the terms "duraplex" and "ultrasonically fused" were his own inventions for presentation of the project to lay audiences. It followed from the choice of duraplex for the roof that the playing surface in the Mapledome, unlike other covered stadiums, would be natural turf, and the presentation included a battery of statistics—mostly about injuries on artificial surfaces—in support of grass. They had been supplied, Jack learned, by Matt Dunlop at Lou's request.

The material in the binder went on to discuss how, with the Mapledome in place, Toronto would have the necessary facilities to host the summer Olympics at a not-too-distant date, for the domed stadium was to be only the centrepiece in a giant waterfront complex that would also include a hockey arena, Olympic-sized swimming pools, a velodrome, gymnasiums, tennis courts, bars, restaurants, and hotels. Much emphasis was given to the notion of "citizen participation," and the availability of most of the facilities for public use, except when the city was hosting special events. That, Lou calculated, was the best way to attract federal and provincial contributions for the complex.

Lou had finished his conversation with Taylor-Steeles by the time Jack got to the final pages of the folder, devoted to the financing of the

Mapledome, and he suggested that Jack simply flip through them quickly. They were the most speculative part of the presentation, especially given the untested nature of duraplex. That, however, did not much concern Lou. The important thing to him at this stage was to whip up civic enthusiasm for this particular project even if, later, it was necessary to switch to a less expensive roof. With the public clearly on side, Lou was confident government and private money would follow. It might take a little arm-twisting, but he was good at that.

"So, what do you think?" Lou asked as Jack finished reading. There was a childlike eagerness to his voice, as if he'd just finished composing a story that he had worked hard on for some time, and now he needed parental approval that it was creative and that he had talent.

"It's amazing, not just the magnitude of the project but the way you've presented it."

"I thought you'd like it, with your artist's eye. That's why I wanted you here for the unveiling."

"But this is too big to be financed entirely privately, isn't it? And if there is public money involved won't there have to be a design competition and open bidding on construction?"

"Not if everyone wants this roof." Lou grinned as he affectionately patted the model on his desk. "Globaltech has the patent for the duraplex process. All we need to do is get everyone thinking 'duraplex' and the Mapledome is a shoo-in. Don't forget, too, this is a design-build approach. Globaltech, Taylor-Steeles, the construction firm, and the architects, Forbes and Elliott, have all been involved from the beginning. If you break them up and hold an open competition, that's when you run into major cost overruns. The financiers—public and private—will all realize that. Hey, what do you think of the name Mapledome? Clever, eh? I figure the Jays and the Argos will move to the complex for sure. The Leafs are the only problem. I want them in the adjacent arena. It will be connected to the stadium by the shopping arcade. But we call the whole project the Mapledome because we want to get people thinking of it as a single entity with the stadium simply the centre. That way we avoid partial funding."

"Clever," Jack conceded. *Maybe too clever?*

"Besides, Mapledome has a nice national ring to it. It will help to get support for the complex across the country." Lou chuckled. "Can you imagine if we called it the Argodome? I mean, I've got a lot of confidence in this duraplex roof, but that would be just inviting a disaster."

They walked together from Lou's office to the Harbour Castle Hotel where they were sequestered in a room one floor up from the reception. While they munched on canapés delivered from the buffet, they watched what was happening on closed circuit television. Members of the media, invited dignitaries, club owners, and senior business executives were milling about a large model of the sports complex, set up in the middle of the room, and studying sketches of the project hanging on the walls. Young hostesses in white blouses, short navy blue skirts, and high white boots were passing trays, and Arthur Philpott, president of Citizens for the Complex, was answering questions from the media. "Yes, I think this is the sort of sports complex Toronto needs if it is to be a first-class city and play in the big leagues... No, it's true the duraplex fabric is totally new, but Globaltech has done substantial laboratory testing in partnership with the construction firm Taylor-Steeles, and the results have been most encouraging... Yes, I think the site we are looking at is ideal for this project. It will ensure the Mapledome plays a central role in the revitalization of the waterfront."

"So, who is this guy Philpott?" Jack asked, biting into a mushroom topped with cheese and bread crumbs.

"An old friend from Commerce and Finance. I asked him if he'd take this on. He's the CEO of Noble Insurance. Having someone like that at the helm is reassuring for people."

"And who are Citizens for the Complex anyway? I haven't heard anything about them before."

Lou turned from the television set in front of him and grinned at Jack as he tapped the side of his head. It didn't seem to him necessary to say anything. Slowly, it all sank in for Jack. Citizens for the Complex was a fledgling organization that Lou was coaxing into flight to lobby for a project that was his idea, and Globaltech, Taylor-

Steeles, and Forbes and Elliott constituted a consortium he'd brought together to build his dream complex. And now, behind the scenes, he was doing the necessary PR to bring his own idea to fruition. It was vintage Lou.

Arthur Philpott had finished answering questions, and with the formal presentation of the project now over, the guests were competitively consuming food and drinks from the buffet as if they were being clocked by the giant electronic scoreboard in the Mapledome. Suddenly, in the middle of the room, a squeal of delight rose above the buzz of the reception, and Lou and Jack turned their attention to another television screen. A column of eight-year-olds, marching two abreast, was breaking ranks as it reached the table with the project model. Wide, shining eyes focused on the Mapledome, giving it perhaps the closest and most favourable scrutiny it had yet received. "Wow! Is this ever terrific," one boy said. "Look how many rows of seats there are in the stadium. And the backs move!"

"Hey, is that real grass?" another asked. "It sure looks like it."

"No, but in the actual stadium, it will be."

"Look at the hockey arena," another boy shouted. "It's bigger than Maple Leaf Gardens. Hey, is that real ice?"

"No, but don't worry; it will be in the actual arena." A rather plump, middle-aged woman answering the children's questions was suddenly square in front of the television camera.

"Jesus!" Jack exclaimed "That's Bev! What she's doing here?"

"Well, you know Bev. She's a real sports enthusiast," Lou responded. "She even goes to Blizzard games."

"Hey, cool!" a pupil shouted. "They're rolling the roof off the stadium. What is that stuff anyway? You can see right through it."

"It's called duraplex," Bev answered knowledgeably. "It's a very special, new material."

"Miss Scott, will you take us to see the Mapledome when it's finished? Please?"

"You won't be in my class then," Bev laughed. "In fact, you'll probably have gone on to another school." She fought hard to hold back a tear. Seeing kids she loved move on was for her the hardest part of teaching. "It takes a long time to build something as big and complicated as this."

"Hey, maybe we can go and see a game. Can we, Miss Scott, can we?"

A television camera panned the children and then focused on Bev again as a microphone was thrust in her face. "It looks super to me, and you can see that my kids simply love it." Her rosy cheeks were bathed in bright television light, and it was clear to Jack that she was excited, perhaps even nervous, not having expected to be interviewed. Still, she spoke calmly and fluently. "Once people learn about Citizens for the Complex and this project, I'm sure there will be widespread enthusiasm for it, just as you see here today. A retractable stadium roof made of this unique new product is just what a northern city like Toronto needs. It will place us on the map as a world leader in innovation and creative design."

As the interview concluded, a receptionist approached Bev and pinned a large blue and white button on her blouse: "I'M FOR THE MAPLEDOME."

"Perfect!" Lou exhaled.

"So, I assume you're responsible for her being here, and getting interviewed."

"Well, I had this guy in my accounting department invite her. He's our only open link to Citizens for the Complex. I figured she might see it as an informative field trip for her class. Worked out well, eh? Good visuals."

"Thank you for not trying to get Susie and her class here, too," Jack said caustically.

"Susie? I've never seen her go to a ball game, much less watch the Leafs."

"So how come you're staying in the background when really you're at the centre of this whole thing? I mean it's perfectly legal to promote a project like this, isn't it?"

There was a look of surprise on Lou's face that Jack couldn't decipher. "It's simple really. It gives us a little flexibility."

Jack nodded, but he wasn't sure what Lou meant, not until several weeks later.

The reception room was emptying, and the media crews were dismantling their equipment. Lou switched off the television monitors and returned his cup and saucer to a cart. "Hey, are you doing anything tonight?" Lou studied the bill for the suite.

"No, I don't think so." Jack anticipated that another of the Pipers' frequent invitations for dinner was about to be extended to the Sturridges.

"So, how would you feel about stopping in at Bev's. If she's home alone, you could congratulate her on how well she and her class performed at the unveiling." Lou hesitated, studying Jack's reaction closely. "Maybe see if you can get her to talk to Cass about taking a positive view of the Mapledome, or if he is there too, you could speak to both of them. I mean, you know Cass, eh? He's unpredictable. He likes sports, but he's not big on public money supporting teams. If the Jays and the Leafs can afford the contracts they sign, then they have the dough to build their own facilities; that's his way of thinking."

"It's not an unreasonable argument."

"Hey, it's no big deal." Lou was quick to sense Jack's resistance. "I mean, don't go if you don't want to. I'll ask Jay to talk to her and maybe to Cass as well. Hey, how about you and Susie coming for dinner at our place?"

It was too late now. The damage had been done. With Lou, there was usually a clear division between business and friendship, but this time, as Jack saw it, Lou had driven recklessly across the line. "Ah... thanks, but I forgot. It's a parent-teachers' night at the kids' school."

"Well, we'll see you soon, eh?" The elation Lou had experienced at the success of the unveiling had vanished, and he added soberly, "Thanks a lot for coming. I really wanted to have you here. It meant a lot to me."

"It was very interesting." Jack was deliberately curt. "Very revealing." As he left the Harbour Castle, however, he suddenly wondered if coming home from England was that good an idea after all.

Chapter 13

Two months after the unveiling, in January 1981, there was another unexpected development in the tangled lives of the Sturridges' old friends. It occurred at a party held by Linda and Jay at the Rosedale home Linda had inherited from her mother. On the inside the house did not look very different from the other staid, red-brick mansions on Chestnut Park, the understated yet privileged dwellings of Toronto's "old money" families. The rooms on the ground floor were wood-panelled with small mullioned windows. Oil paintings of living and departed relatives and of bucolic scenes in Britain and Canada hung on the walls, their details subtly enhanced from below by discreetly shielded lights. From end to end, two walls of the den were covered with polished oak bookcases, containing old leather-bound tomes and voluminous sets of reference works, rarely disturbed except for dusting. And in the expansive drawing-room, there was a large inglenook fireplace with two wooden stools inside where guests could sit, if somewhat uncomfortably. The exterior of the house on this particular evening was, however, in stark contrast with the rest of the homes on this quiet, park-like street with its conservative residents of impeccably decent taste and manners. For, in the middle of the front lawn, Linda had erected an eight-foot-high papier mâché model of a circumcised penis. With its flesh-coloured wrinkles and folds and prominent blue veins, to the arriving guests it looked extremely realistic. And for added effect, Linda had sprayed patches of the scrotum and the surrounding snow-covered ground with a blood-red stain. While Jay had had reservations about the whole enterprise from the moment Linda had broached the idea, she had been insistent that they celebrate Lou's recent vasectomy by throwing a party for their friends in his honour.

"Well," Jack said to Susie as they passed the sculpture on the way to the front door. "We're here to bear witness to the last, triumphant stage in Sally's campaign to ween Lou from his Catholic origins."

"I think it's something bigger than that for Linda," Susie responded.

Jay greeted them at the door, looking, they thought, a bit sheepish. Now forty, he still had an innocent youthful face and his blonde hair effectively camouflaged the whispers of white forming on top and at the base of his sideburns. Dressed in a red and white-striped shirt with no jacket for cover, it was evident that he was beginning to sag a little above his belt. After his last birthday, he had started to worry about his weight, not so much any longer because he valued an athletic build, but simply for reasons of health—to stave off the incipient signs of aging. Linda had converted him to eating largely organic foods with lots of vegetables and fruits, and he had developed the habit of anxiously weighing himself every morning—when the scales were most likely to give him an encouraging result.

As Jack and Susie moved towards the living-room, a waiter passed them glasses of champagne. "I know a guy who gets these terrible pains every time he pees, and it's over a year since he had his operation." It was Cass talking to Lou in the doorway, but he stopped momentarily when he saw the Sturridges and they all exchanged greetings. "No way I'd go through an operation like that, man, no way. I know another guy whose sex life was ruined. Can't get it up anymore. Maybe it's purely psychological, but what does it matter? If you can't get it up, you can't get it up."

Cass was in his usual expansive mood and dominating the conversation. He was also the only one who had declined a glass of champagne and asked for a beer, which he was drinking straight from the bottle. "Hey, can you imagine Jay having a vasectomy? He'd need years of therapy afterwards." Cass slapped Lou on the back. "No, if someone had to do it, better you than Jay, old buddy, that's for sure." Through it all, Lou just grinned good-naturedly. But smartly dressed in grey slacks with an open-neck pale blue shirt and red ascot, to Jack and Susie he didn't look at all like a suffering, post-operative case. "You know, Jay better keep his guard up. Spooky might just take a knife to him herself. No, it's not for me, that's for sure. No one is messing with my dick—not like that anyway."

"Where's your sense of social responsibility?" Linda passed by carrying a tray of hors d'oeuvres. "I better have a talk with Marcia. I'm sure she'd be delighted to have you done. Where is she anyway? I haven't seen her since you arrived."

Cass just shrugged his shoulders indifferently. "Maybe she's in the basement, setting up an operating table, I don't know. I'll keep as far away from her as I can."

Sally briefly joined the group, looking glamorous in a white blouse and beige suede pants with a large gold belt and buckle. *Imitation? Not likely*, Susie decided. "What's new? Oh, God, nothing much. You know me. I'm working on plans for the garden, enlarging the rose beds, that sort of thing." She and Lou had recently moved to a new ranch style home off Bayview Avenue where the house and garden sprawled over two acres. "The boys keep me busy too, and then there's the United Appeal." She had been appointed to the board on Cass's recommendation, calculating that the Pipers' connections would be a real asset when it came to fund-raising. "And, of course, Lou's job always means a lot of entertaining."

"Yeah, sounds like Pinky is into as much shit as ever," Cass commented.

"Yes. He's just the same," Sally said, exchanging glances with Lou. "A bit more restless maybe. Always looking for new heights to conquer. You know Lou. Anyway, I'm sorry, I'm going to take him from you. There is someone I want him to meet. Talk to you later."

Cass studied the Pipers as they walked out of the room. "You know, Sal has a rich, deep voice, almost as if she's talking through an empty tube of paper towelling. But take that effect away and she sounds a lot like Spooky. She's been singing some pretty loony tunes lately. I think Spooky has some kind of hold on her. She's even seen her analyst."

"But when she was shown the proverbial couch, she declined to recline," Jack interjected. "Lou told me."

"What's wrong with seeking professional help to get in touch with your feelings?" Susie offered, although she too had been struck by Sally's emerging admiration for Linda's unconventional behaviour.

Cass chortled. "Now that Pinky has been neutered, Sally isn't going to be feeling much of anything,"

"Hey, Cassie! Jack! Susie Q! How are you guys?" As Bev joined them, she stuffed a large blue notebook back in her purse. In it, she had collected the names and addresses of hundreds of people she had met since high school.

"Hi ya, Scottie, baby. How're you doing?" Cass pecked her on her bright red lips, and her eyelids, heavily brushed with black mascara, fluttered coquettishly. She was, Jack thought, like a doll in a display window, desperately hoping to be the one who would be taken home and loved forever.

"I'm awesome, just awesome. Super party."

"Yeah, for everyone but Lou with his wounded pecker. You seem stoked as always."

"Oh, you know the effect seeing you has on me."

Cass took Bev by the hand. "It had to be you who wrote those chain letters we used to get; you know, the ones that said, 'Within five days, send six postcards to the person whose address is at the top of this letter. Delete that person and add your name and address to the bottom. Then send copies of this letter to six of your friends. Within one month, you will receive, ah…forty-six thousand postcards or something like that. Break this chain and misfortune will strike you. Belinda Wintermeyer did, and six weeks later she died of pneumonia.'"

"That's good, Cassie," Bev squealed. "But you know I'd never write anything as grisly as that. Not little old lovable Scottie."

"No, I guess not. Whoever broke the chain would just get a time out. Hey, you guys, hang on a minute. I gotta go to the can."

"I need to as well," Bev said, and they squeezed their way through the crowd in the living-room.

Jack decided to do the same, but there were so many people waiting by the downstairs bathroom that he went up to the second floor. Cass and Bev had had the same idea and Bev was just coming out of the bathroom when Jack arrived. While he and Bev stood in the hall, waiting for Cass, through the door they could hear his muffled voice singing, just as he used to do at the Ojibway and in university.

If you're going to Linda's Rosedale
Be sure to wear some armour o'er your pair.
If you're going to Linda's Rosedale
You're going to meet a horny fella there…

Bev grinned at Jack and giggled. They heard Cass noisily clear his throat, spit into the toilet, and flush. "Great house old lady Osterman gave Spooky, isn't it?" Cass said as he emerged and Jack went in after him. Through the door he heard Bev answer, "Oh, it's super… Hey! Where are you taking me?"

"On a private tour of the bedrooms."

"Cassie-pooh! We can't. Not in the middle of the party."

"Why not? Perfect time. At a vasectomy party. Wow! Lou would go ape if he knew."

Jack shook his head as he left the bathroom. *I guess Bev doesn't care if someone finds out. But Cass? Does he really love her? He could have left Marcia years ago, but he never has.* He found Susie back in the living-room, and joined her conversation with their hostess about writing, though he was too distracted by what he assumed was happening upstairs to make any meaningful contribution. Linda had submitted several articles to *Cosmopolitan* Magazine, and for the first time one had been published under her maiden name, much to Jay's relief: "YOUR BODY IS YOUR BODY!"

After sexual intercourse, have you ever considered whose
side of the bed you're usually on — whose half of the sheets
are rumpled and soiled? Yours. Right? Have you ever stopped
to consider the implications of this for female liberation?

So focused were the two of them on writing that they didn't notice Marcia come into the living-room and, hands on her hips, survey it carefully, presumably looking for Cass. Not spotting him anywhere, she left, and Jack followed her out to the hallway where he saw her mount the stairs to the second floor. Susie gave him a quizzical look when he returned to the living-room, his lifted eyebrows warning to be prepared for an explosion. Several minutes passed before suddenly, in the distance, they heard a muffled shout. Later, Jack told Susie that it sounded to him like a woman crying, "fucking whore." The three of them moved towards the hallway, arriving just as Marcia reached the bottom of the staircase. Without looking at anyone or saying a word, she immediately marched to the vestibule and out the front door, slamming it hard behind her.

According to what Marcia subsequently told her lawyer, she found Cass and Bev in a guest bedroom at the rear of the second-floor hallway. Cass was allegedly lying on the king-size bed on his back, propped up against a pillow, and Bev was kneeling above his crotch. "We weren't having sex," Bev had contended; "we were just fooling around." Whatever really was going on was immaterial. After that night, Marcia wrung a confession from Cass and learned that he had been cheating on her for years. Incensed, she threw him out of their house. After a week's reflection, living in a downtown hotel, Cass decided to move in with Bev, leaving Marcia free to file for an uncontested divorce.

"So, Bev has at last got her wish," Jack commented to Susie the day they received the news, "but I'm not sure it's really what Cass wants. We shall see."

* * *

Two weeks after the vasectomy party, yet another twist arose in the changing lives of the Sturridges' friends. Linda invited Susie and Jack to dinner—for a simple casserole prepared by Jay with the help of their children, Elizabeth and Sigmund. The Sturridges assumed the invitation was because Linda and Jay wanted to discuss what was happening in the Cass-Marcia-Bev triangle. That turned out not to be the case, though there was some similarity between the direction the conversation followed and the earlier cocktail party with its sudden, public exposure of Cass's infidelity.

"Wait a minute, please Jay," Linda said firmly. "Let me be the speaker and you the listener. Do you fully appreciate what I just said. Sixty per cent of women regularly fake an orgasm when having sex."

It was after dinner and they were all in the kitchen cleaning up. "Shhh, Linda." Jay looked anxiously out the door to see where the children were and then shut it.

"Do you realize what that figure is telling us?"

"Wait a minute. How reliable is this—"

"You wait, please. I'm the speaker."

Jay glanced at the Sturridges with a look of embarrassment and resignation. Clashes between him and Linda were not uncommon. Susie and Jack had become aware of that since returning from England; Jack described these moments as following a sort of predetermined dialectic by which Linda advanced to a higher level of human understanding. They did, however, always make him anxious and on edge, as if he were watching a precocious child about to pat a stray dog. "Please don't get angry," Jay appealed to Linda.

"I'm not angry. I'm just trying to be assertive. You see, that's the problem with that sixty per cent. They're not assertive about their sexual needs, and as a result they're being exploited. Just think how degrading it is to pretend to have an orgasm. Imagine feeling you have to pretend!" Linda had dried the same crystal bowl twice while she was talking, and her intense voice was becoming shriller. She was still as thin as she had been at university, with the same long, dark hair—*like warmed-over spaghetti, stained black with squid ink*, Jack thought. But now her hair was flecked with threads of white which Linda made no effort to hide. She was wearing a long, batik skirt of orange and brown cotton and a coffee-coloured sweater with no brassiere. Susie knew as well that Linda had given up shaving her legs and underarms and no longer wore make-up. "And what about their lovers? What does it tell us about them? Doesn't it prove that most men still see women as convenient wall sockets? You just plug in when you want some quick electricity."

"Wait a minute, please," Jay interrupted again. "May I be the speaker for a moment. Let's take this conversation upstairs where the children—"

"Damn it," Linda cried. "You're not hearing what I'm saying." And at that moment the crystal bowl in her hands slid to the floor at Jay's feet, shattering into several pieces. He jumped back in surprise, involuntarily covering his eyes. "What I'm telling you is that

I'm not coming—not like I should."

At that moment, Elizabeth and Sigmund rushed into the kitchen. "What happened? We heard a crash." Everyone was staring at the jagged pieces of crystal on the floor. "It's nothing," Jay tried to sound calm and casual. "Mom just dropped a bowl." "Yes. Sorry about that. Very stupid." Linda turned to the children. "Jay and I are having an argument about our sexual relationship." She had recently taken to using first names with Elizabeth and Sigmund, asserting that she was not on a parental power trip. "I'll explain the problem to you later."

Jay shut his eyes tight and lifted his head towards the ceiling. Differences with Linda over the most appropriate methods of child-rearing were not infrequent. It was, however, clear to the Sturridges that the children were used to these confrontations, for, apparently unperturbed, they quietly returned to the television in the den. "I'm sorry," Linda said again as she swept up the pieces of the bowl. "I'm not angry. It's just that we were not relating. I guess I wasn't being very direct either. I still haven't learned how to express myself freely." She put the broom and dustpan away. "You're right. Let's go up to my loft and—"

"Oh, gosh, Linda, no," Susie said. "We really should be going. The baby-sitter—"

"No please, I want you to stay." Linda took Susie by the hand. "You know how I value your opinion. I'd like your reaction to what I'm going to say... Jack's too, in fact."

With some reluctance, the Sturridges followed Linda and Jay to the third floor where Linda had a self-contained apartment—"a space for her ego," as she put it. There was a den with a desk at the front and a bathroom and kitchenette at the rear. There was even a rollaway bed in the den and some nights when she was really into her writing, Linda would sleep there so she wouldn't have her "thought processes" interrupted by the chatter of the rest of the family. It was also the room and bed to which she would retreat when she was going through an emotional or intellectual crisis.

The loft was a complete mess that night. There were books

spread out all over the floor of the den and on several chairs, open at passages of immediate interest to Linda, and the rough draft of a manuscript spilled out of a wastepaper basket. Even the walls around Linda's desk were a clutter of notices, reminding her of plays, concerts, and meetings she wanted to attend. She had also taped to the walls quotations from some of her favourite authors: Carlos Castaneda, Marian Engel, and Erica Jong. And directly in front of her desk, she had tacked up a folder announcing some extension courses she was considering taking.

Transactional Analysis for Couples
Ways of giving and receiving strokes. Provides opportunities for establishing stroking patterns, and will offer modifications to the norms where desirable.

The Dream Group
Emphasizes practical day-to-day use of dreams. Applies techniques derived from the Senoi, the 'dream' people of the Central Malay Peninsula.

Love Is Everywhere
A weekend of Body Mind, developing positive, preventive lifestyles through Shiatsu, 'Rolfing' exercise, Feldenkrais, Esalen Massage, Trager Mentastics, est, self -healing. Participants should have previous group experience with some knowledge of elementary bioenergetics and Gestalt therapy, which will be used to move through blocks. The group will not be primarily problem-solving, but a celebration of our possibilities within our human condition.

Nothing strange about this place, Jack thought to himself as he looked around the den. *Not if you're in San Francisco.*
Jay had hired a cleaner who came in twice a week to look after the first two floors of the house. Linda had agreed to that arrange-ment, although she rebuked Jay for what she regarded as an anal tendency due to poor toilet training. The cleaner was not, however,

permitted to enter the loft. Indeed, the Sturridges doubted that Jay ventured there very often either, and probably only after a long confinement when they imagined him creeping stealthily up the stairs to make sure Linda hadn't fallen into a deep trance from which she might never wake.

The four of them cleared away the books from the rollaway bed and chairs. Then Linda sat on the bed with Jay, holding him by the hand, while Susie and Jack settled in chairs. "What I'm trying to tell you," she said slowly and gently, "is that I think we need to open up our marriage."

"No-o-o-o!" Jay breathed. "You don't mean—"

"Yes. I think we both need it. We're suffocating each other, Jay, and it's manifesting itself in our sexual relationship."

"But, I thought… I mean, I had no idea—"

"I'm not saying you're at fault. I don't think either of us is. It's just something that has happened. Sex is like tending a garden. You can't go on growing the same plants in the same soil year after year and expect them to continue to bloom the same as ever. You have to keep mixing in new nutrients."

Organic fertilizer, she means, Jack thought. *That's the only additive she'd consider.* He wasn't, however, completely surprised by the turn the conversation had taken, but, like Susie, he felt embarrassed being a part of such an intimate moment.

"But, no-o-o-o!" Jay gasped again. "I thought everything was okay. I mean you've seemed happy. Happier lately than ever before. Your writing is going well, and you've got lots of outside interests and stimulation."

"But not sexual." Linda stroked Jay's hand lovingly. "I think we've reached the point where our marriage is mature enough to benefit from greater freedom. It will draw us closer together. It will make us more appreciative of each other and our needs. Don't you think I'm right, Susie?"

Susie looked completely flummoxed as she groped for a response. "No…I mean, gosh, it's not for me to say…I…I mean, Jack and I would never… It's…it's a dangerous... It's—"

Jay came to her rescue. Linda had in reality already taught

him to listen and what he was hearing now sounded like a rationalization. "Are you telling me... I mean, is there someone?"

Linda shook her head.

"No? Well, there's no one I'm seeing either, and I've no interest in finding someone." He sounded relieved, almost hopeful again. "So why risk it?"

"But don't you see that this is unnatural? We should be attracted to other people. It's only archaic customs that are holding us back from fully and freely expressing ourselves. We're blocking each other's development and self-awareness." Linda was speaking quietly and soothingly, so much so that, to Susie and Jack, she almost sounded convincing. "We've simply got to agree to do something about it. We need to start right away to explore the possibilities."

Chapter 14

There was a lot to talk about a week later when the Sturridges dined at the Pipers'. It was Lou who invited them—to make amends, Jack assumed, for suggesting he visit Bev and try to persuade her to lean on Cass to take a positive editorial view of the Mapledome project. The surprising development at Linda's vasectomy party was, however, naturally on everyone's mind and that was the first topic to get an airing. Sally shared the Sturridges' reservations about Cass and Bev managing to live together happily over the long term. Given Cass's impetuous personality, they feared the outcome would be the same as between Cass and Marcia, and that poor Bev would be the victim this time. Lou, however, took a more optimistic view. He was delighted for Bev's sake that she had at last snagged Cass and inclined to think their relationship would last. "Believe it or not, guys do change," he argued. "Look at me. I went to bed with a lot of women before Sally and I hooked up. But I've been faithful ever since. Bev will make sure that happens. She'll do everything she can to keep him happy."

"God!" Sally roared. "Is that how you see me? Catering to your every need? Well, I certainly haven't done the things Bev apparently has to satisfy her man!"

It was, however, the Sturridges' disclosure to the Pipers of Linda's open marriage proposal that commanded the most attention. "I don't know. Maybe extra-marital sex can work with them," Sally offered insouciantly. "Linda needs a loose rein to be happy."

"But sex is too intimate a thing for a married couple to share with others and still maintain their relationship," Susie insisted.

"That sounds a bit old-fashioned to me."

"And you like a flower child," Jack interjected.

"That would be me, wouldn't it?" Sally laughed. "Blooming after everything has withered." Lou winked at Jack and his lurking smile indicated he wasn't really surprised at Sally's reaction to the news.

They were sitting in the expansive living-room of the Pipers' new Bayview home, having a pre-dinner drink, served in Lou's crystal cocktail glasses, engraved with a stylized "L.P." The room had a tastefully subdued character. For her initial décor, Sally had chosen largely whites and tans with a smattering of black for contrast. Even the paintings and drawings fitted the colour scheme perfectly, for Sally wasn't averse to selecting art on that basis. *All I need to know is what colours are coming next and I'll have a ready market,* Jack thought cynically. Every object in the room from the golden fan, concealing the interior of the fireplace, since it wasn't in use, to the white and yellow carnations on the rosewood coffee table seemed to have been set in place with geometric precision to ensure proper balance. Indeed, even Sally, attired in a tweed jacket and skirt from Hazelton Lanes, and a fawn blouse with a walnut brown silk scarf, was the perfect match for her surroundings. Yet, despite the overall elegance of the room, there were a few concessions to Lou's less impeccable taste. Tucked away on two corner tables, there were foot-high marble statues of Triple Crown winners Secretariat and Seattle Slew. And, on a third, there was a brass bowl full of what were called "security pills"—capsules containing "rare 22 karat placer gold from the legendary Coal Creek Mines of Alaska," designed for instant relief from the pain of recession. Unable to resist the advertisements for them in the *New Yorker* magazine, Lou had bought them to distribute to business associates for their amusement.

"Actually, I'm surprised that Linda didn't make this proposal before now," Sally continued. "Open marriage isn't exactly an *avant-garde* idea."

"But Jay could be crushed by this," Susie persisted. "He'll feel rejected."

"It's not rejection. In the end, it will bring them closer together."

That's pretty much what Linda said to us, Jack thought. *Maybe Cass is right about her influence.*

"What do you think?" Susie appealed to Lou, but he just shrugged his shoulders and rose to move to the dining-room.

Later, after dinner, Sally took Susie to her greenhouse to show her the plants she had potted for her spring garden, and Lou and Jack retired to the den for a cognac. There, Sally's pastel shades yielded to teakwood panelling and a green leather sofa and chairs. It was one of the smaller rooms in the house, but already Lou's favourite, cramped though it was by having to accommodate a television set, elaborate stereo equipment, and a large desk at which Lou often worked in the evenings. Jack calculated that he liked its claustrophobic atmosphere at the end of the day—that it reminded him perhaps of the cluttered Italian kitchen that had been at the centre of his childhood home. "It won't work, Susie's right." Without preamble, Lou reverted to their pre-dinner conversation as they settled on the sofa. "Loyalty. You've got to have loyalty. It's the only way."

"So, do you think Susie and I should talk to Linda again?"

"I don't know. Theirs has been a crazy relationship from the start. It's bound to end someday somehow."

"It's hard to stand by and do nothing while they risk messing up their lives, that's how Susie feels."

"It's a time for doing nothing." Lou got up to put on a Dizzy Gillespie tape. Jack couldn't help but admire his calm in the face of the unsettling developments in their friends' lives. But that, he knew, was typical Lou, always unflappable whether dealing with a human or a corporate problem. Jack could see it in his long, smooth fingers as he turned the cassette slowly over in his hands and then eased it gently into the tape deck. He could feel it in the room as Lou sank slowly back on the sofa and mellow jazz flowed through the speakers. "Don't worry about Sally either. It's just a passing phase. Mid-life crisis or something." He paused for a sniff and sip of his cognac. "You know, I've been thinking of giving her a few grand to start up a kitchen boutique or something... But I'm not sure it would make any difference. She has money of her own after all."

"No, it probably wouldn't."

"Well, I'll think of something."

They sat quietly and contemplatively staring at their cognacs until Lou jumped up to fetch a sheet of paper from his desk. "Hey, look at this." He sounded cheerful again, matrimonial matters behind him. "It's a memo the boys left for me the other day. Can you beat it? They've even designed a company logo."

At the top of the soiled piece of paper there was a carefully inked drawing of a candle with a long wick. Inside the candle, Scott Piper had carefully printed an artistic "J" and "S" joined together. One paragraph of text followed.

> Memorandum: To Dad
> Urgent
> Jeff and I have formed a company. We are going to
> sell firecrackers and cherry bombs on the black market
> at school. We need your help. As you know, you can't
> buy them in the stores here. Can you find a foreign supplier
> and smuggle them into Canada for us? We need them
> several weeks before Victoria Day next year. If
> you will do that, we will cut you in for 20 per cent
> of the profits.

"Aren't they something," Lou chuckled with pride.

"What are you going to do? Ask for forty per cent?"

"I was thinking of fifty as an initial negotiating position... You know, I worry about them sometimes. They've always had everything they could possibly want. I don't know how that will affect them, their readiness to work hard, their drive."

"Based on this evidence, I don't think it will be a problem."

Lou laughed again. "Well, we'll see how tough they are in negotiations... Oh, here. This is something else I wanted to show you." He passed several sheets of paper to Jack on which his secretary had typed up letters he had dictated to her at the office. With a red felt pen, he had inked in some last-minute changes. One of the letters was addressed to the *Toronto Daily News*. In fact, several days later, Jack read it in the paper, unchanged from the draft he was handed in Lou's den.

Matt Dunlop's column on November 12 ("The NFL Likes Domes") raises an important consideration in the emerging enthusiasm for the construction of a major sports complex on the waterfront. Certainly, if Toronto is ever going to obtain an NFL franchise, the first thing it is going to have to do is build an appropriate all-weather facility. Now is the time to act.

Another letter was addressed to the mayor.

For several weeks now there has been much discussion in the media about a proposed waterfront sports complex. I am sure that the vast majority of Torontonians would agree with me when I say that this is not a matter on which there should be any disagreement among the citizens of this great city. The long-term economic advantages to Toronto and, indeed, the entire metropolitan area from the early construction of the Mapledome would be incalculable. I trust that you and the members of city council will give careful, positive consideration to the desirability of supporting this project. The Mapledome is a sports complex that the citizens of Toronto earnestly want and have the right to expect to see come to fruition.

In recent days, Lou had been composing letters to the media, City and Metro Council, and the provincial premier's office, extolling the virtues of the Mapledome project. They had then been distributed to various individuals and organizations for copying, signing, and submission. A number had been sent to Globaltech, Taylor-Steeles, and Forbes and Elliott in expectation that employees of the consortium firms could be enlisted by senior management to participate in Lou's creative manufacture of public opinion. But he hadn't stopped there. He'd inveigled friends at other companies to distribute letters to their employees and, of course, Arthur Philpott at Noble Insurance. In fact, he'd even asked Jay to do the same at Universal Consulting Services, knowing Jay would feel obliged to help, since it was Lou who had landed him his job. He'd declined, however, to pass any of his drafts to his own employees at Piper, Langford and Jones. Jack was beginning to realize what Lou meant by having "flexibility" if his firm stayed in the background. *Of course, it's also the way to save his hide if anything goes wrong.*

Lou waited expectantly for Jack to finish reading. "So, how much does Sally know about what you're doing?"

Lou was taken aback, having expected only praise. "A little. She likes the project."

"But does she know about these letters?"

Lou shook his head.

"So she doesn't know Jay is involved with them?" There was no response. "I think you should tell her... Oh, and what about using Bev to turn Cass around on the project? Did you persuade Jay to talk to her? Does Sally know about that?"

Lou simply drained his glass of cognac and stood up. "I think it's time we found the ladies, don't you?" He put his arm around Jack's shoulder as they left the den. "I don't ask Sally what ingredients go into one of her lemon chiffon pies. I just enjoy what comes out of the oven. And she doesn't ask me what goes into making a deal."

"That sounds pretty sexist."

"Maybe, but that's how we've always managed things."

* * *

A few weeks later, Lou received an unexpected jolt that severely tested his habitually composed demeanour. The *Toronto Daily News* broke the story of a nefarious letter-writing campaign in support of the Mapledome; not only that, it was the lead story on the front page.

SUPPORT FOR SPORTS COMPLEX A HOAX; ONE AUTHOR BEHIND LETTERS

The recent, apparently spontaneous outpouring of public support for a major sports complex on the

Toronto waterfront has been a carefully orchestrated deception, *News* reporters have learned. An examination of letters and briefs in favour of the Mapledome project mailed to Toronto newspapers and various municipal and provincial officials has revealed that at least fifty-nine of the pro-dome letters and briefs submitted in recent weeks were probably drafted by one individual. The link has been established with the aid of the crime laboratory in the Attorney-General's office by analyzing recurring words and phrases.

Toronto insurance executive Arthur Philpott, president of Citizens for the Complex, the group pushing for construction of the multi-million-dollar scheme, yesterday repudiated the suggestion that his group is in any way involved in a letter-writing hoax. "No one could possibly be engineering the public support for the Mapledome. It's simply too extensive for that to be credible," he said. However, according to the crime laboratory…

Cass phoned Jack shortly after the first edition of the paper reached the streets to crow about his exposé. "The shift in public opinion was just too big and sudden to be believable. We were getting a lot of pro-dome letters. So were the other papers, and petitions were flooding into city council. It's happened before, you know—carefully orchestrated campaigns, disguised as spontaneous public opinion. Remember Ron Haggart's stuff in the Telly on the lobbying for the Spadina Expressway?"

Jack could picture Cass sitting triumphantly in his austere office overlooking Front Street. Chrome-plated chairs with purple seat covers would be pulled up haphazardly at a rectangular arborite table dotted with plastic coffee cups, discarded at the end of an editorial meeting. He knew the only character in the room was provided by framed, original sketches, penned by the *News*'s famed political cartoonist Alistair MacGregor, that hung on the restless white walls. His favourite was one of Pierre Trudeau, dressed in army fatigues, doing a pirouette. In a bubble were the words, "Just watch me." The first time Jack had seen the cartoons, he'd felt uncomfortable realizing how similar they were to his own art and how he could have made life easier for Susie by pursuing the same career path as MacGregor.

"We don't know if it's one person behind all the letters, or two or three," Cass continued. "The kind of analysis the crime lab is doing for us is a tricky business."

It was clear to Jack that, with his letter-writing, Lou had rekindled Cass's interest in the Mapledome and handed him another reason to oppose it. And with Cass's energy and investigative talents, that was a dangerous situation for Lou, and Jay as well.

"You know something? I fucking love this. It's the most fun I've had since I was a reporter. I feel like a caged lion suddenly sprung loose, know what I mean? I'm back in the jungle stalking my prey and the scent is growing stronger. I'm gonna phone Lou and arrange a game of tennis. I feel like I can slaughter anybody right now, even fucking Borg."

Jack was taken aback by the mention of Lou's name. *Does he suspect he's involved, or was this coincidental?* "I can see the headline already," Cass added. "'Mapledome Mystery Writer Talks.' But how to track the bugger down and unbutton his lips? That's my problem."

After their conversation, Jack called Lou to tell him about the phone call. Lou had already read the *News'* article and was relieved by Jack's reassurance that, so far, Cass did not know the source of the letters. Nevertheless, he asked once again if Jack would go and see Bev and find out what she knew about Cass's investigation.

"You mean ask her to work as an undercover agent for you?"

Jack's sarcasm wasn't lost on Lou. "Yeah, sort of, I guess. But hey, this is serious. It's not just my ass that's on the line. There's Jay's, too. And I can't send him back to talk to Bev, not when Cass is sniffing blood."

Afterwards, Jack realized that things might have played out differently if once again he'd declined to get involved. But, for the sake of equanimity among his old friends, he wanted to get the Mapledome behind them, and the best way to achieve that seemed to be to persuade Cass to drop his editorial opposition to the project and his investigation into the alleged letter-writing campaign. He wanted Susie to go with him and, in fact, to be the one to ask Bev about the *News's* investigation, since it would seem a more innocent inquiry coming from her. But Susie was opposed to going. "I don't understand what all the fuss is about. Who cares about this project? It's just a sports complex."

"Lou is obsessed with it. I think he sees it as a monument to his father."

"And I don't understand why Jay is involved either."

"It's a payback for—"

"Nor why you're mixed up in this, too. I simply don't get it. You go if you think you must, but leave me out of it. And be careful, or none of you will be on speaking terms when this is over."

* * *

"Jackie! Hi." Bev planted a kiss on his cheek as he stood at the door. "What a surprise! Come on in!"

"I was on my way home from the studio and thought I'd just drop in and see how you two love birds are getting on."

"Awesome. Cass is still at the *News,* but come on in. I'll fix us martinis."

"No thanks. I can't stay long. Maybe just a cup of tea."

"Sure."

Jack followed her into the kitchen where she plugged in the kettle. The room had the usual Beverley gleam, but without her characteristic tidiness. On a counter by the sink was a large, yellow plastic bowl filled with a grey, glutinous substance and beside it an index card with a typed recipe from a file box for making playdough. On a sheet of wax paper beside the bowl was a little model of a man with a baseball bat in his hand and another of someone running with an oblong-shaped ball under one arm.

"Hey, very artistic!" Jack said as he picked up one of the figures.

"Oh, they're just samples for my art class, so the kids can see what you can make with this stuff." Bev quickly twisted and patted some dough into a third person, legs out-stretched on skates with a stick in one hand. "My kids are going to make a papier mâché model of the Mapledome."

"Really?" Jack felt relieved that the subject had come up so naturally and that he wouldn't appear to be prying.

"Yes. These are the sketches we'll be working from."

Bev led Jack to the kitchen table where she had spread out several blueprints of the sports complex: the exterior façade of the main entrance, a vertical perspective of the dome, and a cut-away of the stadium interior.

"So, where did you get the drawings?"

"From Citizens for the Complex. I joined the group, you know."

"Really?" Jack did his best to sound surprised.

"Yes, at the unveiling. I'm hoping the group can use our model for publicity."

"Good idea." Bev poured him a mug of tea and they moved to the living-room. "So, does Cass know you joined the group?"

"Oh sure. He saw the TV coverage of the reception. But that was before…before…you know, the breakup and he moved in. He doesn't know about the model I'm making. I'm not sure he'd like it. I'll hide it before he gets home."

"So uncovering the letter-writing campaign has made him more negative about the project, eh?"

"Like totally."

"And Cass keeps you abreast of the investigation?"

"Every night. It's always on his mind." Bev climbed onto her ladder to reach the upper shelves of her record collection.

"Maybe you can get him to understand that support for the Mapledome is much too extensive to all be phony."

Bev had pulled the record she was looking for from the rack, but now she just sat on the top step of the ladder, staring at Jack with a puzzled expression. "Jack... You…you're not *telling* me to do that, are you? You're not somehow involved in this thing?"

"Me? No, no. Like you, I just think the Mapledome would be great for the city. It would be nice if Cass saw the thing the same way we do. I mean, it would be great if somehow he were persuaded to drop the investigation and moderate his opposition."

Bev dropped the record dejectedly onto her turntable and sank into an easy chair. "That's almost exactly what Jay said to me a couple of weeks ago."

Right away, Jack felt awful, smothered under a blanket of self-loathing. Bev had been exploited too often not to sense it was happening again. He wanted to say he was sorry and to forget what he had said. He wanted to leave—to crawl home to Susie and apologize to her for going. But all he did was sit silently listening to Bev's stereo, thinking about how the Mapledome was driving his friends apart. He had no idea how much time elapsed before Cass was suddenly standing in a trench coat in the middle of the living-room.

"Jack, you old bugger! What are you doing here?"

"Cassie!" Bev kissed him. "I didn't expect you this early." She was still dressed in old blue jeans and a grey sweatshirt, and the lines on her puffy cheeks had not been powdered away.

"Hi, Cass," Jack said. "Just dropped in to see how you guys are doing."

"Sure, sure. Bird dog!"

Bev glanced towards the kitchen door and then clapped her hands together. "Hey, why don't you guys go up to the den. It's cozier there. I'll get you a drink, Cassie, and join you there. What would you like? A martini?"

"That would be great."

It was in the second-floor den that Bev spent most of her time when she was at home alone. That's where she had the desk at which she corrected her class's work and wrote letters to her friends. Her sewing machine was also there, set up on a bridge table, and there was a glass cupboard with the cups and ribbons she had won in high school, the sweater she was wearing the night Neil Diamond touched her on the arm, and the scarf she bought in Memphis that was a replica of the one Elvis wore at his famous Hawaii concert. The walls of the den were blazing red, but not much of the paint was visible between the rows of photographs and two-foot-high posters plastered from ceiling to floor. There were photographs of her classes in every year of primary and secondary school, of the graduating class at Trinity College, of high school and university reunions, of the gang at the Ojibway Hotel, and the weddings of Sally and Lou, Linda and Jay, and Susie and Jack. There were posters of Eddie Fisher, Pat Boone, Chuck Berry, the Everly Brothers, the Beatles, the Rolling Stones and, of course, Elvis Presley and Buddy Holly. At the bottom of the last two, she had tacked on bands of black paper on which she had glued purple lettering: "BUDDY HOLLY LIVES!" and "ELVIS: 1937-1977, LONG LIVE THE KING!" There were also two speakers that Cass had installed years before to connect the den to the stereo downstairs so that Bev could shatter the silence that had so often crept into her life before Cass moved in.

"So, how's the investigation going?" Jack asked. "Any new leads since we talked?"

"No, not yet. But give me time. I'll bust this thing wide open."

"So why are you so determined to kill the project anyway?" Jack tried to sound casual, as if he were only vaguely interested in Cass's response. "You like sports. You know the Jays need a better home than Exhibition Stadium. And the Gardens is aging."

"It's the principle of the thing. Public money is bound to be involved, and I don't like that. And now it's evident the support for the project is phony."

"All of it?"

"I don't know. But I aim to find out."

Jack knew he couldn't risk saying more without arousing Cass's suspicions, so he changed the subject. "Hey, have you heard about Linda's proposal to Jay that they open up their marriage?"

"Yeah. Fuck. Why wasn't Marcia like that?" Bev arrived with his martini and he attacked it vigorously. "But Linda? For that dipstick to put the canoe in the water? I'd paddle her behind if I were Jay. And she's still working on Sally, you know. I saw her at a United Appeal meeting last week. She's still babbling boutique, The Pewter Pot or some shit like that. Next thing we hear she'll be jumping into bed with Jay and it will be with Linda's blessing." Bev emptied the remainder of the martini jug into Cass's glass. "You know, I used to think Sally and Jay would make the perfect couple. Attractive rich girl marries handsome and aspiring middle-class boy. They have two beautiful children, live in a four-bedroom house in a nice neighbourhood, and go to church every Sunday. Only Jay proved to be more unconventional than we expected. He married Linda, the rebel with a dozen causes, while Sally chose her father." Cass howled with laughter. "Of course, she did have to do a little cosmetic surgery on him. Sally is the one who should be living in Rosedale with all the other bleeding-heart Liberals. Linda ought to be downtown in Regent Park. Or out on Ward's Island. Yeah, Ward's Island, that's the place for her, with the last of the Marxist-Leninists."

And who did you marry? Jack wanted to ask. *The boss's daughter in order to get ahead?* There had never seemed to Jack any other explanation—unless, of course, behind Marcia's flaccid and boring exterior there had lurked a sexual vampire.

Cass stared for a moment at his empty martini glass and then jumped up. "What the hell, the night is young. I think I'll fix myself another."

"Oh, Cassie, sit down. You're tired. I'll get one for you." Cass, however, was already out of the room and Bev chased down the stairs after him, Jack following, afraid that Bev might have left the plans she was using for her Mapledome model on the kitchen table. She had not, but, unfortunately, when she had hurriedly crammed them into her ironing cupboard after Cass arrived home, the end of one of them had slipped out and was wedged in the door.

"Hey, snook'ems," Cass said, spotting it. "Your ironing is calling you. It must be piled up big time."

Before she could stop him, Cass opened the cupboard to stuff the protruding drawing back. But, instead, all the plans came sailing out along with the three figures Bev had made out of her playdough, stuck to one of the drafts.

"Hey! What the shit are these? They're plans for the fucking Mapledome!"

"I'm using them to make a papier mâché model at school." Bev was red in the face, terrified of angering Cass.

"And you keep them with your ironing board...along with these little jocks?"

"I…I…was just working on the model before you and Jack came in."

"A model of the Mapledome? Are you crazy?"

"Cassie, you know I like the project. I've liked it all along. Jack does too, don't you, Jack?"

"Holy motherfucker! Has the whole city gone bananas?"

Immediately, Bev regretted extending the conflict to Jack. She flung her arms around Cass and buried her head in his chest. "Please, Cassie, can't you just forget about this damned thing. It doesn't really matter who is supporting it, or if it gets built. There are much more important things for the *News* to worry about."

"No, I want to know." Cass held Bev back from his body. "Jack, are you…hey, were you planning to—"

"Cassie, please! I don't want this stupid thing to come between us. I'd die if someone got hurt. Why can't you forget about it? Why can't we get things back the way they used to be with everybody?"

"No, I want to know. Jack, you… No…no…" Suddenly—too suddenly, Jack worried—Cass's disposition changed. He pulled Bev close to him again, and she cuddled against his chest, sniffling. "Hey, no, you're right. What the shit, it doesn't really matter, does it? If you guys want to support this thing, what the hell is it to me?" He kissed Bev on the forehead. "Come on. Let's all have another drink and forget about it. Hey, what do you say we get tickets for the Jays' home opener this year…while the Mistake by the Lake is still around?"

* * *

Cass's suspicions were indeed aroused that evening. Mulling things over in his mind after Jack went home, everything started to fall into place: the slick presentation of the complex—too professional to be the work of amateurs in Citizens for the Complex; the clever writing of letters and briefs by one or two authors; Bev's enthusiasm for the project; and, finally, the unexpected visits to Bev's house first by Jay and then by Jack. That very night, he drove back down to the *News* and pulled from a bookshelf in Matt Dunlop's office the sports editor's copy of the promotional binder for the Mapledome. Huddled over his desk in his office, he read through the early historical pages, so artfully designed to establish the thoroughness of the research on the project. "Yeah," he muttered out loud. "They stink of Pinky." When he got to the Mapledome's innovations, including the description of the proposed transparent, retractable roof, he stopped reading for some time. *Duraplex. What the shit is it anyway? Sounds like some kind of fucking condom Pinky invented.* Then Cass focused on who held the duraplex patent: Globaltech, the engineering firm in the Mapledome consortium. That's when, suddenly, he got really excited. *Globaltech. Taylor-Steeles. Forbes and Elliott. Of course! Why didn't I read all this shit before. The answer has been right here in Matt Dunlop's office all along. Lou and the three firms are behind all of this. Maybe others as well, like Jay's and Arthur Philpott's.*

The next day, Cass ordered his city editor to hire a private investigation team to come up with a list of the employees of all the firms he suspected might be involved in the letter-writing, and, two weeks later in early April, he had his answer. Matching the names on the list with the signatures on the pro-Mapledome letters received by the *News* revealed that ninety per cent of them had been signed by employees of the three consortium firms plus Jay's Universal Consulting Services and Philpott's Noble Insurance. "Duraplex!" Cass shouted the name with joy when he and his reporters finished their calculations. "They'll wish it was a fucking condom before I'm finished with them. I'm going to give them a dose that will shrivel their profits."

There was, however, only one letter in the pack that had been signed by an employee of Piper, Langford and Jones—ironically sent on his own volition by the man in the accounting department who had contacted Bev about attending the unveiling. It was a flimsy basis for linking Lou to the scheme, let alone implying that he was the mastermind behind the nefarious manufacture of public opinion. But Cass was determined to get him, especially since he was convinced that Lou had been playing him for a sucker ever since the unveiling, tricking him and all the media with the pro-dome letters and briefs, and using Bev, Jay, and Jack to coax him away from his public duty to oppose the scheme. This was his moment to show who, in the end, was the cleverer. But more important even than that, it was his long-awaited opportunity to get even with Lou—to avenge himself for his loss in the Barbie Bigelow Affair. "Piccolo, you turkey!" he shouted loud enough for everyone in the newsroom to hear him. "I'm gonna fucking get you."

Chapter 15

"Now this is really weird. Wait till you hear it," Lou confided to Jack. "It's about last night, just hours before I learned that Cass had the goods on the letter-writing and was about to spill the beans in the *News*. Around six, I got this call at the office from Linda of all people, inviting me to dinner with her and Jay. Just me, not Sally. She said there was something confidential to discuss 'for my ears only.' So, what could I do? I felt I had to go."

Lou was speaking to Jack late in the evening of the next day—the one on which the *News* published its bombshell story about the sources of the pro-Mapledome letters and briefs. Jack and Susie had gone over to the Pipers' at Lou's urging to discuss how to handle the crisis. After an intense and sometimes heated discussion in the den, Sally had stood up abruptly, grabbed an overcoat from the hall closet, and walked out to her garden. Susie had followed her, knowing that this was where Sally liked to go when she was distraught, and anticipating that she needed comforting. It was an early spring evening with only Sally's snowdrops and crocuses blooming. It was chilly, too, and the flagstone paths that criss-crossed the garden were wet from a heavy dew, yet with the aid of coats a long stroll was still manageable, especially for two distracted women. Lou and Jack had stayed behind in the den and Lou felt more comfortable now telling Jack what had happened at Linda's the evening before.

"She greeted me at the door and led me into the living-room where I expected to find Jay, but he wasn't there, and only two crystal glasses were sitting on a silver tray by the bar. Jay, she claimed, was tied up with work at the office and wouldn't be in until late, so it was just the two of us for dinner plus the kids. I guess their presence was supposed to reassure me, and it did briefly. As Linda poured us drinks, Sigmund walked in and set a match to the grate. I thought he looked a bit uncomfortable at first, but he said hello in his usual friendly manner and as his fire blazed to life it gave the room a welcoming feel. And then Elizabeth came in with a tray of hors d'oeuvres and greeted me warmly. It all seemed a bit much, but—"

"But, you knew that Linda had some unconventional ideas about child-rearing, right?" Jack interjected.

"Right. So, at first, I shrugged off what was happening. But then Linda handed me my drink and sat down on a divan by the fireplace, motioning to me to join her. Stupidly, I did that and right away it was clear I was dealing with a new Linda. I caught the smell of perfume—"

"And you knew she never used it."

"Never, I was pretty sure. And her hair. You know how it usually looks pretty straggly?"

"Like a black ball of yarn that's fallen off a sewing table and unravelled."

"Yeah, well last night it was freshly washed and set, sleek-looking like Sally's, with waves rolling against her back. And that's not all. She was in a mauve silk dress with a large black bow at the waist and, as she crossed her legs and the dress climbed to her thighs, I noticed that her skin was freshly shaven."

"So now you knew she was seducing you."

"Well, not exactly, I wasn't sure what the hell was going on. I knew this all had to do with her open marriage proposal to Jay. But I wasn't sure where I fitted in. I mean, shit, I'm the last guy you'd expect her to make a play for. We've never been that close. So, I still thought maybe she just wanted to talk about the idea, maybe get my thoughts on who to go after."

"Christ, Lou, this is the first time I've ever heard you sound naïve. With your reputation with women, you were a logical choice."

"Hey, come on. That was all in the distant past. Anyway, we talked for a while, but the topic of intercourse never came up. Then we had dinner. It was quite a meal, considering how she and Jay are both so careful now about their weight. A lobster bisque, followed by veal almondine and a salad of mixed greens, avocado and pear. I told her she shouldn't have gone to so much trouble, and she answered that it wasn't, not for me. Her dark, crazy eyes were latched on mine in that freaky way of hers. That's when I began to feel uneasy again, especially with Elizabeth serving us and Sigmund pouring the wine, a Pinot Noir I think. It seemed bizarre, but I thought maybe Linda was training them so that when she actually tried to seduce some guy, they would be able to assist her."

"Well, Linda certainly would have told them about her conversation with Jay and how they planned—or at least she planned—to open up their marriage."

"Anyway, after dinner we went back to the divan in the living-room. Sigmund restoked the fire and Elizabeth brought us liqueurs. Then they wished us a pleasant evening and went upstairs. Linda kicked off her high heels and tucked her feet under her on the divan. By then I'd lost patience with her, so I told her I knew about her open marriage proposal to Jay and wanted to know if they were still planning to go ahead with it. 'Oh, yes,' she said, 'I'm just getting started.' She leaned gently against me as she reached for the cigarette box on the table in front of us, and moments later the smell of marijuana was mingling with the cedar smoke from the fire. She urged me to have a drag—to feel amorous the way she did. But by then, I'd had enough of this shit, so I said firmly, 'Hey, I don't know what you've got in mind. But let's be clear about one thing; if you and Jay are going to have sex with other people, that's your business. But you can count Sally and me out of any plans you may have.'

"'Ah! Sally and Jay, of course!' she cried. 'Why didn't I think of that. What a natural combination!' Linda shook her hair from her face and edged closer to me. 'No, I was thinking of Linda and Lou.' Her eyes roamed all over me, kind of like a doctor's examining a patient, and then she added that Sally would be delighted if we had sex because it would liberate her to do the same. I told her that was absurd and that neither Sally nor I wanted anything of the sort. But she wouldn't buy it. In fact, she added that she felt she and I had a lot in common."

"Well, that's certainly bullshit," Jack interjected.

"Then she said we should try and get in touch with our feelings about each other and explore where each of us was emotionally—

that sort of shit—because she thought we were ready for each other now. She reached to take my hand, but I pulled it away and told her to stop, that this was ridiculous. But still she persisted. She leaned towards me—far enough for me to see down the front of her dress—and whispered that she thought this night was going to end more pleasantly than any we'd shared before. 'Actually, this farce is going to end right now,' I said, standing up. And, ironically, that's exactly when it did, for at that moment there was the click of the front door closing, and I glanced towards the hallway. Linda was still sprawled across the divan, but with that sound, she lifted her head and turned her eyes in the same direction. Jay was standing there, staring into the living-room with a confused expression on his face."

"Kind of like a late-night reveller who had wandered into the wrong party, I imagine," Jack offered.

"Yeah, exactly. 'Lou,' Jay said, clearly puzzled. 'I didn't expect to find you here.'

"'What are *you* doing here?' Linda said sharply. 'That's more to the point. You were supposed to be working late.'

"Jay's jaw snapped open with sudden comprehension. It was only then that he thought he knew why I was there. So he apologized and explained that something had come up; he'd had a call from Bev and had to get home quickly to deal with it. He didn't just sound apologetic; he sounded defeated and his face was ashen. Still, he repeated that he was sorry to have intruded and just to forget he was there. He was going to have a shower, but that he needed to talk to me later.

"I rushed over to him and pressed a hand on his shoulder to explain why I happened to be there, but he interrupted me. 'Hey-y-y. No-o-o,' he said. 'It's fine. Linda and I agreed to this. I'm not upset. It's something else I need—'

"'Jesus, Jay,' Linda shouted at him. 'Will you shut up and listen.' She was silent for a moment, and then she apologized, and added softly that I was there only because she had invited me over for a talk.

"'But you were on the sofa together,' Jay said, confused. 'You—'

"'Yes,' Linda said slowly. 'I had plans, not Lou.' It was one of those moments I appreciated her frankness. Jay sank onto the staircase. At first, I thought it was because he was relieved I wasn't about to screw his wife, and then I thought maybe it was because he was disappointed to discover that Linda really was serious about sexual experimentation. But actually it was neither of those; it was because of the phone call he had got at the office. And now that there was no need to leave Linda and me alone, he blurted it out. Bev had called him to say that Cass had just got home bursting with excitement. The *News* had linked most of the pro-dome letters to employees at the consortium firms. But that wasn't all. They were going to name Universal, Noble Insurance, and Piper, Langford and Jones as involved as well. They were publishing the story in the next edition.

"I sat down on a chair in the living-room. I could see the walls of the Mapledome suddenly collapsing, as if a wrecking crew had just lit a hundred sticks of dynamite around it. Linda asked Jay what he was talking about as she dropped onto the stairs beside him. She didn't understand. She'd never taken any interest in the project, never asked Jay anything about it, and he had never explained how he was involved."

"Just like Susie," Jack interjected.

"So now, Jay filled her in, and what he told her shook her out of her self-absorption. It was as if the whole bizarre evening up to then had not happened. Her attention was now completely on the dilemma we were all in. To tell you the truth, I think she was relieved. I don't think she really wanted to have sex with me. It was just that, after making her open marriage proposal to Jay, she didn't know how or where to begin. Maybe I became the candidate because she calculated Sally wouldn't mind—that, like her, she was titillated by the prospect of sex with another man."

"Or maybe she really did see you as the great Don Juan."

"Well, if she did, it was with horns now. She turned on me pretty quickly with a rant that went like this, 'Well, you got Jay into this mess. How are you going to get him out of it? You may lose this stupid project, but he stands to lose his job. Men! Jesus! You're so devious, so manipulative. You seem to enjoy screwing each other more than you do women. You're sick, sick, sick.'

"I got up from the chair and poured myself a drink, and then I went to the phone in the first-floor den. I called Cass and luckily managed to reach him right away. 'Hey, buddy,' I said. 'I've heard about the story you're planning to run tomorrow—how employees of several firms, including mine, are involved in some letter-writing thing. I'd drop it if I were you. Let the whole thing go. Remember those essays you bought from my store at university? I still have my records of every transaction made. It would be pretty embarrassing if it got out to the media that you, Managing Editor of the *News*, submitted plagiarized papers to get your degree. Could cost you your job, don't you think? Which is worse: phony A's or phony letters to the media? I suggest you drop your story unless you want the public to decide that one for you.' Cass didn't answer. There was just a long silence on the other end, and then he hung up."

"Jesus." Jack started pacing around Lou's den when he'd finished recounting all that had happened at the Walters' the evening before. "What a fuck-up. I don't know who has been hurt the most by this, you, Jay, or Cass. All of us, I guess."

* * *

Despite Lou's intervention, the *News* chose to run Cass's stunning exposé of corporate manipulation as its lead story the next day. In one important respect, however, it was an amended version of what Cass had originally intended. Lou and his firm were never named as among the conspirators. On the other hand, Jay's company, Universal Consulting, was cited, although Jay himself was not disclosed as the executive who organized the letter-writing by Universal's employees, nor as the person who had tried to persuade Cass directly and through Bev to support the project's going ahead.

While the Mapledome's future was now clearly in doubt, Lou's own reputation was still basically intact. Jay's rested on the outcome of an internal investigation by his company of how it had become entangled in the promotion of the project. And, once more, Cass had failed to exact full revenge for the Barbie Bigelow Affair.

Chapter 16

Leaving Toronto, the Sturridges' first stop was at Yonge and St. Clair Avenue for breakfast—fruit and yogurt for Susie and the once-a-month traditional English fry-up for Jack that Susie would allow him. Even in England, she had ruled out bread fried in bacon fat. Now, however, not only was he down to one such breakfast a month, but sausages and home fries had also been eliminated. Jack was careful not to complain too loudly about the restrictions for fear Susie would start using a calendar to keep more careful track of the frequency of his high-fat indulgences.

After breakfast, it was another arduous back-route drive out of the city. First, they went north on Avenue Road and, as they crossed Eglinton Avenue, Jack commented, "You know, when I was a boy, Jay and I used to ride our bikes out this street to little Malton Airport to watch the planes taking off and landing. The last part of the trip was through open countryside."

"Were they bi-planes then?" Susie teased him. "I'm surprised Jay didn't fly out—in that plane you told me about."

"No," Jack laughed. "It never got off the ground. Kind of like Jay himself."

At Wilson Avenue, they turned west and followed it to Jane Street where they headed north once more, following it out of the city, past miles of sterile warehouses, shopping malls, and housing developments, past Canada's Wonderland where Jack and Susie had forever failed to take their grandchildren on a day outing of stomach-churning rides, and past rows and rows of new brick homes that surrounded a mosque, largely hiding it from view. Several years earlier, it had stood conspicuously alone in a farmer's field like a two-seater plane that had made an unexpected forced landing in unfamiliar terrain. It was a route that revealed the relentless spread of suburbia from year to year and led Jack to comment, "Too many people. Something has to be done about it. Without population control, we'll never be able to save the environment before it's too late."

"Yes, dear," Susie yawned. She had heard Jack on this subject many times before. "Tell that to everyone opposed to family planning and abortion."

"In fact, everyone who doesn't accept the scientific explanation for the creation of the universe—everyone who believes in an afterlife."

"What about a beforelife?" Susie tried to distract him. "I'm not sure our kids realize we had a life apart from them before they were born."

"Certainly the grandkids don't, but then they have only a half a life anyway. The other they've surrendered to their devices."

"So, if you really are concerned about over-population and its impact on the environment, why don't you get active like Linda?"

"I don't know. It's just not in my nature, I guess. Nor in yours for that matter."

"My, you're really a barrel of fun to travel with today, aren't you? Dissing religion, dissing the grandkids and me as well as yourself. You—"

"Okay, so maybe I'm wrong," Jack retreated slightly. "Suppose there is an afterlife, but this is what it's like: all you get to do is sit on a cloud and look down at what your descendants are doing generation after generation. Imagine Shakespeare listening to his great-great- great- great- great- great-granddaughter talking: 'Me and Lucy would have went to the show, but she was, like, bummed out, so we just laid around getting stoned and stuff.' How long do you think Will could take that before he'd cry, 'Forsooth, 'tis time I breathed no more?' Five hundred years, tops, that's what I reckon."

"Ten in your case."

"Most probably." Jack leaned on his horn, angry at a driver coming towards them who had passed a car when he shouldn't have and forced Jack to slow down and drive onto the shoulder. "Idiot! This isn't Italy and he's not in a Formula One race... So here's an arrangement that I don't think would be too bad. Suppose we were alive for only three months of every year, but in exchange we got to live four times the normal lifespan. Not a bad plan, eh, if you're Canadian, since all we get with decent weather anyway is July, August and September. So, you're alive for those three and blank for the others, but you've got time in the three months of living each year to catch up on everything that happened in the other nine. Just think, if you lived to eighty, you'd have three hundred and twenty summers. Bliss! Now, the only problem is you've got to decide when to start living, since you can choose any date in history. So, the big question is, how far back in time do you want to go to start? Of course, that depends on how many years you are prepared to gamble on living in the future, given the current state of the planet."

"Not many if one's a pessimist like you."

"Oh, I don't know. I'd kind of like to be around to see how things play out, good or bad."

"You're nuts, you know?"

"I was just trying to change the topic from the unfortunate outcome of the Mapledome scandal that we were talking about over breakfast."

"Couldn't you have thought of something more upbeat than wild speculations about life and death?"

"Well, maybe we just should have stayed on the Mapledome because, to be upbeat about it, I suppose you could say that the outcome of Cass's exposé in the *News* could have been even worse than it was."

When Jane Street ended, the Sturridges turned west to Highway 27 with the aim of following it and various side roads north to the town of Coldwater at the edge of Georgian Bay. "How do you mean worse?"

"Well, Cass held back the information he had about Lou's firm being involved in the Mapledome project. If he'd included that, it could have been a lethal blow to the reputation of Piper, Langford and Jones. As it was, only rumours circulated, mainly in the ad industry, that Lou was involved in the scheme, and they didn't do him and his firm much harm. There were always rumours about Lou. Of course, Cass took quite a risk publishing as much as he did. Even though Lou's firm was left out of the article, Lou might have exposed his university cheating anyway to show his loyalty to Jay."

"What does it say of Lou that Cass was confident he could get away with naming Universal Technologies in the article?"

"That corporate needs run deeper than friendship, I guess."

"Poor Jay, he was the real loser."

"I don't know; everyone lost. Cass failed to bring down Piper, Langford and Jones, and he was so pissed off about it that he was hard on Bev. That's when their relationship started to deteriorate. The same with Lou and Sally's. Remember how angry she was at him that night when we went over to discuss Cass's article?"

"Yes. She was in her bedroom when we arrived and didn't come out for some time."

"Lou took us to his den to talk. I remember so well walking down the hall to it and passing the boys' doors. Scott had pasted a sign on his, 'Piper and Piper Enterprises Ltd. Please knock before entering.' It got me wondering if Lou had already supplied the boys with firecrackers to stoke their entrepreneurial drive."

"I'm sure Sally would have put a stop to that idea."

"That's assuming Lou told her about it. He would have been breaking a business confidence, and I don't think he would have done that. Not a good example to set for the boys. We passed Jeff's room, too. The door was open, and in the light from the hall we could see the poster he had tacked on the wall by his bed."

"You mean the one with a blow-up of his impish, freckled face? Even with braces, he had an infectious smile. What was it that Jeff had printed on the poster? I remember it made you laugh even though we weren't in any mood to."

"At the top, in thick, black lettering, he'd simply asked the question, 'Jeff Who?' and, at the bottom, he had printed, 'Jeff Piper of Piper and Piper, That's Who!' So young to be so politically aware. No wonder Lou was proud of them both."

"I'm not so sure about Sally, though."

Jack shifted uncomfortably in his seat, summoning to mind as many details of that evening as he could muster.

———

He and Susie had been in the den talking to Lou for about twenty minutes when Sally suddenly burst in, saying she'd just got off the phone with Linda. She stared angrily at Lou who was slouched in the leather seat by his desk, and never even acknowledged the Sturridges' presence. She simply lit into Lou right away for entangling Jay in the Mapledome business. There was a mixture of anger and dejection in her voice as she asked him what drove him to operate the way he did, why he involved their friends in his schemes, using them for his own ends. Lou swallowed hard before he answered that that was how business worked. He scratched someone's back one day, and they scratched his another. Linda just didn't understand.

Eventually, Lou motioned to Sally to sit down, but she wouldn't. Jack remembered that she looked plainer than usual that evening with her hair brushed straight for the night. Yet, there was still an ethereal movie star quality about her as she stood in front of Lou in a white satin negligée. She was carrying a magazine in one hand that she had apparently been reading in bed when Linda had phoned and suddenly she tossed it onto the carpet like a rejected screenplay. "How could you do this to Jay?" she asked sharply. "You must have known there was a risk he'd lose his job if it got out that he was involved in your scheming."

Lou answered that he never thought Cass would name Jay's firm in the article after he threatened to expose his cheating. But she didn't believe him and shot back that all he was trying to do was save his own neck. Then she really stabbed him, shouting. "How could you let this happen to Jay when your friends have always meant so much to you—you who are always talking about the importance of loyalty?" Lou didn't respond at first. He just stared at Sally for a long time and then at Jack. At last he'd closed his eyes and rubbed his index fingers in the corners, lost in thought. Sally knew she had hit him where it really hurt.

The Sturridges were about to turn onto Highway 400, for, at Coldwater, they had no real option but to follow it for the last hour to

Parry Sound. "You know, if we live much longer, we'll be doing trips like this all the way on the 401 and 400 again—in a self-driving car."

"Scary."

"No question. It will be like we felt hitch-hiking through France that first summer we were living in London. Remember how the people who picked us up drove like maniacs, darting in and out passing cars?"

"Yes, and we couldn't get them to slow down. They didn't seem to follow our French."

"We thought they were drunk, psychotic, or suicidal."

"No, I'd rather stay as we are on the back roads and not have to worry about a computer going haywire."

Jack laughed. "You may think I'm sick, but actually I'm pretty resistant to viruses." As they drove up the entrance ramp, he drifted back to that night at the Pipers'.

———

Jack remembered that eventually Sally sat down, curling up in a corner of the couch. She told Lou she used to believe him when he said he wanted to be rich just so that he could give their kids the things he didn't have growing up, that it wasn't just success that he wanted—that love and compassion came first, but now she didn't know. Then she buried her head in her hands and began to sob. Lou moved to sit beside her, but he didn't say anything for some time. No one did. Lou just stared out of the den window into the dark night, and Jack wondered if he could see his father standing in the family kitchen in an undershirt and suspenders, saying "Piccolo Construction. Hey, that sounds good. Piccolo Construc- tion." Or maybe he saw his mother by the kitchen sink, placing a bouquet of stolen, wilted carnations her Luigi had presented to her in a jar. Then at last Lou admitted to Sally that she was right, that he'd been pushing the Mapledome too hard, letting it get to him, which wasn't good. Unfortunately, however, he didn't just leave it at that; a few seconds later, he added that he thought his threat to Cass would protect Jay as well as himself, but he had been wrong. Still, he didn't want Sally to worry about Jay because he'd look after him whatever happened. That remark threw Sally into a rage. She leapt off the couch and shouted, "Of course! You'll look after him, won't you—you, the big fixer! Fucking men. You just don't get it, do you?" Sally charged out of the den, grabbing a coat from the hall closet to throw over her nightie. Susie followed her out to the garden, leaving Jack and Lou in the den, hashing over all that had happened at the Walters' the night before.

———

"Before we went to the Pipers' that evening, had Lou told Sally about how Linda propositioned him?" Susie asked.

"No. In fact, I'm not sure he ever did. I don't remember the subject ever coming up in conversation again. I think he just let it go for Linda and Jay's sake."

"I doubt that Linda said anything about it on the phone to Sally. I don't think she thought it was something she had to apologize for. As she saw it, Sally wasn't the least concerned about who was in bed with whom."

"I remember after you and Sally left the den, we discussed Linda's behaviour and the details of the article in the *News*. When we finished, Lou pulled from his desk drawer the foot-long model of the Mapledome I had seen in his office before the unveiling. Maybe it was another copy, I don't really know. He turned it over and over gently in his hands and I realized that he had concluded that the project was finished—that there was no way any investors would touch it now that it was embroiled in scandal. We just sat silently for some time, and I imagined that in his mind Lou was watching his complex rise on the waterfront amidst a sea of steel girders and spidery cranes, a proud edifice like the Taj Mahal. I know he planned to have seats at mid-field for football, a box on the first base line for the Jays, and another at centre ice in the arena to watch the Leafs. In his mind's eye, the Stanley Cup, the World Series, the Super Bowl, even the Olympics would all be at the complex one day. I know he looked forward to entertaining all of his friends there—at pre-game luncheons in the lavish stadium restaurant."

"Gosh," Susie interjected. "Even us. We'd have had to go?"

"Well, for the meals at least. You and Linda could have ducked out afterwards. Bev, he knew, would be ecstatic to get invitations and he'd be able to get autographs for her kids of all of the players in every sport. I know, too, that he had envisaged a gigantic gala opening. Bands, dancers, a torch parade, and, as they rolled back the duraplex roof for the first time, a massive display of fireworks. He would have expected that the finale would be followed by an awed silence among the hundred thousand spectators—until suddenly, spontaneously they would break into thunderous applause. I'm sure Lou anticipated that even Cass would come to love the Mapledome. The facilities for the press were, after all, to be second to none. And, in his heart, Cass loved spectator sports. As for Sally, I suppose he imagined she would enjoy the social prominence that would be entailed in attending all the events the Mapledome hosted. And himself? While he had kept his firm out of the consortium and any public connection with the project, he would have hoped that once the complex was complete and everyone was in love with it, word would slowly circulate that it was really he who was responsible for its construction—that it had been his tenacity and ingenuity that had made it happen despite all opposition. I think he felt that knowledge of his own role in the project would spread privately—in hushed, confidential conversations in the stadium restaurant and in the secluded bars after the games, that a sense of gratitude for his vital part would spread quietly without any media or other artificial hype. That's the way Lou likes to have things happen."

Jack paused as he looked out the window at their first good view of Georgian Bay near Port Severn. "Huh! The water is higher than I thought it would be. Lou will be pleased about that. Less likely anyone will prang up on that shoal near their dock… I'm not sure how long Lou and I went without speaking at that point, but looking back it seemed like ages. Eventually, however, Lou stopped fingering the Mapledome model. He pulled a silk handkerchief from his pocket and carefully polished the transparent roof. Then he rose slowly from his desk chair and carried the model to a cupboard. 'My dad would have liked it,' he said softly. Then he stooped down and packed the model away in a box in the corner of the bottom shelf. His monument to his father."

"Gosh, what a sad moment. That was it? The project just died?"

"Yes."

———

The *News'* report of corporate intrigue killed any hope of public financing, although the project was probably too big and expensive anyway, especially with the technology for the retractable roof untested. Soon after, a group called Ontario Dome Boosters emerged in place of Citizens for the Complex and site plans for a stadium sprang up all over Metro Toronto. In 1984, the provincial government finally announced a mixed public-private financial arrangement to build a domed stadium by the CN Tower. Lou tried to nuzzle his way into the Sportsmen's Club, the consortium of financial backers that was initially responsible for the private component of the costs. But they wouldn't have him. Later, he tried to get Piper, Langford and Jones associated with the group that eventually won the design competition for the SkyDome. He offered to prepare pro bono a dramatic video for their presentation to the Ontario Stadium Corporation. But it was the same story. No one in sports familiar with the Mapledome fiasco would touch him because of the rumours he was the invisible hand behind that project. So Lou went back to focusing on the less glamorous work of the firm.

———

"It was shortly after the exposé that Sally started spending more and more time in New York, wasn't it?" Susie asked.

"Right. I've always wondered if we could have prevented that happening."

"But how?"

"I'm not sure. Maybe I should have adamantly opposed his involvement in the Mapledome, especially the letter-writing campaign and his entanglement of Jay. That's what particularly upset Sally... Anyway, business in Toronto was a little slow for Lou for a while, so he turned to New York to take up the slack. He spent quite a bit of time there himself, but not as much as Sally."

"Do you think he wondered if something were drawing her to Manhattan beyond all it had to offer culturally?"

"No. Not at first at least. I think he felt simply that she was angry with him over what had happened and just needed to get away and have more time on her own. He knew she was searching for something else in her life—something more fulfilling than raising the kids and running the house. That's why he encouraged her to open a boutique or something in Toronto. He proposed it again after the Mapledome collapse, but she seemed to have lost interest in the idea. It was clear, though, that she was looking for something new and different to do. It may have been Linda's influence on her…or maybe Linda's psychiatrist's."

"Jack, she only saw the doctor once; she felt too uncomfortable to ever go back."

"Linda must have been very disappointed."

"She was only trying to help her, but Sally's never been the type to bare her soul."

"Well, eventually, she certainly bared her breasts for that guy in New York."

"Jack!—"

"When, though? Some time after the reunion in eighty-eight."

The traffic on the 400 was light that last week of August, and Jack was able to steal occasional glances out the window at the scruffy, stunted trees along the edge of the highway. "Fuck, I miss old sixty-nine. They've cut a route with practically no views of water. Tourists must wonder why they've driven all this way when the scenery is so boring… Ah, there's a sign with Bobby Orr's picture. It means we're closing in on Parry Sound." Jack rolled down his window and shouted, "Hey, Bobby, how are the knees?"

"What's wrong with his knees? They look okay in the picture."

Jack stared at her, bemused. "Oh, nothing that a surgeon couldn't fix." Then he drifted back to the Mapledome. "You know, I was never a fan of domed stadiums, even with retractable roofs. No more mud bowls and fog bowls. And only when the roof is open on a warm summer evening are you likely to see a little plane flying above the stadium, trailing a long banner, 'Susie, I love you. Will you marry me? Jack.'"

"If you had proposed that way I'd have been too embarrassed to answer."

"So, good thing I waited for you to pop the question."

"Oh gosh, not that line again!... I've never understood why the outcome of Cass's exposé affected him so badly. After all, he did manage to kill the Mapledome. He got his revenge for the Barbie Bigelow Affair."

"Yeah, but it wasn't a complete victory. I think Lou realized that about Cass—that it wasn't over yet. It was as if Cass had had a break in hand against him late in the final set and then an indiscretion from his past had caused him to double fault and the match had slipped away. Lou figured Cass was going to go on chasing down every ball until he had the opportunity to complete his revenge—to be first in the rankings."

"How sick!"

"No question. But it wasn't just his failure to expose Lou as the real villain in the Mapledome scandal that weighed on him. I think he really did feel bad about the impact of the *News'* story on Jay. That's why for some time he avoided seeing any of us. He was too embarrassed about what he had done. In fact, it was Lou who reached out to him rather than the other way around."

"It's amazing that he did."

"I know, but that's Lou. And, despite what had happened, I think he missed Cass's jovial presence, especially in the gloom after the collapse of the Mapledome. So, eventually he invited Cass to play tennis again at the Toronto Lawn Tennis Club, but Cass declined. I remember we saw Cass and Bev occasionally, but the others didn't. And when we were with them, Cass never gloated over his story in the *News*. It was clear he had mixed feelings about having published it. He seemed a changed man—frustrated that Lou had eluded him, wracked by doubts over his behaviour, and uncertain about the future. He started drinking more heavily, and not just beer, but hard liquor."

"Yes, Bev was worried about him and tried to get him to cut back, but he wouldn't. He just got angry at her, and that gradually affected their relationship."

"I think the problem was he had always liked Bev as a good times gal. But there were things about her that had always bugged him—her excessive energy and enthusiasm, her nostalgia for the fifties, the pop music she always played loud on the stereo—"

"Even her passion for her school kids," Susie added. "I think he believed that would disappear if he agreed to have children. But after Stephen, he didn't want any more, even though that poor boy spent most of his time with Marcia. When Stephen was with them, Cass could tell from the way Bev reached out to him what a good mother she would be, and that just unsettled him more."

"So, in the depressed state he was in after the exposé, what had only been petty irritations with Bev became amplified and he got increasingly critical of her."

"Verbally abusive really. We saw it at the reunion in eighty-eight."

"No question. By then, the writing was on the wall. Ah! Good old Parry Sound," Jack declared as they approached the exit to the centre of town. "Shall we stop for a cup of tea, maybe split a sandwich? We've plenty of time. Jeff isn't meeting us at Pointe au Baril until four."

"Sure."

"But let's go up the hill by the old railway station first and have a peek at the Bay."

They parked in front of the nursing home at the top of the hill and walked to the guardrail for the view. Ring-billed and herring gulls were using the stiff westerly wind blowing in the sound to hang almost motionless over the water far below them. Sometimes, however, like revellers who'd overstayed their invitation to cocktails, gulls would excuse themselves and leave the others at the airborne bar to dip and dive for mouthfuls of bugs. Jack turned around to face the sterile brick walls of the nursing home. "I loved the old Belvedere Hotel that was on this site in fifty-eight. It burned to the ground three years later, and Parry Sound lost a building of which it could be justifiably proud. Even with the view, though, I don't fancy moving into the nursing home, do you?"

"Not here. Hopefully not anywhere."

They drove to the bakery on James Street and ordered two teas and a chicken salad sandwich to split. Susie frowned as she returned to the conversation that had taken them all the way from Maine to Parry Sound. "I guess Jay and Linda were affected just as badly as the others by what happened, weren't they? After all, Jay lost his job. No one else did."

"That's true. Universal thought he showed poor judgement, pushing the Mapledome without the company knowing. Of course, true to his word, Lou looked after him and took him under his wing at Piper, Langford and Jones. But that was tough for Jay to take. I'm sure he thought he looked like a loser, something he dreaded more than anything else. But he put on a brave face. Do you remember how, a few weeks after he got fired, he invited me over to go jogging with him?"

"Only vaguely."

Jay started running regularly after the exposé, clearing his mind by listening to music on his Walkman while he ran along the leafy streets of Rosedale, past the homes of people who had "really made it." He was jogging his way through his mid-life crisis, Linda contended. The evening Jack ran with him, he found that Jay had reverted to his old defensive and self-absorbed self. He told Jack that he didn't mind being fired—that he had got as much out of Universal as he could, and that it was time to move on. Working for Lou was great, he claimed, because it was a whole new experience and Lou gave him a free rein. In fact, however, he only stayed a year and a half at Piper, Langford and Jones because Linda hated his being there. She was furious with Lou for enmeshing Jay in the Mapledome scandal, and it took her several years to forgive him.

Right after asserting he was happy working for Lou, Jay asked Jack if he knew that Henry Phillips had become a Queen's Counsel.

Clearly, that realization had got him thinking that maybe he should have stayed in law, that it was the right profession for him after all. Contemplating that possibility led him to pound the pavement harder, and Jack was having a hard time keeping up with him. There was an intense look about Jay. His clear blue eyes were fixed on the road ahead and he was squinting slightly as if that helped him to concentrate on his performance. He looked like a slightly overweight version of the Jay of old in his track shoes, grey pullover and pants, with a white towel wrapped around his neck. It was as if he were trying to get back to his old football condition, not just put behind him all the tactical career errors he had made since then. "Maybe I should have stayed in Ottawa," he mused, contradicting what he had said about law. "I could have moved to Industry, Trade and Commerce. It would have been less political and kind of like being in business. But…" He trailed off at that point, yet Jack knew what he was thinking. Linda hated Ottawa. It was too small a town and too incestuous for her to be happy there.

Jay moved on to Cass, but by then Jack was puffing hard, and wasn't sure how much farther he could go. They had only covered a couple of kilometres and Jack didn't want to call it quits before Jay had unloaded everything that was on his mind, so he willed himself to keep going. Cass, Jay said, was someone who really got to him, becoming Managing Editor of the paper with the second highest circulation in the country even though he had the ethics of a psychopath. "But I think Cass has peaked, don't you? I mean he's gone farther than I ever expected he would. But he's peaked. He's peaked too early."

Jack was really wheezing now and he knew that he would have to stop at any moment. But suddenly it was Jay who jerked to a halt. A sharp pain knifed through his chest and he rubbed it nervously until at last with relief he passed wind. "Maybe I shouldn't be jogging," he worried, "not until I have a checkup."

Up to that point, Jay hadn't said anything about Linda—about the open marriage business or her reaction to the Mapledome fiasco. Jack was sure he wanted to talk about her, so he asked him how things were between them, and he said ruefully that they could be better. "She's so complicated I don't know if I'll ever fully understand her."

Complicated? She's a maze without an exit.

———

Jack reminded Susie of Jay's comment about Linda, and she remarked, "It's odd that he said that. When I talked to Linda right after Jay was fired, it sounded like she was handling the situation well and being very supportive. I mean, she did tell me that for the first few nights after the exposé, she stormed about her loft hurling her books to the floor. She said she'd never forgive either Lou or Cass for what they had done to Jay. But, so far as Jay himself was concerned, she said she was determined to help him get over losing his job and to feel positive about the future."

"Well, the situation was much easier for her." Jack finished his half of the sandwich and downed the last of his tea. "After all, she didn't give a shit about Jay being fired. She wasn't the least interested in his job or anything about business. I'm sure she saw the whole thing—the Mapledome scheming, the exposé, the firing—as some kind of competitive, male macho thing."

"That's true. All that concerned her was its effect on Jay's psyche and their own relationship. She knew that he was pretty depressed after the firing—even after going to work for Lou, much as he tried to hide it."

"Is that why she abandoned the open marriage idea after just that one night?" Jack asked.

"No. I think it was because she couldn't really get into it—certainly not with Lou, hardly her choice for a lover."

"No, just someone who was convenient. Anyway, Jay's view of the state of their relationship was a lot different from the impression Linda gave you. After his stomach stitch passed, we walked on for about a half-hour until he sat down on a ledge at the front of someone's lawn and wiped his forehead with his towel. That's when he told me that, at first, after the blowup, Linda had been very supportive like you said, but gradually that had changed. Linda had come to the conclusion that neither of them was where they ought to be in terms of their emotional and intellectual development. Apparently, she contended that that accounted for their failure to get on with opening up their marriage. She was simply too dependent on Jay. He was a crutch she constantly leaned on to the point where he was smothering her identity."

"Oh, gosh!"

"Familiar, eh?"

"Very."

"Whenever it's calm, you can count on Linda to blow wind into the sails... Hey, do you want another tea?"

"Is there time?"

"Sure. On the new road, it's a much faster ride from here to Pointe au Baril than it used to be."

Jack got them two more teas and a cookie, but Susie declined her half. "I'm sure I've put on weight with all this time in the car and no exercise. I hope the water will still be warm enough to swim at the Pipers'."

"It'll be warmer than Higgins in September, especially with an offshore breeze."

"But not than Muskoka."

"No. Lake Joe would be warmer, but that's partly because Linda's presence heats it up. Anyway, while we were sitting on that ledge, Jay told me that Linda had started going to reparenting sessions. She learned about them from her transactional analysis instructor and was hoping they'd help her get to the bottom of her stunted development."

"Buried deep in her past, you mean? Yes, I remember her doing that."

"Well, what really troubled Jay was that she wanted him to go too, since she claimed that he had the same problem she did. Poor Jay, you know how impressed he's always been by Linda's eclectic interests and how open he is to suggestion? Well, not surprisingly, he agreed to join her after work at her next session."

"I'd forgotten about that."

The meeting was in a beat-up old building on Jarvis Street and, when Jay arrived, there was a woman sitting in a chair at the entrance in sandals, cut-off jeans, and a red T-shirt. Printed on it was a large, flowering plant of marijuana. He wanted to ask her if he was at the right place, but she never looked up at him and just went on mumbling a mantra. So he pushed the door open and noticed that, at the far end of the dimly lit lounge, there were some old couches and chairs that had been gathered in a circle. He couldn't hear anyone talking, so he thought perhaps the group had finished or was on some kind of break, and that just a few of the participants were hanging around waiting for things to get started again. Then, on one of the couches, he noticed a middle-aged man with a heavy white beard who was, in fact, talking, but very softly and slowly. All the others, Jay assumed, were simply listening to him. He moved closer and that's when he saw in the man's arms what he thought was a large baby doll. So he crept still nearer until he realized he was wrong. Cradled in the man's arms was Linda, wrapped in a soft woollen blanket, with one hand resting gently on the man's chest. In her mouth was a baby's bottle, filled with milk. Linda's eyes were shut, and she was sucking contentedly on the rubber nipple.

"Linda?" Jay shouted as he moved into the centre of the group. "No-o-o! What are you doing?" Her mouth dropped from the bottle and, as she turned her head towards Jay, she screamed—a blood-curdling scream was how he described it to Jack, like a baby with an unbearable spasm of colic. Jay called her name again and reached out to touch her, but she turned away and buried her head in the crook of the instructor's shoulder, crying. The instructor politely asked Jay not to bother her, but to sit down with the others and he'd explain what he was doing after the session was over. But Jay couldn't bring himself to do that. He just stood staring at Linda open-mouthed and confused. Jack could easily picture how he must have looked—like a boy whose helium balloon had suddenly and stealthily slipped from his fingers and was now a small speck, disappearing in the sky. Jay stumbled out of the room and down the stairs, vomiting when he reached the street.

"After he finished telling me about the reparenting session, Jay confessed that he didn't know what to do next. He said he knew he should go back again with her, and go through the whole thing himself, but he didn't know if he could. We both just sat silently on that ledge while Jay went on wiping his face with his towel. But then he said more brightly, 'Hey-y-y! What if you and Susie came with us? That would make it way easier to do.'"

"Gosh, I'd forgotten you told me that," Susie exclaimed.

"Yeah, I didn't know how to answer him, but eventually I said something about our not wanting or needing a session like that. He looked at me a little forlornly, and I knew he was disappointed, but I could also see that gradually he understood. I don't think he'd ever thought much about our own relationship before that moment, but over those few seconds he did, and, after a little reflection, he answered, 'No, you don't need that, do you?' That was all he said, and we got up to walk home."

"Oh, poor Jay!"

"I think that's when he finally recognized that he and Linda would never have a stable, conventional relationship. That's why, when she announced a few months later that she was going on her own to Pune, India, to the ashram of Bhagwan Shree Rajneesh, Jay seemed relieved. Wasn't that guy called the 'sex guru' or something?"

"Yes," Susie confirmed. "He favoured much more open attitudes towards human sexuality. That's what drew Linda to him in her search to uncover what was holding her back from sexual experimentation."

"I think Jay still loved her in a way and he certainly admired her intellectual curiosity, but the constant turmoil in their lives was wearing him down. After she left, I think he found a calm in his daily life that he hadn't experienced in years."

"His own Buddhafield."

"Kind of," Jack laughed. "While she was away, it was quite a burden for him looking after the kids, but I think he found it less stressful than when Linda was there. Besides, Lou was very understanding at work, letting Jay leave early to be with the kids at the end of the school day, and work from home if one of them was sick."

"But Linda's absence was hard on the kids." Susie broke a small corner off Jack's cookie and absently nibbled on it. "I'm sure they felt rejected even though Linda told me she wrote them long letters every week, reassuring them of her love and explaining that she had to get her own life in order before she could be a good mother."

"So what happened in India that led Linda to come back after only nine months?" Jack asked. "I've forgotten."

———

It turned out that Linda's time as a Rajneeshee corresponded with a bad patch for Bhagwan. He was having problems with Indian officialdom and they got so bad that he fled to Oregon. Linda stayed on for a while, assigned to the ashram's public relations department where she apparently wrote glowing copy about Bhagwan in an effort to preserve his reputation. But she didn't feel the same about the place without him there. "I ceilinged at the ashram, but the lights didn't come on," she lamented. Apparently, however, what she wrote for the media was so good that one of Bhagwan's disciples contacted her to join the Oregon entourage. But she decided to go home instead because she missed the kids and Jay, too. It was just as well she did because the Oregon ashram became entangled in criminal investigations, even an assassination plot. Bhagwan was eventually deported, and after being denied entry to a number of countries, he went back to Pune and Linda flew home to Toronto. It was the start of what she called their cocooning period.

Linda's return coincided with Jay's leaving Lou's firm to open up a bookshop on Harbord Street with Linda, New Age Voices. That, however, led to new differences between them right away. Jay thought they should offer a wider selection of books than they did — that they should carry all the best sellers at least. But Linda resisted yielding to what she viewed as establishment, capitalist thinking. So the shop retained its narrow focus and never showed a profit. That really bothered Jay. He worried about what Lou must think of him, running a failing enterprise.

Linda, however, didn't care. Money wasn't an issue for her. Her mother had passed away and left them a sizeable inheritance. Everything could have been fine for them, except Linda felt increasingly unfulfilled. Susie and Jack were never quite sure why—whether it was because she was no longer getting many of her articles published, because the bookshop wasn't doing well, or because she didn't like running it with Jay. Whatever, she felt her true identity was being stifled, and that that was a consequence of living in a male-dominated environment. She was determined to prove to herself that she could make it on her own—that she could be, as Jay would have put it, "a winner" without relying on anyone else, especially a man. And the strangest part was that, now, she wanted to make it in conventional society. Linda put aside all her interest in history, art, and archaeology and all her experience writing and went back to university to get a degree in business. On top of that, she told Jay she wanted to separate. And no sooner had he moved out to an apartment in the Annex than she threw out her batik skirts and took to wearing grey pin-striped suits and carrying a Samsonite briefcase. Linda was all Stanislav method, in Jack's view. She went deep into every role she played.

Lou in particular was tickled by the reincarnated Linda. After she got her business degree and landed a position with Wellington Securities, he loved to phone her and ask her for investment advice. He was impressed by how quickly she learned the business and how well she managed to get on in such a male-dominated profession, especially considering she was forty-six by then. So far as Jack knew, Lou never acted on her investment advice, but he did get a kick out of hearing her crisp analyses of hedge funds, companies to short, and those expected to increase their dividends.

———

Jack finished his tea and critically surveyed the walls of the bakery. They were covered in paintings and framed photographs of Georgian Bay: trees, rocks, water, and boats, its fundamental elements, interpreted with only moderate variety. "See. This is why I've never painted here. Too many artists doing the same sort of thing."

"Yes, but your work would have been different. I can imagine you painting the Belvedere Heights nursing home burning down and the old hotel rising from its ashes."

"Hey, now there's a good idea. Maybe I'll have a crack at it."

They were silent for a few moments while Susie nibbled the last of her cookie bite and finished her tea. "After Jay moved out, it was strange visiting him in the Annex, wasn't it? It must have been quite a change for him living in that little apartment after Rosedale." "Yeah, but at least he found it peaceful there." Jack stood up to leave. "And he had Sigmund with him, so he wasn't lonely, and he'd already got pretty good at parenting while Linda was away in India."

"I don't think it's ever a satisfactory arrangement to split children up if you don't have to," Susie said, rising. "But Linda was determined to keep Elizabeth with her and free her from a male-dominated environment."

"At least they were close enough that the kids could visit back and forth between the two homes. In fact, the four of them often spent the weekends together on Chestnut Park, didn't they?"

"Yes, and when they did Jay and Linda slept together. Linda told me she found their sexual relationship more satisfying after they separated. So all could have been smooth sailing again if Linda hadn't been nagged once more by doubts about the choices she had made. After she'd mastered it, the investment business bored her, and she was eager to start writing again."

"But there must have been more to her doubts than that for her to go as far as she did," Jack said as they reached the car.

"The main thing was that, deep down, she missed living with Jay."

"Missed having him to boss around you mean?" Jack began fumbling in his pockets.

"Maybe, but I also think she was afraid of losing him."

"Why?... Fuck! I must have left the keys in the café. Wait here and I'll run back."

"Take your time. No falls please. Not like last winter on Summerhill."

"That was because people don't bother to shovel their walks any longer."

"So why was Linda afraid of losing Jay?" Jack asked again when he got back to the car.

"Because she got it into her head that he and Sally were having an affair."

"That the flame had been re-ignited?" Jack started the engine and turned left past the post office to drive out of town.

"Yes. She knew that Sally and Lou's relationship had been damaged by the Mapledome business—that they were quarrelling a lot and that Sally was spending more and more time in New York. She convinced herself that, whenever Sigmund stayed with her in Rosedale, Jay would fly off to New York to meet up with Sally on the pretext he was going to buy books for the store."

"How likely was that when New Age Voices was already significantly in the red?"

"Exactly. But that's what Linda decided was happening. She claimed there was a new glow to Sally whenever she returned from New York. Linda was sure that Sally had a lover there, and that the person was Jay."

"So that made her jealous?"

"Yes, and aware again of the fact that she loved him and didn't want to lose him."

"So that's what led to the crisis."

"Yes."

"Christ, I remember it so well. It was just a couple of months before we were all to go to the Pipers' for that first reunion in 1988. What a prologue for that unhappy gathering."

Chapter 17

It was around eight o'clock one evening in June 1988 and the Sturridges were having a drink on their deck overlooking the garden when the doorbell rang. It was Jay in his track suit. He had jogged to their home from his apartment in the Annex and was breathing heavily, but more than that Jack and Susie were struck by his strained, anxious face. His appearance seemed to have transformed from youth to middle age almost overnight. "Are you okay?" Jack asked anxiously.

"Me? Oh, everything's okay with me. I've come about Linda." The Sturridges led him out to the deck and Jack fetched him a beer. "I've just been talking to her on the phone. In fact, it's the third time she's called me today. I'm kind of worried about her."

"Why? What's she calling about?"

"Well, I'm going up to the Pipers' cottage on Saturday for a week, and Elizabeth and Sigmund are coming with me. But she doesn't want Elizabeth to go because she says she doesn't want to be left alone. I can't figure her out. One minute she's telling me that I'm trying to take Elizabeth away from her and the next that she needs more fathering. All I'm doing is taking the kids on a short vacation. Elizabeth always spends part of every summer with me. That's been the arrangement ever since we separated. One minute, Linda tells me everything is great with her life—the market is booming and she's really busy. The next she says she hates her job and wishes she never got into business. Then she tells me she really misses me, and can't I at least come over and sleep with her. I've done that a few times, you know, but I don't think it's a good idea. I mean, we're only separated, but we should be getting divorced. That doesn't help us complete the break and get on with our lives."

Susie and Jack both nodded in agreement. "So, have you talked with Elizabeth about how her mother is?" Susie asked.

Jay nodded. "All I ever get out of her is, 'Oh, you know, just the same,' delivered in a flat, bored voice. I asked her, too, if she and Linda missed Sigmund and me and all she said was 'Do I miss my bedtime story? Duh!' I'm not sure what she meant, but it kind of spooked me. I think she's seen so much emotion from Linda that she's just shut down. I don't know what she's really thinking, or what she feels."

"Gosh, that is a worry," Susie concurred.

"Anyway, what really got me the last time Linda called tonight was when she said that she didn't know if she wanted to go on living if she was going to have to spend the rest of her life alone. That really shook me."

"Of course, it would."

"You don't think she meant it, do you? I can't imagine that she'd do something to herself. I mean, she can be pretty emotional, but she's always a bundle of energy and there's never enough time for all she wants to do. I don't think she's the type who'd cut her life short, do you?"

Not under normal circumstances, Jack thought to himself. *But if she'd been at Jonestown, she'd probably have drunk the Kool-Aid.* It was, however, Susie who answered vaguely soothingly, "I don't think so either, but I suppose you never know exactly what's going on in someone else's head."

"Anyway, that's why I came over. She really upset me with that line. I had to talk to you."

"Would you like me to go and see her?" Susie was certain that was what Jay wanted to hear.

"Hey-y-y, that would be terrific if you wouldn't mind. It would be better than my going over. We might just start fighting. Besides, I'm trying to loosen the tie."

It was close to ten o'clock when Susie arrived at Linda's. Elizabeth met her at the door, dressed in a plaid flannel shirt, blue jeans, and brown leather combat boots. Her hair was dyed orange and she had a ring in her nose and two more attached to her lips. When, right away, Susie asked her how her mother was, she displayed the same indifferent attitude Jay had described: "A bit spazzed. You'll see."

"Does she seem tense or depressed?"

"We've all got our problems."

Sixteen she is now, I think. I'm so glad I teach elementary school. It was clear to Susie she wasn't going to learn much from Elizabeth, so she tried a different subject. "Are you looking forward to going to the Pipers' cottage next week?"

That simply induced a shrug. "Been there before. It's no big deal." Elizabeth started up the stairs to her own bedroom. "You'll find her in the loft. Oh yeah, and shout if you need anything."

When Susie reached the third floor, Linda was standing by the window next to her desk, apparently transfixed by the swaying branches of a maple tree on the front lawn. To Susie's surprise, she was wearing a floor-length brown homespun dress; she had not, after all, thrown out all her former wardrobe in favour of corporate garb. One of Linda's arms was pressed tightly against her flat chest, and with the pale, fretful fingers of her other hand she was absently twisting a shock of her tangled hair. She turned towards Susie when she heard her approach, and Susie caught sight of the single strand of hair that had escaped Linda's clutch and chased across her taut, white mouth. From there it rose level with her swollen eyelids and disappeared in a fold of pallid skin.

"Susie!" Linda cried. "How wonderful of you to come." As she kissed her on the cheek, Susie detected a mixed odour of unwashed hair and alcohol, and that worried her because normally Linda drank very little. "I'm so glad you're here. This house is like a tomb. I hate it. I can't stand it anymore."

From her desk, she picked up the glass of Scotch and water she had been drinking. The ice had dissolved in the warmth of the June evening and the glass was wet. It had left a ring on the magazine she was using as a coaster, and Susie couldn't help but notice that it was open at an article on primal scream. It was clear that a reversion had occurred in Linda's evening reading habits as well. "I can't stand being alone. Why doesn't Jay understand that? Why doesn't he think of my needs?" She gulped at the drink and then resumed her pose at the window, dark and still, with the thin, tortured lines of a Giacometti sculpture.

"He is thinking of you," Susie answered. "In fact, he asked me to come and see you. He's worried about you...about your health."

"My health? Fuck my health. Why didn't he come if he's worried about me? Why is he going to the Pipers' next week, and taking the kids? It's always their place. I could take some time off. We could all go to Muskoka." Suddenly Linda whirled around from the window to face Susie. "Do you know what I think? I don't believe Jay really is going there. It's a ruse. He's dropping the kids and going to New York to shag Sally."

"Oh, Linda, you know that's simply not true. He's not seeing Sally. He wouldn't leave the kids alone at the Pipers', and he certainly wouldn't take them to New York if he were meeting Sally there."

When Elizabeth had gone to her bedroom, she had turned on her stereo and, through the floorboards, the relentless throb of her favourite rock band was penetrating the loft. Suddenly Linda tore out of the room and screamed down the stairway, "Turn that fucking shit off! Now! I don't want to hear it again. Ever!" She slammed the door of the den, and the beat immediately died away. "She's turning into a zombie," Linda said to Susie. "I don't know what to do with her." But then she abruptly left the room and ran down the stairs to Elizabeth's room. She was gone for several minutes during which Susie walked to the top of the stairs to try and hear what was happening. Eventually, she heard Linda's voice in the hall, coming towards the stairway. "Just don't play that stuff around your father, please. You know how he hates it," and as she climbed the stairs the music started up again, but more softly.

"I'm worried about her, Susie." Linda walked back into the den. "She needs Jay. I'm no good for her." Her eyes began to drip as if spilt black ink were running out of the wisps of hair traversing her face. "But I don't want her to go to the Pipers'. I don't want to be alone." She retrieved her glass of Scotch from the coffee table and placed it on the table next to her bed. As she lay down on her back with one forearm across her eyes, she wailed again, "I don't want to be alone, damn it. I want Jay and Sigmund here."

"You're not alone." Susie sat down on the bed beside her. "Elizabeth is here, and— "

"Why won't he try to understand me. I understand him. I've given him space when he needs it, but now we should be together. Has he thought about Elizabeth and Sigmund? What about their needs?"

Linda flung herself onto her stomach and lay there for a long time, sobbing, while Susie gently patted her head. "He is thinking of them. He's thinking of all of you."

Linda rolled over again and propped herself up on one arm as she opened the drawer of her bedside table. Her damp, matted hair fell like a black curtain across her face as she unscrewed the lid of her bottle of sleeping pills.

"You shouldn't be taking one of those," Susie scolded. "Not when you've been drinking."

"Fuck that." Linda fingered the pill in her hands and then popped it in her mouth, washing it down with the rest of her Scotch and water. She put the bottle back and lay down again. Quickly, Susie pulled the drawer open and snatched the bottle. "I'm taking these until the morning."

Abruptly, Linda sat up. "You don't think I'd—"

"Of course not. But you need to be careful. In the middle of the night you might forget that you've already taken one. I'm going to stay for the night too, just in case you need me to talk to."

Afterwards, Susie wondered if, by taking the bottle of pills, she had actually put the idea of suicide in Linda's head because at that moment she suddenly seemed transformed. "Hey, I'm okay... I'm okay. I feel better now." Linda lay down again on her back. "It's great that you are staying. It will be like old times—like back on the *Homeric* with you looking after me." Mistakenly, Susie thought it was knowing that she would be in the house that had calmed Linda. "What was the name of that bitch in the other lower? I've forgotten. In fact, I'm not sure I ever knew. Anyway, it was she who got fucked, not me. Always someone else."

"Oh, Linda, you—"

"Those were fun times, though, weren't they?... Hey!" Linda sat up again. "Maybe we could go back to Italy together, just you and me. Find another Dominic and Alfredo and really get laid this time. Well, maybe somebody better than Alfredo for you."

"We don't need that." Susie stroked Linda's hair. "Our lives are very good, you know. We've been incredibly lucky. Look at all the things you've done already—Thailand, Laos, India, your writing, the bookstore, business. We have a lot to be thankful for, and—"

"Yes, I guess some of it was good."

"Don't talk as if it's over," Susie protested. "There are more good times to come. We're only forty-eight."

"Only? Two years to fifty. I feel like Methuselah already." Linda laughed as she said it and Susie felt encouraged that she was relaxing, especially since she lay on the bed again, staring at the ceiling. "How's Jack?"

"He's fine."

"You're lucky, Susie. You found a nice guy. Like totally."

"I know I am. We both are."

"And he's very talented. Please tell him I said that."

"He's always appreciated your support." Susie was relieved that Linda seemed to be shifting from focusing exclusively on herself.

"Oh, listen. When you're talking to Lou, tell him to buy Futuretel. There's a rumour it's going to split two to one."

"He'd rather hear it directly from you."

Linda dropped the subject. "Sally seems more open. She's not repressing her feelings the way she used to. Tell her... Tell her, Jay... Shit, I've forgotten what I was going to say."

It was obvious to Susie that Linda's sleeping pill was taking effect. "Look, I'm going to go to bed myself now. Would you like me to stay up here? I don't mind sleeping on the floor."

"Oh, my darling Susie. You'll never change. No. No, thank you. Have Elizabeth put you in Sigmund's room."

"Are you sure? I don't mind sleeping here if you'd feel better knowing I'm right next to you."

"It's okay. I'm fine now, thanks." Linda repressed a yawn. "You go to bed. Elizabeth will get you anything you need."

"Well, you be sure to call me if you feel you need me—if you want to talk some more or anything."

"Thanks, Susie. Thanks for being the same old you."

Susie kissed her on the forehead and went downstairs to Elizabeth's room to explain that she was staying for the night. "You might as well crash in Sig's room. I'll get you a wash cloth and towel. How early are you leaving in the morning?"

"Probably around seven. I'll have to go home and change for school, but I'll come back tomorrow evening to see if your mom needs me here."

"Well, there's juice in the fridge, coffee, and shit," Elizabeth said as she closed her door.

Susie called Jack from the phone in the kitchen. "She doesn't seem fit enough to be left alone, and she says she wants me here."

"You're an angel to do that on a week night."

"You'll explain to Catherine and Tom in the morning why I'm not there?"

"No problem. They'll understand."

"It's hard to tell what's going on in Linda's head. Her mood kept changing and I seemed to be talking to decades of her all jumbled together like the strands of her hair. Gosh, it's messy."

Susie went to bed in her underwear but couldn't fall asleep for a long time. She kept running through her conversation with Linda, trying to sort out what was wrong with her and how much risk there was of her doing something foolish. And, when at last she dozed off, she awoke again with a start not long after. It was utterly silent in the house, yet she had an image in her head of Linda standing on a large, empty stage, screaming, "Jay, where are you? Elizabeth? Sigmund? Susie? Where are you?" She sat upright in bed, assumed she had been dreaming, and tried to recollect what had happened next in her nightmare. Had she heard a loud thud above her? Possibly. Coming from the hallway…of the…of the third floor? Yes. That was it! Susie leapt out of bed and ran up the stairs, shouting to Elizabeth at the same time.

On the floor, just outside the door to the den, she found Linda spread out motionless on her stomach. Her hair was hanging from her head like strands of seaweed on a beach. The bathroom door behind her was open, and through it Susie noticed an empty bottle of pills lying on the tiles. She had no idea what they were, but she realized right away that she had forgotten to check the cupboard in the bathroom to see what other pills Linda might have stowed in her loft.

Susie and Elizabeth dragged Linda to the bathroom toilet, lifted her by the waist and shook her. Then Susie stuck her finger down her throat, trying to make her vomit, while Elizabeth phoned for an ambulance.

To Susie, it seemed like hours that she knelt on the bathroom floor desperately trying to revive Linda. "Come on! Come on!" she kept shouting.

"I've phoned Dad as well," Elizabeth reported as she returned to the bathroom. "And Jack." She quietly studied Linda for a few seconds and then added detachedly, "Already dead, it looks like to me. Grody!"

"Come on! Come on!" Susie cried again.

Within no more than fifteen minutes of Elizabeth's call, the ambulance arrived, and a medic started attending to Linda.

Chapter 18

The Bay was still calm that August morning in 1988. Only scattered patches of ripples told Jack that by afternoon the wind would probably rise to ten or fifteen knots out of the west. The sky was clear, the cerulean blue of a barometric high, and the pines and granite ledges had the sharp lines of impending autumn. The climbing rays of the sun bathed the spindly, thirsty shafts of grass at the front of the Pipers' cottage in ochre, and the lichen clinging to the pink-tinted rocks looked like paint carelessly splashed from cans of orange, black, and ash grey. Two loons, which seconds before had been floating quietly near the shore calling to each other in ancient, melancholic notes, flew overhead, now shrilly sounding an alarm. And far away, the source of the impending danger was increasingly audible. There was the hum of an outboard heading out Hemlock Channel to the open, driving the birds to the shelter of the outer islands. As the boat drew closer, the voices of its occupants rose above the incessant whine of their engine and were borne clearly across the slumbering water.

"We'll shoot out past Caroline Island and still fish for a while before lunch. Then we'll take our catch somewhere down Mud Channel and fry 'em up on the rocks."

"Sounds great to me."

"Afterwards maybe we'll go out to the McCoys and latch into some big motherfuckers to take home."

"Excellent. I hear there are some real bazookas out there."

"You better believe it. Not a smallmouth under three pounds."

"What about walleye? I'd like to snaffle a nice six-pounder."

"Listen, you just tell me what you want, and I'll take you to it... Hey, whaddya say we crack open a couple. It's the best way to get rid of a hangover."

"I'm with you. Fuck me, I really tied one on last night."

"It's from Pine Haven Cottages." Lou lowered his high-powered binoculars. "Couple of months and those guys will probably land on our island duck hunting."

"Pine Haven is for sale, did you know?" Sally sipped from her mug of coffee. It was still cool sitting in the varnished deck chairs on the smooth granite at the front of the cottage and Sally was wrapped tightly in a quilted eiderdown.

"What are they asking?"

"Six hundred thousand, the Winslows told me."

"That's not bad considering the number of buildings at that place."

"A lot cheaper than Maine," Susie interjected. She was sitting next to Sally in a mauve woollen sweater and jeans, enjoying her second cup of tea.

"No. But how can the sort of person who would want to run it ever afford the payments they'd have to make?" Sally dropped her eiderdown and disappeared into the cottage, freshly repainted the preceding summer in the same colours the Pipers always chose: grey with white trim. She returned with a plastic jug and slowly watered her tubs of petunias and geraniums. Near them was a flagpole, hewn from a local white pine and rising twice the height of the cottage. Cass had run up the Maple Leaf first thing in the morning, but it was drooping listlessly from the top of the flagstaff.

"There goes the Planters' launch." Lou raised his binoculars again. "Looks like it's on its way in to the Ojibway... I'd love to have one of those. There're so few of them left. But Sally won't let me."

"Shepherds are beautiful, I admit." Sally didn't look up from her watering. "But the upkeep is terrific, and you have to treat them gently. That wouldn't happen with the boys."

"No, a rubber dinghy would be better," Jack concurred from his chair beside Lou.

"I wonder if they'd be interested in selling."

"Lou!" This time Sally lifted her head and glared at him.

Lou's glasses moved from the water to the naturally weathered steps leading down to his own boat. The sun was already gleaming off the smooth cedar planks of the floating dock Lou had had built two years earlier. With the water level on the Bay changing every year, he had finally given up on docks built on cribs with their tops at a fixed height. Floaters were more practical and in the long run less expensive, an argument he could use with Sally to persuade her he had earned himself a Shepherd. Bev was stretched out on a towel on her stomach, reduced to playing solitaire because Cass and Jay wouldn't join her in a game of Hearts. Jay was lying on the diving board in a pair of faded cut-offs. Despite the early hour, he was already covered in suntan lotion; fear of skin cancer was another emerging anxiety. Lou's white Whaler with its twin 70s was tied securely to the dock rings, and Cass was sitting in the bow seat examining the depth finder that Lou used to locate schools of bass. Not that he fished much—never more than once or twice a summer—but the equipment had caught his fancy. On the starboard side of the boat there was an antenna that Cass had extended. He'd turned on Lou's CB radio and was listening to the messages from cottage to cottage traditionally transmitted in the morning. Sitting in the deck chairs above the dock, Lou and the Sturridges could just catch the exchanges.

"Sandy Harbour calling Westerly, come in please."

"Westerly here. Go ahead Sandy Harbour."

"We've got a message for you from Jock O'Reilly. If you're going into Parry Sound today, he'd like you to pick up a case of gin for the rendezvous. They're a little low."

"That's a big ten four, Sandy Harbour. Will do."

"Paradise Island, calling Loafers Lodge," another transmitter broke in. "Do I have a copy?"

"This is Loafers. Go ahead, Paradise."

"Let's go to twenty-one."

"Loafers going to twenty-one."

"Paradise Island going to twenty-one." Cass turned the dial to continue to follow the conversation. "Hey, you racing today?"

"Ten nine."

"You racing today?"

"We can't. Our centreboard is broken. But we'll see you at the rendezvous."

"Breaker two one," a voice interrupted.

"Go ahead, breaker…"

"I should get a VCF." Lou turned from the dock to Jack. "Better range and less interference. And I'm thinking of trading in the Whaler for something faster. What do you think?"

"I like the Whaler. It's perfect for the Bay."

"Hey, that's the Mercers' boat. I haven't seen it all summer." Lou trained his binoculars on the water again.

Sally stood up from deadheading the geraniums and shielded her eyes against the increasing glare on the water. "No, theirs is a cedar strip. That's the Greers'. They just bought it last month."

She sat down in the deck chair beside Susie again, the plastic jug in her lap. For the first time, Susie noticed how much Sally's appearance had changed. The skin on her hands was stretched tight and blue-grey veins criss-crossed the surface like the tangled branches of a bramble bush. There were dark half-moons under her eyes and her lids looked puffy as well. Sally had flown in to Toronto from New York only the day before and then immediately taken another flight from Toronto Harbour to Parry Sound. There, a pilot familiar with the Bay had flown her to the Pipers' cottage. Sally wasn't particularly happy to be there, Susie sensed, but, nevertheless, she had made a big effort to get to the cottage on time for Lou's sake. This fact, plus the absence of the glow that Linda contended signalled that Sally was having an affair, led Susie for the moment to suspend judgement on the state of the Pipers' relationship. "What are we going to do about the rendezvous?" Sally asked Lou.

"Go," he said flatly, still studying the disappearing boat through his glasses. Jack could tell, however, that the water traffic wasn't the only thing on his mind. He seemed distracted, absorbed in an end-of-summer assessment of where things stood in his career. Piper, Langford and Jones was chugging along quite nicely both in Toronto and New York, but there was nothing exciting or glamorous going on with the firm. He had been missing the Mapledome project badly for several years now, Jack surmised, and he needed something new like that to spice up his life.

"What? *All* of us go?"

"Why not? You want to go, don't you?" Lou turned to Susie and Jack.

"It doesn't matter to us," they answered together.

"Are you sure that isn't the Mercers' boat?" Lou asked Sally.

"Maybe they painted it."

"Paint over a cedar strip? *They* wouldn't do that!... We can't all go. Bev? Cass? I mean it's not intended as a hotel staff reunion."

Lou rested his binoculars on his red pullover and for a long time the four of them stared silently over the water. It was a solid sheet of rippled tinfoil now, and the flag was stirring at the masthead. "Oughta be a good wind for the race," Lou said at last.

"Mmmm," Sally murmured. She realized it was pointless to argue against going to the rendezvous that would follow it. Lou was oblivious to the embarrassment she felt at the thought of arriving with a mixed bag of uninvited guests who clearly didn't belong in the Ojibway crowd. If any of his friends wanted to go, that was fine with Lou; they would all go together. It had been his idea to have all of the old gang at the cottage at the same time—to clear the air so to speak after everything that had happened, affecting the intimacy of their friendship. All of them had been at the Pipers' on different occasions, but they had never been on the Bay together since the Ojibway in 1958. It was time—past time, Lou concluded, to get everyone there and start afresh. He wasn't going to precipitate a new division by separating his friends into those who were rendezvous-acceptable and those who were not. Sally finished her coffee, but as she got up to take her mug to the kitchen, the Sturridges saw her glance towards the guest cabin thirty yards from the main cottage, nestled at the edge of the woods. "What about Linda?"

"She won't want to go."

"No. I suppose not."

On the small, unscreened porch of the cabin, Linda was sitting in a wicker rocking chair. Her face was pale, but her long black hair, heavily flecked with white and grey, was neatly brushed and hanging straight around her shoulders. She looked completely composed. A large notebook was resting in her lap and she was writing rapidly, totally absorbed in her work.

"Hey, what's with Spooky anyway?" Cass turned off the CB as the Sturridges walked down to the dock, leaving Lou sitting in his deck chair and Sally tending to her flowers again. "I hear she slashed her wrists and ran screaming all over Toronto in the nude."

"No, it was nothing like that," Susie answered defensively. "She inadvertently took an overdose of sleeping pills."

"Inadvertently? How the shit do you do that?" Cass climbed out of the Whaler and joined the others on the dock.

"I think she woke up several times in the night and took a pill or two. She was disoriented and, each time, she forgot what she had done before."

"Sounds like bullshit to me."

"Cassie!" Bev scolded him.

"Susie knows," Jack intervened. "She was there. In fact, she helped save Linda."

"Shit, Susie, I thought you had more sense than that."

"Cassie! That's a terrible thing to say."

"Oh, come on! Lighten up. I was just joking... So how's she doing now?"

"She's recovering well. She's resigned from Wellington Securities and she's started writing again." Susie didn't mention that Linda had had some sort of religious epiphany when she was unconscious from the overdose and that the article she was currently writing was about that experience: *Life Begins with Death.*

"Her recover? How do you recover when you've been a total ditz all your life?"

"Cassie, stop it! You can't say things like that."

"Oh, fuck, I can say what I like. Hey, Linda," Cass shouted in the direction of her cabin. "Wanna hear a joke that'll make you laugh your tits off?"

"Cassie! Please!"

There was no response from the little porch.

"Oh, I see you've already heard it."

"Cassie, that's awful. You really mustn't talk like that." Bev's face was red with embarrassment and she was casting anxious glances at Susie and Jack.

"Ah, shut the fuck up, bitch, you're bugging me."

The Sturridges walked to the end of the dock to distance themselves from Cass, leaving Bev to deal with him on her own. As they moved, they heard Bev say, "I wish you wouldn't speak to me like that, especially in public. It's embarrassing." She rubbed her bare foot against his thigh, coaxing him to show his better nature—to be his old self.

"And I wish you'd get the fuck off my case. You're turning into Little Goody Two Shoes."

Susie had decided to provide to Cass the best explanation she could of the dramatic episode with Linda. In fact, however, she had actually convinced herself that Linda wouldn't have taken the pills at all if she herself hadn't put the idea in Linda's head by taking the bottle from her bedside table. As it was, she saw the attempt as half-hearted at best. She doubted Linda would have taken the risk she did if she and Elizabeth hadn't been in the house. On top of that, it seemed clear that Linda had called out to them soon after swallowing the pills. Admittedly, she hadn't rushed down to them right away to tell them what she had done. But Susie decided that that was because she wanted to be rescued—she wanted someone to come to her rather than the other way around. Indeed, later, Susie had learned that Linda had called Jay first, before shouting out to her and Elizabeth, but apparently, in her confusion, she had dialled the wrong number. For Susie, the whole sequence of events pointed to one specific intention on Linda's part—to draw Jay back home to her, and that is what had happened—for the short term at least. But now the Sturridges were witnessing another relationship that was in trouble and that saddened them both—for Bev's sake in particular.

Bev picked up the playing cards from her towel and returned them to their package. To show Cass how much he had hurt her feelings, she walked out on the diving board and sat down next to Jay. "Hey, I get my kids back next Tuesday. Isn't that awesome? Wow, I love September."

"No-o-o! I hate it. The end of summer." Jay sat up and rubbed some more suntan lotion on his face and chest. "How do you stand being around so many kids all the time? Two are more than enough for me to handle and it's only part time."

"I love it. They're so cute. One of my kids from last year came around to see me the other day. Raymond Parker. He has the cutest dimples. He brought me a chocolate bar. Of course, he'd eaten half of it by the time he got to our house."

"That's kids for you." Jay was only half listening. His mind was on the future, what was going to happen with Linda, what he was going to do himself. With Linda planning on returning to writing full time, should he bother keeping New Age Voices open, or should he shut it down, and if he did what would he turn to next?

Cass got up from the dock and retied one of the bumpers on Lou's Whaler. It was hanging too low and the fibreglass finish was being scuffed by the dock. Jack was struck by how at ease he seemed to be toying with one of Lou's favourite possessions despite the way he'd destroyed Lou's most precious one. But then Lou had had Cass and Bev to the cottage two or three times since the Mapledome's demise in an effort to mend their relationship; it was clear this tactic had worked. Of course, Jack surmised that Lou had another motive as well for being nice to Cass: it was best to keep him in his sights, should he be looking for a way of completing his revenge for the Barbie Bigelow Affair. "Hey, I could do with a beer," Cass shouted. "Anyone else want one?"

"Cassie, no!" Bev climbed off the diving board and tried to throw her arms around him. "Don't start drinking. Not now, it's way too early."

"Hey, Jay, you want a beer?"

"No thanks."

"What about you, Jack?"

"Not before sundown."

"Sundown? Shit, I plan to be wasted by noon."

Cass started up the stairs to the cottage and as he left Jay rose from his towel, stretched, and plunged into the water from the end of the diving board. He swam a few strokes and then climbed out by the ladder. "I was just figuring it's thirty years since that summer at the Ojibway." Jay rubbed himself vigorously with his towel.

"Yeah, that's why Lou got us all here," Jack answered.

"Kinda makes you think, though, doesn't it? Will we all be

around to do it again in another thirty?"

"Oh, stop it, Jay-Jay," Bev scolded. "Don't be so morbid."

Cass returned to the dock carrying two open beers. Bev was back at her towel and deck of cards, and he stooped to kiss her on the forehead. "Sorry about that, Scottie baby. I didn't mean what I said." Jack and Susie looked at each other with relief. He walked to the end of the dock and offered Jay one of the beers, but he declined. "You know, I'm fucking sorry about that article on the Mapledome. Did I ever tell you that? To your face, I mean. Yeah, I hated naming Universal. But what could I do? I had to do my job as a journalist."

"Sure," Jay answered unconvincingly.

"But I avoided naming you, eh?" Cass started on the beer he had brought down for Jay. "And I never thought it would cost you your job."

"It's water under the bridge now," Jay answered. "I'd had enough of Universal anyway. I'm happy with what I've been doing since."

Jack and Susie could hear most of the exchange and they knew it was the closest that Cass would ever come to an apology, yet it had taken him more than seven years and a few beers to make it.

After Jay's response, there was an awkward silence on the dock as if no one had anything else to say to anyone. But Bev filled the void. "Hey, you guys, let's go over to the Ojib. The dock will be really busy now." She hauled her chubby body from her towel. "It would be neat-o to just sit there and watch all the boats come in, see if there is anyone we recognize."

Cass had moved from the diving board back to the Whaler and was wiping down the decks with a damp sponge. "Naw. There'll be no one there we know."

"Sure there will." Bev flicked her towel at him and started up to the cottage. "I'm going to see if Sally and Lou want to go. You can drive, Cassie, just like old times."

"Wanta go?" Cass asked the others.

"What do you think, Jack?" Jay asked as he watched Bev slowly climb the stairs, his expression mixing patronizing fondness and bemused incomprehension.

"Susie and I are game, but you guys decide."

"I feel too beat to bother really," Jay said as he applied a fresh layer of lotion.

Cass tossed the sponge onto the floor of the Whaler. "I'll go and see what Lou thinks."

***

In the end, there wasn't the interest to mount a trip to the Ojibway Hotel, and Sally went on her own to the rendezvous in the Pipers' second boat, a blue bow rider.

"I'm thinking of closing New Age Voices," Jay said. "It was really Linda's thing not mine. But I don't know what to do next. I think I'm cut out for business, but I just don't know what area to get into."

"You can always come back to Piper, Langford and Jones, if you want."

It was early evening now and Jay, Lou, and Jack were sitting in the deck chairs at the front of the cottage. Susie had gone to talk to Linda in her cabin about how her writing was going, Bev was in the kitchen, and Cass was sitting alone in the stern of the Whaler having a martini. Lou had been in his deck chair most of the day, leaving it for only brief interludes, and he'd chosen not to go to the rendezvous with Sally in order to be with the others. Everyone had joined him at one time or another at the front of the cottage. To Jack, it was as if he were the Godfather, receiving his minions in his outdoor office, dispensing advice, issuing instructions.

"Maybe what I'll do is turn New Age Voices into a full-fledged bookstore, make it the flagship in a chain."

"Risky business these days," Lou answered. "Why not something a bit more general: books, music, and a coffee shop?"

"Or books and art?" Jack suggested.

"Hey-y-y, I like that idea. Maybe all four. I wonder what…" Jay's earnest voice trailed away, and Jack noticed him looking in the direction of the cabin where he and Linda were staying. "You know I've moved back in at Chestnut Park, eh? Ever since…ever…"

Lou and Jack silently nodded.

"She wants me to stay, did I tell you? I mean permanently… but I don't know. We've gone through so much. I guess I still love her, but I don't know how much more I can take. I'm pretty happy living on my own. It's way more relaxing, and I think it's worked out pretty well for Sigmund, too… Maybe not for Elizabeth, though."

"I don't think you should stay at Chestnut Park," Jack advised. "I'm sure it's helped Linda get back on her feet having you there the past two months. But if you stay together at some point the shit is going to hit the fan again. What do you think, Lou?"

"I think it's time to make the separation official and then divorce, but with custody of the kids if possible."

"No-o-o! Really? That might send Linda around the bend again."

"Or you, if you don't," Jack cautioned.

"Hey… No-o-o." Jay wiggled his feet nervously, slowly digesting their unsentimental advice. "Hey, can I ask you guys a personal question?"

"Shoot."

"So, how often do you do it… I mean, you know…?"

"What's the matter? Having trouble?" Lou was unable to repress a grin.

"No, no. No problem. Just curious what the average is."

"Hey, come on fella," Lou laughed. "You know I've never been average. Better hear Jack on this one."

"I've never counted."

Lou reached over and patted Jay on the shoulder. "Don't worry about it. Everyone hits a dry spell now and then."

"Hey, I'm not worried, guys. I don't want you to get the wrong impression. I was just curious—"

"So, I presume you've been sleeping with Linda again since you moved back in?" Jack interrupted. "Maybe that's the problem. She's put you through so much, she's snuffed out the candle, so to speak."

"No-o-o! Hey, no-o-o." Jay rose from his deck chair and started down to the dock. "Talking to you guys is depressing. I need Cass to tell me a couple of jokes to cheer me up."

Lou and Jack sat silently for several minutes while Lou occasionally glanced through the binoculars that were still hanging around the collar of his red pullover. They had always been comfortable together not talking, each knowing that the other would speak when he felt he had something worth saying. Jack surveyed the rolling Bay without the aid of glasses; the wind wasn't dropping with the sun the way it usually did and whitecaps had formed on the crests of waves that had been even in the afternoon. "Sally is going to get bounced around a bit coming home."

"Yeah, but I'm not worried. She's good at handling rough water." Lou glanced at his watch. "Huh, I thought she'd be home before now. Must be a good party." He put the binoculars to his eyes again and this time pointed them in the direction of Hemlock Channel. "Ah, I see her coming now. I better go light the barbecue." When he got back, he said, "You know, maybe I should have really pushed Sally to open that shop she used to talk about, the Pewter Pot I think she was going to call it. Now she's no longer interested in the idea... Well...I'll think of something, I guess."

There were several bursts of raucous laughter from the dock and it appeared that Cass was, indeed, cheering Jay up with jokes as he poured himself martinis from the jug resting beside him. Bev could hear them all the way from the cottage and left the kitchen to join them, hoping for a good time that Cass wouldn't spoil. Shortly after she reached the dock, Linda and Susie walked onto the porch of the cabin where the Walters were staying. Linda was dressed the same as she had been all day, except that a brown sweater was now draped over her slender shoulders. Jay saw them come out and looked anxiously towards the cabin, unfortunately alerting Cass to their presence. "Hey, Linda!" he shouted loudly "How is the article coming?" In their different locations, Susie and Jack tightened, realizing that Jay had been indiscreet enough to tell Cass what she was writing about.

When no answer came from the cabin porch, Cass repeated, "Hey, Linda, how's it going? Have you died yet?"

"Oh, Cassie, no! Please!" Bev cried as she tried to smother his mouth with her hands.

"Oh, my! No answer! Thank the good Lord." Cass pushed Bev away from him. "Come on, leave me alone, you fat little fart. I'll say whatever the fuck I please... Hey, everyone! That isn't Linda on the porch. It's her ghost. Three cheers!"

"Oh, Jay-Jay, I'm so sorry." Bev buried her face in her arms and sobbed. "Cassie, go to our room. Go. Please. You need to sleep it off."

"I'm not fucking going anywhere. But you...you can go to hell. I don't want to see your ghost even."

"Oh, Jesus! Why is this happening to me?" Bev puffed out her cheeks, and air rattled between her lips as she pulled herself up from the dock. "Sorry everybody, I really am," and she started up the steps to Linda's cabin to apologize.

Cass downed the rest of his martini in one gulp and climbed the steps to the deck chairs, waving his empty jug. "Sorry about that, Lou," he said as he passed. "Totally unrehearsed."

Lou and Jack watched him disappear into Linda's cabin and then come out hauling Bev by the arm. A little later, they could be heard quarrelling in their bedroom in the main cottage until finally the room went silent.

"Have you seen him like this before?" Jack asked Lou.

"Yeah, but not this bad."

"What do you think we should do?"

Lou just shrugged. "Not much we can. I don't think he's drunk enough yet to pass out, but he probably will pretty soon." They sat silently reflecting on the situation until Lou picked up the pad of foolscap that had been lying by his chair all day. At the same time, he handed Jack a crimson leather folder. "Here. Have a look at this. I'd like to know what you think." Lou began writing notes on his pad while Jack perused the folder. Inside it there were several sketches of twelve-metre yachts in boisterous flight across heavy seas. All of their hulls and sails were painted in creative combinations of red and white and little designs of maple leaves had been skilfully brushed on in various strategic locations.

"Your art department?"

"Yeah, they did them up for me last week."

"They're good. So what's up?"

"I'm trying to get a bunch of guys together to mount a challenge for the America's Cup. We've never won it and we haven't been the challenger since eighteen eighty-one. Here. What do you think of these?" Lou passed Jack the top sheet from his pad of foolscap. On it, he had jotted names that had come to him while he spent the day in his chair: CHALLENGE NORTH; ONE CANADA; ICEBOUND; SNOWBLOWER; CANADIAN CAPER; TRUE NORTH; ON GUARD; MAPLELEAF FOREVER. "I think I like ON GUARD best. What about you?"

"Sounds too much like a deodorant."

Lou laughed hard at that—harder than Jack had heard him laugh for some time. "Yeah, you may be right. How about MAPLE-LEAF FOREVER? I really like that one, too."

This is vintage Lou, Jack thought to himself. *He's like a teenager setting out to write a book. He has the title and the dust jacket design already, but there's nothing yet to go between the covers.* Lou had no organizing committee, no financing, not even a skipper. Jack recognized that some people would say that that was typical Lou—just a lot of big ideas and fancy packaging. But he saw it differently. It was Lou picking himself up from the Mapledome collapse at last and thinking big and bold again. It was a risk-taker planning to be in on a project from the inception—the person who would put all the parts together and make things happen.

Towards the open, there was the sound of an outboard slapping against the waves as it beat its way towards Hemlock Channel, and Lou raised his glasses to watch it. One moment its varnished bow was riding high out of the water, and the next it plunged out of sight into a deep trough, drenching its two passengers in a thick white spray. "I wonder if they caught anything." Lou studied the boat through his binoculars. "It was pretty rough out there for fishing."

"Hey, Pinky-pooh!" Bev burst out of the cottage and hurried towards Lou's deck chair. "I've got a great idea! Let's all go over to the Ojibway and roast wieners at the campfire on the back of the island." She was struggling to lighten the atmosphere after the embarrassing outbursts from Cass—trying to get those awkward moments out of everyone's thoughts. "We could sing some of the old songs. You know, a few drinks, a few laughs. Wouldn't it be fun?" Lou grinned at Bev and put an arm around her shoulder. "Wieners? Well...ah...Sally got some steaks at the Station. Filet mignon. I've lighted the barbecue."

"Oh... Oh!" Bev hid her disappointment behind a brave smile. "That sounds super!"

Chapter 19

"Hey, that's where you probably would have taught, if we'd ever settled in Parry Sound." The Sturridges were passing William Beatty Public School on their way out of town.

"You mean you actually thought of our living here?"

"It passed through my mind. Way cheaper housing than in Toronto. We could have bought a big house with plenty of room for a studio."

"But you've never painted the Bay."

"Maybe I would have if we'd lived here. Do you think you would have liked it?"

"Me? Those long winters?"

"The kids on that playground look happy."

"Oh, teaching here would have been okay. It's…"

Jack laughed. "A road fortunately not taken, I guess. We've been lucky. Not many wrong turns."

"You know that night Linda attempted suicide was probably the worst moment of my life. I felt so helpless waiting for the ambulance to get there, and angry with myself for not sleeping in Linda's room. I'm sure I could have talked her out of taking the pills. I should never have left her alone."

"It wasn't the sort of thing you'd think Linda would do. Sure she's kooky, but she's too involved, too active to have really wanted to end her life. And look how quickly she bounced back. By the time of the reunion, she was forging ahead as if nothing had happened apart from acquiring a good storyline."

"Gosh, that reunion was awful. Cass was terrible. I hope this one won't be as bad, but I have to confess I'm rather dreading it."

"Well, I'm sure Cass won't be there, and Jay may change his mind about going if he learns Linda plans to show up with her new lover. I must say, though, that after the last one I never thought there'd be another. I'm sure there wouldn't be if it weren't for Lou."

"But why, after all that Cass has done to him, is he so forgiving?"

"Nostalgia, I guess. We've shared a lot together, both good times and bad. Lou likes being with people he knows well. For him there's a comfortable predictability to it—"

"Even when their behaviour is unpredictable?"

"So it seems. He forgives the faults of those he's closest to. Maybe we're all like that. We want the companionship of old friends because of all the memories."

"Mmm." Susie didn't sound convinced.

"You know how we've talked about where it would be best to be in a major disaster like a pandemic or nuclear war even?"

"Yes. Maybe we should have that conversation again. I do feel threatened; those awful attacks on Yonge Street and the Danforth haven't helped. There's so much happening on the planet that isn't good. Everything is changing so quickly."

"Well, maybe the best place to be in a disaster would be at the Pipers' cottage. It's in a pretty isolated location and Lou has an instinct for survival."

"In that case, I hope it's not winter."

"We could fish through the ice. No, when I picture the Bay it's always in summer. I see Lou and Sally in yellow sou'westers standing together by the helm of their Boston Whaler as it crashes through five-foot rollers. Lou is at the wheel, struggling to stay on course, and Sally is anxiously scanning the bubbling water for shoals as they weave through a fleet of islands that could be frigates and destroyers on patrol. The Whaler passes near a steep, rocky promontory where a single, defiant pine clings to the stingy soil, stooped with its back to the wind and its outstretched arms trembling—the limbs of an old man stubbornly taking his constitutional. Did I ever tell you that I read once that, in the old days, the priests of Quebec City feared that if young settlers caught sight of the Bay they would forever be lost to church and duty? So an edict was issued that anyone who dared dip a paddle in the Bay just for pleasure rather than for faith or commerce would be flogged in the central square of the city. And on a second offence, they would be banished to virtual serfdom in the galleys of Toulon."

"Well, I'd have been safe," Susie answered. "I've never paddled on the Bay."

"Nor have I... Oh, wait a minute. I forgot. I did once in fifty-eight. I took Mary-Anne Thompson out by canoe to Hole-in-the-Wall."

"And what pleasures did you engage in?" Susie gave Jack a severe school-marm glare.

"Oh! No, I dipped my paddle for faith only—faith that you would come along."

Susie smiled. "In any case, I think you could do with a belated paddling right now... No, your image of the Bay is too bleak and wild for me. I prefer Higgins even on a foggy day when we walk the beach and ghostly apparitions suddenly appear and then slowly vanish again. I love that taste of salt on my lips, the feel of soft wet sand between my toes, and the swooshing sound of the receding waves."

"Like Dover Beach?"

"Yes, but softer. And I like the way I can walk up the road and be back in warmth and sunshine right away."

"Buying corn at the vegetable stand. I like all of that, too. And Muskoka. There I see a swinging, canopy-covered couch on a wide verandah. Through the dapple-green leaves of maples and the curling white bark of birch trees, I catch glimpses of a glassy stretch of water. It starts at a boathouse and dock near the cottage and halts a mile away at a cyan-coloured bluff that calls out for childhood exploration."

"I see you examining the scene with a brush in hand. You're holding it at eye level, pointed towards the horizon, deciding what you need to add to the picture for perspective."

"In the foreground I'd paint a red canvas canoe, gliding across the black ink surface, rippling the silken sheet and sending out circles that slowly widen until they brush against bleached driftwood lying on a scrap of yellow, sandy beach."

"No need to paint the picture. I can see it clearly."

"No, I wouldn't really. You know, I love them all. Maine's rugged coast and frigid surf contrast with the beachcombers and languid teenagers stretched out on the warm sand, listening to pop music. Muskoka climbs beguilingly into my memory and curls up with the seductive charm of a young lover."

"Not Mary-Anne Thompson again, I hope!"

Jack just laughed. "But it's the Bay that I find particularly special. It battles incessantly for my undivided attention, repulsing all distractions."

"My, how poetic you are this afternoon! Was your tea laced with something?"

"No, but I may need it to be tomorrow. I feel a nuclear winter coming on, and we won't be toughing it out alone with Lou and Sally."

"So it wasn't long after the reunion in eighty-eight that Cass and Bev split up, was it?"

"No, they stayed together for another year or so in Bev's house, but their relationship just went on deteriorating."

"Because of Cass's drinking."

"That was the main problem, but I'm not sure what caused him to drink more and more until he was an out-and-out alcoholic. I don't know what a psychiatrist would say, but I think it was the outcome of the Mapledome exposé. It just kept eating away at him for years. He was frustrated that he had not got complete revenge for losing out to Lou with Barbie Bigelow. At the same time, he felt guilty that his article in the *News* had cost Jay his job. But he was angry with Jay as well, and with Bev and me for acting, as he put it, as Lou's secret agents. So he developed a persecution complex, and it grew worse the more he drank."

"And he dealt with it by verbally abusing Bev."

"Yeah, but there may have been another problem behind the drinking. I'm not sure he ever really loved her, and the longer he lived with her the more her personality irked him."

"Poor Bev. At least in the end, she had the courage to toss him out of her house."

"No question, it was really hard for her to do. Despite all that had happened, I'm sure she still loved him, but she realized he was ruining both their lives. The thing that always amazed me was how Cass avoided losing his job at that time. Everyone at the paper must have known he was an alcoholic, including the publisher, Horace Aitken. Maybe it was because editorial rooms are full of drunks, and you can't cobble together a competent staff without them. I don't think Cass ever fit the image Aitken had in mind for the managing editor of his paper. But he knew he had a nose for news and how to present it dramatically. Besides, Aitken was aware of Cass's charitable work, something he had always done without any prompting, and he felt that was good for the paper's reputation. So he kept Cass on—longer than he should have, as it turned out."

"To Lou's detriment, in particular."

"Yes, and his friendship with all of us... Hey, the town of Nobel is just off to our left now. On the old road, we used to pass right through it. That's where they manufactured explosives and other munitions during the Second World War. There's a lake just past the road that is still out of bounds because of all the unexploded stuff on its bottom."

"Odd that the Nobel Peace Prize should carry the name of the man who invented explosives."

"Yeah, just like the Rhodes Scholarship honouring a racist and an imperialist. The world is full of contradictions, not just our friends... So it was you who found out first what was going on with Sally, wasn't it?"

"Yes, she invited me over—just for tea, I thought."

––––––––––

That was in June of the year after the 1988 reunion. Sally was stretched out on a sun cot by their pool, toying with a four o'clock gin and tonic. She had slipped the straps of her bathing suit off her shoulders to tan them evenly with the rest of her body and was absently examining the sun spots on her arms. As Susie sat down, she looked sheepishly at her drink and then laughed resonantly as she apologized for "bending the elbow a little early like a typical Bayview woman." She had been doing that lately, she said, and when Susie asked why, she answered, "Ah, that's why I wanted to see you. I'm afraid I've gone and done something rather stupid." Then she told Susie about the handsome young man she'd met at an agency party in New York several years earlier. It was, in fact, Max Gardner, the head of Lou's New York office who had introduced them, the man Lou stole the Ripples Chocolate account from when they were both at Warnick and Redfern. "Payback time," Jack had said when Susie had first told him about her talk with Sally. "Advertising executives are always stabbing each other in the back."

According to Sally, Mehmet Kadir was a handsome, talented graphic designer from Istanbul, ten years her junior, but she found him charming and attentive. It wasn't long before they were jumping into bed with each other whenever Sally went down to New York. Max Gardner presumably knew about the affair, but he never said anything to Lou.

"So Sally and Mehmet were in New York together right before the reunion in eighty-eight?" Jack was having a hard time focusing on the road after so many hours driving on top of the distraction of conjuring up the past. "Linda was right about a glow on Sally's face."

"Yes, and partly responsible for the affair happening. Her view of extra-marital sex challenged Sally's conventional thinking and awakened her libido."

"The irony is Linda never did have sex with another man."

"No. Who would have thought it would be Sally who would risk everything she had for a fling? She knew it was crazy. Maybe when they first met she was going through some kind of pre-menopausal crisis. Whatever, Mehmet swept her off her feet. Sex had never been like that for her before, she confessed."

All went well for Sally for about five years, but then Lou arrived in New York unexpectedly one Friday night. He wasn't supposed to be coming for the weekend until Saturday and Sally didn't know why his plans changed—whether he was simply able to get away from work earlier than expected, or if it was because he finally suspected that Sally was up to something and wanted to find out what was going on. When Lou suddenly burst through their New York apartment door, she wasn't in bed with Mehmet, but they were sitting together on a couch with a half-empty bottle of wine on the coffee table in front of them. For Lou, that was all the evidence he needed and he acted swiftly. He told Mehmet to leave, and then he and Sally had it out. Lou gave her an ultimatum and then he left to catch a late plane back to Toronto.

———

"So it was the Sunday of that very weekend that Sally called you over to talk?"

"Yes. She told me that Lou was willing to forgive her this one time."

"One time? Christ, the affair had been going on for five years."

"I know. It was amazingly understanding of him under the circumstances, but, as you know, his condition was that the affair had to end immediately, and there must never be another one, or else it was all over between them. You'll never guess what Sally said to me next."

"What? I don't remember ever hearing."

"'God! I don't know what to do. Catholics are so rigid!'"

"She really said that?"

"Yes, because I remember responding rather stupidly that surely Lou wasn't really a Catholic any longer as if that were somehow relevant, and Sally just said, 'Well…' Only then did I add more sensibly that it hardly seemed rigid for anyone to expect their spouse to be faithful."

"And what did Sally say?"

"I can't remember, but it was clear that she was in real turmoil and hadn't yet made up her mind what to do. She admitted that it wasn't like her to get into a mess like this and that she realized the consequences of leaving Lou would be grave. She guessed she still loved him, or 'deeply affectioned' him at least as Linda would have put it, but it wasn't the same as it was with Mehmet. Lou was so preoccupied with work, it didn't seem like she was with him even when they were together. She said she felt neglected, an afterthought, and that sex with him was like taking a meeting."

"Oooh! Not what he'd have wanted to hear. So, you advised her to end the affair, didn't you?"

"Yes. Both for her own sake and the boys'. And I reminded her how much she had to be thankful for, how Lou had been a good and loyal husband and father. It would be foolish, I told her, to throw it all over for an uncertain future with a much younger man who lived in another country."

"'I knew that's what you would say,' Sally answered me. 'But I guess I needed to hear you say it.'"

"Good for you. You helped save their marriage."

"Well, I don't know how important my advice was. But she and Lou did stay together. And they both tried to forget about Mehmet, though not entirely successfully in either case."

"No, their relationship has never really been the same since then, has it?"

"No, but she made the right decision, don't you think, especially for the boys?"

"No question. But I do feel guilty that we didn't do more to prevent the affair."

"Well, what's done is done. There's no point torturing yourself about the past, but gosh, I do wonder how they'll be with each other at the reunion, especially if Lou's health is worse."

"Hey, there's the road that goes down to the reserve… What's its name…begins with an 'S', I think." Jack started running through the alphabet for the next letter. "D…e…f….g…h. H! That's it! The Shawanaga Reserve. That's where the guides lived who worked for the hotel. They were terrific. Every morning, they would come over to take the guests out fishing. I always remember the day the hotel opened being down on the dock with Cass and Jay at the gas pumps. We were in our uniforms for the first time, and when the guides saw us in those green bow ties, all I remember is rows of white teeth flashing at us."

"What a picture!"

"Cass took off his tie and wrapped it around the neck of one of the guides. He offered him his khaki shorts as well. It was the sort of thing he could do very naturally, not like — "

"Oh, gosh!" Susie interrupted. "I just remembered we were to text Lou and Sally when we left Parry Sound. I forgot all about it. Apparently Scott is going to come into the Station to pick us up."

"We'll be there before he is. But that's okay. It will give us time to relax and stretch our legs before…before God knows what."

Susie got the cellphone out of her purse and with the aid of the stylus tapped out a short message that disguised their forgetfulness: "En route from Parry Sound. See you soon."

"That's nice of Scott to do that for his parents. Would Tom?"

"Of course he would."

"I suppose. Thanks to Narinda and her strong sense of family."

"Jack! That's not fair. Our kids feel as close to us as the Pipers do to Sally and Lou."

"Well, at least they tolerate us. And not because they're waiting patiently to inherit a fortune."

"Now you're not being fair to Scott and Jeff."

"Probably not. Do you ever think of all the questions you failed to ask your parents about their lives — what it was like living through the Depression, what they did for entertainment before television, why Aunt Maria left Uncle Bert, and did Uncle Will really run away from home and join a circus? When you finally became inquisitive, they were dead or too old to remember. I wonder if our kids will feel that way someday about us."

"Oh, stop it! Can't we talk about something more positive?"

"Like how, after Linda's suicide attempt, Jay moved back in and stayed despite Lou's and my advice to the contrary?"

"At least that's a bit better. Actually, things went well with them for quite a while."

———

Linda and Jay didn't close the bookstore, but instead expanded their inventory so that they could compete better against the chains. And, at the same time, they got into selling art. Linda was thrilled with Jay for proposing that idea, since now the store combined two of her principal passions. They even added a tea and coffee bar where you could buy snacks, and they renamed the place New Age Books and Art.

On the surface things seemed fine, but Linda was still intensely jealous. For some reason, she hung onto the idea that Jay had rekindled his old romance with Sally. So she watched over him like a lioness zealously guarding her only male cub, tracking his every move. That became particularly apparent at a cocktail party the Pipers had when Lou first got involved in Toronto's bid to host the 2008 Summer Olympics.

It was in the spring of 2000, and it was a large gathering that included a lot of people the Sturridges didn't know as well as all the old gang from the Ojibway, except for Cass. Jack was never sure if he wasn't invited because of his drinking problem, or because Lou wanted to talk up Toronto's Olympic bid and he was fearful that, if he did so in Cass's presence, Cass would suspect he was somehow involved.

Jack remembered standing with Susie and Lou on the Pipers' flagstone patio, surveying the guests spread out in the garden below. They were thickly clustered on his immaculate green grass, his "centre court," as he called it, and around the swimming pool. But, farther away in an area of flowering shrubs and sandy pathways, there were only scattered knots of people engaged in intense conversations. Jay and Linda were there, and Lou's mouth stretched wide when he noticed Linda's appearance. She was wearing a blue silk dress, short enough to show off her slender legs, and they were tucked seductively into open-toed shoes of a matching robin's egg blue. It was Linda in corporate garb again, co-owner of a bookstore, and dressed to hold on to her man.

As the three of them walked down the steps from the patio, Lou glanced upwards, drawing the Sturridges' attention to the solar panels on the southern slope of his roof that he had just installed. He was the first in his neighbourhood to get them and to add a whirlpool and sauna to the deck of the pool. As they walked towards the end of the garden, Lou's white loafers seemed to spring out of the lawn as if, for him, the weight of gravity was less than for ordinary mortals. He was wearing a navy-blue blazer and white pants neatly pressed, and he had a signet ring on one finger with a seal that he had designed and registered as his family emblem. Wafting softly through the garden, carried by speakers Lou had installed behind bushes, was his favourite jazz music, performers like Stan Kenton, Art Tatum, and Ray Charles. Sally had appealed for a live band for the party, but Lou was proud of his speaker system and argued that it was better at delivering a sweet sound to all corners of the garden.

As the three of them approached Linda and Jay's group, a bearded man was making an assertion about abstract art—about its not having had a purposeful direction since Rothko and Pollock. Right away, Linda forcefully disagreed with him, contending that the revolution that Kandinsky had started wasn't over yet, and that the man was neglecting later developments like hard-edge geometric abstraction and digital art. Linda spotted Lou grinning beside her and stopped abruptly, her tight mouth curving down. "I agree with you," he said to her surprise. "That's why I'm still investing in abstract art, painters like Michael Goldberg and Kazuo Nakamura." Linda rolled her eyes at Lou the way she used to at Godfrey Wincanton and turned to talk to someone else—about Arica and the liberation of the true self from the ego.

Linda was, of course, aware that Lou was knowledgeable about art and that the Pipers had a good collection of contemporary paintings. What irritated her, however, was that his outlook was totally different from hers. Art appreciation to Lou was literally art appreciation—a question of how fast the price of works was rising relative to the TSX composite.

Somehow, Jack and Susie got separated at that point. Jack wound up in a conversation alone with Lou and Jay, while Susie spotted Sally farther down the garden and went to speak to her. From there, the two women moved on to the greenhouse where, later, they had a startling encounter with Linda.

Lou put an arm around Jay's shoulder, and as he led him and Jack away from everyone else, he asked Jay about the Feldenkrais exercises Linda had him doing. Jay was embarrassed that Lou had learned about them but admitted that he found they were good for dealing with tension. Another plus for him was that they were supposed to reverse the symptoms of aging, a notion that amused Lou immensely. As they were chatting, a server offered them canapés from a silver tray. Jay munched slowly on his, but he didn't like it. Too late he realized it contained shellfish, high in cholesterol. It was then, out of the blue, that Lou said, "Hey, I told you guys I'm working for Win-2008, eh?" In fact, he hadn't said anything to either of them about his involvement and he knew full well that he hadn't. Jay said that the name sounded like an early retirement investment strategy, but Lou explained that it was a group gunning to hold the 2008 summer Olympics in Toronto. That was a crazy idea, Jay thought, given that China was bidding and with Asian and developing country votes, it was likely to be a shoo-in.

"Every bid has its problems," Lou answered enigmatically, but then he added that Toronto had a lot going for it—multicultural city, compact site on the waterfront, democratic decision-making processes, and the sympathy vote as a four-time loser.

That led Jay to wheeze, "Since when has sympathy been a characteristic of IOC members?"

Lou shrugged, and reminded Jay that everyone thought Athens was a natural for the centennial games in 1996, but in the end, Atlanta was a pretty easy winner. Jack asked him what his role was, and he said, "Oh, just adding some shadow. You know, bringing a little attention to the problems with the other bids, especially Beijing's."

Pretty quickly, Jack got the picture. Lou was going to head up a sort of dirty tricks division, sowing doubt in other countries about the suitability of Beijing for the Games: the problems of pollution, heat and smog, and China's record on human rights. Maybe nose around for information on China's construction plans for various facilities, uncover the flaws, and do some strategic bad-mouthing in the ears of IOC representatives. It wouldn't be that different from the role he'd played in the Mapledome project, only then he was dealing in positives and this time it was negatives.

Ever since the collapse of that project, Lou had been casting about for something else big and public to latch onto. When his efforts to find a role in another stadium project failed, he got the idea of taking a run at the America's Cup, the scheme he told Jack about at the reunion in eighty-eight. But, as it turned out, there just wasn't the interest among the people he knew in the yachting set to launch an entry. That's when he turned his attention in 1990 to the Toronto Ontario Olympic Council and its bid to hold the centennial Olympics in 1996. But they wouldn't have him in their group for the same reason as the stadium proponents: his rumoured connection with the Mapledome scandal. At that point, Lou figured he was finished with getting involved in showy projects and that he would have to concentrate on the ho-hum work of the firm. But then, much to his surprise, he was approached in 2000 by people associated with Win-2008. Enough time had now elapsed since the Mapledome fiasco that they didn't see any risk in involving Lou. Besides, after four failed bids in the past, they realized they needed someone like him on board—to do the nefarious, underhand work that seems to arise with every Olympics bid.

"Hey," Lou said casually to Jay in the middle of the conversation, "maybe you could help me a little." He made it sound as if the idea had just come to him rather than it being the reason for telling them both about his involvement. Lou explained that he was flying out to Beijing the following week to talk to some of the people involved with the Chinese bid. He wanted to see if he could pick up any information on their plans for various facilities. And then he asked Jay if there was anybody at the embassy he knew from his time at External who might be able to help him. He needed a contact there—somebody who could set up some meetings for him with the right people. Jack was shocked that Lou would ask even that much of Jay after the disastrous outcome of involving him in the Mapledome business. It showed, he concluded sadly, just how little he understood the depth of his friend's determination to win.

Jay answered that it was inconceivable to him that Lou could get that kind of information as a member of Win-2008. "No, no," Lou smirked. "The Chinese won't know I'm with them. They'll think I'm there representing Canadian companies that assume Beijing is going to win and want information about the city's proposed facilities to help them tender for contracts."

Now Jay and Jack got the full picture. Whatever information Lou got from the Chinese, he'd immediately pass on to the Win-2008 office so that they could look for weaknesses to broadcast and to use in the wording of their own Olympics plans to show their superiority.

"Sorry," Jay finally said. "There's nobody I know at the Beijing Embassy. I can't help you." Jack didn't know if that was entirely true, or if Jay was simply too cautious to risk being burned again by Lou. Anyway, Lou dropped the subject at that point, but not before he added that what he had told them was strictly confidential. He wanted them to go ahead and talk up the bid to everyone at the party—help him get all the city on side, but he didn't want anyone else to know that he was directly involved. Unfortunately, Lou overlooked Jay's penchant to talk, especially if he thought he had interesting gossip to pass on, and, even more seriously, he underestimated, despite the passage of over forty years, the depth of Cass's obsession to get even with him for the Barbie Bigelow Affair.

———

"When our conversation about the Olympics ended, Jay went up to the house with Lou to examine a painting he was thinking of selling via New Age Books and Art. And I went looking for you, who seemed to have vanished completely from the party."

"Yes, I'd gone with Sally to her greenhouse. She wanted to show me some of the plants she had started there. They looked terrific, especially her nasturtiums which she'd grown from seeds. When I complimented her, she said that at least gardening was something she could do well, better at least than successfully conducting an illicit affair."

———

That comment surprised Susie because she assumed Sally was over Mehmet. After all, their relationship had ended a decade earlier. Sally guessed she was but admitted to Susie that it hadn't been easy—that she thought of him often. Then she added that she didn't think she and Lou should ever have had kids. Anticipating a long conversation, Susie sat down on a stool from where, as it happened, she wasn't visible from outside the greenhouse. "What do you mean?" she responded to Sally's assertion. "You've both been great parents." But Sally insisted that Lou had been too preoccupied with the firm and that she hadn't had the understanding and patience the boys needed. Susie told her that she thought that was nonsense and that what she seemed to be saying was that, if it hadn't been for Scott and Jeff, she would have left Lou for Mehmet. She never answered but, looking at her, Susie could see why Mehmet would have found her appealing. Even though she was sixty by then, she was still attractive—in a country club sporty way. She was in a brown velour dress that slipped beguilingly off one shoulder, and tan leather boots that had low heels for walking on the grass, the sort of person you might see in a box at the Royal Winter Fair.

When at last Sally spoke again, she said in her self-deprecating manner, "Anyway, wouldn't you know that having chosen to have kids I'd be conventional about it? Two boys with freckles who needed braces... God, Susie! If Lou needed the Mapledome for his father, what kind of a monster are the boys going to have to come up with for Lou?"

Susie assumed it was a rhetorical question and responded by asking how things were going with her and Lou. She said that they were okay; they lived their separate lives, but they ate together most evenings. She and Susie were silent for a while and Sally started picking dead leaves off one of her plants, until eventually she asked Susie what she thought of the idea of her opening a flower shop. Susie told her that was a terrific idea; it would give her something new and exciting of her own to occupy her time now that the boys had left home. "If I do, I think I'll call it the Perennial Centre." Sally laughed sonorously. "That's me. Perennially the same!"

It was at that moment that Sally saw a figure dart quickly along the wall of the greenhouse to the end where she and Susie were. The knob on the greenhouse door twisted back and forth urgently, but the women were at the opposite end from where they had gone in and the door was obviously locked. The whole frame shook as the weight of a body pressed against it. "Who is it?" Sally shouted. Susie got up from the stool and, through the panes, she could just make out a person kneeling down a few steps from the door, but then the figure approached the greenhouse again. Sally called to wait, that she was coming. But it was too late. A rock sailed through the window beside the doorknob, sending a shower of glass onto the greenhouse floor. Instinctively, Susie and Sally clutched each other and drew back. A hand reached through the jagged hole and turned the key on the inside. They could see it was a trembling white hand with red fingernails, blackened by chunks of wet earth. The door flew open, and there was Linda, her dark eyes wild with rage and her blue dress splattered with mud and blood. "Linda!" Sally cried "Linda, what on earth…?"

"Sally!" Linda whispered faintly. "Susie!"

"Linda, are you all right?" Susie asked.

"Sally. Susie," she repeated. "I…I thought…I mean…I was looking for…" She covered her carefully painted lips with her shaking hands, smearing them dark brown. "I…I must be drunk. I thought you were…were…" Her face was white, and her voice was quivering. "Jay... Where is Jay?" Suddenly Linda's legs buckled, and Susie and Sally grabbed her by the arms. Only then did they notice that a red stream of blood was running down the palm of Linda's right hand. It didn't look too serious, but they knew they needed to get her to the house to clean and dress the wound. So they walked slowly from the greenhouse back towards the party, propping Linda up between them, while Sally reassured the guests they passed that Linda was okay; she'd simply fallen on the uneven grass. "Gee, you never know what's going to happen when the Pipers have a bash," they heard one guest say as they walked past him. "Remember that night Jonesie chug-a-lugged a mickey of Scotch and fell flat on his face in Sally's rose bushes?"

"After that incident in the greenhouse, I left Sally with Linda in an upstairs bathroom, and went to find Jay to tell him what had happened," Susie recollected. "He was by the pool where the remnants of the party were gathered. And that's where I found you too, you silly boy."

"Yeah, Jay and I were talking about Lou's involvement in the Olympics bid when we heard someone singing by the diving board. We wheeled around to look and there was Bev, with her arms around a guy called Skippy, one of Lou's old bellboy buddies from the Ojibway. They were stumbling out to the end of the board rocking precariously back and forth. Bev had lifted her party dress high up one leg, exposing her thigh to the gawking guests, and she was belting out one of her old campfire songs, but with different lyrics.

Oh, I ain't got my philanderin' honey,
That's why I'm feeling real rummy,
So we're walking the plank
Right into the tank
Side by side.

"*Don't do it, Scottie, for Christ's sake*, I said to myself. *Don't make a fool of yourself.* It was the sort of stunt she was inclined to pull whenever she felt rejected—her way of showing everyone just who was the life of the party. The two of them stood tottering at the end of the board and then Bev tumbled backwards into the pool, pulling Skippy along with her. Her arms and legs flailed the air like a turtle flipped over on its shell."

"Ouch! Jack! What a terrible image."

"Sorry, but that's exactly how she looked. They floated for several seconds treading water awkwardly under the weight of their clothes while several of the guests applauded. 'Come on in! The water is great,' Bev started shouting. 'Come on! Everyone gets dunked.' But no one budged and eventually Skippy climbed out by the ladder. Bev desperately searched the edge of the pool for familiar faces and Jay and I instinctively backed away, but she saw us. 'Jay-Jay, Jack! There you are! Come on in.' I knew Jay would never do it, but I just couldn't leave her in the pool alone. I felt so sorry for her. So I draped my jacket over a chair, kicked off my shoes and dove head first into the pool. When I surfaced, Scottie waddled over and pecked me thankfully on the cheek. Then we struggled to the ladder and got out. 'Oh, I'm having a ball.' Bev rubbed a towel vigorously through her curly hair. 'Isn't this a fabulous party?'"

"My brave, handsome lifeguard, coming to the rescue," Susie said. "That was certainly quite an evening."

"No question. I think it was while Sally was drying our clothes that Bev mentioned to me her plans to leave her school and go to Uganda to teach."

"Really? I don't remember. But the date seems about right."

"Yeah, she left in the middle of that summer and was gone until 2008, the year that Beijing hosted the Olympics."

"Too bad for Lou that Bev and Cass didn't stay together. Maybe she still would have gone to Africa and Cass might have quit his job to go, too. Then things would have turned out differently."

"I don't think he would have—not without having completed his revenge... Hey, the place doesn't look any different since the last time we were here." The Sturridges had reached Pointe au Baril and Jack drove down to the dock, where they unpacked the car. He left Susie sitting on a bench beside their luggage and the carton of wine while he parked the car in a lot near where the station had been in the days when the town and the Ojibway Hotel were serviced by the railway. Then he walked back to the dock and sat on the bench with Susie, waiting for Scott to arrive. "Do you have your glasses? Both pairs? You didn't leave one in the car, did you?"

"No," Jack answered indignantly. "I have them... That was really brave of Bev to go to Uganda, wasn't it? She could have just retired. She'd reached her pension maximum. We talked about doing something like that ourselves, didn't we?"

"Yes. But you were too afraid of getting amoebic dysentery to risk doing it."

"Was I? I would be even more now... Would you have gone if it were you and I who'd split up?"

"No." Susie took Jack's hand in hers. "I would have been more like Linda. I would have stayed in Toronto and jealously stalked you everywhere, begging you to come home. What about you?"

"If you'd taken off like Bev, I would have followed you all the way to Ouagadougou and back, pleading with you to give me one more chance."

"Gosh! That sounds like an awfully long way. I'm impressed."

"Ah! There's Scott's boat coming down the channel." Jack took a deep breath. "Are you ready for this?"

Chapter 20

Rumour spreads around the nation's capital the way the acrid, sulphuric odours of the E.B. Eddy Match Company once pervaded the downtown. It's borne by the lungs of bureaucrats talking to their counterparts in other divisions and departments, swirling with increasing intensity and diminishing accuracy. This time, rumour had it that Jay Walters, former foreign service officer, was trying to involve the Canadian embassy in Beijing in sabotaging the Chinese bid to host the 2008 Olympic Games—not that he had simply been *approached* to help with Toronto's bid, but that he was actually involved.

How the rumour started was not entirely clear, but Lou and Jack eventually concluded that it must have resulted from Jay talking to one of his old colleagues at External Affairs not long after the cocktail party at the Pipers'. Jay, however, never admitted that that was what happened; there just seemed to be no other credible explanation. Most likely, Jack believed, Jay hadn't intended to disclose anything about nefarious Canadian activity related to the Olympics; it was just something he let slip out during the course of a conversation. And, given the way rumours spread, the information quickly became inaccurate. Lou's name was apparently omitted after the initial transmission at least, and only Jay was identified as trying to solicit the help of the Canadian embassy in Beijing in an effort to discredit the Chinese bid.

Not surprisingly, this juicy bit of news eventually reached the Ottawa Press Club and from there it spread to media outlets in general, including the *News*. As soon as Cass heard this gossip via his Ottawa bureau, he naturally thought of Lou. Ever since the Mapledome, he'd automatically put every story that even vaguely hinted of scandal through a kind of Piper filter just in case it had legs, and since this one appeared to involve Jay and a flashy project like the Olympics, it had a hint of promise. Several news outlets checked out the leak in Canada, but only two papers sent reporters to Beijing to sniff around for information, and one of them was the *News*. Much to Cass's frustration, however, nothing was uncovered. The embassy denied that anyone from Canada had been aided in seeking contact with Beijing Olympic officials, while members of China's Olympic Committee refused to comment on any meetings they might have had with foreign visitors pertaining to the Games.

For the moment, Cass's investigation was stymied. But he wasn't prepared to give up. And several months later, he was handed an unexpected and unusual gift. Just weeks before the IOC was to meet in Moscow in July 2001, to select the winning bid, the mayor of Toronto made an appalling blunder in attempting to explain to reporters why he was unenthusiastic about going to Kenya to seek African support. "What the hell do I want to go to a place like Mombasa for?" he declared. "I just see myself in a pot of boiling water with all these natives dancing around me."

Not surprisingly, the comment received strong criticism around the world, and especially among African delegates to the IOC, who were critical to the Canadian effort to win the Games. So Lou was immediately dispatched by Win-2008 to do what he could to repair the damage. On a whirlwind tour of a number of countries, especially in Commonwealth and francophone Africa, he drew attention to Canada's historic ties with them, and to its long and generous role in providing them with developmental assistance, unencumbered by the strings attached to aid from so many other countries. Finally, he made the point that, in stark contrast to China, Canada was a democratic, multicultural country that had opened its doors to thousands of immigrants from Africa. These arguments, it was hoped, would be enough to undo the damage caused by the mayor's shocking and ill-timed remarks, but that was now clearly problematic.

The African tour had brought Lou's link to Win-2008 out in the open, and, as a result, Cass assigned a reporter to track him wherever he went on the continent, but so far nothing had been uncovered of significant media interest. It was simply the kind of innocuous tour any bidding country would have mounted under the circumstances. But then an unfortunate event occurred in Kenya that changed everything and landed Cass the story he was hoping for all along. An item came over the wire services about the death of a member of the Beijing Olympic Committee in Nairobi. Apparently he stumbled on the sidewalk outside his hotel and fell smack into a passing truck. In accordance with instructions Cass had circulated regarding anything pertaining to the Olympics, one of the *News*'s assistant city editors dutifully circled the piece and placed it in Cass's in-basket. Right away, he phoned his reporter in Africa with instructions to get "his ass to Nairobi" right away and find out everything he could about the deceased. "I mean if he took a crap before he left the hotel, I want to know about it."

Fortunately for the *News*, the Beijing Olympic official, a Mr. Ho Chou Dao, had not been travelling alone, but with his executive assistant who was still in Nairobi. When the reporter located him, he learned that the Chinese were in Nairobi simply to explain the details of their bid to members of the Kenya Olympic Committee. Mr. Ho, however, had also been involved in informal talks with several other people during his visit and a review of those names disclosed that he had met with a Mr. Lawrence Piper, a Toronto businessman, although the assistant contended that the meeting was purely social. They had met for drinks in the bar of the hotel where they were both staying immediately before Mr. Ho's fatal accident. Asked what had prompted the meeting, the executive assistant explained that it had occurred simply because the two had met before in Beijing. Now the *News* had the information it had been unable to obtain earlier. Lou had, indeed, been in Beijing and on a visit clearly related to the Olympics, since he had met there with Mr. Ho. But pressed as to what had transpired at the Beijing meeting, the executive assistant would not commit himself. Cass's reporter was, however, well trained in the tricks of the journalistic trade and persisted with his questioning. "Can you tell me if Mr. Piper was in Beijing on behalf of Toronto's Olympic Committee, or in some other capacity?"

"I believe the latter," the executive assistant confirmed.

"In that case, might Mr. Piper have presented himself as representing Canadian firms that were exploring the possibility of tendering on certain of the Olympic facilities, should Beijing be awarded the games?"

"I cannot say," the Chinese official had responded.

"But is that not a plausible explanation for him to have advanced for his visit?"

"Yes... Yes... It's certainly plausible."

People never forget where they were the moment they learned of the assassination of President Kennedy, or of the two hijacked planes flying into the Twin Towers in New York. In the same way, Jack knew he would never forget where he was when Lou called him just hours after he got home from Nairobi. It was about the article that had just been published on the front page of the *Toronto Daily News*. Jack was in his studio about to apply the finishing strokes to a painting of Jean Chrétien and Paul Martin boxing in a ring erected inside a coffee shop. Chrétien was holding a milkshake in one hand and easily fending off his opponent with the other. It was a painting that Jack never finished. He put down his brush and rushed to Lou's office, grabbing a copy of the *News* at a stand outside the building.

TORONTO OLYMPICS REP MISREPRESENTED SELF IN TALKS IN BEIJING, MET WITH CHINESE OFFICIAL IN NAIROBI BEFORE HIS SUDDEN DEATH

Jack quickly scanned the article as the elevator climbed to the twenty-fourth floor of the TD Tower.

> Toronto businessman Lawrence Piper, who is associated with the the city's bid to host the 2008 Olympics, allegedly presented himself to Chinese officials in Beijing as a representative of Canadian companies seeking Olympic contracts. Subsequently he met with one of these officials in Nairobi immediately before the latter's sudden death outside the hotel where both men were staying. Police are still investigating the cause. According to the executive

assistant of the deceased Chinese official, the meeting with Mr. Piper in Nairobi was purely social and resulted from their acquaintance in Beijing. The assistant did, however, acknowledge that, in so far as the meeting in Beijing was concerned, it was plausible Chinese officials had agreed to meet with Mr. Piper because they understood he represented Canadian firms interested in bidding on some of the proposed facilities.

Sources knowledgeable about the bidding process for Olympic Games have, however, informed the *News* that, since Mr. Piper is associated with Win-2008 and was not in Beijing representing the interests of any Canadian firms, he was probably seeking information that could be used to discredit proposed Beijing facilities and thereby aid Toronto in its own Olympics bid. That kind of activity is not an uncommon practice, sources indicated.

Mr. Piper is president of Piper, Langford and Jones, a diversified Toronto advertising and consultancy firm with offices both in Toronto and New York...

"It's utterly preposterous," Lou was on the phone telling a journalist when his secretary showed Jack into his office. "It appears that the *News's* reporter asked leading questions. He put words in the mouth of Mr. Ho's assistant. Officials in Beijing knew full well that I was there on behalf of Win-2008. I never had the least intention of deceiving anybody, or...or ferreting out information to help Toronto's cause. That's a ridiculous notion. Mine was strictly a courtesy call, designed to maintain an amicable relationship between our two cities during the competition."

Jack had never seen Lou look so old. His face was ashen and his lips a pale purple. It was obvious his mouth was dry from the clicking sound he emitted as he spoke, and Jack had Lou's secretary bring him a glass of water. "No, I wasn't even with Mr. Ho when he was hit. I walked out to the front of the hotel with him and said goodbye. But then I went back inside because I had another meeting… I have no idea what happened. From the press reports, I assume he slipped off the sidewalk and fell into the path of a passing truck. There's nothing more I can tell you."

Lou hung up. "That was the *Calgary Herald*. The phone has been buzzing ever since the *News's* first edition hit the streets." He looked at Jack almost beseechingly. "It isn't true. You realize it isn't true, don't you?"

"What isn't?"

"I didn't push him. I wasn't even there when it happened."

Now Jack knew, however, that the *News* had figured out correctly what Lou had been up to in Beijing. The paper's evidence was flimsy, but Cass had chosen to publish the story anyway.

"This hurts. This really hurts." It was never entirely clear to Jack what Lou meant—that he was angry and upset that Cass would do this to him, that he loathed all the publicity, or that he was concerned about the impact of the disclosure on the future of the firm; perhaps all of them.

Because Lou had been with Mr. Ho immediately before his death and had engaged previously in discussions with him in Beijing, it was natural that, in their investigation, the Nairobi police would want to satisfy themselves that no foul play had occurred. So, the next Saturday, following a request from Interpol, Lou was interviewed at home by two Toronto police officers. Lou asked Susie and Jack to be present as support for Sally. It was quite a scene, with media people all over the front of the house, looking for photos and interviews. But they found Sally remarkably calm through it all, unlike the way she had reacted over the Mapledome exposé. She knew, of course, that Lou was in no way involved in Ho's death, but up to then she had been in the dark about his visit to Beijing. Yet she didn't seem upset or angry over the nefarious nature of his mission. All she said was, "I thought I knew why he had gone." And then she laughed, "I understood he had a meeting with a client of the firm." After that, she changed the subject. "I talked to Scott in St. Petersburgh. He's made it from Paris on his bike. He wondered if he ought to end his holiday early and fly home, but I told him I didn't think it was necessary, do you?"

"No," Jack answered. Only later, after discussing that moment alone with Susie, did the two of them agree on why Sally was so calm in the midst of this latest crisis. After Lou's ultimatum about her affair with Mehmet, she had reconciled herself to two realities. She wasn't ever going to leave Lou, and he wasn't going to change; he would always be scheming. When Sally arrived at an understanding of a situation, she could live with it whether or not she liked it. There was, they realized, a fatalistic quality about her, so she remained calm at this dark moment in their lives. Indeed, she was even able to laugh. She wasn't happy about how everything had turned out, but at least she could laugh.

Lou's meeting with the police provided more fodder for the *News* and another embarrassing headline.

TORONTO BUSINESSMAN LOU PIPER QUESTIONED IN DEATH OF CHINESE OLYMPICS OFFICIAL

Once again, the details of Lou's deceptive activity in Beijing and of his African tour to bolster flagging support for Toronto's Olympic bid were repeated.

It wasn't long, however, before the Nairobi police completely cleared him. Lou did have a meeting with another person right after his drink with Mr. Ho, and that person had confirmed that he met Lou on the front steps of the hotel right after he said goodbye to Mr. Ho, and then they went together directly to the bar. There wasn't even anything to suggest that Lou might have attempted to get Mr. Ho drunk and that that had been the cause of the accident. His executive assistant confirmed that they had had only one drink together.

The completion of the police investigation meant there was a third round of media stories under headlines like "POLICE INVESTIGATION CLEARS PIPER OF SUSPICION IN NAIROBI DEATH."

In the end, however, this later publicity worked to Lou's advantage. Cass would have been better off, Jack realized, confining his stories to Lou's activities in Beijing. For, once he was cleared of any wrongdoing in Nairobi, interest in what had transpired in Beijing evaporated. Most people had never clearly distinguished between the two incidents, so when the Nairobi investigation ended, in the public's mind at least Lou was off the hook. On top of that, the media as well soon lost interest in the Beijing angle; the implication of wrongdoing on Lou's part was vague and not very newsworthy in light of the transgressions that usually accompany the Games. Instead, until the Moscow vote was held, what interest there was in Toronto's bid largely reverted to the mayor's stupid outburst and the damage it had done to the city's chances. Lou did, however, lose his position with Win-2008. Despite the good efforts he had made on their behalf in Africa, they felt obliged to drop him from the team because of the reports of his alleged activities in Beijing. But that meant little. The decision of the IOC was now too close at hand for him to do anything more for Toronto anyway.

Not surprisingly, Cass went berserk when he realized what was happening to his big exposé. The Teflon man was prancing away again. His hands were a little sullied, but with each passing day the grime was a little less visible. Cass saw the Olympics business as his last chance to get even with Lou, so he was determined to keep the story alive by any means possible. But the method he chose was so reckless that it seemed unlikely that even Cass thought he could get away with it. More likely, he just didn't care any longer what the consequences were. He just wanted to get Lou—to use the power of the press while he still possessed it whatever the consequences. So, with the Olympics story dying and Lou still on his feet in his bullet-proof vest, Cass spilled what he had never published about the Mapledome. He wrote the story himself and never cleared it with the publisher, Horace Aitken.

PIPER WAS MYSTERY MAN BEHIND MAPLEDOME PLOTTING

Lawrence Piper, the Toronto consultant who recently employed devious means in Beijing to obtain information useful for Toronto's bid for the 2008 summer Olympics, was responsible for secretive activities to boost an ill-fated sports complex in the city in 1980. Mr. Piper, president of Piper, Langford and Jones, was the person behind an extensive letter-writing campaign designed to give the impression of widespread public support for the waterfront project with which he was directly associated. The project, known popularly as the Mapledome, collapsed when an investigation by the *News* revealed the attempt by interested parties to present a false impression of the degree of public support for the undertaking. Mr. Piper's role in the manufacture of public opinion was not, however, disclosed at the time.

Mr. Piper was recently cleared of any suspicion of wrong-doing in the sudden death of a Beijing Olympics official in Nairobi...

Over protests from the city editor, the story ran in the first two editions, until Horace Aitken learned about it and had the article pulled. Even Cass wasn't so bold as to make it the headline story, but it ran in the top right-hand corner of the front page along with a head-and-shoulders photograph of Lou.

Once again, Jack raced to Lou's office after he read the piece in the *News* and found him dealing with an incessant string of phone calls.

"Yes, I've read the article. The *News*'s story is totally unfounded... No. There's not one shred of evidence connecting me with this so-called letter-writing campaign... Yes, one of my employees did submit a letter to the press, but it was his own decision to do so. I knew nothing about it at the time... But I've never denied it. My firm did some informal work for Citizens for the Complex on a pro bono basis. Our involvement, however, pertained only to the initial public presentation of the scheme. There was nothing inappropriate in that. Citizens for the Complex would have been foolish to have acted without professional advice... Come on! The Maple-dome has been dead for over twenty years!"

Eventually, there was a short break in the calls and Lou said to his secretary, "No more for now, eh? Tell them I'm tied up until five-thirty." He looked drained, but better than Jack had expected to find him—better even than he had when the first story about his activities in Beijing had come out. "I think that ought to do it," he said to Jack.

"You mean satisfy the media?"

"No, I mean that ought to be the end of it." Jack still wasn't sure exactly what Lou meant, but then he added, "Cass doesn't have anything left to hit me with."

"No. I think you're right."

"Sally called." Jack waited patiently for him to elaborate. "She said Jeff wanted to know what he should say to the media if anyone called him." Lou grinned with paternal pride and Jack couldn't help smiling himself. He was, however, astounded at how calm Lou was, considering that he loathed any kind of publicity and was obviously concerned about the damage the media reports could cause to his reputation and that of the firm. It was as if he were in a storm he always knew was coming, and there was nothing he could do but wait for it to break, and then attempt to ride it out. Now the eye was passing, and Jack guessed that that was a relief to him. "Sally has taken it all very well," Lou added. "She's been a peach. I'm a lucky man, Jack, a lucky man."

Chapter 21

Sally came down to the cottage dock to meet Susie and Jack when they arrived from Pointe au Baril. She looked well, they thought, no obvious signs of stress, though it was clear she'd only managed with make-up to wrestle to a draw the creases and blemishes that had gradually formed on her skin. In recent years, she'd taken to wearing her hair shorter; it was cut above the shoulders now, but there were the same gentle waves she had always had at the base, and the colour was similar, a realistic blend of brown, grey, and white. "Thanks, sweetie," she said to Scott. "You'll come by tomorrow, won't you, in case anyone wants to go over to the Ojibway?" She pushed the bow of his boat away from the dock and hugged the Sturridges. "God! It's hard to believe he's retired already. This is the first summer he's staying up after Labour Day."

"Gosh, are we really that old?"

"Well, he's stopped working pretty early. I don't think Jeff will. Lou certainly never did."

"So, how is he?"

As Jack asked, Sally's eyes shot up to the front of the cottage where Lou was sitting as usual in his favourite deck chair, wrapped in a blanket. When he and Susie also looked up, Lou gave them a wave. "Not well, as I'm sure you've guessed. You know the cancer has metastasized. First, it was to his bones, but now it's in his lymph nodes too. He has what they call spinal cord compression as well."

"So what's the prognosis?"

"Six to nine months."

"Oh no, Sally. That's awful."

"The doctors think this will be his last summer. That's why he wanted to get everyone together."

"We were afraid that might be why, but we weren't sure because it's also thirty years since the last reunion."

"God! Is it really? It seems like just a few years. No. We never thought of that. There's been so much going on."

"Is there nothing that can be done? Some kind of experimental treatment?" Susie asked.

"They've been doing all they can—hormone therapy, chemotherapy, radiotherapy."

"What about going somewhere in the States?"

"He won't contemplate it, not so long as Trump is in power."

"Good for him." Jack put his arm around Sally's shoulder and they climbed the steps together. As they reached the deck chairs, Lou stood up, holding on to an armrest for support. With his stooped back, he looked as if he had passed eighty winters standing there, fastened to the granite like a beloved old white pine whose imminent fall everyone dreaded. Lou held out his hand, and Jack was pleased to discover that his grip was still strong. His eyes were clear as well, but his face looked puffy and drained of colour. With one hand, he patted Jack on his back and then he turned to Susie and gave her a warm hug.

"You look well," she said encouragingly.

"Bullshit." Lou grinned. "But thank you."

———

After Cass's article exposing Lou's role in the Olympics bid and in the Mapledome scandal, Piper, Langford and Jones went through another rough period. There was an investigation into Lou's conduct by Advertising Standards Canada and while nothing came of it, things were slow for the firm for several years. As a result, Lou did some reorganizing. He closed the New York office and cut some of his staff in Toronto. While business gradually picked up, it was never the same as it had been at its peak, and none of the firm's projects interested him the way the Mapledome and the Olympics had. The advertising business was also changing as the Internet and social media increased in importance; the focus now was on targeting individuals and groups with messages directed specifically at them. Lou found it hard to keep up with the transition, so in 2010, at age seventy-one, he turned the reins of the company over to Jeff. He did, however, maintain an office at the firm, and continued to go in three or four times a week until he was diagnosed with prostate cancer in 2013.

The adjustment to having Lou at home more of the time was not easy for Sally, especially after his diagnosis. They spent a lot of time seeing doctors and going for treatments. On other days, they followed their own routines. Sally kept busy with her garden, various charities, luncheons, and bridge games with her female friends. Lou spent a lot of time reading and increasingly, after 2013, brooding on the past, especially the failure of the Mapledome and the Olympics bid. Both tended to come up frequently in his conversation at the dinner table, though Sally wasn't interested in either. Overall, she felt rather bored with their life and wished she had got around to opening the flower shop she had contemplated to provide some stimulation; it might even have been good for Lou, she thought, because it would have given him a diversion.

———

"Jackie! Susie Q! Hi!" Bev suddenly bolted out of the cottage, raced to the deck chairs, and flung her arms around the Sturridges. "It's great to see you. It's been way too long."

"Over a year, I guess."

"Yes, not since that ball game the Jays lost in the bottom of the ninth."

"Yeah, one of many." Jack turned to Lou to include him. "We tried to get you and Sally to go, but you wouldn't."

"No. I hate that place." Only two or three times since its construction had Lou set foot inside the SkyDome, later renamed the Rogers Centre—only when for business reasons he had been obligated to make an appearance in one of the private boxes. For him, it was a form of silent protest against the building of a stadium that he deemed vastly inferior to the Mapledome.

"You're looking well," Susie said to Bev. She did, too. While she had put on still more weight, her facial skin was rosy and smooth for her age. That, however, only served to hide a new problem: she had developed type 2 diabetes and was vainly struggling to stay on a diet low in sugar and carbohydrates.

———

After returning home from Uganda, Bev had kept busy working for two charities involved in developmental assistance projects in Africa. Susie and Jack saw her once or twice a year, usually for dinner or when she suggested going to some sporting event. In 2014, however, Cass had his first stroke and that changed Bev's focus entirely. From the time they broke up until that year, they never saw each other at all. But when Bev learned about Cass's stroke, she went to see him in hospital, initiating a very different connection between them. She helped nurse him back to reasonable health, feeding him at first, attending his physiotherapy sessions, participating in his speech lessons, and later, taking him for short walks, while he leaned alternately on her and his cane. They weren't living or sleeping together, but they were seeing a lot of each other and without the acrimony that had characterized their relationship when they were together in the same house.

———

"Cassie is here," Bev beamed at Susie and Jack.

"He is?"

"Yes, he's on the porch. Come and see him."

"Is he…is he still drinking?" Jack asked.

"No… No. He's…he's… Well, you'll see. Oh, it's so good you've arrived. Now everyone is here!"

Everyone? Jack and Susie exchanged glances.

They found Cass alone on the screen porch where Bev had left him. The Sturridges hadn't seen him either since the ball game at the Rogers Centre, but they knew he had had a second stroke six months before the reunion and was in pretty bad shape. But that had not fully prepared them for what they saw now. Cass was sitting in a wheelchair, his torso slumped to one side and his head resting on a pillow. It looked as if he had fallen asleep when Bev had left him to greet the Sturridges, for his eyes were closed when they stepped onto the porch. But when Bev spoke gently in his ear, "Look who's here to see you," they opened, though one only partially. He stared at Jack and Susie as if momentarily confused, but then his mouth turned into a vague, misshapen smile. "Ghack… Shushie," he mumbled and then added something that was totally unintelligible.

"How...? How did you?" Jack was about to ask Bev, but he turned to Cass instead. "Good to see you, old buddy. We're glad you were able to come." He walked over to Cass's chair and patted the bald crown of his head. Again Cass muttered something that Jack couldn't catch.

"I think he said it's good to see you, too," Bev translated and then, as she wiped drool from the side of Cass's mouth, she added, "Scott has been terrific. He met us at the station with two of his friends, and the three of them carried Cassie up to the porch. Wasn't that super of them? Pinky was determined to get Cassie here."

"Nothing will keep you out of boats, will it?" Jack joked to Cass, but this time there was not even an attempt at an answer.

Immediately after the publication of the story linking Lou to the Mapledome scandal, Cass was fired by Horace Aitken. The earlier articles about Lou's activities in Beijing and his meeting in Nairobi with Mr. Ho just before his death had worried the publisher considerably, since the imputed wrongdoing on Lou's part was based on very flimsy evidence. But when Cass published the Mapledome piece, more than twenty years after the scandal, without Aitken's approval and with just one letter that only vaguely linked Lou and his firm to the letter-writing, it was too much for him to take. Fearing a libel suit, he insisted on the paper publishing a retraction and then he fired his maverick managing editor. Cass went without work for over six months and, during that period, he hit the bottle even harder. Ironically, it was Lou who eventually got him a job, writing ad copy at Warnick and Redfern. Whatever faults he had, Jack and Susie agreed, Lou could never be accused of meanness of spirit. And loyalty was his touchstone—to his family, his firm, and his friends. Lou had even made clear to the Sturridges years before the reunion that he felt partly responsible for Cass's firing—that he had provoked it, not by seducing Barbie Bigelow—he didn't take it back that far—but by his surreptitious activities related to the Mapledome and the Beijing Olympics that tantalized Cass but left him short of outright triumph. So, once again, despite what Cass had done to him, Lou reached out to him. "It's the perfect job for you," Lou had said to Cass when he phoned him about the position at Warnick and Redfern. "You're such a great bullshitter."

Cass, however, lasted less than three years at Warnick and Redfern before they let him go because of his high absentee rate when he went on binges. After that, he worked only intermittently on copy editing assignments, and even that stopped by 2009, so he was doing nothing over the five years before his first stroke. Cass's own view of his downward spiral differed from this account, and his was the version he planted in the sympathetic ear of Bev after his first stroke: "Aitken didn't want to fire me. He liked the way I pursued both those stories aggressively. It was just that he was afraid of the *News* getting into a long and potentially costly libel suit." That was the interpretation Bev dutifully relayed several times to his more sceptical friends, and she did so once again at the reunion.

———

Bev moved away from the wheelchair and said quietly to Susie and Jack, "Poor Cassie, I blame the way Horace Aitken treated him for both of his strokes. He should have supported Cass rather than leaving him to take the fall for the paper. If you want good, tough investigative journalism out of your staff, you have to stand by them even at the risk of libel… Hey, get a load of this." Bev turned cheerful again as she lifted a large object off a table by Cass's wheelchair. "As soon as Lou got up from his nap this afternoon, he brought this in for Cass. Isn't it wonderful?"

Bev was holding a large silver cup, engraved with the words: TORONTO LAWN TENNIS CLUB TWO PLAYERS' SINGLES CHAMPION, BOB CASSIDY, 1966-1980. "I could tell that Cassie was really touched when Lou presented it to him. He mumbled something that we couldn't catch, but Lou pretended he'd heard it. He put his hand on Cassie's shoulder and answered, 'you win some, you lose some.' Wasn't that just perfect?" Bev suddenly clapped her hands excitedly. "Hey, isn't this super news, too—about Jay and Linda?"

The Sturridges stared at each other mystified. "What?"

"Haven't you heard? They're back together."

"Back together? How—"

"Well, at least for now they are anyway. They're staying in the Pipers' new cabin, the big one they built after our last reunion."

"So, what about Linda's new partner? Didn't she come?"

"No, she didn't, and there's more to the story than that. They've broken up altogether."

"Where are Linda and Jay now?"

"They're napping."

Several deep grunts and then a strange, guttural sound emanated from the direction of Cass's wheelchair, indicating that he was doing his best to follow the conversation. Bev laughed and explained, "I think he said, 'my ass they are.' Anyway, you'll see them later and I'm sure Linda will fill you in."

As they left the porch, Jack pressed a hand firmly on Bev's shoulder. "You're terrific, you know. You always have been." Bev beamed back at him, her eyes dampening.

* * *

The next afternoon, Scott came by in his boat to take anyone who wanted to go over to the Ojibway Hotel. In the end, only Jack and Jay were keen on having a look at the old place. There was no question of Lou or Cass going and Linda had no interest in visiting a hotel with which she had no personal connection. Susie was prepared to go to be with Jack but decided to stay in order to have a private chat with Linda. Sally considered going, but at the last moment changed her mind, saying she would rather stay at the cottage and read. When, however, Jay asked her what book it was that was so engaging, she laughed and confessed, "A flower catalogue, wouldn't you know? God! How I've let my mind go—to seed no less!" The biggest surprise was that even Bev chose to remain at the cottage in order to be with her "sweet'ems." But she did ask Jack and Jay to bring her back an ice cream cone, "a staff portion, please."

Susie spent most of that afternoon talking with Linda on her cabin porch, where she had been busy drafting a letter to the *Globe and Mail*, in support of the Leap Manifesto of the NDP's left wing, especially its call for radical action to address the issue of climate change. "I promised Elizabeth I'd get it done this week." It wasn't the first time Linda's activism made Susie feel guilty. But the feeling passed as they started reminiscing about old times together—especially the trip to Europe in 1958, their years at university, Linda's visit to the Sturridges' flat in London, and the wedding in Muskoka. "I wish I could get you and Jack to come to Lake Joseph more often, instead of always going to Georgian Bay."

"Well you know how Jack feels about the Bay."

"Yes, but you should have a say. Why do we always yield to what men want to do?"

"Do we?" Susie asked.

Linda didn't answer. "You know, I think my favourite time may have been that trip to Europe. It was wonderful meeting you. Everything seemed to hold so much promise then."

"But what about later when you and Jay got together?"

"Oh, that was good, don't get me wrong. But our relationship has never been like yours and Jack's. We've always had issues." Then Linda talked about the erratic path of their lives in more recent years, even though Susie already knew most of the details. First up was how she and Jay decided to close New Age Books and Art in 2010. "Nobody in the trade was doing well by then. For indies like us it was clearly over unless you were prepared to work yourself to death for a pittance." After that, Linda went back to writing, albeit with only limited success; the magazine market had changed and, by and large, publishers were looking for manuscripts from younger writers. Jay, however, was at a loss as to what to do and spent most of his time walking, jogging, and at the gym, trying to stay in shape. Susie knew all about that because Jay would sometimes phone Jack to go for a run or a hike. "Anyway, after we closed the store, we went in separate directions. We simply weren't connecting any longer. And then I met Stephanie."

———

That was in 2011. They met at an exhibit at the Art Gallery of Ontario, standing in front of a painting that they both liked. "Now that's art that I can relate to," Stephanie said to her. "It speaks to me at so many different levels. It seems to have access to my deepest thoughts."

"Such as?" Linda asked her.

"That we should go and have a drink together."

They did, and before the night was over they were in bed together. It was totally different from sex with Jay, Linda contended, because it was an equal partnership. "Besides, I was infatuated by her. She was a real vampire. All she had to do was part her luscious, quivering lips and I'd start to come." That didn't last, however, because age was against Linda.

A few weeks after they met, Linda told Jay about Stephanie and gently asked if he would leave because Stephanie was going to move into the house on Chestnut Park. In making the request her conscience was clear, she told Susie, because there were no longer kids at home to worry about. On top of that, she was deeply in love, or thought she was, while, in her view she and Jay weren't relating.

So Jay obligingly moved out again and found an apartment near Yonge and St. Clair. He and Linda did stay friends and got together for dinner sometimes, even with Stephanie present.

In 2015, however, Linda learned that Stephanie had another lover she had been seeing for over a year, and, after a stormy argument, she kicked her out of the house. "It took me a long time to grasp it, but really women are no different than men," Linda was now convinced. "Both sexes can be insensitive, ungrateful, and deceitful." This realization did not, however, stop Linda from having another fling, this time with a French woman named Jaqueline, who was almost twenty years her junior. She was an assistant editor at a woman's magazine and she had called Linda the preceding summer, inviting her in to discuss a manuscript Linda had submitted.

———

"I fell in love with her at first sight, or at least I thought I had, kind of like it was with Dominic. Or maybe it was just that she was interested in my article. Anyway, it was all pretty dumb from the start. She's so much younger, so innocent really. Ours was almost like a mother-daughter relationship. No orgasms—not for me at least. Just a lot of snuggling. But by this summer I realized I had to end it. Beyond the physical, we weren't really relating. I felt it wasn't fair to her to carry on, that I was blocking her own development. Of course, it didn't help that, in the end, the magazine turned down my manuscript."

"So, are you really back with Jay now, or is this only for the reunion?" Susie asked.

"I don't know. I'd like him to come back. I hate living alone."

"Is that reason enough?"

"Of course not. I still love him. I really do. We have our differences, but we're good for each other. He steadies me, and I diversify his life—keep him from falling into a rut."

"Gosh, Linda, I'm not sure it's a good idea. It's always ended badly before. Why not go on seeing each other, but living separately? Lots of couples do that nowadays and it can work very well. That way you'll both have more independence when you need it."

"Be a LAT couple you mean?"

"A LAT couple?"

"Yes. Living apart together."

Susie laughed. "Trust you to know. But I think that's the perfect solution for the two of you."

"Oh, Susie, I do love you," Linda smiled, "but you're just so practical!"

***

It was quiet at the Ojibway dock when Scott let Jack and Jay off for a walk from end to end, while he went to the gas pumps to fill up. Only a few boats were tied up near the hotel, and no more than three or four people were walking along the dock from the grocery store and gift shop to load their boats with their purchases. At both stores, there were signs offering sales at prices that brought the goods close to what one might pay in Parry Sound. No one was in the deck chairs by the Ojibway Club sign, close to where, sixty years earlier, Jack had sat on the rocks sketching. The tub of geraniums beside them looked tired and neglected. The once-scarlet flowers were scarred and drooping, their petals black and brown in desperate need of deadheading. Overall, there was a melancholic, end-of-the-season feel to the place. "When we were kids and later working at the Ojib, did you ever imagine our lives ending up the way they have?" Jay asked as they seated themselves in deck chairs after their walk.

"No, I never thought mine would be so good."

"You serious?" Jay stared at Jack, genuinely surprised. "I mean, no offence, but your art never really caught fire."

"I didn't expect it to. I was never the new Riopelle or Colville. But Susie and I have had a wonderful life."

Jay gazed past the channel markers in front of the hotel. There were no outboards heading towards the dock. "Yeah, I guess you have. Me? I always thought I'd be a prestigious diplomat, or a big-time lawyer or businessman. But that's not the way things turned out. I'm not sure where I went wrong. Life just threw me a lot of curves."

"Well, you've had a pretty good run all the same. Things certainly haven't been boring."

"No, I'll grant you that."

"So, what gives with you and Linda? Are you together again, or what?"

"I don't know. She wants me to move back in, but I can't decide. We seem to get on better when we're not on top of each other."

"Then why change it?"

"Because she's good at twisting my arm."

Jay's bony fingers, nails chewed short, were nervously tapping the armrests of his chair. His face was no longer boy-like, but Jack noted enviously that when he looked at himself in the mirror, Jay would probably recognize the person staring back at him. His earnest blue eyes shone as brightly as ever with a childlike combination of innocence and bewilderment. His hair, on the other hand, did disclose his true age; it was white and patchy like the cumulus puffs drifting over Ojibway Island. Yet, on balance, given his appearance, Jack concluded that Jay was likely to outlive the rest of them.

Jay and maybe Linda too, alone together getting under each other's skin.

"I mean, fuck, Jack," Jay continued. "I feel I'm wasting my time, just waiting to die. I haven't been able to jog since my knee replacement, and what the shit is the point of going to the gym all the time at seventy-eight? No one is going to be impressed by my abs, certainly not Linda. She's good for me; she gets me doing things, and I think I can help her when she's down."

"That's great. But you don't have to be living in the same house for that to happen."

"Hey, no-o-o-o! I think I've heard this sort of advice from you before… Shit, you and Susie have managed to live together all these years. Why can't it work for us?"

Jack realized it was useless to continue the argument. "Well, Scott is ready to go. No point hanging around any longer. Let's get an ice cream cone for Bev and bugger off." They did that, but the cone was half melted by the time they got back to the cottage.

* * *

When they arrived, Lou was the only one outside, sitting in his deck chair, wrapped again in a blanket. He had gone inside for meals and an afternoon nap, but the rest of the time he had stationed himself in his favourite place where, from time to time, others had joined him. No one, however, had spent any time down at the dock, or in the Grady-White Lou had purchased a few years earlier as a replacement for the Whalers he had always bought in the past. And no one had gone swimming either; the water was way colder than any of them had remembered it being just before Labour Day.

Jay went to find Linda, and Jack sat down in the chair next to Lou. It was the first time that they were alone together all weekend, and Jack found Lou in a surprisingly reflective mood for someone who normally looked forward. "You know the SkyDome was a big mistake," he said without any preamble. "The dimensions are all wrong. The foul lines are too close to the stands and the outfield isn't deep enough. It's a hitter's ballpark. Lots of pop fly homeruns. Those wouldn't have been problems with the Mapledome; we had a site with a lot more room. Besides, the place we're stuck with isn't big enough for track and field, and it's not the right shape for soccer either. Those were handicaps for us bidding for the Olympics."

Out in the open, they could hear the drone of an outboard heading towards Hemlock Channel on water that looked like maple syrup that had flowed out of the rocky shore and was now splattered in air bubbles that had formed as the viscous liquid tumbled into the Bay. Lou raised his binoculars for a closer look. "But the fix was in anyway, you know. Ever read the book by the guy who was China's sports minister and president of their Olympics committee at that time?" Lou lowered his glasses. "According to him, the Chinese struck a deal. In exchange for their supporting Jacques Rogge's candidacy to head the International Olympic Committee, the Europeans agreed to back China's bid for the Games. We had the better proposal, but we needed those votes to win. And then look what happened! All those doping scandals. More athletes were stripped of their medals than in any previous Games. It was a shambles."

It wasn't characteristic of Lou to dwell on the past, and Jack tried to get him off it. "So, what are you working on now?"

"Now? You kidding?" But at least Lou grinned good-naturedly. "I'm working on staying alive, that's all."

"But you've got that pad of foolscap with you."

"Yeah. I'm drafting a few changes to my will."

"Hey, come on. Don't sound so defeatist. It's not like you. You may still outlive us all."

Lou raised his glasses and trained them on the outboard again; it was drawing near to the cottage. "Don't bullshit me, Jack. You've talked with Sally." They were silent for a few moments and over the water they could hear the voices of the two men in the outboard as it approached Hemlock Channel. At last, Lou added, "You'll stay in touch with Sally and the boys, eh? They'll want to talk to you and Susie, get your advice from time to time."

Jack just nodded.

The outboard was close to the tip of the Pipers' island now and a tern was dipping and diving off its starboard bow as if piloting it into Hemlock Channel.

"We needed a bit more wind."

"What we had was out of the north. The west is best."

"Worms would have been better than minnows at this time of year."

"It's too late in the season. July is perfect."

"Wait till next year, my friend."

"Fuck me, you better believe it!"

Chapter 22

"Gosh, that wasn't as bad as I thought it would be," Susie exclaimed as they drove away from the dock at Pointe au Baril. "No, that's how I feel, too. It was certainly better than in eighty-eight. No one got angry, there wasn't any shouting, no dramatic scenes. Everyone seemed pretty mellow."

"Yes, but I'm glad it's over. It was all pretty depressing. Everyone seemed so old, so...so defeated."

"Oh, I don't know. Bev was her usual self. And Jay and Linda were looking ahead...even if only to another calamity."

"But it hardly seemed like a happy, nostalgic gathering."

"No. Time has certainly taken a heavy toll," Jack agreed. "You know, all weekend I kept thinking about this new science of neuro-imaging—the development of computers capable of probing our brains for our innermost thoughts—how we're on the verge of a society where nothing will be private any longer, not even our most hidden secrets and desires."

"How scary!"

"No question. But wouldn't it have been interesting to know what everyone at the reunion was not just saying, but actually thinking, and what random images were flashing across their minds?"

"I'm not sure. There would be nothing for you and me to speculate about any longer, nothing to misinterpret. Whatever would we talk about? I must say, though, I would like to know if Sally really does have Mehmet out of her head, or if he still keeps popping into it when she feels bored or frustrated."

"Especially now with Lou so ill."

"Ouch! That's not what I was thinking."

"Linda's is the brain I'd most like to see into. It's got to be so scrambled I doubt any computer could make sense of the data collected."

"Jack! You know that's not fair. She's just a little eccentric. Fundamentally, she's a very sweet person."

"Yeah. Sweeter than Cass, the poor bugger, I'll grant you that. Gee, I wish we hadn't just got back from Maine, but were going there now. Wouldn't it be uplifting after so much gloom and portents of the end?"

"It certainly would. Even if we found the water too cold to swim, the salty air would be refreshing, cleansing in a way."

"So, maybe we *should* go—get to Toronto and just keep on driving, pretend we're young again."

"That would be wonderful. I'd do it in a flash if it weren't so far. But I don't think our bodies could handle another trip that long, not right now."

"Probably not."

In Elmvale, they stopped at a coffee shop for a pee stretch and a cup of tea. "I've got it! I know what we can do," Jack said as he carried their cups to a table. "We can fly down to Portland and rent a car there, or just take a taxi out to Higgins."

"Hmm. That's a possibility, I guess. But the cottage is all closed up for the winter. It would be quite a chore opening it again just for a short visit. And we couldn't stay long. I've got cataract surgery at the end of September, remember."

"So, we'll stay at the inn. It's got to be a lot more comfortable now that it's all been refurbished."

"And a lot pricier, too."

"Hang the expense. We deserve a splurge while we can still enjoy it."

"Do you really mean it?"

"I do."

"Gosh! I'm excited at the prospect already."

Jay reached across the table and brushed Susie's bangs to one side as if preparing her for a portrait session. Her sapphire eyes were shining at him in the same indecipherable way they always had, but this time he was pretty sure he grasped their meaning. "What do you most want to do when we get there?"

"I don't know... Oh, yes, I do. Walk the beach from end to end, holding your hand."

"While we talk about everyone we know?"

"Yes," Susie laughed.

"Me, too. Hey, would you like another tea while we plan the trip?"

"Sure"

"How about a cookie to go with it?"

"No thanks. Just a tea."

Jack took their cups to the counter and along with the teas he bought a chocolate chip cookie. As he sat down again, he split it and handed half to Susie. She studied it for a moment, looked up at Jack and smiled. Then, as she took a bite, she gently kicked him on the leg.